WARM
ON A COLD NIGHT

WARM
ON A COLD NIGHT

G. E. Lapington

St. Martin's Press
New York

WARM ON A COLD NIGHT

Library of Congress Cataloging in Publication Data

Lapington, G   E   1935-
    Warm on a cold night.

    I.   Title.
PZ4.L314War   1980   [PR6062.A64]   823′.914   80-51104
ISBN 0-312-85618-0

WARM
ON A COLD NIGHT

One

The two women went out by themselves that evening. Curtains moved as they walked down the street, eyes watched them go by in their high heels, silk stockings, faces made up to perfection. They were both thirty-two, but felt eighteen, June a chubby blonde, Bella slim, raven-haired, beautiful.

It was the first time that the two Americans had been unable to get out of the camp on a Saturday night. But that was no reason for Bella and June to stay at home. Whatever happened on the other six nights, to them Saturday night was the only night of the week. They had to go out, had to go somewhere, could not stay at home on a Saturday night.

There was a dance on in the town, but they did not go there. It would be full of GIs and servicemen on leave. Instead, they took a twopenny bus ride to the Plough, a pub just outside the town. The bar was always full of old men, so they went into the smoke room. There was a dartboard in there and Bella enjoyed playing darts. She was good at the game and could have played for a team if her interest had been constant. But her interest was in men and if there was not a man to play against then she would play June, whose darts often fell short and stuck in the floor.

It was not often that she played against June. For Bella there was always a man. That evening he was young, and had only one arm. She saw that he had his own set of darts on the table in front of him and she beckoned him over. While they were playing, June got into conversation with a little fat man who looked about sixty. He was buying her drinks in small glasses and could hardly believe his luck, because June and Bella were good-looking enough to be particular about who bought them drinks, and whose arm they went out on at closing time.

When they had finished playing and had sat down, Bella said: 'You throw a good dart.'

'It's knowing where to put the ones I'm not throwing,' he said. The man had had to take each dart out of the top pocket of his jacket to throw it.

'Where did you lose your arm?' Bella asked bluntly. Only a woman who looked like her could look a one-armed man in the eye and ask him that question, in that manner.

'In the Atlantic,' he replied. 'Convoy escort. Torpedo.'

'You manage all right,' she told him sympathetically.

'Couldn't go back to painting and decorating though,' he said. 'They got me a job in an office.' He grinned. 'Never thought I'd work in an office. Up at the parachute factory.'

'Get away. My friend works there.' She looked across the room but June and the old man had gone. Bella said: 'My husband is in the RAF.'

'Is he? Good number?'

'He's a pilot. Flies Hurricanes.'

'Pilot. That's the thing to be.' The man was impressed. 'You need your head screwed on the right way for that.'

'Oh, he's got his head screwed on the right way,' Bella assured him. She felt annoyed that June had gone off with the old man.

'Where is he stationed?' the man asked.

'He's in North Africa. Showing Rommel the way home.'

'He's seeing some action then,' he said enthusiastically.

'Fighter pilots usually do,' Bella said drily. The man was hero-worshipping, but she knew the hero and he did not.

The smoke-room door opened and June stood there and beckoned to Bella. She went across to her. 'Oh Bella, that man I was with, he's been taken bad. Oh, come and see to him, Bella.'

'Which man? That old fellow?'

'Yes. He sort of collapsed,' June explained. She looked sorry for herself.

'The things you get up to,' Bella hissed. She went back to get her handbag and said to the one-armed man: 'I won't be a minute, duck. My friend's not feeling well. I'll be back in a jiffy.' She left her drink on the table.

It was getting dark outside. 'Well, where is he?' Bella snapped.

6

'Up the road in the park,' June said. She sounded like a child who had done something wrong and was about to be found out. 'We were on the grass and he sort of . . .'

'Oh come on,' Bella said. She gave June a look of wild annoyance and set off along the road.

There were no railings around the park. They had been taken down for salvage early in the war and the place had been neglected since. Bella walked across the grass and peered into the gloom. 'Where is he, then?'

'Over there, by the bushes somewhere,' June said, pointing vaguely.

Bella opened her handbag and took out the small torch she carried to find her way in the blackout. 'If anybody sees us shining this light over here . . .'

'There he is,' June squealed, and set off towards a dark mound on the grass by the bushes.

The man was lying on his side. His breathing was laboured. Bella switched off the torch and said to June: 'What happened, then? How far had you got exactly?' She knew June of old. If you were pleasant and had the money, she was yours.

'Well, we were on the grass like, and he sort of got overexcited. We hadn't done anything much, but . . .'

'Even the thought of it was too much for him, was it?' Bella spat the words at her.

'Oh Bella,' June said sorrowfully, 'it wasn't my fault. After all, he gave me two quid.'

'He'd better have his two quid's worth then, hadn't he?' Bella snapped. 'Are you all right, dad?' she said to the old man. 'Can you get up?'

The old man groaned. They got either side of him and helped him up. His eyes were shut. He leaned against June.

'Oh God, I don't know if it wouldn't be better just to leave him here,' Bella said, half to herself. She took the man's wallet from his inside pocket, looked through it by the light of the torch and said eventually: 'Hm, he's got a posh address. Come on, shall we see if we can walk, then?' she said to him, and they guided him out of the park and back along the road. There was a low wall outside the pub and they sat him down. 'You sit with him,' Bella told June. 'I'll go inside and ring for a taxi.'

7

She did not come straight back out after she had telephoned. Instead, she stood just inside the doorway where she could make out June and the old man sitting on the wall. She lit a cigarette. She was hot with anger inside. She had known June since they were children together, and she had not got one ounce wiser in all that time. June's level had never risen above the very basic things in life. One of the basics was that you cannot live without money, and that every woman has something to sell.

Bella went outside into the darkness. She walked across to them and said: 'How are we feeling now, then?'

'He's bucking up a bit,' June said cheerfully. The man said nothing.

The taxi came down the road. Bella went to the kerbside and waved it down. She opened the door and June helped the old man get inside.

'What's up with him?' The driver had the sort of face that would turn milk. 'If he's drunk he can get out. I don't want him being sick in my cab.'

'Shut your face,' Bella snarled at him. 'He's had a giddy spell. Nineteen Belvedere Drive. How much?'

The driver looked at her, was caught by her unblinking, challenging eyes. Belvedere Drive was at the better end of town, where all the nobs lived. He could have got three shillings out of the old man if he had been alone, but he dare not try it with her. 'Two bob,' he said meekly.

'Here's half a crown. Keep the change and take him right to the door.'

He took the money and drove off. They stood on the kerbside and watched the dim red rear lights of the taxi disappear into the darkness. Then June said: 'Shall we go back in, Bella?'

'Go back in? What, now?' Bella said tartly. 'The evening's finished for us. You've seen to that. I'm off home. Come on, let's see if we can get a bus.'

They walked down the road to the bus stop and stood there in silence. On the wall opposite, someone had painted in diminishing white letters: 'Open the second front now.' Bella read the words over and over again to herself until she was interrupted by June saying apologetically: 'I'll pay the fares, Bella. I'll give you the half a crown.'

8

'I don't want the half a crown,' Bella said stonily. 'Honestly, I don't think you'll ever change. You mess up everything. What happened when you went to London? Supposed to find us somewhere to live. When I turned up with the kids, what did I find? Half of fighter command queueing outside your door. Honest June, if there had been six more like you in London in nineteen forty, then the Luftwaffe would have won without firing a shot.'

The bus came then. June paid their fares. She never let Bella's attitude upset her. She just ignored it. It was the only way she knew to show her gratitude. Bella could always get her out of a jam. It was a gift she had. And she soon cooled down. By the time they were turning the corner of their street, finding their way over the uneven pavement by the light of the torch, Bella was saying: 'You'll come in for a cup of tea then, duck?'

June sat at the kitchen table and lit a cigarette. Bella put the kettle on and sat down opposite her. She took something out of her handbag. June looked and said: 'Oh Bella, you didn't. That's his wallet. You didn't take his wallet?'

'Yes I did. I'll give it him back on Monday. Make the old devil sweat over the weekend.'

June sat there mystified. There seemed to be no object in taking it. The kettle began to sing.

'There's twelve quid in here,' Bella said. 'Identity card. Oh, and look, he had his party balloon.' She held up a contraceptive packet. She had not got the man's address from his identity card. Fortunately, she had first come across a small white card in his wallet. She looked at it again, in the better light of the kitchen, and said to June: 'You know who he is? Town clerk. Mr Shanklin, town clerk. No wonder he lives in Belvedere Drive. Half a quid to look at the houses up there. Lucky I saw this, wasn't it? I might have left him there on the grass if I hadn't.'

June became frightened. 'What if he goes to the police? Oh hide it, Bella.'

Bella laughed. 'Can you imagine him doing that? "I was lying in the grass with this young lady, officer, and when I got up I found she'd pinched my wallet."' The kettle began to spit on the gas stove. 'Make the tea, love, will you?' Bella said. 'Warm the pot.' Then she went on: 'There might be a

9

reward. After all, twelve quid and a pigskin wallet. Look at that.' She took two five pound notes out of the wallet. 'You don't very often see them on their own, never mind in pairs. At least, we don't.'

June brought the cups and saucers and put them on the worn oil cloth covering the table. 'The things you do, Bella. And then you go on at me.' She poured the tea.

Bella looked pensive. 'You know, I was just thinking. That man I was playing darts with. He only had one arm. He works in the office at the parachute factory. Do you know him?'

June shook her head.

'You must know him,' Bella insisted. 'He's only got one arm.'

June sat with her elbows on the table, the cup held in front of her mouth. 'They all seem to have three pairs of arms to me,' she said.

'Well, anyway,' Bella went on, 'I thought if he can get a job in an office, after only being a painter and decorator, then so can I.'

'It's not only getting an office job, it's doing it,' June remarked.

'Oh, we are bright all of a sudden, aren't we?' Bella said indignantly. 'Well, Mr Shanklin the town clerk might be able to help me in that direction.'

'You're not going to ask him for a job, are you?' Bella never answered, just looked at her, and June went on: 'He'll probably want you to lie down on the grass with him first.'

'Oh, you are coarse,' Bella said emphatically.

'You ought to come up the parachute factory with me,' June said. 'Important work, making parachutes.'

'No thank you,' Bella replied. 'Too much responsibility. It's bad enough at the laundry, all that steam and mucky clothes. But at least we don't risk killing anybody.'

June had no ready answer to that remark. Instead, she said: 'What about that Derek Pobjoy who was going to get you such a good job in the dyeing room?'

'Well,' Bella replied uncertainly, 'it was one thing having the job and another thing paying the price for it.'

'What on earth do you mean?'

'People like Derek Pobjoy don't give things away. And

what he wanted me to do in return for a job in the dyeing room – well, I've done a lot of things in my time, but there are some things even I stop short at. I'd rather put up with the steam and the mucky clothes.'

June lived next door. When she went home, Bella stood on the doorstep until she had gone through her own front door. Then she went upstairs, looked in on the children and went into the front bedroom. She closed the blackout curtains and lit the candle that stood on the bedside table. She never bothered with electric light bulbs in the bedrooms, was having no air-raid warden shouting at her if a chink of light was showing. A candle was sufficient. It gave enough light to undress by. When she was in bed she heard a drunk singing crazily in the town, a clock chime in the distance, an aeroplane drone overhead. Then she went to sleep.

Two

Bella had a lie-in the next morning. It was Sunday and there was no need to get up. She had a packet of Camel on her bedside table and as she reached out for them she knocked over the photograph. She was always knocking it over, never knew why she kept it there. She stood it up again, lit a cigarette, put the lighter back on the table and glanced at the photograph.

He was good looking, Leslie Rigby, looked fine in his RAF uniform with his pilot's wings. He was tall and slim and had a natural aloofness that it had taken an alley cat like Bella to overcome. But Bella was more than good-looking. She was beautiful. He had fallen in love with her, had married her. They were both eighteen and she was pregnant. In his mother's eyes, that had been the only qualification for her marrying her son. In Bella's eyes that had been the only way to escape from being one of a family of ten in a drab Manchester backstreet, to marry someone better off, to marry Leslie Rigby, an only child with a widowed mother. Love never came into it. Escape was the thing.

She lay in bed until ten o'clock. She heard the children get up, caught the smell of hot fat drifting up the stairs. When she got into the kitchen Rita was frying a piece of bread. 'Oh mam, I was going to bring you up a cup of tea,' she said.

'Never mind, love.' Bella poured her own tea. 'Has the paper come?'

'No,' Rita said. 'We owe him three and seven and he won't bring us another paper until we pay up.' Rita was the image of her mother, her features, her black hair. But she was going to be taller than Bella. She was as tall as her already.

'Oh damn, I thought I'd paid him. I'll go over to Mrs Bragg's when I've drunk this. Better keep up with the war, if nothing else.' She stood in front of the mirror and brushed her hair.

Whatever Bella might want in life, she could not create a home. Her kitchen was a barren, dismal place. The grate had not seen black lead, and it still contained the cold remains of the last fire of winter. They had a little mud garden with a dustbin and a drooping washing-line. The row of houses at the back of them had been bombed before they went to live there, and now there was just an open space giving them the view of some railway sidings and the foundry which was always issuing smoke, always out of focus in a thin mist. It was the sort of outlook Bella was familiar with, but one which she could never get used to. She was always thinking of the day when she could run away from it.

She put on an apron, put her purse in the pocket and said to Rita: 'I'm going over the street then. Where's our Ronnie?'

'Out playing,' Rita replied, spreading sauce on her fried bread. 'I wish I had an egg to go with this.'

'You had it for tea yesterday. You can only eat it once. Get the potatoes started for me, love, will you?'

Bella found Ronnie out in the street. He was ten, quiet like his father, forever flying around the place with arms outstretched being a Hurricane. She gave him five shillings and sent him to the newsagent's. 'Bring me the change,' she yelled, as he flew off down the street.

Mrs Bragg lived almost opposite. Bella opened the front door and called: 'Megan, you there?' before going in. Mrs Bragg had a shiny brass door knocker, tiles in the hall that had been done with Cardinal Red, a front room which was always locked to preserve her best furniture.

Bella went into the kitchen. It was neat, with little brass ornaments glinting on the mantelpiece and a photograph of Petty Officer Bragg, grinning.

'Can I have a look at your Sunday paper?' she asked. 'Ours never came. I've sent our Ronnie down to the shop, but it's ten to one they've none left.'

'Of course you can,' Megan said. She was Welsh, quiet, with plain brown hair done up in a bun at the back of her head, and the only similarity between her and Bella was in their ages. She gave Bella the paper.

13

Bella spread it out on the table and sat on the edge of a chair. 'Bomber Command have again struck at strategic targets deep in Germany,' she read out loud. Then she commented: 'Well, for all their striking at strategic targets, it doesn't seem to bring peace any nearer. They said in nineteen thirty-nine that it would all be over by Christmas. Here we are in nineteen forty-three and I expect the Germans will still be sinking the ships with all our dried fruit in them next Christmas.'

'Well I hope not,' Megan said dismally, 'for all our sakes.'

'It looks like Rommel's had his chips now, doesn't it?' Bella went on. 'I reckon it's all over bar the shouting. I wonder where they'll send Les after it's finished.'

'Should think he'd come home,' Megan said.

'Well, that's as maybe,' Bella remarked, disturbed at the thought. 'I reckon they'll go somewhere else after North Africa. Don't you?'

'I'm sure I don't know,' Megan said, as if afraid to commit herself. Then, as Bella leafed her way through the newspaper: 'I had a letter from Arthur yesterday.'

'Did you, love? Oh, that's good. How is he?'

'Fine. Sent a photo. Look.' She handed Bella a snapshot. He was wearing baggy white shorts and a grin. He was a plump man whose waist looked wider than his chest. 'They cut a lot out of the letter though, look.' She held the letter up to show Bella the great gaps where the censor had been with his scissors.

'I know what that is,' Bella said confidently. 'That's places he's been to. They always cut that out. When Les went to North Africa on that troopship, they cut pieces out of his letter just like that. It was all the places the ship had stopped at. You know what I think? I think he's coming home.'

'Oh, I don't know,' Megan said miserably. 'He might be going in the opposite direction. You heard from Les lately?'

'No,' she replied. 'And I know what he'll put in the letter when he does write. The same that he puts in every one. Why don't I go to Manchester to see his mother? You'll catch me doing that, too.'

'Be a nice change,' Megan suggested.

'No it won't,' Bella replied fiercely. 'Three years we lived

14

with her after we got married, right until Les finished his apprenticeship. As soon as he had a wage coming in, we moved out. I saw to that. He didn't get bad money, being a motor mechanic. Lots of jobs on the side. His mother never let me forget that she kept us for three years, me and Les and our Rita.' She fell silent then, stopped herself saying things that Megan would not believe. She could not tell her that it had been a marriage of want, not of love, or that Mrs Rigby had never stopped reminding her of the fact. She could not tell her that she had taken Mrs Rigby's generosity without thanks, and had never called her mother. 'He got a job at the aerodrome eventually, you know, did Les. That's where he learned to fly. He didn't learn in the airforce. No, when he joined up in nineteen thirty-nine, he already had his pilot's licence. We had a car and all, you know, before the war. Trouble was, everywhere we went his mother had to come, sitting there in the back passing remarks.'

'Good of her to keep you for all that time though, wasn't it?' Megan remarked tentatively.

'Was it be buggered,' Bella said loudly. 'She had plenty of money. Her husband had been manager of a shoe shop. They owned their own house. I can't imagine how anyone could have so much and be so nasty.'

'I always hope me and Arthur might be able to do better than this,' Megan said. 'I mean, they're nice little houses, it's a nice little street, but I always fancied living somewhere where I could see a few trees, have a proper bit of garden for the boys. Don't suppose we will though. I think the war has spoilt the chance of having things like that.'

'You never look on the bright side, do you?' Bella said, sounding cross, just as if she was telling off June or one of the children. 'Things will be better when the war's over, not worse. You read too many books, that's your trouble. You need a change, stuck in the house reading all the time. I keep asking you to come out with me and June. They have nice dances up the camp. Real polite those Americans, real nice boys. You'd enjoy it. You don't have to start anything. After all . . .' She paused, not quite knowing how to put it. 'Well, a lot of them are married as well, you know. They can't wait to show you the photos of their wife and kids.'

'I don't think I would feel right, somehow,' was all she

15

said.

Bella knew that wild horses and a promise of unconditional surrender by Hitler would fail to get Megan to go to a dance at the camp. She was happiest with a book at her own fireside. She had two on the window sill, both partly read, with the corners turned down to keep the place. Once she had gone into the library to change her books and had left her shopping bag there with the week's rations in it. When she had realized and had gone back for it, it had gone. But Bella, without a second thought, had gone halves with her and had seen Megan and her two small boys through the week. Practically every week since then there had been something from the camp to eke out the rations, sometimes a bit of lard, or butter, or sugar, all of it stolen, all of it welcome, to say nothing of the cigarettes Bella gave her. She had forty Camel there then, on the mantelpiece behind Arthur's photograph.

Ronnie came to the door with the newspapers just then and Bella went home. She closed Megan's front door behind her and crossed the street back to her house. It was a dull street, even if Megan thought it was nice. Terraced houses with sticky tape criss-crossed over the windows against bomb blast, a W painted in white on the wall of the air-raid warden's house.

Bella was on the run from streets like that, from the sort of life that was lived in them. Leslie Rigby had offered her little alternative. Her life had remained unchanged, while he had gone about achieving the things he wanted in life. That was not the way she had wanted things to be. She had never wanted to be just a housewife, looking after the children, cooking his dinner for him every evening when he came home from work. She had wanted romance, some of the fine things in life. But all she had got from Leslie had been an evening at the flying club, the shabby clubhouse where all the talk was of aeroplanes, where all the drinks were warm, where everything smelled of oil and petrol. She had wanted something with class, with dim lights, a band playing, waiters, ice in her drink. If it had not been for the children she would have gone, left him. For years her mind was on escape. No one knew then that there was going to be a war, a war that would bring separation and opportunities.

When Bella got back into her kitchen, there was no one there. 'Rita,' she shouted. 'Rita.' But there was no reply. The frying pan was still on the gas stove. Rita's greasy plate was on the draining board.

Bella lit a cigarette. There was an enamel bowl in the sink, still full of the soapy water that either Rita or Ronnie had washed in. She tipped it away and filled the bowl with water from the tap. Then she put it on the kitchen table, got the cardboard box in which she kept the potatoes from the pantry floor, and counted the potatoes out into the bowl, dropping them in so that the water splashed out on to the oil cloth. She got a knife and began peeling them. The ash dropped from her cigarette into the bowl.

The nearest she had got in those pre-war days to the sort of life she had wanted was on the one night every week that she went out with June, one night when Manchester was theirs, when they went to a club in the town, when she felt single again, when there were men who took an interest in them, drinks from tall slim glasses, a taxi home afterwards, the door held open for them. But for her one night a week had not been enough. She had wanted it all the time, for ever.

She looked up from peeling the potatoes, looked out of the window. Someone had let their pigeons out, and they were flying in a tight flock in a great circle across the sky, the circle moving gradually sideways until they were out of sight. A cat sat on a broken wall on the bombsite, methodically washing itself. The bombing, the war, had meant death and pain and sorrow to so many people, but to Bella it had meant escape, freedom. At the outbreak of war, Leslie had been posted to the south of England and Mrs Rigby had never believed for a minute that Bella's reason for going to live in London was to be near him. But she had taken the children and gone, with June. Then the bombing had started. They went to Birmingham and got bombed there as well. She was achieving nothing. She was forever on the run, forever trying to escape, forever seeking freedom.

One Saturday morning Bella caught a train which took her south from Birmingham. At the third or fourth stop, after the train had travelled through miles of open country, she got off. She bought the local paper, looked for accommodation being advertised, found nothing. So she went into a pub and had a drink, and even amongst the lunchtime crowd she could attract attention, was soon talking to someone, being bought another drink. The man had a word with the barman, who gave her a name on a piece of paper and said: 'He might be able to help you. He's a Jew mind, but he's quite pleasant.'

An hour later Bella had a house, paid a week in advance, and went back to Birmingham to fetch June and the children.

It was a small town. It seemed an unimportant place. They decided to settle there, make some sort of life for themselves until peace came again. Bella had run enough. From home, from Mrs Rigby, to London, to Birmingham, to this little town. It would have to do for the time being. After all, there was a war on.

Three

The Americans were coming at tea time. As soon as Sunday dinner was over, Bella started getting ready. In the kitchen the sink was in an alcove and she had rigged up a curtain across it, behind which she could go with a kettle of water to wash. They had no bathroom and she would strip off and do it all in a bowl of water. Rita was in front of the mirror, combing her hair. Her friend Anne was coming round to tea. Bella encouraged friendships. You never got anywhere without people, she reckoned. Even so, there were some people life was better without.

There were occasional bouts of bad feeling in the house at that time. Rita had the chance to go to the technical college to take a secretarial course that autumn. Both she and Anne had qualified to go, and Anne's father had signed the form straight away. But Bella was having none of it. Rita was fourteen, and she wanted her at work in August.

'Mam,' Rita started, 'we've got Miss Nicholls at school tomorrow.'

'Hard luck for Miss Nicholls,' Bella said from behind the curtain.

'She never asked me for my form last week. What have I got to say if she asks me tomorrow?'

'Now don't start, don't start,' Bella said, sounding agitated. They had been having this argument on and off for a month.

'But mam, I'm the only one who hasn't . . .'

'I told you to say you were not going. I'm not having you at the technical college until you're sixteen. Work my girl.'

'But mam, I want to be a secretary. I don't want . . .'

'You'll be what I say,' Bella snapped. 'I'll get you a nice job in the Co-op, serving. I know the manager. I'll fix it. Now be satisfied.'

'I won't go, I just won't go,' Rita cried. All her emotions were in her throat.

'You're going to work even if I have to drag you there every damn morning,' Bella screamed. 'If I've told you once, I've told you a hundred times.'

'I bloody well won't,' Rita yelled back, tears in her eyes.

Bella flew from behind the curtain in her petticoat. She screeched with rage and flung her sopping face flannel at Rita. It went right across the front of her clean white blouse.

'Ah, my blouse,' Rita cried. 'You bugger. I'll write to gran, I'll write to gran.'

Bella flew at her again, but Rita was out into the hallway and through the front door before her mother could lay a finger on her. 'You just dare,' Bella yelled out into the street.

With those few words, all the life and joy had gone out of Bella. Her mother-in-law was one of those people without whom life was a lot better. If Rita did write to her, she might be down on the first train, full of fight and argument. She was the only person who had ever matched Bella in an argument, and the only other thing they had in common was an ability to ignore each other completely. Letters, cards and gifts came for the children at birthdays and Christmas, without a mention of their mother. And whatever Leslie wrote about his mother in his letters to Bella, it was always ignored. She had never called her mother and had never made any reference to her in writing.

Bella went back into the kitchen, picked up the face flannel and flung it into the bowl of water. Her whole body felt weary with anger.

Rita raced off down the street, past the children on their way to Sunday school, the tears drying on her cheeks, the wet mark drying on her blouse. She desperately wanted to go to the technical college. For her, there was too much at stake to give in easily. She wanted to be a film star, and how could she turn up for a screen test and tell them she worked at the Co-op? You had to be a secretary, or a hairdresser, or a mannequin.

Anne lived a couple of streets away. Her father was sitting in the sunshine outside the back door, a newspaper across his knees. He had been in the army and had been wounded at

Dunkirk. He had almost died. It showed in his face. It was lined and his eyes looked old and tired. He was only thirty-five, with all the age of a long life past in his face. 'I wish I had your energy, Rita,' he said, as she stood there puffing. 'Somebody chasing you?'

'No,' she said. 'Mam went for me. She still won't let me go to the tech.' She liked him. He was calm and said sensible things, the opposite to her mother.

'Great opportunity,' he said. 'Opportunities are the things, they don't occur too often in life. Got to grab them, you know,' he told her wisely.

'She wants me to work at the Co-op.'

'Hm.' He looked away with his tired eyes. 'You want to get our Anne to talk to her.'

'I'm going to write to my gran. They hate each other. That's why my mother chased me. She hit me with the flannel.'

'You're a bright one, you are,' he said jovially. 'I can't see anyone holding you back.' His face was wreathed in a smile and he said: 'Do you want a twopence ha'penny stamp?'

She laughed and went past him into the house.

The Americans arrived early that afternoon. They both came into Bella's house first. Chuck was ten years younger than Bella. He was tall, strongly built, with a boyish face and piles of fair wavy hair. Bill was even taller, lean and dark, and when he saw that June was not there he went next door.

Bella started to lay the table. Few of the cups matched, all of the saucers were odd. Even she could not get new crockery in wartime. Chuck could see that there was something wrong with her and it took no effort at all to get her to tell him about it.

'Jesus,' Chuck said. 'You still fighting about that?' He had heard them arguing about it several times, but he had taken no notice. He was quiet, minded his own business and he did not want the quarrel spreading to him. But she wanted his sympathy and he knew she was in the wrong. 'You sure are low on sense sometimes,' he told her.

'Am I?' she said tartly. 'Thanks for telling me.'

'Do you know how much they pay for working in an office? Do you know how much they pay a secretary?' Bella never answered, and he went on: 'Why the hell do you think it takes two years to learn how to do the job? Anybody can serve in a store.'

'I suppose your father has loads of typists working at his factory,' she sneered.

'I guess so. And I know they get better money than the girls who wear overalls and work in the plant.' He stood behind her and put his hands on her shoulders. 'Look, Bella, she'll hold it against you. We are young, all of us are young. We've got a lot of life to get through yet. You mess it up now and you mess it up forever. She's a great kid. She deserves the chance. I guess some folk would give their right arm to see their kid have the chance.'

Bella stood there, still, hearing his voice and feeling his warm, soft hands on her shoulders. It would have been different if he had said it without touching her. But she seemed to feel all the depth of meaning come into her body through his hands. She did not know why she had wanted to deny Rita her chance. Bella was too fond of herself ever to find wrong in herself. It never entered her head that she might be jealous of her own daughter, that she was frightened that even Rita might stand in the way of her getting out of that life of poor streets and terraced houses which, for all her running, still encompassed her.

Rita and Anne stood outside in the street for a while, tentative about going in. Anne was plump. She had on her best dress, a white one with blue polka dots that did not make her look any thinner. She was frightened to death of having to ask Rita's mother to let her go to the technical college. To her, Rita's mother was small, fierce and beautiful, with eyes that went right through you and lit up like a flame.

'Can you imagine me going for a screen test and telling them I serve on the bacon counter at the Co-op?' Rita was saying. 'They'd all laugh. I'd die of shame. Oh, come on, let's get it over with. It's either you or my gran.'

They went inside then, into the kitchen. 'Hi there,' Chuck greeted them.

And Bella said: 'Oh Rita, love, there you are. Now where's that form I've got to sign for the tech? I can't find it. You try and find it before I go out, love, and I'll sign it for you. Now go next door and tell Auntie June tea's nearly ready, will you, love?'

Rita stepped backwards to the kitchen door. She could neither blink nor shut her mouth. As she went out into the hallway Chuck winked at her, but she could not decide whether it had been her grandmother or Chuck who had been the force that had made her mother change her mind. And she was not going to ask, just in case it was changed back again.

June came in with Bill and Mavis. Mavis was eight, father known only to June. She was the result of one of those times when June had drifted away from Bella, as even good friends occasionally do.

'Mr Fisher at home?' Bella asked June.

'Sleeping it off somewhere, I think,' she replied. 'Just put him something on a plate, love.'

At first, June had lived with Bella in the house she had found after that Saturday train journey. Then Mr Fisher, who owned the house next door, had lost his housekeeper. She had left suddenly and June had taken her place. It was only after she had moved in that June found out why her predecessor had left. Mr Fisher was addicted to cider and was hardly ever sober. But she tolerated him for various reasons, saw his good points clearest of all. Although he was a nuisance when drunk, when he was sober he was as pleasant as any other old man of sixty. He worked at the foundry, never missed a day, drunk or sober, ate his meals and let June live there free. He gave Mavis all his sweet coupons and sixpence pocket money every week, and most important of all, never questioned Bill's presence there, even when he appeared in the kitchen of a morning, yawning and fresh from June's bed. Occasionally, Mr Fisher would take a couple of cider flagons into the coalhouse and get drunk lying on top of the coal. Sometimes it would be the outside lavatory. Then June and Bella would get him into the house and put him to bed. They never minded. Their upbringing had been anything but genteel and although they found it difficult to go upwards in life, they found no problem at all in going down to their old level, to deal with the sort of situation that was common to their background.

Bella had a nice spread for their tea that afternoon. Had they, like everyone else in the street, been limited to living on rations only, it would not have gone beyond bread and jam. But Chuck and Bill worked in the stores, so most of it came from the camp. They saw to it that Bella and June always had something to make the rations go further. And on the table there was best butter, a great piece of cheese, jam, jelly made from crystals, biscuits and a small piece of ham. Chuck had given the ham to Bella to cook, and Bella was no great cook. The ham had turned out the colour of mahogany and she wondered what it would do to the carving knife. But, to her amazement, it sliced beautifully and was pink and succulent inside. Anne was hypnotized by it. She watched Bella carving. 'Are you hungry, love?' Bella asked.

'Starving,' Anne admitted.

'Starving?' June burst out. 'Look at the size of you. How do you get that fat on rations?'

'It's only puppy fat,' Anne replied meekly.

'How many puppies have you ate then, love?' June said and everyone laughed.

But Bella saw Anne's face grow long. 'Take no notice, love. They're only pulling your leg. I was fat when I was your age – and she was.' She pointed at June with the carving knife. 'Here, love, have a sandwich.'

Anne took the ham sandwich and her teeth snapped into it. Two bites and it was gone.

At six Bella, June and the Americans went out. Mavis and Ronnie went into the street to wait for the Band of Hope, who sang hymns in the street every Sunday night. Upstairs, Rita got out her film annuals and she and Anne lounged on the bed, gazing at them.

Anne said: 'You know, I'm cut between Clark Gable and Eric Portman. I don't know which one I'd like to carry me off into the night.' She paused and mulled over the choice. 'Both I suppose,' she admitted.

Rita brought her back to reality. 'I can't imagine either of them fancying us. You've got to have a figure like my mother.' She slid off the bed and looked at herself in the oval dressing-table mirror. 'Look at me. I'm just like a boy.' She looked down at her chest and had an uninterrupted view of her feet.

They went outside then, on to the bombsite at the back of the house. 'They do concerts and plays at the tech. I'm going

24

to join in that straight away,' Rita said. She picked up a half brick and hurled it with all her might at the only bit of building left standing at one end of the row. 'Then, when I'm a secretary, I'll save a bit out of my wages every week for drama lessons. You can go to evening classes for that. And then I'll go to London for a screen test. I've got it all worked out.'

'Look at Mr Fisher,' Anne said. 'He'll fall off in a minute.'

Mr Fisher, in his old fawn mac and his cap, was cycling in a haphazard fashion along the alleyway that once divided the bombed houses from those that still stood. He managed to ride in through the open gate and was lost from their view behind the garden wall. There was a crash and a cry as he fell off.

'Oh, had we better go and see to him?' Anne sounded concerned.

'No,' Rita said, throwing another brick. 'He's drunk. He's probably ridden into the linepost again. Serves him right.'

'I think we ought to,' said Anne. 'He might be hurt.'

'Oh, come on then,' Rita said reluctantly and they meandered over to the gate. They looked through and the bicycle was lying on the ground by the linepost. They went up the garden path and into the kitchen. Mr Fisher was sitting at the table. 'Are you all right, Mr Fisher?' Rita asked.

He did not answer, just grinned at them, chuckled a bit, his eyes sparkling.

'Do you want a cup of tea?' Rita tried.

'You went and caught a flea? That's clever that is. Went and caught a flea,' he chuckled.

'Oh, come on,' Rita said. 'The drink's sending him deaf.' And they went outside again.

With the two Americans, Bella and June caught the same bus that they had taken the night before, but they paid an extra halfpenny and went a bit further this time, getting off in a leafy country lane. They walked along hand in hand, then climbed a gate and went laboriously up the side of a hill. The men's shoes slipped on the grass, the women struggled in their high heels, and they laughed and joked as they went on upwards. When they got to the top they had a view right over the town. They could pick out the Plough at the foot of the hill, and the little park where June had been in trouble the previous night.

They sat down on the dry grass, watching the sun setting and the clouds turning pink. Then June and Bill got up. 'See you at the Plough,' they said and wandered away with their arms around each other.

As they disappeared behind the blackberry bushes, Bella said: 'She'll regret it. She's got her best silk stockings on.'

Bella and Chuck lay on their backs on the grass, silent with their own thoughts. Chuck was going to be Bella's escape, the escape she had always been seeking. His father owned thousands of acres of land in California. They grew fruit. They had their own factory where they canned it, he had told her. A big house, servants, cars, a swimming pool in the garden. Leslie Rigby was yesterday. Chuck was today. Chuck was tomorrow, a sparkling new tomorrow, an end to all her running. It would all end in a big white house in California, a house on a hill, with apple orchards and peach trees.

'What's it like, an orange grove? What does it smell like?'

'Oranges,' he said.

'And peaches. There's nothing so luxurious as a peach. You don't know how lucky you are.'

'I do,' he said definitely.

'Oranges, peaches, California, all that sunshine. Lovely.'

She was quiet again then. Never before had she been so close to escape. But there was one difficulty, one thing that might spoil it all. It was the children. In all the dreamy conversations she had had with Chuck about going to America when the war was over, never had either of them mentioned the children. The trouble was, and she admitted it to herself as she lay there on the grass, that her escape, her real escape into a new life, had always been very much for herself. Somewhere in the dreams there had always been a man, but never anyone else. But lately, however far she let her mind wander away from reality, the children suddenly appeared right in the midst of her imaginings, as if demanding consideration, as if demanding to be included. She sighed a deep sigh. The only comfort she could get was in hoping that by the time the war finished the children would be older, nearer to their own independence and able to live their own lives.

Chuck drew himself up on one elbow. He looked down at

her. 'What are you dreaming about now?' he asked her. 'What do you want most – me or those orange groves and all that sunshine?'

'You every time,' she replied, and added, a little untruthfully: 'I'd have you and Manchester in the rain, and be satisfied.'

He said: 'You dream too much,' and kissed her firmly on the lips.

Four

Usually Bella set off to her job at the laundry at eight o'clock, but the following morning at that time she was still engrossed in the *Daily Mirror*, with her third cup of tea.

'Not going to work, mam?' Rita asked her.

'Not today, love. Going about a new job. I've signed your form for you. Tell that Miss Nicholls it's my fault you're late taking it.'

Rita sat and listened to the radio doctor, wondering if her mother was going to finish with the newspaper so that she could read Belinda, but when it was half-past eight and time for her and Ronnie to go, she was still reading it, a cigarette going, her feet up on a chair. Rita dared not say a thing. She had vowed not to risk crossing her mother until her acceptance at the technical college was secure.

When Bella went into the gloomy entrance of the town hall, she looked her best. Best costume, best shoes, best stockings and a hat with a brim that came down over one eye. The receptionist, with horn-rimmed glasses and hair that looked as if it had recently been stirred by a strong wind, thought, in the bad light, that it might perhaps be Hedy Lamarr coming in. On her appearance alone, Bella got as far as the town clerk's outer office. There she found Miss Hackett, wrinkles, chins and a black dress.

Miss Hackett stayed seated behind her typewriter. 'You can't see Mr Shanklin without an appointment,' she said.

'He'll see me,' Bella said calmly. 'Just tell him I'm here, love.'

'You cannot see the town clerk without an appointment,' she said firmly and, she thought, finally.

'He lost his wallet on Saturday night, didn't he?' Bella said, just as firmly.

'I'm sure I don't know,' Miss Hackett replied, as if it were none of her business anyway.

'Well he did, and I found it, and I'm not making an appointment to give it back to him,' Bella said, with the sound of aggression coming into her voice.

'Then you can give it to me and I'll give it back to him.'

Bella leaned forward and fixed the woman with her eyes. 'I could go and hand it in at the police station and then he'd have to go down and claim it. And the police would apologize for bothering him and say that they had no alternative, being as you refused to let me give it back to him. So how about it, love?'

Miss Hackett wilted under Bella's gaze. Those eyes went right through her. 'Oh,' she moaned, standing up. 'It is most irregular.' She turned to the large polished door behind her, stepped towards it and said over her shoulder: 'What did you say your name was?'

'I didn't. But he saw me on Saturday night. You just tell him what I look like. He'll remember me.'

'I'm sure he will,' Miss Hackett grunted, knocked on the polished door and went in.

Bella stood there and waited, while Miss Hackett told the story and gave her description. She came out of the town clerk's office and said brusquely: 'You can go in.'

There he was in his big office, behind his big desk, little, fat and frightened to death. He invited her to sit down. She looked at him and smiled. She guessed that he was scared stiff of blackmail, yet thankful that she was not the little blonde.

'I understand you've found my wallet,' he said softly.

'That's right, love,' Bella replied, and just to let him know exactly where he stood, she said: 'After you'd been on the grass with my friend. I had to take it out of your pocket to find your address. You won't remember – you were all overcome at the time, sort of. I couldn't have put it back properly. It was on the pavement after we put you into the taxi. He got you home all right, did he? I paid him half a crown.'

'Oh yes, yes.' Mr Shanklin felt weak with fear. He put his hand into his pocket.

'No, that's all right, love. I don't want the money. After all, you gave my friend two pounds and you didn't get anything for it, did you? Anyway, you were all buttoned up and that, and my friend said you hadn't.' Bella reckoned she had him now.

'No. You were very kind. I have a slight heart condition, you know,' he said pathetically, touching his waistcoat just where his heart was. 'I had omitted to take my pill that day.'

'There now,' Bella said with mock sympathy. 'You should be more careful. You could have caught a chill on that damp grass.'

Mr Shanklin was now fully prepared to die instantly of a heart attack, or of anything else that would get him away from this dark, attractive woman and her embarrassing conversation. But before anything else, he said meekly: 'You have my wallet?'

'Oh, I was forgetting, love,' Bella said, acting as if she really had forgotten. 'Here we are.' She took the wallet out of her handbag and gave it to him.

'You must allow me to . . .' he began, taking the money out of the wallet.

'No, I wouldn't hear of it,' Bella insisted. 'You put that back this minute.'

'But it's only right. You have been most honest. A reward is the least I can do.'

'You put it back,' Bella said again. 'After all, you've already paid out two pounds to my friend and got nothing for it but a heart attack and a taxi ride home.'

Mr Shanklin was more frightened now than he had been when she had first come in. As town clerk he dealt with a lot of people, important people. But this woman, who looked as if she had stepped straight out of a glossy magazine and who spoke as if she had stepped straight out of a north country backstreet, she had him cornered. He had his wallet but she had him – right in the palm of her hand. 'If you won't take a small monetary reward,' he said, 'then all I can offer you is my sincere thanks.'

'Well, there is something,' she said, and saw his worried face become even more worried. 'I wonder if you could fix me up with a job?'

'A job?' he echoed. If that was all, then it could have been worse. She could have asked him for anything. 'What sort of a job?'

Bella moved in the chair, made herself a bit more comfortable. 'I work in the laundry, you see,' she began. 'But it's not my sort of work at all. All that steam and mucky clothes. No, I want to get back into an office.'

'You work in an office normally, do you?' The worst was over now, he felt. His voice, totally of its own accord, became a little stronger.

'No,' Bella admitted. 'But when I worked at the mill up in Manchester, I had to go up to the office a lot. Forewoman I was. I was always up in that office. I could have slid into a job in that office as easy as you like, but – forewoman. Few were called to be a forewoman.' She was lying like mad. She had had four looms like all the other girls and had only been up into the office once, when she was threepence short in her pay one week.

'You never actually worked in the office then?' he said cautiously.

'I'd never worked in a laundry either, love, but they'll miss me when I've gone.'

'You can't type then?' he tried. There was a chance that he might be able to reassert himself, he thought, if he was careful.

'No,' she said. 'But I know how to.'

'You can't type, but you know how to?' he queried.

'That's right. I've never actually done it, but I've watched them for long enough up in that office. Oh, I know how to do it. Yes, you just press those keys and that. I could soon pick that up.'

'Would you know anything about filing?'

'Filing? I can tell you, I was up in that office so much that I knew their filing system better than they did themselves. If I'd have waited for them to find anything, well – I'd have been there all day.'

'You've never done any actual filing then?' he asked, with the faintest feeling of confidence returning.

'Well no, not actually.' Bella looked across the big desk at him. He looked calmer now. And she knew why. She knew that the town clerk, of all people, would know when someone was trying to bluff him. She knew that to be town clerk he would have to be clever. But he was still a rat, he was still in her trap, and if needs be she would let the spring snap down

31

on him. She would tell him quite bluntly that unless he fixed her up with a job, all sorts of people would find out that he consorted with prostitutes. 'But I'm very adaptable,' she went on. 'I'll do anything, from typing and filing to making the tea. Just as long as I can get back into an office. You'll always find me presentable. I don't go to extremes – who can with clothes rationing? But I always believe in being presentable. And I get on with people. Receptionist, I could do that. Just up my street.'

'I'm afraid we have a receptionist,' Mr Shanklin said.

'Afraid is the right word,' Bella remarked. 'That girl downstairs with glasses and hair like dying grass?'

'She is my niece,' he said and thought his troubles would soon be over.

Bella fixed him with her eyes. Where other people smelled disaster, she scented triumph. 'Well, you do surprise me. If you were selling things and that young lady was on your counter looking like that, you'd soon go out of business. If anyone else had told me she was your niece, I would never have believed them.' And now she decided to nail him. But the nice way. 'When I picked you up off the grass on Saturday night and shone my torch over you, I thought – well, he's a gent. Nice bit of cloth in that suit you had on. Pre-war? You shouldn't have been doing that sort of thing in a suit like that. They have a hell's job getting grass stains out of cloth at the laundry. And when I saw you were the town clerk – well, it all fitted. Class. It was a taxi home for you. If it had been one of the usual sort my friend picks up, I'd have left him there. And your wallet? If it had belonged to anyone else I would have dropped it straight in at the police station. But you know what the police are, they ask so many questions. And me, I'm as straight as a die. Bella, I said to myself, you are going to have to keep this one under your hat.'

Mr Shanklin felt that he was back where he had started. She might have helped him up off the grass, but in every other respect she had pushed him flat on his back. He was now going to have to think solely of himself. 'Well, my dear, if you'd like to leave things with me, I'll see if we can find a little position that you can fill.'

'Oh, that's real nice of you.'

'We did have a young man leave us recently, called up. We

didn't intend replacing him. But, well – I can't decide these things entirely on my own. So if you'd just like to leave it with me, bide your time for a week, say?'

'I'm very grateful,' Bella said. 'I'm sure you'll find me very useful. And I'll tell you what. I'll get acquainted with your niece and give her some tips on how to look after her hair. We can't have her looking like that, not with the town clerk as her uncle, can we?'

On the Friday of that week Bella had a letter from the town clerk offering her the job of part-time temporary clerical assistant at the town hall. The hours were nine until three, Monday to Friday, 'the duration of employment not to extend beyond the cessation of hostilities, in order to re-accomodate employees returning from active service.' Bella deciphered this with the help of Rita's dictionary and said to June: 'What it really means is that when we win the war, then I get the sack as a victory present.'

June could not believe that she was the cause of Bella's good fortune. 'Did you tell him about Les?' she asked. 'Did you tell him he was a flight lieutenant and had his own Hurricane?'

'No,' Bella said. And she went on disparagingly: 'They make anybody an officer in wartime. It all depends on whether they've got a uniform to fit you.' Then she wrote her letter of acceptance to Mr Shanklin.

There was a dance at the camp that night. Before they went, Bella and June both tucked a paper carrier bag underneath their coats. The bus took them to within sight of the camp gates. Chuck and Bill were waiting at the stop. When they were inside the camp, they slipped the bags to the Americans.

Bella enjoyed the dances at the camp. They had a good band, a good dance floor and the men were a revelation. They had a well kept look about them, the sort of look that slums and the depression had kept from their British counterparts. It seemed as if those men, with their well filled cheeks and outdoor complexions, really had fed like they did in films, on ice cream and steaks. Their uniforms were smart, they fitted as if they had been tailored. But what captured Bella most of all were their manners. They knew how to treat women. They were polite and attentive to all the girls, they left no one out, there were no wallflowers at the camp dances. Bella was in her element. For her it was a foretaste of what was to come.

But June was unimpressed. 'Be a bit different if some of our fellows were here,' she would reply to a remark from Bella. 'What price their good manners then?'

Before the war, when the British army had occupied the camp, there had been an expansion programme. New buildings had gone up. Then war broke out, and it all stopped. At the far side of the camp, near the boundary fence, was the lecture room. It had been finished and fitted out, but the purpose for which it was required had evaporated with the German advance through Europe. It stood isolated beyond the grassy mounds of the air-raid shelters. Officially it was unused. No one went near it. But when the dance was nearly over that night, Bella and June went outside and strolled casually in the moonlight towards the air-raid shelters, and when under their cover they went on to the lecture room.

The door was unlocked. Inside were several couples enjoying each other's close company. It was all very innocent. Of the couples that the war had brought together, not all had access to a place to be alone in. Many were like Bella, married with children. Some girls had parents to whom Americans were foreigners, and they had to keep their friendships as secret as if they were married. The lecture room was for them.

Bella and June sat down in the gloom in a corner to wait for Chuck and Bill. The room had big windows that reached almost to the ground along one side, and curtains that were never drawn. There were no lights. They never needed lights. The two Americans were not long in coming and the four of them went outside again and walked away in the darkness. The sound of the band came over the still air. The moon had gone behind the clouds. Everything was black. For a while there was nothing but them and the music.

Some distance away from the lecture room they stopped. The men lifted up the boundary fence. It had been cut loose from the posts and they went underneath into the adjoining cemetery. They gave Bella and June the two carrier bags which they had packed full of cigarettes, and said their good-nights there amongst the gravestones.

Bella was not afraid to walk through the cemetery. June was petrified and clung on to her arm. It was no comfort to June to know that there was a lot of going to and fro through the cemetery, that the lecture room was in almost nightly use, that the fence had been loosened purposely to give access to it. She still trembled with fear every time she had to make that short walk between the graves. 'For heaven's sake, loosen your grip on my arm,' Bella hissed, trying to pull free from June's grasp. 'You're stopping my circulation. And don't walk so close. If you kick my ankle again, I'll kick you back.'

The men would have gone with them to the cemetery gate but Bella knew what that would mean. They would stand and talk and the longer they stood the harder it would be to get June away from Bill. They would miss the bus they wanted to catch and would have to go on the one with all the girls from the dance, conspicuously carrying the bags full of cigarettes. As it was, coming out of the cemetery they were able to approach the bus stop from the opposite direction to the camp, and that bus, the one before the dance ended, was empty.

Bella and June took only small amounts of food or cigarettes out of the camp. The larger amounts that Chuck and Bill got their hands on they disposed of themselves, to contacts Bella had found for them. But now and again Bella wondered about Chuck. She knew that in America there was less class distinction, but she often wondered why, coming from so much wealth and independence, he was only a private. It did not seem realistic either that someone from his background should be so involved with smuggling goods out of the camp and on to the black market. Yet it seemed to occupy both him and Bill as much as any legitimate work did. They had a system whereby a quantity of goods disappeared while travelling that short distance between the back of the truck and the stores. If it was never booked into the stores, then it could not be stolen from there. It worked well. And Bella had a friend who had friends who had shops. For them too, as for Bella and June, it was a risk, but if they got caught it would be something that they could get over, something that would only affect them for a while. For Chuck, she

35

imagined, the consequences would be greater. There was his family's good name to consider, their reputation, his own future. She could not understand it. But then the bus started up and lurched away from the kerbside. June offered her a cigarette and her train of thought was lost.

Five

Megan did not go out very often. She went to the library, she went shopping, she went to chapel. And occasionally she went to the cinema, with Bella, June and the children. They were going that Saturday. Bella called down the hallway, then went into Megan's kitchen, talking as she went. 'It's my treat,' she said. 'Celebrate my new job. Be ready, mind. Early doors.'

Megan, who was shy and vulnerable and uncertain of herself, felt safe in Bella's company, felt protected by her striking appearance, her aggressiveness, her popularity. She felt as safe with Bella as she did with her husband. To Megan, Arthur Bragg was a little like Bella. He too was extrovert, experienced and forceful. He had thrown his protective shadow over her and had shielded her from being overwhelmed by the world she had found herself in when he had married her and taken her away from the close familiarity of the Welsh village where she had lived. He had found that ordinary, unimportant town for her to make a home in when the bombing had struck Plymouth. And although he was in the navy and was away at sea, she felt no fear for him. He had the same tough exterior, the same resilient character that she knew Bella had, that she thought would make them both indestructible.

Megan powdered her face and put on a bit of lipstick. She wished she had the courage to go to a dance with Bella. She kept asking her to go. But it seemed a wrong thing for a married woman to do, and anyway, she knew that the moment she became separated from Bella she would feel lost and out of place, and would want to go home. Megan had no courage at all and was only brave enough to feel longing to do the things Bella and June did. She knew her limitations and admired her two friends for seeming to have no limitations. They were like two characters out of a book, doing the sort of things that only people in books did. And of all the books she had read, none excited her as much as the sight of Bella and June walking off down the street with the two Americans, tarted up, noses in the air, walking off into an evening that would bring them enjoyment, romance, the thrill of doing what they should not.

There were three cinemas in the town, but when Bella took them they always went to the Palace. It was always her treat, and although Megan knew that Bella was a friend of the manager, she found it hard to believe that they all went in for nothing. There were nine of them going that day.

It rained that morning, but it had stopped by the time they set off to walk into town. It only took ten minutes. They went into a pub called the Unicorn for a drink before going on to the cinema. There was a passageway at the front where they could leave the children, and a small girl was waiting there with a baby in a grubby pram.

Bella led the way into the saloon bar. She had put the cigarettes that they had got from the camp into a large leather shopping bag and brought it with her. She put it under the table and went to the bar to get the drinks. She was a long time away. She seemed to know everybody and everybody knew her. She stopped to talk, refused offers of drinks, stood laughing at something the barman said to her.

Megan and June sat at the table. Megan did not have the gift of conversation and June never knew what to say to her. They sat there in silence for a minute and then a man approached them from behind, put his hand on June's shoulder and said: 'Hello, June. When are you going to leave that Yank and come back to me?'

'Go on,' June said, and she grinned at Megan.

'Have a drink? What are you having?' the man asked June.

'Bella's getting them,' June said.

'Oh, all right,' he said. 'Be seeing you.'

He moved away, and as he turned to go he glanced at Megan. She saw his expression. It seemed to tell her that if she had not been there, he would have been able to get off with June, and it made her feel awkward and in the way.

Bella returned then with the drinks. In the books Megan read, the ladies either drank champagne or cocktails with unreal names. Megan always had a shandy. On the handful of times that Arthur had persuaded her to go into a pub, that was what he had bought her. Bella and June each had a glass of beer, which they drank in great mouthfuls while Megan sipped her shandy.

After their one drink, Bella picked up the leather bag and they went on to the cinema. It was raining again and all the shops had their awnings out. As they hurried along, Anne asked the question that Megan dared not: 'What have you got in that bag, Mrs Rigby?'

'Five pound notes, duck. I robbed a bank this morning.'

There was a long queue outside the cinema, waiting for the first house. They were huddled against the wall to keep out of the rain. But Bella never stood in a queue at the Palace. She led the way past and as they went up the steps a man at the front of the queue said aggressively: 'Hey, there's an end to this queue.'

They all stopped. Megan froze with fright. But Bella turned and said firmly, affronted by the remark: 'Yes, and there's a war on. Why aren't you in uniform?'

'I'm doing my bit,' the man said awkwardly.

Then the plump woman with him said loudly: 'He's got a bad leg. You'd send a cripple to the war, would you?'

And Bella snapped in a voice that could be heard right down the queue: 'Yes, I know. There were hundreds of your type suddenly found they had a bad leg in nineteen thirty-nine. I'll bet it will be well enough for you to dance a jig on victory night.'

And they went on up the steps, through the swing doors into the foyer. From up on the wall, Clark Gable looked straight down from his photograph into Rita's eyes. They were all there on the wall, Myrna Loy, William Powell, Leslie Howard. And one day, she thought, Rita Rigby.

Archie, the commissionaire, in a green uniform with tattered cuffs, conducted them up the grand staircase. Megan noticed that Archie, a lanky boy who was judged to be too daft to serve in the forces, was now carrying the leather bag. He held open the door to the restaurant for them and said: 'I'll keep your seats for you, Mrs Rigby. How many of you is it?'

'Nine of us, duck. Where's his nibs?'

'In the projection room. I'll tell him you're here, Mrs Rigby.'

'Don't bother him duck,' Bella said. 'Just pop the bag into his office.'

The restaurant was no longer open to the public. It was closed for the duration. The little round tables, the cane chairs and the potted palms were still there, but it was used as a rest room by the usherettes now and all the ashtrays were full of cigarette ends.

They sat down to wait until the performance started. Rita and Anne sat by themselves near the windows, looking out into the wet street at the people still queueing outside.

'Why did your mother say she had five pound notes in that bag?' Anne asked. 'She gave it to the commissionaire.'

Rita knew what was in the bag. She also knew that she should not tell anybody. From the time they had left Manchester she had been keeping her mother's secrets, mostly about men. In her mind she had a whole compartment of things that she was not to tell her father. 'It's laundry,' she said to Anne. 'She takes some washing to the laundry for the manager. He's not married. He's a Jew, you see, and he can't marry anyone but another Jew, and there aren't any around here.'

'Why did she say it was five pound notes then?'

'Because he's a Jew,' Rita emphasized. 'Some people don't like Jews.' And then, to get off the subject, she said: 'I made three shillings at school last week. That's the most I've ever made.'

'You must have stolen a lot of your mam's fags to make that much,' Anne commented.

Rita glanced across to see if her mother were listening. She was selling cigarettes for twopence each to the girls at school, and she got a penny a stick for the chewing gum which Chuck gave her. Rita saved all the money she got. She bought savings stamps with it at school. Her intention was to buy a long frock. She would never become a film star without a long frock. After her screen test, she imagined she might be asked out to dinner by a producer or a director to discuss her acting, and she would have to have the right things to wear.

'I didn't take any of my mother's fags,' she said softly. 'You know when Chuck stays the night and he sleeps on the sofa in our front room? Well, I found a packet of Lucky Strike down the side. They must have slid down there somehow. And he'd only smoked a few. They were a bit squashed, but nobody minded about that.'

'I don't know how he sleeps on that sofa,' Anne said. 'It's so small. His legs must hang over the arm.'

They pondered over the matter in silence, imagining that Chuck really did sleep there, knowing nothing of the occasional early morning rush down the stairs he had to make when he and Bella had dozed off again after the alarm had gone.

Then Rita said dreamily: 'You know, I'm thinking of changing my name when I'm a film star. I just can't imagine Rita Rigby up in electric lights outside one of those big cinemas in London. I might call myself Isabella Ackerman.'

'Isabella Ackerman?' Anne pulled a face. 'I don't like that. Who on earth would call themself Isabella Ackerman?'

'That was my mother's maiden name,' Rita said and she gave Anne a look that might have belonged to Bella, the hard set mouth, the fire in the eyes.

They took their seats, always the front row balcony left-hand side, near to the toilet because of Mavis. It was a Bette Davis film. Rita enjoyed her films. She reckoned that if she could act as good as Bette Davis, and grew up with her mother's looks, stardom was hers.

During the interval, the manager, Mr Jerome, came down the aisle. He leaned over Bella and said quietly: 'In the office at the end of the programme.' Then he said to Rita: 'Bette Davis,' and smiled at her, showing all his gold teeth.

Mr Jerome owned the house Bella lived in. It was his name that had been written down for her in the pub on that Saturday lunchtime. He also owned the Palace Cinema. The cigarettes would go to a friend who owned a tobacconist shop. And anything else Chuck and Bill managed to get out of the camp he could usually dispose of to one friend or another who happened to be in the appropriate line of business. He was now the main agent for anything they could get their hands on. And he owed it all to Bella, Bella who had come to see him one Saturday afternoon about a house to rent, Bella who had befriended him, a German Jew with a clipped Teutonic accent, who had been interned briefly at the beginning of the war. Bella had told him what people had told her about him. That before the war, when he had fled from Germany, he had landed in England with a suitcase full of money and with banknotes sewn into all his clothes. Of course she never believed it, she had told him, but nevertheless she decided to make a friend of him, just in case.

Ten minutes before the programme ended, Bella left her seat and went to the office. The door was ajar. He was inside. It should have been a brief transaction. He paid a shilling for twenty and sold them to his friend for one and six. But when Bella counted the money, she found she was ten shillings short.

'But Bella my dear, here, look.' He opened the small suitcase into which he had put the cigarettes. 'See? Two hundred fewer Camel than Lucky Strike.'

'I brought the same amount of each,' Bella snapped.

'My dear, you can see . . .'

'You did that to me once before,' she went on, her voice rising. 'Don't you twist me. Now come on.'

'But Bella.' He shrugged and showed his palms.

'Look.' She jabbed him on the lapel. 'Just you watch out. If I tell Chuck and Bill, they'll give you a right working over.'

'My dear, why should I do such a thing? We are friends, you and I. Do you think I would jeopardize everything for ten shillings?'

She gave him a look of hate, unblinking, right in his eyes. 'Yes – well,' she said uncertainly, 'I don't know about that. But what I do know is that there's a war on, and your lot got us into it.' And she went out and slammed the door.

He mopped his brow, sighed and sat on the edge of his desk. He had only himself to blame. He had caught Archie red-handed the other time, the first time he had decided to help himself to the cigarettes. It was too late to do anything about it now, the time to act had gone. Archie had called him an old Jewbag and had threatened to tell the police. He might be daft, but he knew the cigarettes were stolen. Mr Jerome had been caught, not Archie. He should have called Archie's bluff, or told Bella – she had an answer for everything. But business is for profit, not loss, he had been taught, and he had passed the loss on to Bella. No one had taught him that one could incur greater losses than financial ones. He had fled from one enemy, and yet even now he was making an enemy of a friend. All for ten shillings. He could not understand himself.

There was a knock at the door. 'Tea, Mr Jerome,' one of the girls called.

Tea, a look at the evening paper, listen to the six o'clock news on the wireless, then change out of the lounge suit he wore for the afternoons, into the dinner jacket he always put on for the evening performance. 'Come in, my dear,' he said, taking the suitcase off the desk and putting it behind the door, by the safe.

The film finished and Bella led the way, blinking from the dark cinema, into the bright afternoon. The rain had stopped, the sun was drying the pavements. Then, just ahead of them, Megan saw the man who had shouted at them from the cinema queue, limping heavily along the street. And she felt the shame of responsibility come over her.

Ronnie wanted chips. They walked down the street to the fish and chip shop. They were not yet open, but they were frying and there was a queue outside already, getting hungrier on the smell. Megan took her purse out of her pocket, but Bella said: 'No, I'll get them. After all, it didn't cost me anything to get you all into the pictures.'

It was only the children who wanted chips. Bella gave Rita one and sixpence to get six threepennyworths, and left the children standing in the queue. She led June and Megan over the road to where there was a seat by the war memorial, by the bronze plaques covered with the names of the dead from the Great War. They could keep an eye on the queue from there.

'Chips used to be a big treat in our house when I was a kid,' Bella said. 'We never got fish with them. Peas maybe, but no fish. With ten kids, what could you expect?'

'That's more than we got in our house,' June remarked.

And Bella said: 'Well, there were fourteen kids in your family, weren't there? I mean, even Jesus Christ with his fives loaves and two fishes couldn't have fed your lot.'

Megan was aghast at the blasphemous thing Bella had

43

said, but Bella took out her cigarettes and offered her one, and as she took it she felt guilty at ever criticizing Bella in her mind, Bella who always paid for the drinks when they went out, who was always first to hand round her cigarettes, who kept her and her two boys in stolen food, Bella who was coarse and adulterous and was probably, for all Megan knew, the salt of the earth.

'There were fourteen of us,' June said, holding out her lighter for Megan and Bella to light their cigarettes, 'but they weren't all my father's. I'm one of his – well, he said I was. But my mother, she was so . . .' She searched for a word. 'Friendly. She had more men than me and Bella put together.'

'You can say that again,' Bella remarked.

'She got off with the coalman once, my mother,' June said casually.

'I'll bet that made a mess of the sheets,' Bella joked.

And as if she had not heard, June went on: 'That cold winter it was. She had our Ernie by him.'

'Your Ernie? She never did,' Bella challenged her. 'Your Ernie is ginger.'

'So was that coalman,' June replied. 'When he had a bath he was ginger. He used to take it out on us, my father, when he'd had a drink. Belt the living daylights out of any of us he could catch. It was having to keep us, I suppose, all those kids, half of who weren't his. It was daft really. We couldn't help it. It wasn't our fault. He never layed a finger on my mother, though. He loved my mother.'

'Everybody loved your mother,' Bella observed. 'That's how she got fourteen children all with different colour hair. Your mother must be the only woman in history who went to a funeral and got pregnant.'

That took Megan's breath away. She let the ash grow long and grey on the end of her cigarette while they told her about it.

'That was when her sister Maude died in Liverpool. Do you remember, Bella? We had to scour every house in the street to get her enough black clothes to go in. They did things properly in those days. She went with her sister Ruby.'

'I also remember,' Bella stated, 'that there was more than

44

one house in the street that sent something to uncle's to raise the money for a wreath and the train fare.'

'That's right.' June smiled at the thought of it, as if it were a beautiful memory. 'Hearts of gold, those people.'

'That was the only gold any of them had,' Bella said, 'except for a wedding ring.'

'So she went to Liverpool with my Auntie Ruby,' June went on, 'and after the funeral, they were walking back to the railway station when it came on to rain. And a man asked them if they would like to step into his hallway until the storm had passed. So they did, and that's how our Lenny came to be born. Couldn't help but be friendly, my mother. Now she might have had doubts about who had caused some of us to come into the world, but not with our Lenny. He was coloured, you see. Just like the man who asked them in out of the rain.'

'He was a lovely lad, your Lenny,' Bella said.

'Even my father liked him,' June revealed. 'He used to say: "Lenny, you're my favourite. You can do no wrong. Because whatever you do in life, they can't blame any of it on me. Anybody can see you're not mine. But whatever you do, be good to your mother, because she's the only relation you've got." He always used to tell him that, our Lenny. He joined the merchant navy, you know. He was on an oil tanker. It got sunk in the Atlantic in nineteen forty-one. All hands were lost. He was the only one my mother and father cried over. He was the only one they were really sure about.'

'He was a lovely lad, your Lenny,' Bella said again.

The ash dropped off Megan's cigarette on to her coat. There were voices, and she looked round. The children were coming across the road, eating their chips.

When they got home that afternoon, Rita put the kettle on for a cup of tea while Anne put the crockery on the table and tried to match the assortment of cups to the mixture of saucers. Bella had gone straight next door with June to tell her of the missing ten shillings, and to give her a half share of the money. To Chuck and Bill, a few thousand cigarettes was regarded as just pin money for the girls.

'Rita, come quick. Rita!' Bella was shouting over the garden wall. When Rita and Anne got next door they saw Mr Fisher, in his fawn mac and his cap, sitting in the outside lavatory, unconscious with drink, cider bottles everywhere.

'Come on, get one arm each,' Bella instructed them.

'Oh mam, leave him there. He can come out on his own when he's sober,' Rita said. It was hardly the training for fame, the background she wanted to recall, helping to carry a drunken old man out of the lavatory.

'Get an arm each,' Bella snapped. 'Do as I say.' Then she turned to Mavis, who was standing crosslegged, and said sweetly to her: 'Go and use Auntie Bella's, love.'

Reluctantly, Rita and Anne took an arm each, while Bella and June took him by the legs. They carried him, too drunk to be aware of anything, into the house and up the stairs, feet first. They were halfway up the stairs when Anne said: 'Mrs Rigby, don't you think we'd better turn him round? The blood might rush to his head.'

'Put some colour in his cheeks,' Bella said and they carried on upwards.

They put him on his bed and June took off his boots.

Later that evening they were sitting in the Manhattan Lounge of the Shire Hotel and Bella was smoking a cigarette in a long holder and feeling very elegant. There were soft lights, a pianist in a dinner jacket with a white carnation, old waiters who came at a beckon and the hint of a tip. Bella longed to sit on one of the tall stools at the bar, but Chuck would not let her. It was expensive in the Manhattan Lounge. Only the better off and the Americans went there. Bella liked that. She liked the atmosphere it gave to the place. She got the feeling there that she was cut off completely from her old world, from her real world. It was what she wanted in life, the things money could buy.

Then June said: 'When you think of it, only a few hours ago we were carrying Mr Fisher upstairs, feet first, boots and all.'

Bella blew a long cloud of cigarette smoke and without looking at June said: 'Leave it behind you, can't you, just for a few hours?' and had the same thought Rita had had earlier, the thought that everything in her past life would be worth forgetting if it could be replaced by the sort of life in which coming into the Manhattan Lounge was an ordinary everyday thing.

46

Six

They had never had anyone like Bella at the town hall before. Even in peacetime they had never had anyone dress as smart. She struck them all with her good looks, her sleek black hair, her bright red lipstick, her high heeled shoes with the ankle straps. She made the office boys ambitious and made the old men have young dreams.

Everyone liked Bella. She brightened all their days, was cheerful all the time, never had an off day. And she worked. She did all the office jobs that nobody else wanted to do, without ever realizing that she was getting the butt end of the job. She was in an office and as long as she could work there she would do anything. After spending hours doing the most mundane job, a job that would have bored anyone else to tears, she remarked: 'One thing I like about office work. It's interesting – keeps your brain occupied,' sounding as happy as a sandboy.

Bella knew that this was her big opportunity. Even if she was still working there when the war ended, when she would have to leave, there would be a reference to leave with. A reference would be a passport to another office job. An office job would enable her to speak on something like equal terms to Chuck's family, who grew fruit and owned a cannery. She would never mention to them the cold, dark winter mornings when she had gone off to the mill, with her clogs clattering on the cobbled road. The talk would be of her office job, as if she had never done any other sort of work.

Miss Hackett always wore something black, because she was still in mourning for her boyfriend who had been killed in the Great War. After nearly thirty years of it she was too old to see the futility of her action. 'What shall I call you, love?' Bella asked her. 'Miss Hackett seems a bit formal.'

'Well, Miss Hackett it is. I don't like all these Christian names being used. Wouldn't have happened before the war. Things will never be the same.'

In her strange way, Miss Hackett was fond of Bella. She treated anyone who wanted to see Mr Shanklin just as brusquely as she had treated her the day she had brought back his wallet. It had not been personal. Soon she developed the same protective attitude towards Bella that she had for Mr Shanklin. When Miss Hackett was around, no one was going to foist just any old job off on Bella. Bella could not understand it. But she had never been lonely.

She was curious though, curious to find out the reason why Mr Shanklin had gone into the little park with June that night, spent two pounds and risked it being found out who he was. She knew she would not find out from Miss Hackett though, even though she had worked for him for ten years, for she was starched stiff with propriety. But Bella admired her. She could actually type and carry on a conversation at the same time, a miracle to one who could do nothing but jam all the keys down.

Bella was given the job of standing in for Eileen, the receptionist, at lunchtime. That was Mr Shanklin's idea. He had not forgotten that she had mentioned her liking for the receptionist's job during their conversation that day, and he felt pleased with himself when the idea came to him. It made him feel safer too, having done this extra thing to please her. The fact that none of the other girls liked standing in for Eileen, that it caused arguments enough, was another matter.

And having got to know Eileen, Bella lived up to her promise to Mr Shanklin, caught hold of a handful of Eileen's wild, dry hair and said with her tongue in her cheek: 'You'd have lovely hair if you looked after it. What ever do you wash it in, static water?' Then she went on: 'Here, I've brought this for you,' and she took out of her handbag a shampoo bottle. It was about one third full. 'There, that's for you. That's proper shampoo. That's pre-war. Heaven knows when you'll be able to go into a chemist again and buy a bottle of shampoo. I've been saving it, but you can have it. I've got the sort of hair that looks nice whatever you wash it in. Eke it out mind.'

Eileen took the shampoo. She got her hair under control.

Bella told her to wear a piece of ribbon around it and she did so. And then she asked her to go to a Friday-night dance at the camp. 'We catch the bus by the cattle market. We'll wait for you at the stop, me and my friend.'

'She won't go,' Miss Hackett said. 'Never in this world. They won't let her.'

'She said she would,' Bella replied. 'She's nineteen. Old enough to please herself.'

'She won't go,' Miss Hackett maintained. 'I'd bet money that she won't go, only I don't bet. I think it's cruel making those horses jump over those high fences.'

Bella went on about the nice men, the band, the beautiful dance floor. 'They put French chalk down. It's real dancing. If you want to jitterbug you have to keep up one end.'

'I don't care if it's polished mahogany. You won't find anyone from Belvedere Drive going to a dance at the American camp, or at any other camp for that matter.'

'Heavens,' Bella exclaimed. 'Does she live up there as well? They must practically own the street.'

On Friday Bella was appointed receptionist for the day. Eileen was absent with a bilious attack. 'Didn't I tell you so?' Miss Hackett said at eleven o'clock, when Bella came up to have her tea. 'Look Bella, the job's the thing. You've got the job. Don't try to take it any further. I've been working in the town hall for twenty years and I've never got involved with any of the higher ups and they've never got involved with me. Everyone here will tell you the same. It's knowing your place and sticking to it. Come home time, they go off to live their lives and we go off to live ours.'

Bella took the hint. She could put a rebuff like that behind her. She was ambitious, and all her thoughts and plans were for the future. She, unlike Miss Hackett, had no longing for anything in the past. She had no dead to remember. All her dead remained dead.

Eileen's small-voiced apology was received politely. And the only hint of bitterness to come from Bella was when she said to Miss Hackett: 'That Eileen ought to do something about her skin. Talk about blackheads. Her nose is like a mushroom bed.'

There were two high, wide doors at the top of the main staircase in the town hall. The first time Bella saw them open she went straight into the room and saw Mr Shanklin standing there alone in the middle of the floor. The place was empty. 'Hello,' she said, 'what's this place?'

'This, my dear? This empty shell is the ballroom.'

'Well,' she remarked, 'I wouldn't fancy tripping the light fantastic in here. Looks like an army has marched over this floor. And those curtains. They're torn to shreds.'

Mr Shanklin looked up at the ragged curtains, drawn back from the high windows. 'Enemy action in nineteen forty-one. Our one and only air raid. And that was a mistake. It was assumed that the bomber lost its way going to a raid on Birmingham. Intended jettisoning its bombs in the countryside to facilitate a speedy escape, but hit us instead.'

'What? Missed all those green fields? He must have had his hands over his eyes,' she said. 'Is that what happened to the street back of where I live?'

He nodded. 'Seven people killed. One bomb fell right there in the square. Early hours of the morning, so no one got hurt there – no residential property. But it blew the windows in and the glass made that mess of our curtains.'

'You were lucky to get the windows mended,' she observed.

'We have a council member in the trade,' Mr Shanklin said softly, as if it were still a secret.

'Well, you won't get any new curtains until the war's over,' she said. 'Not to fit those big windows. Might as well lock the place up and forget it.'

'We can't do that, Mrs Rigby,' he said. 'I only wish we could. We have Mr Bevin, the Minister of Labour, coming in a few weeks time. We've got to entertain him somewhere, and all the civic dignitaries and all the heads of our local industries. War or no war, everyone wants to get in on this sort of event.'

'You have got a problem there, haven't you?'

He sighed. 'What with the Ministry of Food taking up nearly all of our ground floor. We could have had it down there.' He walked around in a little circle, then said: 'To think that in nineteen thirty-four, the King – Duke of York he was then – and his wife, the Duchess, were entertained in this very room. They walked through those doors on to a floor that shone like glass. The mayor, the sheriff, everyone dressed in their regalia. We had two men dressed as footmen just to open those doors. Scarlet coats, wigs, everything. We got the clothes from a theatrical costumier's in Bristol. Cost a fortune, Mrs Rigby. Expensive business, opening a door for a royal duke – if you do it properly, that is.'

'Good job you got him when he was a duke then, love. It must cost more to open a door for a king – properly.'

She left him then, looking miserable, and went down to relieve Eileen who was waiting to go to lunch.

Although Mr Shanklin was frightened of Bella, frightened of what she knew about him, he liked the look of her. He could not help sneaking glances at her. If only he had seen her first, he used to think to himself, instead of the little blonde, that night in the Plough. But Bella, he reckoned, would be worth more than two pounds. It would be worth two pounds just to be with her. From his passionless wife, to the women he paid for love, to Bella, was an age and another world, was something he could not put a price to. His fear and his feelings were not relieved by looking at her, but he could not help it, he could not help thinking about her, could not drive out of his mind the fantasy of being rich enough to install her in a flat somewhere and visit her at night.

The following morning he called her into his office. 'What I want to ask you, Mrs Rigby, is whether, in the event of us having a reception in the ballroom for the Minister of Labour, you would be willing to assist?'

'Only too glad to help, duck,' Bella replied. 'What do you want me to do?'

'Let me explain,' he began. 'It being wartime, we feel that with our limited resources – because of rationing and other restrictions – we cannot have a sit-down meal, or even a buffet – that least of all. We envisage a mad dash by some people for the food. Therefore, we require the services of someone like yourself to take the food and drink round on trays. That way we shall have fair shares for all, I think. What do you say?'

'Delighted. You don't need to ask twice. I'll see no greedy beggar hogs the lot.'

Mr Shanklin adopted a bemused expression and said half to himself: 'Well, that's one problem solved.' And then he explained to her: 'The firm which normally organizes the civic functions has gone out of business owing to the war, otherwise we would have proper staff waiting on the guests.'

'Beats me what you'll give them to eat and drink,' Bella remarked. 'After all, you will be feeding all the nobs, won't you?'

'Yes, well I think we shall be able to manage something,' he said darkly. 'And one of the aldermen is a wine merchant – he has graciously offered to provide the liquid refreshment.'

'Good job a bomb never fell on his shop then, isn't it?' And she smiled, but Mr Shanklin did not find it funny.

'The other thing is, Mrs Rigby, that we wondered if you could find someone else to help out. The snag is, you see, we rather hoped you would do it on a voluntary basis. Funds are low and . . .'

'And there is a war on,' she finished the sentence for him. 'Of course, we'll do it just for the fun of it. I'll ask my friend June. She'll do it. You know her, she's the one you got down on the grass with that night.'

'Oh no, no.' Pain, anguish, they all showed in Mr Shanklin's face at the very mention of that night. 'I really don't think so. No.'

'I've got it then,' Bella said, having enjoyed her little joke. 'I'll bring Rita, my daughter. She's fourteen is my Rita, but she's tall, taller than me going on. She's going to the tech in the autumn. Shorthand and typing and that. I like to see the young ones getting on, having the opportunities we didn't have – or at least, some of us never.'

'That's settled then,' Mr Shanklin said. 'I'll tell the custodian. That will be you and Rita – yes? And the custodian and his wife.'

Bella went towards the door, then turned and smiled the smile that taunted him, that haunted him. She said: 'Do you know, I'm looking forward to it already. If there's anything I enjoy it's a bunfight, especially a posh one.' Then she said: 'But you're going to have to do something about those curtains.'

The difference between working full-time at the laundry and part-time at the town hall eventually began to manifest itself in a way that had not entered Bella's head in the excitement of getting the job. Financially, she was not so well off. She had got more money at the laundry and there had been overtime. She would not have gone back there. She reckoned that the financial loss was far below the gain in status she was enjoying, even though this elevation in her class of work raised her up more in her own eyes than in anyone else's. But just as Rita was saving up for a long frock, so Bella was saving up for that trip to America. There had to be no snags when the time came. She was thirty-two, at that age in life when time starts going by faster. She had to have a few pounds in her pocket, just in case.

But Bella could not begin to save. If she had had something to start with she would have been able to, but that first five shillings, those two half crowns in a cocoa tin on the top shelf in the pantry, they seemed so insignificant. By Thursday she was tipping them into her hand to see herself through until she got paid on Friday afternoon. If she could find a five pound note in the street . . . if she went on the game for a few nights. The Americans had caused the price to rise so much that she could have made a fortune. If June could ask two pounds . . . But she would not do that because of Chuck. In a small town like that, she knew that once you went on the game the word got round. She took a cigarette out of a packet of Camel, lit it and wondered why, when she had smoked five cigarettes out of a packet of twenty, there were only twelve left.

One night, in the lecture room, in Chuck's arms, awkwardly seated on a chair that was designed to prevent anyone bored by a lecture from falling asleep, she had an idea. She knew how she could make some money. And at the same time, she thought, she might be able to do Mr Shanklin a favour which would not be beyond repaying.

She would need June's help and she was bursting to tell her. There were too many people who might overhear on the bus, so she contained herself until they got home and were drinking tea in the kitchen. 'You know those curtains I was telling you about in the town hall ballroom?'

'The ones that got all torn in the bombing?'

'That's right.' Bella was looking pleased with herself already. 'I know where I can get some new ones.'

53

'You never can.' June put down her cup. 'In wartime? For great big windows like that?'

'I can. I shall have to pinch them mind,' she said frankly, 'but they're not being used, so it won't be much of a loss.'

June's mouth was agape. 'Where from ever?'

'From the lecture room,' Bella replied simply. 'You'll have to help me, mind.'

'I'm not pinching any curtains from the lecture room,' June said definitely. 'I didn't know there were any curtains there, anyway.'

'Well, there are and they won't be missed. Even you haven't noticed them, although the only light we get in there is the moon. It's money, June. They must be worth – well, pounds. And if I can do the town clerk a favour and get him some curtains, it might help me on a bit. I'm only working part-time, after all.'

'Oh, I don't know,' June said unhappily. 'Why don't you tell the town clerk they've got some curtains going spare? Then he could buy them off the Yanks.'

'You dim twit,' Bella said angrily. 'I'm not supposed to know they are there. I'm not supposed to know the lecture room even exists. None of us are.'

Bella was quiet for a while then. Her eyes focused on nothing as her imagination worked. 'What I've got to think of is this,' she said eventually. 'There is a war on. What if something should happen to Chuck? Well, I'd still want to go to America. This country isn't going to be worth living in after the war. It's bad enough now. All the bomb damage, the widows, the war orphans. America, that's the place. They don't know there's been a war over there, except for the GIs who are fighting it. No bombing, no rationing. If I keep in with old Shanklin, they might not get rid of me when the war's over. If I still need to go on working for a while, that is. And think of our Rita. If she's going to the tech, then he'll be just the sort to know when it comes to getting her a job. Yes, you've got to look to the future and that's what I'm doing.' She was quiet again then for a minute, before saying sharply to June: 'Well, what about it? Are you going to help me pinch these curtains or not?'

June did not answer. She sipped gloomily at her tea, looking down at the table, avoiding the piercing look Bella was giving her.

Then Bella said fiercely: 'The things I've done for you. What about the time I got you off that banana boat on the Manchester ship canal? Stowing away. Going to live on a tropical island in the West Indies. Going to live in a little grass hut on the beach.'

'Well, I was only eighteen, Bella.'

'And what about that seaman you were going to share your little grass hut with? Horrible. He was horrible.'

'It was dark when I met him Bella. He didn't look too bad . . .'

'It was dark when you met him and it was dark four hours later when I got you off that boat. If it hadn't been for that second officer, I don't know what would have happened to you. At least there was one gentleman in the merchant navy.'

June gave in then.

Bella had it all worked out. The next time they went to the lecture room they would do it. They would not involve Chuck and Bill. They might say no. But first, Bella said to Rita as she came in from school one afternoon: 'Rita, go down to Mrs Sadler's will you duck? Tell her Auntie June wants to borrow her pram.'

'Wants to borrow her pram?' Rita queried.

'That's right. That old one she fetches her coal in.'

'What do you want it for, mam? You're not going over the foundry to pinch coal again are you, like you did last winter? It's dangerous going over those railway lines in the dark. Auntie June said she wouldn't go again.'

'Of course not, silly,' Bella said, laughing. 'Tell Mrs Sadler Auntie June has bought a roll of lino from Bentley's, and they can't deliver it because their horse is sick. And love,' she called as Rita went out, 'put it in Auntie June's back yard.'

Among the murmurings and the moans and the soft words in the lecture room that night, Bella was tense in Chuck's arms. Chuck did not notice. He fed off her like a bee feeds off a flower. All at once she said: 'Let up a minute, love. I shall have to go and spend a penny.'

The men never used the toilet. It was reserved for the girls. They all used to crowd in there before they went home, tidying themselves up by the light of a torch. It was in the corridor outside. Bella groped her way out through the huddled couples, opened the toilet door, but did not go in. Just by the door was a window which opened on to the boundary fence. She caught hold of the handle to open it. It would not move. It had not been opened since the place had been built and Bella hurt her hands trying to get it to move. But she was not easily beaten. She put her shoulder under the handle, braced her arms down on the window sill, gritted her teeth and pushed. There was a loud squeak that seemed to sound right through the building as the handle went up and Bella rubbed her shoulder and blinked her watering eyes. She pushed the window open half an inch, then went back to Chuck's loving arms.

Bella and June caught the bus home at ten o'clock and as soon as they got there they changed their clothes. 'Put on your slacks and your mac,' Bella instructed June, 'your daps and a headscarf.'

It took them half an hour to walk to the cemetery, pushing the empty pram. They had to leave it at the lych gate. The gate was always locked and the only access was by a little stile. There was a big moon that night and all the marble crosses and angels stood out white above the graves. June was frightened to death. She clung on to Bella as they walked along the gravel path past the thick black yew trees. Bella was oblivious to the atmosphere. She said: 'Les used to say these were the sort of nights the Luftwaffe liked. They could find their way there and back easier.'

They went under the boundary fence and along the back of the lecture room. 'Now look,' Bella said to June, who was silent with fear, 'you don't have to come in. You stay out here. If anybody comes, slip away quietly.'

'Oh, I won't leave you, Bella,' she replied, fear of having to go through the graveyard alone governing her thoughts.

'Do as I say,' Bella hissed. 'If we both go to jail, who's going to look after the children? Now, give me a bunk up through this window.'

The bright moon lit up the middle of the room. She could pick her way, without stumbling, through the pairs and clusters of chairs that had been arranged to accomodate the lovers. In one corner, Bella knew, there was a step ladder. Someone had stumbled against it in the dark one night and it had fallen on them. She felt her way around the dark walls until she found it, then dragged it to the windows and erected it. It was a rickety thing and she clung on to the curtains as she went up the steps. The curtains were hung by large rings on a thick rail. The rail moved as she put her hand underneath it. It lifted clear of the bracket holding it. Then, as she adjusted her position on the steps, she inadvertently let the rail slope downwards and the curtain fell off the end, making a clatter as the rings hit the floor. It was easy then. She got the others down in the same way.

The curtains were heavier than Bella had imagined. They were bulky too, as she discovered when she gathered the first one up to take it out. When she got to the open window she could not see June. She whistled and June unfolded herself from the crouching position she had adopted, over by the boundary fence. 'I've got the curtains down, love,' Bella said. 'They're heavy. I'll bring them one at a time,' and the rings rattled against the window sill as she passed the curtains out. June remained silent, still mute with fear.

The last thing she did was to put the steps back in the corner. Then she climbed out through the window and pushed it shut. The unlatched window, she hoped, was the only clue she had left.

The bulky curtains were awkward to carry. Bella wanted to stop in the graveyard and fold them up but June was too scared and they had to make two journeys from the boundary fence to the lych gate where they had left the pram. Then Bella had to line the pram with newspaper because of the coal dust that coated it. It all took time and the longer it took the more nervous June became. Her hands shook so much that she was no help at all. And the curtains filled the pram. Bella pushed them down as best she could but they still formed a great conspicuous mound. Finally they set off through the empty streets, feeling secure eventually in the blackout and the dark shadows of the buildings.

Once she was away from the graveyard, June regained her composure. Bella noticed this and taunted her gently. 'What are you going to do if a policeman stops us?'

'I'll leave all the talking to you, Bella, like I always do.'

'I don't know why, honestly. I shall never forget the time that man exposed himself to you in the park. What was it you said to him? "What are you showing off about? I've seen bigger ones than that."'

They laughed at the memory of it. 'And he ran away,' June said, 'he ran away.'

Seven

Despite what she knew about Mr Shanklin, Bella realized that he was important. No one went marching into his office to see him, even if Miss Hackett was not there. People made an appointment to see him. Miss Hackett had an appointments book specifically for the job. And that morning he was fully booked, just because Bella wanted to see him.

She was on duty at the reception desk when he came back from lunch. 'Have you got a minute, love?' Bella said to him. He came across to her and she went on: 'You know your awful curtains up in the ballroom? Well, I know someone who's got some for sale. I've got you first refusal.'

'Have you?' he said, with an air of disbelief. 'Who's got curtains to fit those big windows, and in wartime too?'

'I've got this friend, you see. He's got a restaurant in Manchester. It had big windows just like yours. Only it got bombed. So as he hasn't got any windows now, he doesn't need the curtains.'

Mr Shanklin looked at her sitting there with her arms crossed over her firm breasts, with her black hair done in a fringe that day and making her look like Cleopatra. He looked at her bright red lips, her bright red nails and her pencil thin black eyebrows, and he did not trust her. What, he wondered, did she want out of him now? He said: 'His windows got blown in, did they, and his curtains never got touched?'

Bella could see through him as clearly as if he were a pane of glass. And she did not like being doubted. Still, she knew she was the only one in the town hall who could talk to him without any respect, she knew she was the only one there he was afraid of. 'He had some spare ones, love,' she replied. 'Those are the ones he wants to sell. He's not so mean as you people, having only ever bought one set.' She let that sink in for a second, then said: 'If you're not interested, love, don't bother. He can make a fortune cutting them up and selling them.'

Mr Shanklin was less unsure of it now. 'How much does he want for them?'

'I can get them for you for about twenty-five pounds. But you'll have to let me know pretty quickly. He's moving down here from Manchester – bought a little place in the country – and he'll bring them with him.'

'Of course, I shall have to consult the council,' he said. It was one thing doing business with her, but the thought of coming into contact with her friend from Manchester was even more off-putting. 'In the meantime, I must ask you not to mention this to anyone. In wartime this sort of thing is not fully above board.'

'Oh, you don't have to worry about me, love. I can keep a secret. After all, you know that better than most people.'

Anyone who could lay their hands on things that were in short supply was thought a lot of in wartime, Bella knew that. She could imagine Mr Shanklin putting on an air of being in the know to those council members he would have to mention it to.

But in actual fact he spoke only to a couple of town hall officials about it, trusted colleagues. The council could not risk being involved in what might be a black market deal. The treasury could not risk forwarding the money to pay. And so, unofficially, the curtains would be purchased. Those who dipped into their pockets to pay for them would get their reward through their job, through the town hall, through the hands of those who gave out the rewards for public service.

He called Bella into his office the following morning. 'How much did you say this friend of yours wanted for the curtains? Twenty-five pounds? What colour are they?'

'A sort of buff colour,' she replied.

'I shall have to see them first. Can you arrange it – discreetly?'

'Of course I can, love. I'll get in touch with my friend and arrange it.'

She was halfway to the door when he said: 'I hope they really are suitable. Even in wartime, one likes to make the right impression. Not only for the Minister of Labour. We have quite a guest list. Heads of local industries, the commanding officer at the American camp.'

She had turned round to listen to him. 'The commanding officer?' she queried, in a voice that was failing.

'Yes. We have invited him and two or three of his staff. We have never recognized the Americans as part of our community, and yet, in reality, they are. I must say he most graciously accepted our invitation.'

Bella went straight to the lavatory and smoked a cigarette. She was so angry and upset that it made her feel sick all day. It was made worse by the fact that she could speak to no one about it except June, and she had to contain herself until she got home from the parachute factory at half past five. Even then, the only relief she got was in talking about the fix she was in. June was no help whatsoever. There were the curtains, under Bella's bed on a carpet of dust and fluff, worth twenty-five pounds one minute and nothing at all the next.

It came to Bella while she was getting ready to go out that evening. She was making up her face in front of her bedroom mirror when it dawned on her, and she smiled at herself with relief. All day she had had to think about it, and yet the most simple solution of all had only just come to her. It was the obvious answer to the problem.

They were to meet Chuck and Bill in the town that night. As they set off down the street, Bella told June, 'I should have thought of it before. It's so simple I feel soft that it didn't dawn on me straight away. They only need dyeing a different colour. Then even if the Yanks do miss them, they'll never recognize them. I'll get Derek Pobjoy to do them for me.'

'Oh Bella, what a good idea.' Even June sounded relieved. 'I wonder how much he'll want?'

'I'll phone him up in the morning. I know Alice on the switchboard at the laundry. She'll put me through to the dyeing room. She's not supposed to, but she'll do it for me.'

If Bella had anything, she had friends. The woman on the switchboard at the town hall was not supposed to let people have personal calls, but for Bella it was all right. Alice at the laundry was not supposed to put through personal calls, but she did it for Bella. But there are friends and friends. And

Derek Pobjoy fell into the second category.

She had to meet him at a pub in the town the following night. Certainly he would dye the curtains for her. Dark blue, just as she wanted. They were on war work in the dyeing room and they had to dye all sorts of things dark blue. And he was not at all interested in whose they were. None of his business. Neither did he want any money for doing it. He wanted paying, but he was not going to take money, not off Bella.

Bella was considerate enough not to bother June with the details that night. She did not want to spoil her sleep. The following morning, Saturday, she told her.

'The thing is, June, this Derek Pobjoy is a bit odd in some ways. That's why I never got a job in the dyeing room. I wouldn't play along with him and his ways. Anyway, if I want the curtains dyed, I'm afraid I'm going to have to give in to his odd ways, for one night, at least.'

June was full of sympathy. 'Oh Bella, I am sorry. All through trying to do someone a good turn. Damn the town clerk, and his curtains.'

'It's not the town clerk you're going to damn, June. It's Derek Pobjoy. You see, he doesn't only want me. He wants you as well. He wants both of us, one each side of him, all bare and naked beneath the sheets.'

'No, Bella, no.' Even June, whose experiences in life were not the sort that could be discussed casually in just any kind of company, was repulsed momentarily by the thought of it. 'Not both of us. Not together. Oh, I couldn't.'

But Bella knew her weak spot. She said: 'Well, love, it's either that or take those curtains back one night. All that traipsing through the graveyard.'

June thought for a moment. 'Why does he want me? You didn't say . . .?'

'I didn't say a thing about you. He didn't even know your name. He asked for you. That little blonde you knock about with, he said. Reckons he's always fancied you – fancies us both.'

'I've never seen him, Bella,' June said. She sounded dazed by it all. 'What's he like?'

'Never seen him? Well he's seen you. He styles himself on Ronald Colman.'

'Like Ronald Colman, is he?'

'I didn't say that. I said he styles himself on Ronald Colman. He's got the moustache, but nothing else. Anyway, love,' Bella said, 'by the time we've finished with him, he might not even have that.'

They went into town together then, June to get the rations, Bella to see Derek Pobjoy at a rendezvous in the Mechanics' Arms. It was a dull looking place in a backstreet. She went into the saloon bar and there he was, looking slightly unclean, leaning against the bar. He bought her a light ale and she arranged for her and June to see him on Monday evening, at his flat. While these arrangements were being made, Bella looked along the counter into the public bar.

'That's Archie, isn't it?' she said. 'The commissionaire at the Palace.'

'That's him. Daft Archie. He's a regular here.'

'They shouldn't let him in,' Bella maintained. 'He's only fifteen and six in the pound.'

'He's old enough,' Derek Pobjoy replied. 'Anyway, he's quite popular here. He gets a few American cigarettes to sell occasionally.'

'Does he now?' Bella tried not to sound too interested. 'How often is occasionally?'

'Oh, now and again. Why, has that American I've seen you about with cut off your ration?'

'I won't tell him you said that, Derek, otherwise you might not be fit for Monday night.' She drank the last of her beer and left feeling more pleased than she imagined she would, wondering what she could do to Archie for stealing her cigarettes.

She walked back through the town and kept her eyes open to try and spot June in amongst the crowds of Saturday shoppers, but she did not see her. But she did see Mr Jerome. She spotted him on the other side of the street and her first thought was to go across and tell him that she suspected Archie of stealing the cigarettes, but the idea went from her mind when she saw the concerned look on his face, when she noticed that he was coming out of the police station.

Mr Jerome saw Bella at the same moment that she saw him. He came across the road to her and began: 'Bella, my dear . . .'

But she did not allow him to say more. 'What were you doing in the police station?' she asked him bluntly. 'You don't supply their canteen from the black market, do you?'

'I will tell you,' he said. 'Come, we will go to the Blue Café and have a cup of tea.'

He was glad to have someone to tell it to and he could not wait until they got to the café but jabbered on about it as they walked down the street. The night before, he had been stopped by the police just after he had driven away from the cemetery with his boot and back seat loaded with food from the camp. They had been watching him, they said. They wanted to know where he got his petrol from to be driving around so much. They seemed not to notice that he had a mound of something covered over with a rug on his back seat, or that the car was weighed down at the back, although they flashed their lights all over it. The one thing Mr Jerome did not have was black market petrol. He only just managed to eke out his ration making night-time deliveries to his customers.

He opened the door for Bella, and they went into the café. They got a table over by the window. The window was hung with net curtains to give a bit of privacy from the street. There were dead bluebottles on the window sill. She did not fancy drinking tea on top of beer. If nothing else, it would give her the wind. But she had left herself no option.

'Then, just when I thought everything was going all right,' he said, 'they asked me for my identity card and I did not have it. I had left it in my other coat.'

'You can go to prison for not having your identity card,' she told him. She sipped her tea. It was tasteless and she thought of the time when you automatically had biscuits with a cup of tea, before Hitler put a stop to it.

'I showed them my driving licence and said I had just taken one of the usherettes home because she had missed the bus, as it was gone midnight. And they said I had to go to the police station this morning with my identity card.'

'Lies,' she said self-righteously. 'You never get anywhere telling lies. Are they taking you to court?'

'No, they just told me to be careful, that next time . . .' He did not tell her that he had had a lecture from an old sergeant, a man who had been a sergeant for twenty-five years and would never be anything else, a man who seemed to get some satisfaction from frightening people with his authority. That, he imagined, was part of the attraction of the job. He had seen people enjoying that aspect of their job in Germany.

'Well you want to be careful,' Bella told him sharply. 'They might intern you for the duration.'

'Me? But I am a naturalized British citizen. I have my papers.'

'That makes no difference,' she warned him. 'After all, you are a German. You were born a German. Papers don't alter that. Anyway, a leopard can't change its spots, even if it has got papers to say it can. So you watch out, my lad, and be thankful you've got friends like me to advise you.'

She drank the rest of her tea. There were no tealeaves in the bottom of the cup, which was hardly surprising, she thought, since the tasteless stuff bore no resemblance at all to the proper thing, barring its colour.

That afternoon, Bella was boiling the kettle for her all-over wash ready for the dance that night, when Mavis ran in. 'Auntie Bella, mam says to come quick. Uncle Fisher's fallen down the stairs and made a mess in the hall.'

'Oh lovie, that sounds awful. Never mind, Auntie Bella to the rescue,' and she took Mavis by the hand and went next door.

Mr Fisher had fallen halfway down the stairs and then been sick in the hall. He had finally collapsed in the kitchen doorway.

'Oh Bella,' June said with concern, 'he's not doing himself any good going on like this. He's going from bad to worse.'

'He's not doing any of us any good. Smells like a four ale bar in here. Go on outside, Mavis, this smell's turning my stomach. I don't know what it might do to yours.'

June got Mr Fisher under the armpits, Bella took his feet and they carried him outside and layed him down on the garden path. The sun was warm. He was sound asleep. Then June started cleaning up the mess.

Bella was standing in the hallway burning a rag to get rid of the smell when she told June the details for getting the curtains dyed. 'Half-past seven. He's got a flat in Unity Street.

65

Above the pet shop.'

'The pet shop? But that place stinks, Bella. It's full of parrots and rabbits and things.'

'If it does stink you won't notice it,' Bella remarked, waving the burning rag about. 'Not with the smell you get in here when old cider Johnnie brings up his guts.'

'What shall I wear? You know what I mean.'

'Look, love, what did your mother teach you? Always put your clean underwear on in case you get run over. Anyway, you know I always like you to be clean and respectable when I take you anywhere, wherever it might be.'

She did not tell June about Mr Jerome's bit of trouble. She considered that they had enough to think about as it was, although Monday night did not cause Bella too much concern. As long as she got the curtains dyed, she could not care less. Things were looking up. If Derek Pobjoy made a good job of them, she might get more than twenty-five pounds. She had found out about Archie, she was sure of that. And after the dance at the camp that night, they went to the lecture room and the window she had got through was still unlatched. No one had noticed. She took the handle in both hands and pulled it down. No one appeared to notice that the curtains had gone either. They were all too interested in other things.

Monday night came. Half-past seven came and they had a drink in the Mechanics' Arms before walking the short distance to Derek Pobjoy's flat. He unlocked the back door of the pet shop and let them in, and the first thing that caught June's eye was a tank full of goldfish with long green weeds in it and air bubbling out from a rubber tube. She was captivated and hardly noticed the strong animal smell, the squawking birds, the whimpering puppies. She gazed at the fish while Bella stood back and wondered why Derek Pobjoy had moved behind the guinea pig hutches. And then she noticed why. He had become physically aroused in anticipation of the event about to take place. 'You need a dirty fawn raincoat to put over that, love,' Bella said to him.

He moved towards the stairs, but June had not heard Bella's remark and she was still fascinated by the goldfish. 'Look, Bella, they've got seaweed and all, and snails.'

'For goodness sake, come on,' Bella said, looking again at

Derek Pobjoy. 'His buttons won't be able to hold it for much longer. Looks like one of us will end up sitting on the foot of the bed with a needle and thread.'

But by nine o'clock they were home again, back in Bella's drab kitchen, smoking and drinking tea. 'Well, I didn't think much of that,' June said.

'You're not the only one,' Bella replied. 'I got all there was going, and I can assure you it was a bit short on quantity and fairly low on quality. I worked it out at ten grunts to the minute, three minutes in all. That's fifteen grunts per pair of curtains.'

'I've never heard such a noise. Sounded just like a pig. No wonder he lives over a pet shop.' They laughed at the tops of their voices, then June said: 'Fancy him going to sleep like that. Sound off. It was hardly worth my while going.'

'Sex has the same effect on Derek Pobjoy as cider has on Mr Fisher. Only Derek needs far less of it to be satisfied,' Bella observed.

And June said: 'Good job it didn't make him fall down the stairs and be sick as well.'

'Amongst all those bloody parrots. That would be just the place for him. To think that I sacrificed a good job in the dyeing room because I was afraid of that. I was told he went to all sorts of extremes.'

'But you wouldn't swap, Bella, would you?'

'No, love, I wouldn't swap.'

The following night, after dark, Derek Pobjoy came to collect the curtains. He had a motorcycle and sidecar and wore a leather helmet and goggles. 'I wouldn't dress like that in daylight if I were you, duck,' Bella said. 'You look just like a German who's baled out.' She felt she could afford to be cocky now.

She had the curtains ready in the hallway. Two nights later, after dark again, he brought them back. Both transactions were brief. Derek Pobjoy, the lover, rejected for military service because of flat feet, destined in his own opinion to spend the war giving a sort of comfort to the wives of men far away – and their daughters – had failed where he needed to have been an outstanding success, between two women who had actually done some of the things of which he made himself out to be the master. Life might never be the same again for him. The last he wanted to see of Bella was her taking the curtains in through her front door.

The curtains looked beautiful, changed from a dirty buff to a deep blue. Bella went into Mr Shanklin's office first thing the next morning. 'Those curtains,' she said. 'There's been a bit of a hitch.'

Before she could say more, he blurted out: 'Oh, don't say you can't get them,' betraying to her the fact that he had let his tongue run away with him.

'I can get them all right.' She looked at him across his big desk and could imagine him boasting in low tones about a certain connection he had. 'The only thing is, the ones I was going to get for you looked a bit shabby. They'd faded with the light. But my friend has some lovely blue ones. I wondered if they'd do?'

'Yes, yes,' he said eagerly. 'As long as they are the right size.'

'Good. They'll cost you thirty pounds then, on account of they're so much better than the others.'

'Thirty pounds,' he repeated quietly. He felt she had tricked him again. 'Very well.'

'Right,' Bella said. 'I've got them at my house. You come round tonight and you can see them. Take them away with you.'

'I don't think I could do that,' he said hesitantly. 'I've layed the car up for the duration. Could you not . . . ?'

Bella leaned over the desk towards him. 'Look, love, I've got the curtains, you want them. The corporation has plenty of transport. So come round to my house at eleven tonight. I shan't be home before. And I want paying in ones mind,' she said. 'I don't want those thin white fivers. Too apt to blow away in the wind. All right?'

Mr Shanklin had very little option. He had hinted to the mayor that he might be able to lay his hands on some curtains, and the mayor had been as happy as if peace had been declared. If Bella had asked him to crawl to her house and drag them away between his teeth, he would have been compelled to do it.

Mr Shanklin arrived at the house self-consciously carrying a large bundle of brown paper. But he was pleased with what he saw. His self esteem rose as he handled the material. To be on the safe side, he had brought a tape measure with him, and in the awkward confines of Bella's front room they measured the curtains. They were ideal.

'Thirty pounds, Mrs Rigby.' He took out his wallet and paid her in one pound notes, got down on the floor and made two parcels of the curtains with the brown paper, tied them with string and went up the road to get a taxi. Bella helped him carry the parcels out to the taxi and after he had gone she went into the kitchen. June was sitting there. 'I'll bet you were dying to come out there and give the little bugger a fright.'

'No I wasn't, Bella. I didn't want to mess it up for you,' June replied.

'Right, there you are. Fifteen quid.' She counted the money out on the kitchen table.

'Oh no, Bella, I couldn't.' June pushed it away. 'No, I'll take five, but no more. After all, it was you who went to all the trouble.'

'Take it,' Bella snapped. But June was adamant. 'Take ten then,' Bella insisted. 'Five for Mavis.'

'All right,' June conceded. 'Five for Mavis.'

'That's been your trouble all along,' Bella rebuked her. 'You're all give. You're too generous. And where has it got you?'

'Where has anything got either of us?' June replied.

Eight

There was a letter for Bella the following morning. It was from Leslie. Ronnie brought it up to her in bed. It was Saturday and she lay in for a bit. She read parts of the letter out to him. 'Blimey,' she exclaimed, 'your dad's been and won a medal. Distinguished Flying Cross. What do you think of that then?'

But Ronnie never stopped to think about it. He ran off to tell it to anyone he could find.

Later on she went across to see Mrs Bragg. 'Megan,' she shouted down the hallway, 'I've had a letter from Les.' She got into the kitchen and said: 'They've given him a medal. Just imagine that. He must have shot down a German at last. He'll be coming home covered in glory. I doubt if he'll ever lower himself to speak to me again.'

She said it all as a joke, but her attitude horrified Megan. She could never comprehend Bella's lack of respect for anything. Everything had to be mocked or denigrated. And she, an officer's wife. Honour and respect. One should follow the other, Megan thought. It was only natural.

'Anyway, duck,' Bella said, 'how about the pictures this afternoon? My treat. Celebrate Les getting his medal. Your boys will love it. "In Which We Serve." All ships sinking and guns going off. Early doors mind.'

Rita did not want to go. 'I don't like war films. And I don't like Noël Coward. He talks through his nose.'

'You're bloody well coming,' Bella screeched at her. 'Anne's coming. You'd like to come, wouldn't you, Anne?'

'No thank you, Mrs Rigby,' Anne said mistakenly.

Bella turned on her. 'Well, you're a fine friend,' she said sharply, as if she were talking to one of her own. 'Who was it loaned you their blue gaberdine mac and a pixie hood to go home in the other night, when the rain came on? And that mac was still damp when you brought it back.'

Anne gave way under the glare of those eyes. 'All right then, Mrs Rigby, I'll come,' she said miserably, looking at the floor.

'Right then,' Bella stated. 'Go home and tell your mother. And take old misery face there with you.'

Bella had the leather shopping-bag full of cigarettes again. The routine was always the same. A drink at the Unicorn, then down the street to the Palace, past the queue standing four deep, and up the steps.

No one shouted out this time. People stared, then looked at each other and murmured. Archie opened the door for them, snapped up such a smart salute with his left hand that he nearly knocked his cap off. June paused at the pay desk to ask the girl there about her sister who had just had twins to one of two men, both of whom were blaming it on a third, and then they went up the stairs to the restaurant.

Archie took the leather bag off Bella and went to Mr Jerome's office with it. When he had gone round the corner into the corridor, Bella went after him. He went into the empty office, put the bag on the desk and put his hand inside. But he had forgotten to close the door.

Bella watched him. 'Archie, get your hand out of that bag. Come out here.'

He withdrew his hand from the bag, turned round quickly, his face white.

'Archie, there are fags in that bag and you've been stealing them.'

'I haven't,' he said simply. 'Not me, Mrs Rigby.'

'You have. You had your hand in the bag then. You've been stealing them. Twice you've pinched fags from that bag and I've had to pay for them. They cost money, Archie, don't you know that?'

He was frightened. Her voice rang in his ears and her eyes never blinked. 'No, Mrs Rigby, no.' He started to shake with fear.

'You've been stealing them and selling them in the Mechanics' Arms. People have told me. I've seen you in there.'

Archie started to cry like a child. He leaned against the wall, buried his face in his hands and cried. He was a six-year-old, with a six-year-old's brain and a man's body. 'Don't hit me, Mrs Rigby. I won't do it again.'

She closed in on him. He saw her from between his fingers and sank to his knees, weeping noisily. 'You know what will happen if I tell Mr Jerome, Archie? You know what he'll do? He'll give you the sack. And you won't get a job anywhere else, Archie. Nobody else will give you a job. They'll put you in the lunatic asylum, Archie, with all the madmen. That's what they'll do. Because you're daft, Archie, you're daft. What are you?'

'I'm daft, Mrs Rigby, I'm daft,' he bawled.

'Right,' she said. 'So you be a good boy in future or you know what will happen to you. Now get up and go and dry your eyes.'

Archie got up and ran down the corridor to the lavatory, leaving his cap on the floor.

Bella turned to go and June was standing at the corner. 'Oh Bella, you are awful. That poor boy.'

'He's a thief,' Bella snapped. 'Needs teaching a lesson. Stealing cigarettes off me.'

'But Bella, it was only a few fags. All that shouting and that boy crying, all over a few fags. You know he's not all there.'

'It's a matter of principle,' Bella said sharply and pushed open the restaurant door.

June blinked. She had tears in her eyes and she dabbed them with her handkerchief before following Bella into the restaurant.

The doors to the ballroom were open as Bella went up the town hall stairs. Inside, a little clutch of people were admiring the curtains. Two women were cleaning the floor. It gave her a feeling of pride that people should admire something for which she had been responsible. She had done little in life that she could be proud of. If only they knew, she thought, that in order to get those lovely curtains she had gone to bed with Derek Pobjoy. The thought amused her and she had a smile on her face when she went into the office.

'He wants you, Bella,' Miss Hackett said without looking up from her shorthand notes, without stopping typing. She smelled the cloud of Evening in Paris and knew it was Bella.

72

'Let him sweat a minute, love,' she said casually. 'I had this letter from my Les on Saturday. He's won a medal. The Distinguished Flying Cross. Here, you can read it. There's nothing private in it.' She handed Miss Hackett the letter.

'Oh, that is good, Bella. I'll bet you're proud.'

'Proud? Well, I don't know. I wonder if it will mean more money?'

'He writes a good letter,' Miss Hackett remarked, 'but being an officer, he would.'

Mr Shanklin appeared in his office doorway. 'Would you come in please, Mrs Rigby?'

'Hold on, sunshine,' Bella said offhandedly. 'I'm just telling Miss Hackett my bit of news.'

'Good news, I hope,' he said.

'Of course. My husband in the airforce has been given the Distinguished Flying Cross.'

He smiled. 'I shouldn't think so, Mrs Rigby. The DFC is only awarded to an officer.'

'Well he is an officer,' she said loudly. 'Flight lieutenant. Flies a Hurricane. Read it for yourself. Give him the letter, love.'

Miss Hackett handed him the letter and he read it and felt very small. 'Very creditable,' he remarked. 'I didn't know your husband was an officer. A wartime marriage?' he queried, his mind full of disbelief.

'No it was not,' she replied indignantly. 'He married me when he was nothing at all, like a lot of people who work here are.'

He felt hot with embarrassment. 'Well, please come in when you are free,' he said meekly.

'I'm coming now,' she said and followed him into his office.

Mr Shanklin felt relieved that he was going to be able to do something to placate her. 'I wondered, Mrs Rigby,' he said, 'whether your daughter would like to wear this dress to the reception?' He had it on his desk, wrapped in the *News Chronicle*.

'Won't her white blouse and navy blue skirt do, then?' she asked him. 'I told you she didn't have a dark coloured dress. Catch a girl wearing a dark coloured dress.'

He pushed the newspaper parcel across the desk. 'This belonged to my daughter, Alice. She put on weight after she got married. She used to be quite slim. And if it fits – well, your daughter can keep it.'

'If she can keep it, it will fit,' Bella stated firmly and took the dress.

'We have some little white frilly aprons for you both to wear.'

'Oh, look quite like a couple of French maids, won't we?' she joked.

But where she was concerned, Mr Shanklin had left his sense of humour on the grass that Saturday night. 'It's the finishing touches that give a good impression.'

'Like having two flunkies to open the doors for the Duke of York,' she commented, 'only cheaper.'

Bella showed the dress to Miss Hackett. 'Cut quite a dash at the bunfight, me and my Rita, won't we?'

'You always look nice, Bella,' Miss Hackett told her. 'I don't know how you do it, what with rationing and shortages. You always make up so nice. And you're never without scent, are you? All the things we can't get.'

'Funny you should say that,' Bella told her. 'It was when we were living in Birmingham. There was an air raid one night, just as me and my friend were setting off home. Been out for a drink. Well, when we came out of the air-raid shelter and made for home, we went down this little backstreet – no houses, just the backs of buildings. Quickest way for us. Anyway, I had my torch and a good job too because soon we were clambering over rubble. And as we were making our way over all these broken bricks and things, what should I see in the light of the torch? Bottles of scent, lipsticks, Palmolive soap, goodness knows what else. It was the back of a chemist shop and it had been blown right out by the blast. There was nobody about, so me and my friend filled our pockets and our handbags with as much of it as we could and made off home. And we decided to go back with a bag each to get some more, but when we got there the place was alive with the fire brigade and policemen. So we had to be content. And anyone who doesn't like Evening in Paris is going to have to put up with it. That's the only scent there was.'

'Palmolive soap,' Miss Hackett echoed.

74

'Yes. We might be poor but at least we're clean. Tell you what,' Bella said. 'I'll save you a tablet of soap for Christmas. Only don't tell anybody. Even Father Christmas can't get Palmolive soap these days.'

Bella wrapped the dress up again in the newspaper and took it home. It was navy blue with white collar and cuffs and Rita loved it. But however thin Mr Shanklin's Alice might have been, her bust had been bigger than Rita's, because that was the only place it did not fit. Bella had to go out in her lunchtime the next day and buy her the smallest brassière she could find. That evening, in her mother's bedroom, Rita put it on. 'It doesn't make any difference,' she complained.

'Of course it doesn't,' Bella said. 'A barrage balloon is no good until it's pumped full of gas. Hang on a minute.' She started sorting about in the bottom of the wardrobe and brought out a shoe box. 'Tissue paper. Do you know, a man on the wireless in nineteen forty said to save tissue paper because there would be a shortage. I can't think why the war should cause a shortage of tissue paper – or why people might want it. Anyway, I saved it and it's going to come in useful. Put some in the cups of your bra, Rita. Fill you out a bit.'

'Hey mam, it says Large Jaffa on this piece,' Rita observed.

'Never mind, love,' Bella said. 'Stuff it in your bra.'

It worked wonders for Rita's figure. The dress now fitted her perfectly. She never wanted to take it off. And when she went up to bed that night, she spent an hour in front of her mirror admiring herself in her brassière, ignoring the fact that it was not full of her but of tissue paper.

On the day of the reception, Bella gave Rita forty Lucky Strike and said: 'Give those to Mrs Truscott at the public baths. She knows me. She'll give you more than five inches of water. Tell her I'll be in later.'

'You know everybody, mam, don't you?' Rita remarked admiringly.

'Don't be saucy. Just make sure you come out smelling sweet,' her mother told her.

Ever eager to make the right impression, Bella booked a taxi to take them to the town hall that Friday night. She booked it to collect them afterwards as well.

June, soft hearted and emotional, blinked away eyes full of tears at the sight of Rita looking so grown up. Her black hair parted in the middle, just a touch of lipstick and a dusting of face powder, the dress, the silk stockings June had given her for Christmas and she had never dared wear, the patent leather shoes Bella had given her for her birthday. The black market added the finishing touches and, as Mr Shanklin had said, it was the finishing touches that gave a good impression.

As they were going along in the taxi, Bella remarked: 'Well, I hope Mr Bevin turns up. We've both had a nice hot bath and we don't want to waste it.'

The food and drink was layed out in an ante-room. Bella and Rita were to take out the drinks and Rita had no qualms about walking out among the gossiping throng with a tray full of little glasses. 'That's Mr Bevin up there,' the custodian told her. 'The one who looks as if he's been in a fight or two.' And off she went with her head in the air, all the way along the middle of the floor towards the man in the baggy grey suit who was so important.

'Look at that,' Bella remarked. 'Not a nerve in her body,' and she felt proud for the second time that week.

When things were well under way and everyone was smoking and talking loudly, and a woman wearing pearls had dropped a glass and then trodden on it, Bella came across Mr Jerome, standing there eating a minute sandwich. 'Well,' she said, grinning at him, 'look who's here. It's amazing where a few free tickets will get you.' She held up her tray of drinks in front of him. 'Hey, are you allowed to go out socializing on a Friday? Or is it Saturday you have to go to the synagogue? No wonder you Jews don't get on with people – you always have to be different.' He knew she was pulling his leg and said nothing, just smiled painfully and glanced around to see if anyone was listening. 'Have you seen my Rita? What do you think of her?'

'A credit to you, my dear, a credit to you. She has a little bit of class about her,' he said ingratiatingly.

'She gets that from me,' Bella said and moved off to the group of American officers. 'Here you are, boys, take the weight off my tray, will you?'

They laughed, drained their glasses and took full ones from her tray. She walked away, looking at the curtains. They looked even better under the light of the chandelier, worth more than she had got for them.

The food soon went. There was not a lot of it. And the empty wine bottles built up in a corner. 'Who's that man up there, mam, the man with the cloak on?' Rita asked.

'That's the mayor,' Bella told her.

'What's that thing round his neck? Did he win that in the war like dad won his medal?'

'No, silly, that's his chain of office. And that's Mr Shanklin by him, who I work for, that little fat man. That's who your dress came from.'

'Oh, he looks generous. He smiled at me ever so nicely when I took the drinks up there.'

'Oh he's generous, Rita. Ask your Auntie June. She knows him.'

When it was all over and everyone was drifting towards the door, the custodian beckoned to Bella and took her along to the kitchen where the food had been prepared. He gave her a flat paper parcel. 'A little bit of corned beef. Don't tell a soul. Black market, I think. I'll have to be careful how I get rid of the tins.'

Bella recognized the tins. They were from the American camp. She said: 'Who got hold of that, then?'

'Highways manager. Don't ask me how. But from what he said to me, it cost him a pretty penny. It would do on the black market.'

Bella said no more, but when they were collecting up the glasses in the ballroom she told Rita about it. 'No wonder old Jerome was here. I expect he supplied it. It couldn't be anyone else. They might think they're important at the town hall, but they're all on the fiddle like the rest of us. There's no honesty anywhere these days.' She glanced at the curtains and said: 'If you ask me, if it wasn't for the Yanks, there wouldn't have been a party at all tonight.'

Before they went home they had a drink themselves in the ante-room. 'Go on, Rita,' Bella said. 'It's sherry wine. Good for your blood.'

Two sips and Rita went giddy. She sat there patiently waiting for the room to stop going round. 'You can have mine, mam. I'd rather have some Tizer.'

'Well, we haven't got any Tizer,' Bella said, taking her sherry. 'Mr Bevin doesn't like it. It gives him the wind.'

By the time the taxi came, Rita was all right again. She walked down the town hall steps straight into the taxi, door held open, feeling just like Greta Garbo. And when they got home she swept out of the cab in a grand manner, but had it all spoiled by the front door being locked and by her mother calling out: 'Have you got sixpence, love? He's got no change.'

'I wish Chuck was staying the night,' Bella said. 'I wish he could have got a pass out.'

They were in the ladies' at the Manhattan Lounge. Bella was examining the top of her stocking. She had laddered it getting ready that evening and had put a dab of nail varnish on it to stop it running. She examined it to see that it had laddered no further.

'I should think he's glad he isn't staying the night,' June remarked. 'You've done nothing all evening but gas about that reception last night. Should think he's heard enough of it.'

'Well I do make conversation,' Bella snapped.

'I wouldn't have done it,' June said. 'Not without being paid. The fuss you went to. A taxi there and back.'

'Look,' Bella said savagely, 'I was among all the nobs. Those are the people to be seen with. The next time they have a bun fight I might be asked again, and our Rita. People will remember me. I'll be recognized. That's the way to get on. That's all I did it for, to get on. For my own benefit. And where were you last night, might I ask? What did you spend the evening doing, or would it be more discreet not to ask?'

June looked away and sniffed. Someone else came in then and saved her from having to answer Bella's question.

Nine

Bella stood there in the kitchen in a dream that Sunday afternoon. It was going to be easy, she felt, to get to America. All she had to do really was save up enough money to buy a ticket. She might not even have to do that. She might go there as a GI bride. There was more than one way of getting there. One of them was bound to work. She dreamed that she had a job with Chuck's family's firm, that she was walking across the shiny-floored hall to the lift which swept her up to her office on the sixteenth floor, an office with Venetian blinds and one of those things like a big goldfish bowl that you could get a drink of water out of in a paper cup.

June's voice brought her back from dreamland. 'Bella,' she said, 'I can't find Mr Fisher.'

'Can't find him? Uncork a bottle of cider. He'll come running.'

'Seriously, Bella. I haven't seen him since yesterday morning. He's not in any of his usual places. I've looked in the coalhouse, the cupboard under the stairs, the outside lavvy. I've put his dinner in the oven.'

'He's not at work is he?' June looked at her blankly and Bella went on: 'Get yourself over to the foundry and see if he's there. Fine housekeeper you are. Haven't seen him since yesterday morning? Go on, on your way.'

June went but she was soon back. Mr Fisher was not there. He should not be there until seven o'clock on Monday morning, they had told her.

Rita and Anne appeared and they all began to look for Mr Fisher. They looked again in all the usual places and asked up and down the street, but no one had seen him. They went over to the bombsite but knew he would not be there, with children playing everywhere.

When Rita and Anne got back to the house, Mavis ran out and said: 'Uncle Fisher's asleep upstairs.'

'Go on, he's not. First place your mother looked,' Rita said.

'He is. He's asleep upstairs. I shouted at him to wake up but he's still asleep. Come and see.'

'All right, clever clogs, come on.'

They followed Mavis up the stairs into Mr Fisher's small, dull bedroom. The window looked out over the bombsite where the children played. Their voices rang shrill and wild up to the bedroom.

The bed stood about a foot away from the wall. The covers were rumpled, as if someone had lain upon it. 'There he is,' Mavis stated, pointing to the gap between the bed and the wall. 'Come on, uncle, get up,' she shouted.

Rita looked into the space. Mr Fisher was laying face down on the floor. There was a peculiar smell. She half-realized that he was dead, but stayed calm, went to the top of the stairs and called down: 'Mam, Auntie June, he's up here. Come quick.'

Bella and June, sensing the worst, ran up the stairs. They looked down at him, the thin body lying there in a small space, dead, as he had been since, with his last distant movement, he had rolled off the bed.

'Why doesn't he get up?' Mavis asked, as they moved the bed further away from the wall.

'Because he's dead, love,' Bella said simply. 'Now go down into the kitchen and fetch your mother's cigarettes and lighter off the mantelpiece.'

When she had gone, Bella and June turned the body over. It was stiff. He had his eyes shut and his mouth open. They lifted him on to the bed. He was still in his working clothes, his soiled dungarees and sweat-stained shirt. 'Well, he died with his boots on,' Bella observed.

There was a moan and a thud behind them. At first sight of the corpse, Anne had fainted. Bella and June looked at her with an air of disinterest, while Rita bent over her and tapped her lightly on the cheeks. 'She's fainted, mam. Shall I throw some water over her?' She had seen Clark Gable do that to a swooning woman in a film.

'Oh God,' Bella exclaimed, 'we'll have a room full of

bodies soon.' Mavis came in with the cigarettes. 'I shall have to have a fag on June, respect for the dead or not. The smell.' She handed June the cigarettes. June had tears streaming down her face but was not making a sound. 'Oh come on, Rita. Let's try and lift her up,' Bella said.

They held Anne beneath her armpits and tried to lift her. They could hardly move her. 'My goodness, isn't she heavy?' Bella complained. 'She doesn't get any thinner, does she? They don't keep a shop, do they?'

They managed to push Anne up into a sitting position and she came round then. One on either side of her, they helped her up. 'For heaven's sake, lean her your way a bit, Rita. She's pushing me over.'

'I think I'm all right now,' Anne said uncertainly, when they got her over to the window.

Rita pushed the window open, letting in the noise and shouts of the children playing on the bombsite. Over at the foundry a locomotive moved slowly along the tracks into a siding, and from the high chimney a plume of black smoke that never seemed to end rose heavily into the still afternoon air.

Bella left June crying in the kitchen and went to the telephone to ring for the doctor. When she got back she took June into her own house, still crying. Mavis, unaffected by any of it, went out to play. Having fully recovered, Anne hung around to see what else was going to happen. She helped Rita make a pot of tea in the kitchen.

Bella, getting down to practicalities, said: 'Do you know how he was fixed, June? How is he going to be buried?'

'By two men with shovels,' Rita said without thinking, and she and Anne got shouted out of the kitchen, out onto the bombsite with the other kids.

The following evening, Bella and June were dressed ready to go out, waiting in Bella's kitchen for Chuck and Bill to arrive, when Mrs Sadler, whose pram Bella had borrowed to bring home the curtains, came in. She lived a few doors down the street, and was an avid witness to the comings and goings of her two good-looking neighbours. She sat down and took a cigarette. 'Choked on his own vomit, did he? Not a nice way to go. Still, he had a bit of money,' she said. 'Don't know where from, but he had a bit of money. Always worked at the foundry. I've known him for years. I've lived in this street twenty-five years. It was really nice here at one time, nice tidy people. But it's gone to the dogs now. I never thought I'd see this street go like it. Scruffs some of them. I'll bet you've known better. Was he insured?'

'Oh yes,' June said. 'At the Co-op. I used to pay it once a month for him, at the office.'

'That was their style,' Mrs Sadler went on. 'Didn't have people calling weekly like we do. His wife was a very nice person. Very tidy. That was what I liked about her.' She flicked her ash on the floor and blew the smoke down her nose. 'A tidy woman,' she repeated, sitting there in a filthy pinafore, hair that had not been combed all day, slippers that were trodden flat at the back. She had five children and a husband who was a dustman. 'Their son is a doctor.'

'He never is,' Bella said in disbelief.

'He is,' Mrs Sadler maintained. 'And their daughter is a school teacher.'

'Get away.' Bella thought she was making it up.

'You look here,' Mrs Sadler went on. 'He had a bit of money, and he never missed work. All the hours that God sent. His son is a doctor. Emigrated to Canada. And the daughter is a teacher in one of those boarding schools. Evacuated the whole school to Wales because of the war.' She took another puff at her cigarette and waited for it all to sink in.

Eventually Bella said: 'What drove him to drink then?'

'Ah well, I think it was like this. His wife died. The kids had grown up and gone away. All he'd ever worked for. I think it turned him a little, that and the cider,' and she tapped her forehead to show them what she meant. 'You get a lot of cider drinkers around here. They all go mad in the end. Never any shortage of cider like there has been of beer. It gets you, you see. Most people steer clear.'

Bella and June nodded in agreement.

Mavis came running in then. 'Mam, is Uncle Fisher still dead?'

'You'll have to tell her,' Mrs Sadler said.

'Uncle Bill's coming down the street,' Mavis said.

Mrs Sadler went home then. Chuck and Bill were told about Mr Fisher's death and in order not to give the wrong impression, when the four of them went out that evening they went by the back door, through the dry desolate gardens and along the path by the bombsite.

Despite the fact that Mr Fisher's body had been taken to the mortuary, June refused to sleep in the house that night. Instead, she slept with Bella and Mavis slept with Rita.

Bill, through a similar difference between the American and the British armies to the one which allowed the Americans to wear well cut, smart uniforms, was able to claim two days furlough. On the second day, after spending the night with June – who was too cut between grief for Mr Fisher and pleasure at having Bill around in the daytime to go to work – Miss Fisher turned up at the front door. June and Bill were sitting in the kitchen under a cloud of cigarette smoke when she arrived, a middle-aged woman, neat in a tweed suit and a black hat.

Miss Fisher showed no surprise at finding her late father's housekeeper to be an attractive blonde, in full make-up at eleven in the morning, nor at her companion being an American soldier. She blamed it on the war and said to June: 'I want to thank you for the kind way you looked after my father. He always spoke most highly of you in his letters to me. His previous housekeeper, you know, left rather a lot to be desired.'

June was in tears again. She lit another cigarette and gulped down the smoke. In all the time she had lived there she could remember Mr Fisher receiving few letters. And she had never posted anything for him. To her there had been only one Mr Fisher – the drunken one. She said: 'He was never any trouble,' as generous to the dead as she always was to the living. 'I shall always remember him sitting in that very chair by the wireless, listening to Tommy Handley. Every Thursday night, with my little Mavis on his knee. She loved her Uncle Fisher. All his sweet coupons . . .' Her voice tailed off with the emotion of it, although she had never seen him sitting there listening to Tommy Handley on a Thursday night. She had always been out somewhere, at the Manhattan Lounge, or the Plough or in the lecture room.

Miss Fisher was unmoved by it all, playing out her part just like June. Her only sign of grief was her black hat. She waited until June recovered before telling her that she would arrange the funeral. June gave her Mr Fisher's insurance policy and she left.

Whatever the occasion, where Bella was concerned it had to be done properly. She and Mrs Sadler had a collection up the street and bought a vase for the grave. She went to a florist and ordered a wreath from herself and one from June. When she came home that day, she said to June: 'Look, if we are going to have any more deaths around here, one of us is going to have to become friendly with a florist. It cost me a fortune in that shop. They can't blame that on the war.'

They went to the funeral in veils and borrowed black. All the street turned out. In the church there were rows of men from the foundry, with work-lined faces and large hands, looking uncomfortable in thick dark suits and stiff white collars. They walked in a long black line behind the hearse as it went slowly through the cemetery, along a path Bella and June knew so well.

As the cortège wound its way through the cemetery beneath the trees, a low branch, stirred suddenly by the wind, hooked one of the wreaths from the top of the hearse. One of the bearers picked it up and put it back in place. June, through her tears and the veil, saw it. It frightened her. She knew what it meant. It was an omen, an omen that meant a personal tragedy for whoever had sent the wreath.

Bella appeared not to notice. She stood there dry-eyed at the graveside and said to June: 'For heaven's sake, stop snivelling.' Then, in a strange attempt to cheer her up, she went on: 'It's a good job they didn't decide to cremate him, isn't it? With all the alcohol he's drunk, he would have gone off bang.'

But there was no consoling June. She needed both hands to cry with and Mavis stood hand in hand with Bella. And as they lowered the coffin into the grave, Bella looked down at Mavis and said: 'Well, love, there go your sweet coupons.'

Later, when the flowers were set out on the grave, they stood around and read the cards. June saw a wreath with some of its flowers crushed on one side, the wreath that had fallen from the hearse. They were yellow flowers. She did not know what kind. There had been few flowers in her life. Then she read the card: 'From Bella, Rita and Ronnie,' and turned to look with eyes hot with tears at Bella, who was combing

Ronnie's hair which had become tousled in the wind.

That evening, before they went out, June went over to see Megan. She had to tell someone. So she told Megan and made her swear never to say a word about it. Megan cringed at hearing of it. She knew what it meant. To her, a falling wreath was as bad as a broken mirror. She spent her life avoiding ladders, touching wood and never ever spoke when going under a bridge. The news took away all her concentration. She kept losing the thread of the story in her library book. She dusted things and could not remember having done so. It was almost as if she had had the curse thrust upon her. At the very least, she seemed condemned, through her knowledge, to sharing it.

Ten

Whatever they thought might happen to Bella, whatever wrath they imagined some unknown power might bring down upon her, life for her went on virtually unchanged throughout that summer. If anything was going to happen to her, June wanted it to happen quickly. But it did not, even when Bella tempted providence by saying: 'You know, that funeral was a bit of good luck really. I can tell Les all about it when I answer his letter.'

'Oh Bella,' June said, 'haven't you answered it yet?'

'I never know what to put,' Bella admitted. 'He keeps on about me going to see his mother. What can I say to that? I'd rather spend a week with Hitler, although there wouldn't be much difference. No, I can fill a page about Mr Fisher dying. I'll write weekend.'

If anything, things got better for both of them. Bella was asked to help out in various departments in the town hall when people went on holiday. Although few of the women were able to go away, they all took a week off in turn, giving Bella the chance to work full-time for several weeks. She started adding a bit to the money she had got for the curtains. Every shilling took her a step nearer to America, a step nearer to escape. Sometimes, when she was at the reception desk in the town hall, she would see in a daydream how real it was soon to become. Germany being bombed day and night, Americans all over the country, barracks full of soldiers all waiting for something to happen. It could not be long. She must be living in her last dingy backstreet before the warm blue skies, the fresh clean countryside, the comfort, the plenty of California.

It was June who had the first shock, a letter from the solicitor who was dealing with Mr Fisher's affairs. She had to go to see him. Bella had to take her, she would not go alone. On the way, she took her into a pub and bought her a whisky to calm her down. June was positive she was going to have to leave the house. She had already arranged to move in with Bella again. And when they got to the solicitor's, those two good-looking women with painted lips and painted nails, skin of the quality that came from either good breeding or good luck, looking, as one of the clerks remarked, like two film stars up for a divorce, she found out that Mr Fisher had left the house to his daughter and Miss Fisher had decided that June could go on living in the house at a rent of one pound a week.

Then the solicitor told her that Mr Fisher, in gratitude for all she had done for him, had left June a hundred pounds. For the first time in her life she held a cheque in her hand. She did not know what to do with it and still had it in her hand when they got out into the street.

June was in a daze. Bella guided her along the street back to the pub, where the whisky was being rationed and they had to have beer, however much money they had. They had an argument then about sharing the money, but Bella bullied her and made her promise to change it into savings certificates. Then Bella said: 'It's one thing him leaving you a hundred pounds, but you weren't much of a housekeeper. You weren't letting him have it, were you?'

June pulled a face. 'Oh no, Bella. I wouldn't have let him. Not for a thousand pounds, never mind a hundred.' Then she said: 'I wonder if he heard all those things we used to say about him when he was drunk?'

'He wouldn't have left you that money if he had,' Bella replied. 'And besides, if you go to the outside lavvy to get drunk and wake up in bed, you know it wasn't the fairies who got you there. Anyway, it was worth every one of those hundred pounds, the things you did for him,' she admitted. 'There are only two things puzzling me. Where did he get all his money from and why was it, when we were carrying him into the house or up to bed, that I always got his feet? I knew the soles of his boots better than I knew his face.'

Bella did write to Les that weekend. It was difficult for her, like writing to a stranger. She had considered everything to be over between them at the beginning of the war, when he had joined up and she had made off for London. But it would have been difficult for her anyway. She did not have the mind nor the depth of feeling for anyone to be able to put such feelings in writing. As it was, she made up half a page about Mr Fisher's death, the other half about June's one hundred pounds and of how she was missing Mr Fisher's ration book, then she started another page to tell him about her new job, Rita going to the technical college and Ronnie growing so tall. At the end she had to put a postscript to congratulate him on getting his medal.

One morning in July, Mr Shanklin came in with the *News Chronicle* in his hand and said: 'We've invaded Sicily. I expect your husband is doing his bit there, Mrs Rigby,' then went into his office.

'He'll be doing his bit somewhere, that's for sure,' Bella said to herself. Then she asked Miss Hackett: 'Where the hell is Sicily, ever?'

'In the Mediterranean,' she told her. 'I expect they'll invade Italy next. It looks like it's turning our way at last, doesn't it?'

'Well, what do you expect,' Bella joked, 'with Montgomery and my Les out there?'

When she got home she read about it herself. There was a little map in the newspaper, with arrows showing where our troops had landed and were thrusting forward. But Bella could still not picture where it was. 'Go up and get your atlas, Rita love.'

Rita brought her atlas down and opened it to the map of the world, so that her mother could get everything into perspective. Bella studied it for a while, then said: 'Now, if that's Italy and they've got to go all the way up there, then right across France and capture these other places before they tackle Germany – well, it's going to take them years. They've got to walk all the way, you know, with Jerry shooting at them as well.' She studied the atlas for a moment in silence, then said: 'You know, I think it would have been better if they had started somewhere nearer to Germany. Up here like.' She ran her finger along the coastline of Europe. 'No,' she concluded studiously, 'I think they've made a mistake there, staring off that far away. I wonder what made old

Churchill come up with that idea? He must have been on the lavatory when he thought of that. Which page is the map of America on, Rita? Find it for us, will you, love?'

Autumn came, and the invasion of Italy, and the men could talk of nothing else. Bella could not lose at darts in the Plough, with the men breaking off every few minutes to argue about some point of tactics.

Rita started at the technical college, was called a student for the first time, and felt herself to be at that strange stage between schoolgirl and adult. As soon as she got her bearings in the huge college building, she set about getting into the drama club.

'I don't really want to,' Anne said. 'I don't think I'm quite the type.'

'Just for fun, do it just for fun,' Rita encouraged her. 'You don't have to go on to be a famous film star like I'm going to be. Anyway, they'll jump at having you. After all, you were the star of our Christmas show at school last year.'

'I don't think I'd dare tell them I was Humpty Dumpty,' Anne said, shocked at the thought of it.

'The kids all loved you. Every school we did it at, they all loved you. And that photo of you in the paper. Admittedly, you were inside that eggshell thing, but those were your arms and legs sticking out. Can't you see it, outside the London Palladium? Ann Phelpstead as Humpty Dumpty. In lights.'

The teacher they had to see was a starved-looking woman, whose hair was strained so tightly back that it arched her eyebrows. 'What can you do?' she asked Rita.

'Everything,' Rita lied bravely. 'Acting, dancing, singing.'

'And you?' she said to Anne.

'I was Humpty Dumpty in our school pantomime last Christmas,' she said apologetically.

'Humpty Dumpty? He fell off a wall, didn't he?' the woman commented, and gave Anne a job helping with the wardrobe and make-up.

Rita, with one hand on the baby grand, sang 'Somewhere over the Rainbow' to an empty hall as if it were full and was taken on immediately for the forthcoming Christmas concert.

One Friday at the beginning of November, on an evening cold and still wet from the day's rain, Mrs Bragg was alone in the kitchen by the fire, with her library book. She had a good blaze going, a cigarette and an easy chair. The boys had gone to the pictures with Rita, Ronnie, Mavis and Anne. It was half term and Mr Jerome had got 'Snow White' again specially. Bella and June had gone to the Friday night dance at the camp.

A knock on the front door disturbed her. She took the torch and went down the hallway. Standing at the door was a tall, slim serviceman. He was wearing a raincoat and she could not tell in the bad light which branch of the services he was in. But he had on a peaked cap, wore kid gloves and was very good-looking.

'I'm sorry to disturb you,' he said politely, 'but I wonder if you could tell me when Mrs Rigby will be home?'

'Oh, well – later on I should think,' Mrs Bragg said apprehensively. Now she could make out the Royal Air Force cap badge. It was bad news. Something had happened, she knew.

But he said: 'Do you know where she is exactly? Or the children? I'm Mr Rigby – home on leave.'

She had read it in a hundred love stories. It kept happening, but it always excited her. In some of the stories she had read, she would have stumbled over her words, given the game away. And he would have latched on to it, become angry, demanded the truth. But in her slow, careful way, she would not be caught out. She remembered the right answers that she could give. As calm as a favourite character, she said: 'Bella has gone to visit a friend in hospital. Her friend June has gone with her. The children have gone to the cinema. My two boys have gone with them. "Snow White" they've gone to see. At the Palace.'

'Ah well, thank you,' he said. 'I'll come back later.' Then, as he turned to go, he looked back at her and said: 'I wonder if you would allow me to wait?'

'Oh no, I don't think so,' she replied quickly. 'I'm alone in the house, you see. Wouldn't be proper.'

'No, of course not.' He smiled, touched his cap to her and went.

At that moment, at the moment of that smile and that

touch of the cap, Mrs Bragg thought he looked just like Robert Taylor. She walked back into the kitchen with an odd feeling of elation inside her, sank into her armchair and looked into the fire where she saw him, tall, slim, kid gloves, peaked cap, smile. Those white, even teeth, that touch of the cap. So that was Leslie Rigby.

Then she came to her senses, the senses that had made her refuse to let him wait. She put on her shoes, her coat and her headscarf. Leaving the kitchen light on, a note for the boys, the latch up, she went out into the cold black night. This was real life. This was life as Bella and people in books lived it. At the cattle market she got the bus. It did not go straight away. She had to sit there, with the excitement of it running right down to her feet. Bella had told her that afternoon that Chuck had a weekend pass and was coming home with her that night. 'Breakfast in bed and that,' Bella had said, laughing.

But Leslie Rigby was an officer. For him, life had been very real. The perilous dog fights of the Battle of Britain, the dangerous routine of strafing Rommel's supply lines in the Western Desert had meant facing death almost every day. Luck and his own ability had brought him through. Ability on its own had made him an officer. And in his calm, orderly mind, he thought of the Bella he knew, the Bella who, for some reason, had flitted to London, to Birmingham, to this place, the Bella who was either out or very flustered when suddenly he turned up on leave. He had learned through the war never to take anything for granted, always to question himself, always to take heed of the instinct that had made him scan an empty blue sky and know the enemy was there.

Instinct made him wait in the shadows that night and watch Mrs Bragg as she hurried off down the street and get on to the bus. The crew were standing at the front of the bus warming their hands on the radiator. 'Where does this bus go to?' he asked them.

'Sherwood Camp,' one of them said. 'The American camp. You want a number seventeen for the airforce camp. Opposite the town hall.'

He walked round the corner to the railway station. There was a taxi rank there. He took a cab and told the driver to stop at the corner. From there he could see the bus and they followed it out of the town, into the empty streets of the suburbs, past the cemetery, almost to the camp gates. He paid the driver and walked along the road in the shadows, following Mrs Bragg.

'She's had a visitor turn up suddenly,' Mrs Bragg said to the sentry on the gate and to her surprise he pointed the way for her. She had not expected to be let into the camp.

'Follow the kerbstones, ma'am,' the sentry said. They were painted white.

Soon she was walking towards the sound of dance music. Just inside the doorway was a soldier who wore a bow tie with his uniform. She said the same to him that she had said to the sentry and the man invited her in, gave her a chair, offered to get her a drink. She declined the offer of a drink and he excused himself and walked away towards the crowded dance floor.

So this is what it is like, she thought, looking from her seat by the doorway down to the dance floor. There was the band on a little stage, with proper music stands with a monogram on them. It was just like it was in a film. All the men were handsome, all the girls pretty. Everyone looked happy, those who were dancing, those who were sitting at the little round tables. She wanted to sit there and watch it all night. For a minute she forgot everything else and felt happy just watching it.

The band stopped playing, everyone clapped and the couples moved off the floor. Then the man who had been at the door stepped up to the microphone and said: 'Do we have a Bella Rigby here this evening, please? We have a message for Bella Rigby, if she will come to the foyer please.'

If it had been worse news, Bella could not have appeared more shocked, been more put out. All the happiness of the evening, all the joy of life was gone. 'Where is he then, Megan, where is he?'

'He went away. Said he'd be back later,' Megan replied. She was looking towards the dance floor. A girl was singing now, 'The last time I saw Paris.' The lights were dimmed and she stood in a spotlight. On the dance floor the couples stood close together, dancing but hardly moving. Megan sat there while Bella and June fetched their coats. The band, the singer, the lights low, couples dancing. This, she realized, was what she had said no to.

Leslie Rigby stood in the shadows and watched them come out of the camp gates. There was a bus at the stop. Mrs Bragg went ahead and boarded it. Bella, June and the two Americans stopped and kissed goodnight. They stood there, close together, until the bus was ready to go. And he watched them from a few yards' distance. When the bus had driven away, he watched the Americans go back towards the camp. He had no quarrel with them. He had been away from home. He had been in a foreign country. He had seen men looking for a bit of life before they went out to face death. A little bit of life could always be bought. Death came cheaper.

There was panic in Bella's house. 'Ronnie, get rid of those Yankee comics. Give them to Auntie June to look after. Rita, hide all that chewing gum.'

June was collecting all the cigarette packets together. Bella seemed to have a half-used packet of Camel or Lucky Strike in every room. There was a shirt and tie belonging to Chuck on the back of the front-room door and the blankets for his unused bed were on the sofa. Under a cushion she found some American newspapers and behind the clock on the mantelpiece were some snaps he had taken on the troop-ship coming over. 'Honest, Bella,' she said, 'it looks like an outpost of the American army in here. It says emergency rations on this packet. What did he bring this for? A midnight feast?'

It was no great task for Leslie Rigby to find his way back from the camp. Walking gave him time to think. And it was better to walk than to stand in the November cold waiting for the next bus. Standing there he would have thought of nothing but the cold. After the Mediterranean he felt it as bad as if he had never experienced it before.

But the walk did not make him think any clearer. When he arrived in the empty, pitch black, cold street, he still had no idea of what he would say or do when he went into the house. As he stood there on the pavement he could hear a voice. It was June, chatting away at the top of her voice in the front room. He had never liked June. In his eyes, she had always behaved as he imagined Bella would have done had he not married her. Men for money, an illegitimate child, no permanent home. June had always been around. She had been with Bella on the first occasion he had seen her. She had been in the background ever since. Even now, he was forced to wait out in the cold until she went home.

Bella was in no way confident that all the traces of Chuck's presence were gone. She was still scurrying around the house checking each room when the knock came on the front door. 'Right,' she said to herself, 'here goes then.' And she went down the hallway and opened the door. 'Les. Well, you're a fine one. You don't give anybody notice, do you?' She stepped back from the door.

He looked at her, stepped over the threshold and took off his gloves. The raven hair, the red lips, the neat, slim figure, the face that did not belong to an alley cat like her, the light, high, strong voice, all the things that had first attracted him to her were just as striking as she stood there looking at him with a half smile.

Bella saw something in his eyes. She stepped back another pace and then he hit her across the face with his open palm. The blow sent her reeling backwards into the kitchen. 'That's for your Yankee boyfriend,' he said in a voice not used to speaking in anger.

Rita and Ronnie stood petrified as Bella fell against the table. He hit her again, the other hand, right into her face. 'And that's for you.'

On seeing the blood spurt down her mother's nose, Rita let out a scream, a long scream that came from deep inside her, a loud, piercing scream that went on and on. She pushed past her father and ran, still screaming, out into the street.

June knew that it would not go well. It was not a premonition, it was common sense. It was bound to happen sometime. She had left the latch up on the front door. Mavis was sitting in front of the kitchen fire in nightgown and slippers, drinking her cocoa. June had filled the stone hot water bottle, slipped it inside an old sock and put it into Mavis's bed. When she came back into the kitchen she heard the scream. It came right through the wall, went right through her and made her shiver. It went on, waned a little, then became loud again as Rita flung open the front door and ran into the kitchen. June caught her in her arms. 'There, there, lovey. There, there,' and Rita stopped screaming and sobbed on her shoulder.

June sat her down by the fire. Ronnie had come in behind Rita and he stood there, his face white, his eyes wide open, unblinking, perplexed. Mavis looked at them, sipped her cocoa and wondered what it was all about.

'Everything's going to be all right,' June said softly, drawing Ronnie to the fire. 'It'll be all right. It's the war. Your father's been away at the war. It does things to people. Just you stay with Auntie June for a while. It'll be all right.'

Rita sat with her face in her hands, still crying. June heard the voices next door, both of them shouting at each other. Then Bella cried out. There were bangs and bumps, doors slamming, furniture scuffing against floorboards, Bella screaming. Footsteps thudded on the stairs, Bella screamed again and again and again. June found herself with her hands cupped over Rita's ears, just as she and Bella had done to the children when there was an air raid on.

Then she could stand it no longer. She said nothing, took the carving knife out of the drawer and ran out of the house. She went through Bella's front door and into the wrecked kitchen. There was blood on the table. 'I'm coming, Bella,' she shouted. 'I've got the carver. I'll kill the bugger.' She went back into the hallway and he came down the stairs, blood on his face from the nail scratches. June lunged at him as he went for the door, scagged his sleeve with the point of the knife and fell sprawling in the doorway. Leslie Rigby ran off into the darkness.

Bella was lying on the floor beside the bed. Her face was all blood. June dropped to her knees beside her, the carving knife still in her hand. 'Oh Bella, what's he done to you?' She was in tears already.

'Help me up, love, will you?' She cried out with pain as she got to her feet. Then she lay on the bed, moaning as she breathed.

'Oh Bella, what can I do?' June whimpered helplessly. 'You're all over blood. Your face.'

Bella looked at her. One eye felt hot and aching and was swelling up. 'I wish there was blood on that knife.'

'I only got his coat,' June said sorrowfully. 'I'd have stuck it in him.'

'Oh my ribs,' Bella moaned. 'I've never been punched in the ribs before. It does hurt, June, it does hurt. He must have won that medal for boxing. I feel as if I've done ten rounds with Jack Dempsey.'

'Do you want the doctor, love?'

'No, I'll be all right. I don't want any doctor. Go and hot up some water and wipe my face. It feels awful. I can feel the blood drying on it.'

'All right,' she said. 'I'll make a cup of tea, shall I?'

'That's right. And June, stay with me will you? Stay with me.'

When she had put the kettle on, June went back home. The children were sitting in silence around the fire. She said to Rita: 'It's all right, love. It's all over now. They've had their little quarrel. I'm going to stay with your mother tonight. She's a bit upset. You and Ronnie can stay here. You can sleep in my bed. How about that?'

Rita nodded. 'Where is he?' she asked dismally.

'He's gone now. He's gone.'

'He shouldn't have hit her, Auntie June, he shouldn't have hit her.'

'Never mind, lovey. You stay there and I'll bring your pyjamas.'

June, who had men for money, who had an illegitimate child, who had never had a permanent home, made tea for Bella, cocoa for the children, put their pyjamas on the kitchen range to warm, filled a hot water bottle for them and put it into the bed, washed Bella's face and made her comfortable, kissed the children goodnight and tucked them in, asked them if they wanted a nightlight, then went back to Bella.

'You put something in that tea,' Bella said dreamily.

'A drop of whisky. Bill brought it for Mr Fisher last Christmas.'

But she was asleep then. June went downstairs and started to straighten the house. Both the kitchen and the front room were in a mess. There was blood on the passage wall, on the front room linoleum. Chairs were overturned, crockery broken. And as she went about the work, she kept saying to herself: 'The children mustn't see, the children mustn't see.'

It was Saturday, with cold November sunshine. June slid out of bed at half-past eight, made a pot of tea and lit the kitchen fire on top of yesterday's ashes. Bella was still asleep, so she went next door and looked in at the children. They were still asleep too. She lit the fire in her own kitchen, then went quietly back to Bella.

'Look at me,' Bella said. 'Have you ever seen anything like it?' She had a black eye and her ribs were black with bruises. There were bruises on her arms, on her back and on her thigh where he had kicked her as she lay on the floor. 'Good job he didn't hit me in the stomach. He might have hurt the little stranger.'

'The what?' June was sitting on the bed with a cup of tea in her hands. 'Bella, you're not? You're not pregnant?'

'I am. The little Anglo-American, Chuck calls it. I don't know what that means. I'll have to look it up in our Rita's dictionary, when I can see out of both eyes.'

June said nothing, just looked at her open-mouthed.

'When you go downstairs, do something for me, will you?' Bella said. 'Just take your carving knife off my dressing-table.'

There was no keeping her in bed. If she had not been marked on her face, she would have gritted her teeth against the pain and gone out that day. Over toast and some more tea in the kitchen, she said to June: 'There's no need for you to look so glum just because I'm pregnant. You look more miserable than you did when you were expecting Mavis. Pregnant, unmarried and not a man in sight when you most needed one. That was you.'

'You didn't tell him then, Bella? You didn't tell him you were expecting?'

'Tell him? I was too busy dodging uppercuts and hitting back to do much talking. Anyway, love, it's all been over between us for years, you know that. I can get a divorce for him hitting me and he can get one for me having Chuck's baby – when he finds out. So, what do they say? All's well that ends well. Who was it said that?'

'Mr Churchill, I should think,' June replied.

'Probably. And another thing, June.' Bella patted her stomach. 'You know what this is, don't you? It's my ticket to America.' And she laughed.

June had a soft look in her eyes. 'Nothing ever gets you down, does it? Look at you. Black and blue and laughing.'

'Story of my life, isn't it? Story of our lives. Any more tea in that pot?'

June took the teapot off the hob. 'It's stewed a bit now.' She poured it out and said: 'What started him off last night, Bella? I mean, he seemed to go straight off the deep end. After all the trouble we took clearing the place up.'

'Followed Megan, didn't he? Clever types, these officers. Followed her up to the camp. Saw it all. Sly as old boots.'

'We've got a foreman at the factory just like that – sly.'

'Make sure he never twists your arm then,' Bella said, feeling her elbow. 'He twisted mine last night until I thought it was coming off. God help the women in Germany if he ever gets his hands on them.'

Bella was quite frank with Rita and Ronnie. They were both horrified and fascinated by her black eye and gazed at it while she warned them that they were not to tell anyone about what had happened, about her black eye. Lots of people had rows, had fights, especially in wartime. It was all the fighting and killing that was going on that was to blame. But it was no one else's business and they were not to say a word about it. Her firm voice and the hard look on her battered face scared them into secrecy.

Bella would not let June leave her. She sent Rita to get the rations. 'What am I going to say,' Rita asked, 'if anyone asks me where you are? Everybody knows you. They're bound to ask.'

'Tell them your father's come home on leave and he loves me so much that he won't let me out of his sight,' Bella said flippantly. 'Now off you go. Don't create problems, we've got enough of them as it is.'

June stayed in the house with Bella all day, just in case Les came back. And in the afternoon, when Ronnie and Mavis were out playing on the bombsite, Bella told Rita about the baby. She told her of her plans to go to America, to marry Chuck. It would all happen when the war was over. She would get a divorce, but probably not until the war was over. Otherwise he might do something silly in his aeroplane. They would probably have to carry on until the war was over.

Rita let it all sink in, sitting there with a sullen look on her face. Then she said: 'If you ask me, mam, everything's going to happen when the war's over. That's all people say. When the war's over. All that's going to happen when the war's over is that people are going to stop killing each other. Other than that, things aren't going to be much different. That's what I think, anyway.' She was quiet for a moment then and sensing that no reply was coming, she said: 'I'm going round to see Anne now. I said I'd go round.' And she went out.

'Well, what do you think of that?' Bella said, almost in a whisper.

They saw Mrs Bragg coming home from town with her two boys later that afternoon and called her in. She had heard Bella screaming right over in her house, she told them, but they did not tell her the part she had unwittingly played in causing those screams. 'You want a bit of steak for that eye,' she said without thinking.

'Right,' Bella replied. 'I'll send our Ronnie down to the Co-op for a couple of pounds.'

Nobody laughed at the joke, but Bella's sense of humour was irrepressible. They sat round the fire, the three of them. Bella opened a packet of Camel and handed them round. She was amused by the look of shock that would not leave Megan's face at the sight of her black eye and bruises, and she said, as if to shock her further: 'Anyway, Megan, you won't have a fuss like I've had to put up with when your Arthur comes home. But just to be on the safe side, next time he comes home on leave, I'll lend you my fancy French underwear. It's all black lace with frills around the legs of the knickers. I got it when we lived in London in nineteen forty. June and me, we worked in this club, evenings. Hostess they called us. Well, there was this Free French airman, an officer he was. He wanted me to stay with him one weekend at an hotel in the country. Now he was quite posh, a count he was. June will bear me out.'

And June nodded. She wished she had had the chance.

'Count something or other of somewhere in France,' Bella carried on. 'Anyway, I said that if he wanted me to go anywhere posh for the weekend, he'd better get me something worthwhile to wear. Name it, he said, and you shall have it. So I named it and I got it. In a posh box with ribbon and French writing on it. They reckon that all sorts of stuff came out of France before the Germans got it. Well, if it did, I got a

99

bit of it. There was a nightie with it too, you could see right through. I ruined that though. I put it on one hot night and went and caught my foot in the hem. Ripped it to bits.' She reflected on it for a minute, drawing on her cigarette, and then said: 'Anyway, where was I? Oh yes, well we went to this hotel for the weekend. Very nice it was. He was nice too. Very nice.' She felt that she had better not tell Megan what was nice about him. 'We had champagne, you know. Have you ever had champagne? No? Well, I didn't go much on it. Put anything in a posh bottle with silver paper round the top and a cork that comes out with a pop and people are bound to make a fuss over it, aren't they? Give me sherry wine any day.'

Megan said nothing. It was more than anything she had ever read in a book and she lost all sympathy for Bella, having seen Leslie Rigby, who had stood on her doorstep and smiled and touched his cap.

The children went over to Megan's that evening, while Bella and June stayed in the house to see if Les came there again. Megan was good with children. She would get them all playing a game on the kitchen table. They would not quarrel or fight. She would stay in the background and quietly supervise things without intruding into their game. They liked her. She was like a favourite teacher at school, possessed of a certain kind of charm. Later she would let them listen to the wireless. Jack Warner was on and he was one of the children's favourites. Megan never knew what it was that the children liked about her. But whatever gift it was she had, she would have exchanged it for the one Bella had, the gift to be able to live life as if she were single, to be attractive enough to bring out such violence in Leslie Rigby, that face at her door, that face in the fire.

'Bolt that back door, June,' Bella said. 'I'll do the front. Make sure the windows are closed.' Then they settled down in the kitchen with cigarettes and a pack of cards. After a while, Bella said: 'I'll tell you what. We'll fill a bucket with water and if he makes a fuss outside the front door, I'll chuck it over him from the bedroom window. If he comes here acting like a tomcat, then I'll treat him like one.'

June filled a bucket three parts full, took it upstairs and stood it by the window in Bella's bedroom. Then she went back down to the kitchen where they went on playing cards, waiting for the knock on the door. 'What are you going to do if he forces his way in?' June asked.

'You're not the only one who's got a carving knife,' Bella replied with determination.

At half-past seven the knock came. June's insides turned to jelly. 'That's him,' she said shakily. 'What are we going to do?'

'Lights out,' Bella instructed. 'Upstairs, come on,' and they crept down the hallway and up the stairs. He knocked again. Bella opened the bedroom window. 'Who is it?'

'Bella? It's me, Les.'

'You've got a neck. Clear off.'

'I want to talk to you, Bella.' He spoke no louder than he had to. He minded whether the rest of the street heard them, even if Bella did not.

'You can talk to me from there. Now what do you want?'

'Bella, let me in for a minute.'

'Not bloody likely. You can stay there and speak. Go on, say your piece.'

'If you don't let me in I'll . . .'

She never let him finish. 'You'll what? You try and get in here and I'll fetch the police. I'll show them what you did to me last night. You'd better get out of it, my lad. I'm sending a letter to your commanding officer about you. See what he thinks of you then.'

He was quiet for a while. Then he said, with an air of exasperation: 'Please, Bella, I just want to talk to you for five minutes.'

'I've had enough of this,' she snapped. 'Either you clear off now or I'll throw a bucket of water over you. Now go.'

'Don't be silly,' he said and still stood there.

That was enough for Bella. She lifted up the bucket with both hands, and tipped the water out of the window. But the arm he had twisted gave way and the bucket went out of the window as well. It missed him and clanged on to the pavement.

He scuffed about in the street swearing to himself. They stood tensely by the window, wondering what he would do. But he just walked away into the darkness.

'He's going. Oh, what a relief. I'll bet he's soaking,' June said.

'It's not over yet. Come on,' Bella said urgently. 'Get your coat on. Follow the bugger. He must be staying somewhere. He'll go back and get dry.'

June was disappointed. She had thought it was all over. 'Oh Bella, what for? He won't come back now.'

'Do as I say. Have my coat, there's no time to go and get yours. And my headscarf. Now go on, otherwise you won't catch up with him.' She pushed June towards the front door. 'Find out where he's staying, that's all. And shout through the letter box when you get back. I might think you're him and kill you, otherwise,' and she pushed June out into the street.

Bella went back into the kitchen. She did not put the light on, just sat down on the hearth rug in front of the fire, sat there for she did not know how long, turning over the burning coals with the poker. Eventually she put the wireless on. It was Jack Warner. He had the audience in stitches singing a comic song. But she switched it off. To her, listening to the wireless was like reading a book. It meant that she had to make some of it up for herself, she had to imagine things. And she could imagine things that concerned her personally, the house she would have in America, the swimming pool in the garden, the big car. But she could not picture the things that were in other people's minds, even when they wrote them down or spoke about them. Make it into a film and then she saw it all.

And so she sat there in front of the fire, just like a child, seeing faces pictured there, watching the flames, yellow, orange, blue, flickering on the red coals, until suddenly she heard: 'Bella. Let me in. It's all right,' June's voice through the letter box.

She put on the light and let her in. 'I'm perished,' June said, making for where Bella had been in front of the fire. 'It's freezing out.' She had something in her arms and she gave it to Bella. 'I came back past the Unicorn, so I went into the jug and bottle and got a flagon of draught. Bad enough staying in on a Saturday night, let alone having nothing to drink.'

'Oh June, you are thoughtful.' Bella kissed her on the head. 'So considerate of Les not to break the glasses last night along with all my crockery, wasn't it?' She poured the beer. 'Now, where did he go?'

'Well, you'll never guess,' June said, getting up from the floor and taking off Bella's coat and headscarf. She pulled a chair closer to the fire and drank the froth off her beer. 'He had to take off his mac, it was so wet. He was standing up in the street shaking it when I went out. Nearly walked into him. Then he walked into town and went into the Shire Hotel. I watched him through the revolving doors. Went up to the reception desk, to get his key I should think. I came back then.'

'He would stay there. Nothing but the best for our Les. You've been a real good kid tonight,' she said laughing, with her black eye shining. 'Father Christmas will visit you for sure this year.'

June grinned, bent forward and poked Bella gently in the stomach. 'He's already visited you,' she said and they laughed as if they had not a worry in the world.

For more than an hour they sat there talking. They drank all the beer. Then, at ten o'clock, they heard a noise in the street and someone cry out. Rita shouted through the letter box: 'Mam, let us in. The door's locked.'

June let them in. Ronnie was rubbing his knees. 'What's up, love?'

'Some dope left a bucket out in the street,' Rita said angrily. 'He fell right over it.'

'Now we'll have less of that.' Bella looked at Ronnie's knees. 'It's our bucket. Your Auntie June was scrubbing the front step for me and it got dark before she had finished. She couldn't find it. Some kids must have moved it. Now go and fetch it in for me.'

'Couldn't find it? It was in the middle of the road,' Rita remarked irritably as she went out. 'Should have tried walking around. Might have fallen over it.'

It was all right while they were all crowded round the fire and the children were all talking at once about what they had been doing over at Mrs Bragg's, but when the clock crept on towards half-past ten Bella had second thoughts about being without June that night. He could get in easily if he wanted to, she knew, and she asked June to stay with her. Mavis was delighted and skipped off to bed with Rita.

The following morning, Sunday, Rita took them up a cup

103

of tea in bed. There were no saucers. They had all been broken when the crockery had been swiped off the kitchen dresser. They did not possess a tray and Rita took the cups upstairs on a dinner plate. 'Sorry, Auntie June, war has broken out on the kitchen front and all our saucers have been damaged by enemy action,' she said.

They drank their tea, then lay in bed smoking. 'I wonder if our Rita will think to bring the paper up,' Bella said, lying there too idle to go to the door and call down the stairs. Then she said: 'I was thinking, June, if you would go to the telephone box for me later on? I'd go myself but I daren't go out with this fat eye.'

'What for?' June asked, tentative about committing herself.

'I thought of ringing the Shire Hotel. Asking if Les is there. He might only have been on a forty-eight. I'd feel safer if I knew where he was.'

'He'd get more than a forty-eight after being overseas for so long,' June said. But she went all the same, later in the morning, and took the flagon with her to get it filled on the way back.

Bella knew it was good news. June was cradling the flagon of beer in her arms and smiling. 'He's gone, Bella,' she said. 'They said he left early this morning. And when I asked if they knew where he'd gone, they said he caught the train to Manchester.'

'Well I'll be damned. He's gone home to his mother.' Bella laughed at the top of her voice. 'Just like Les. You know what his trouble is? He left his brains in his flying helmet.'

But June felt that Bella's flippant remark was far from the truth. Leslie Rigby was shrewd, she knew. That was why he had booked into an hotel, as if he knew something were going to happen. He had almost caught her before. It was a relief to have it happen and get it over with. June was glad that he had gone. She felt that Bella had now had the amount of bad luck allotted to her for her wreath having fallen off the hearse. From now on, she thought, everything would be all right. She would have the baby, get a divorce and go to America and marry Chuck.

Bella's thoughts were running along the same lines. With the niggling fear that Les might turn up again gone from

104

inside her, she once more became preoccupied with the future. At every gap in their conversation that morning her thoughts went over to her imaginary life in an imaginary country. For Bella believed, just as everyone else did, that the America she saw at the pictures was the America that Chuck came from, that Bill came from, that all those boys up at the camp came from.

June and Mavis stayed to dinner that day. 'Bring your ha'porth of meat round and put it with my ha'porth,' Bella told her. 'Look at it,' she said, as she put the two small rations of meat into the oven. 'If you'd have given that to the cat before the war, he'd have thought he was hard done by.' And she gossiped and dreamed as they got the dinner, drinking the beer, smoking, moaning at her aching ribs and every now and then sitting down and putting a cold wet flannel on her black eye.

That afternoon Anne came to call for Rita. It was teatime. The table was layed. 'Like a camel to water,' Bella said to herself.

Anne looked at Bella and said: 'Oh Mrs Rigby, what have you done?'

'Had a little accident, love.'

Then Anne looked at the table. 'Where are all your saucers, Mrs Rigby? And the handle's gone off that nice cup with the flowers on that you always have your tea in.'

'As I said love, I had a little accident. I'll tell you what happened. I was feeling a bit off colour, so I thought I'd have a lie down. But as I was up to my neck in work, I thought I'd take the washing-up with me and do it in bed. Anyway, as I was coming downstairs with the bowl full of crockery, I fell, broke all my saucers, knocked the handles off most of my cups and gave myself a black eye. Now don't go and tell anybody what I've done, will you, love? They'll never believe you.'

June started giggling and Rita said: 'Oh give over, mam.'

Anne sniffed, looked at the floor and said: 'I've come to ask Rita if she'd like to come to our house for tea.'

'Heavens,' Bella exclaimed, 'what's happened? Did your mother get two lots of rations by mistake?' And realizing that she had upset the girl, she took a packet of Lucky Strike off the mantelpiece and said: 'Here, love, give these to your dad.

105

Tell him to have a good cough on me,' and redeemed herself.

When the girls had gone, June said: 'Honest, Bella, the daft things you say. I don't know how you think of them.'

But before Bella could retaliate, a voice said: 'Rita says the coast is clear,' and they looked round to find Chuck poking his head round the door. Bill was behind him. Once again, for Bella and June, life was complete.

Before she went to bed that night, Bella said to Rita: 'I don't know what to say really. I can't go to work with this eye. And I shall look daft wearing sun glasses in November. Yes, you'd better say I've fallen down the stairs. Then if one of them does call round, I can explain away my black eye. Oh, isn't life complicated? I shall miss the money.'

Then in the morning she said: 'Now you tell the receptionist who you are and don't speak to anyone but Miss Hackett. You'll know her. She's got the sort of face that looks as if it fell off the outside of a cathedral. She's got more wrinkles than a pound of prunes. And you're sure it will be all right, being late for college?' She enjoyed saying that last word more than she ever imagined she would.

'Of course it will, mam,' Rita said and set off.

'The image of your mother,' Miss Hackett said to her.

'Our little waitress,' Mr Shanklin called her.

And they watched her walk away, jet black hair, dark eyes beneath long eyelashes, lips red without lipstick. The image of her mother. But with something in her manner, something in the way she looked at people, something in the way she walked that made her different. She was a little bit more refined. She had just a touch of elegance. There was a mention of aloofness about her. Her mother's looks, they agreed, but the rest of her had come from someone else.

They missed Bella that week. They missed her entertaining chatter, the bit of colour she brought to the drab town hall, the smell of perfume she always left behind her. 'It's just like when the sun goes in,' Miss Hackett remarked to Eileen on the reception desk, Eileen who had been struck almost as much by the sight of Rita as she had been on first seeing Bella.

Eleven

Until her eye was better, Bella only went out after dark. She and Chuck wandered around the unlit streets with their arms around each other, while she talked on and on about going to America. And on the nights that he could not get out of camp, she sat in front of the kitchen fire roasting her shins and smoking, and pictured herself on a liner going to America. She did not picture the baby, just herself standing on deck with a cigarette and her coat draped around her shoulders, just as she had seen Joan Crawford in a film.

There was still a dark mark under Bella's eye on the Friday morning when she went into the town hall and told them she would be back at work the following Monday. She had reached the point where she could stay in the house no longer. Although it was too early for her pregnancy to be visible, and bearing in mind the fact that she had carried small with Rita and Ronnie, she did tell them at the town hall that Les was stationed back in England, so that it would not be too big a surprise to them when the baby did start to show.

The lecture room in winter was too cold for Bella and June. Only the most hardy and the most desperate spent their evenings there. The smoke room of the Plough was more inviting, with a fire crackling in the hearth and a taxi home afterwards. And when they went to the Manhattan Lounge, Bella wore the fur cape that a man had given to her in Birmingham in nineteen forty-one. She used to wear it into the lounge, then stand there while Chuck took it from her shoulders and hung it over the back of her chair. It made her feel grand. That and her long cigarette holder put her into that other world for a while, that world to which she was only ever a temporary visitor.

107

A fortnight after her fight with Les, Bella had a letter from him, a letter offering forgiveness, a letter that said they would start afresh as soon as the war was over. But Bella was having none of it. It was all over, she wrote back. They would make it official when the war ended. Or sooner, if he wanted to. She was not offering forgiveness. Anyway, she did not want to see him again. She put that in twice. He was stationed in the south of England, which was far too close for comfort. 'If you make a nuisance of yourself to me,' she wrote, 'then I'll write to your commanding officer.' 'Rita, dictionary. How many m's in commanding officer?'

'Tell him I'm in the Christmas concert at the tech, mam,' Rita said.

'You write and tell him yourself. I'm only sending him bad news, not good.'

Rita was having dreams about her future just as her mother was having dreams about going to America. But for Rita it was to be stardom, her photograph in the foyer of the Palace Cinema, her own story of her rise to fame in *Picturegoer*. She had a solo singing spot in the concert, as well as a place in the line of dancers. On a cold night she stood on the stage in the assembly hall singing 'Oh Johnnie' at the top of her voice, while the starved-looking teacher walked around shouting: 'Look out front, look out front,' and: 'Project girl, project,' which Rita did not understand. But she went on singing and did what they told her to do with her hands and could almost hear cheers from the empty hall when she had finished.

One afternoon she brought home the dress she was to wear. That evening she put it on to show her mother. It was a short little thing which did not catch sight of her knees and had little puffed sleeves. She put on her best silk stockings for the second time ever and went downstairs.

On seeing her, Bella said commandingly: 'You're not wearing that. Get it off, my girl. It shows all your legs. Look at you. I've never seen anything like it.'

Rita said nothing. She was going to wear it. She looked down at her legs and June said: 'It's all right, Bella. She's got lovely legs.' And without thinking, in her usual way: 'She follows you for legs, Bella, doesn't she? You always had nice legs.'

108

That did it. Bella said: 'Yes – well,' and Rita knew that Auntie June had won the day for her.

The following week Bella was touting tickets for the concert around the town hall. Although, it was not so much for the concert. It was for Rita. That was who they were going to see. Miss Hackett bought one and then said she would have another as she was taking Eileen. Mr Shanklin bought two, as long as they were near the front because Mrs Shanklin was a bit deaf. Bella did not believe him. She said to June: 'Dirty bugger. He only wants to get a good look at our Rita's legs. You want to watch out, June. He'll be wanting his two quid back.'

Rita sang her song without a fault and did her part in the dance routine perfectly. She looked out front, she projected and she smiled. It all came naturally to her.

They did three evening performances of the concert to a packed college assembly hall. In that town, other than the cinema and the public house, there was no place to go of a winter's evening. And Rita played the part of the star to the utmost at home. 'That spotlight on me when I'm doing my song. It's too bright. It's doing something to my eyes. They'll have to dim it down a bit, otherwise I just shan't go on.' She had done one performance.

Then it was: 'Don't talk to me, Auntie June. I'm saving my voice.'

'Just like our Ronnie with his foreign stamps,' Bella said to June, quietly, so that Rita did not hear.

But Bella was so proud of her that she took it all seriously on the surface and kept her comical remarks for others to hear. On Friday afternoon, she said to Miss Hackett: 'Well, I hope you like the show tonight. Quite frankly, I'll be glad when it's all over. It's like sharing a house with Greta Garbo. No wonder none of them stay married for long.'

Bella went to see the last performance of the concert on Saturday night, along with June and Chuck and Bill, in seats right down the front, ignorant to the remarks that were passed by people sitting further back to whom the sight of women with American soldiers was something to be whispered about and viewed with disdain.

They had time for a drink in the Wheatsheaf afterwards, then they stood talking in the cold under the plane trees by

109

the cattle market until the bus came at half-past eleven to get the Americans back into camp by midnight. Bella and June walked home alone by the light of Bella's torch and as they walked along, Bella said: 'Do you know, after seeing our Rita up on that stage, I really think she could be an actress or something. I mean, most of us wouldn't have the nerve, would we? Just imagine our Rita being a film star.' She thought of it for a while, then said: 'Although, I don't think film stars are all that they're cracked up to be. You take that Humphrey Bogart. He's got the sort of face that makes me think his feet smell.'

When they got into Bella's kitchen, she put on the kettle for a cup of tea. June sat by the dying fire and lit a cigarette. Rita had made herself a drink before going to bed and her unwashed cup was on the draining board, with lipstick on it. Bella stood by the gas stove waiting for the kettle to boil and said: 'I hope she gets on, our Rita. She had a good report from the tech this term. I want her to take all the opportunities that come along.'

'That's a good one,' June said. 'You didn't even want her to go to the tech. The arguments you had . . .'

'I didn't know what it meant, did I?' Bella snapped. 'But seeing her report,' she went on calmly, 'seeing her up on that stage, I want her to take all the opportunities that come her way. Not like me. I've let all mine slip by.' The kettle began to steam and she made the tea.

'You haven't, Bella. You're going to America, aren't you? That's an opportunity you're not going to let slip by.'

'It's my last chance though, isn't it? I can't afford to let anything go wrong.' She handed June her tea and sat down at the opposite side of the fire. 'I have missed some chances, you know. Do you remember that chap who wanted me to get a divorce and marry him? That chap who used to come round in a little van selling disinfectant and lavatory cleaner and things. About seven or eight years ago.'

'I remember,' June said. 'Lived with his married sister.'

'That's right. He used to spend every Wednesday afternoon at our house. I never had to buy any disinfectant for eighteen months. Talk about being paid in kind. That was when Les worked up the 'drome. I reckon everybody in the street knew I was carrying on with him, except Les.' She

110

paused for a while, sipped noisily at her tea, then said: 'I should have buggered off with him, you know. Talk about a missed opportunity. That was his own business too. A little gold mine.'

'He got killed, didn't he?' June recalled. 'Wasn't he the one who got killed at the fair?'

'That's right,' Bella said, in a voice quiet with recollection. 'That dreadful accident when the chairoplanes went out of control. He got flung out of his chair, sailed right through the air and landed bang in the middle of one of those sideshows where you have to shoot a ping-pong ball off a jet of water to win a china dog. Killed outright.'

'It was lucky you didn't go off with him then, Bella,' June said. 'You might have been killed too.'

'If I had gone off with him,' Bella replied, 'then we wouldn't have gone to the fair, that's for sure. He went with two mates. One of them got hit on the head by a piece of metal and it sent him funny. Never worked again. I always remember that afternoon. I did Les a couple of bloaters for his tea and he saïd: "These bloaters are a bit dry, aren't they?" And I said: "They shouldn't be. They've been in the sea all their lives and there's nothing wetter than water." Then I heard the boy push the evening paper through the letter box and I went to the front door to get it. And there it was, headlines on the front page. Talk about having a lump in the throat. I felt as if I'd swallowed Blackpool Tower, ballroom and all.'

'The things you would change if you could have your time all over again,' June said.

'I hope our Rita isn't sitting in a back kitchen over a dying fire at one in the morning saying that when she's our age,' Bella said. 'I hope I never do again, either.'

Twelve

It was New Year nineteen forty-four and everyone started on afresh about how much longer the war would go on, how much longer they would have to put up with rationing. Before Christmas the newspapers had been full of reports of air raids on Berlin, but now the Germans were bombing London again. The second front became the favourite topic once more. 'I don't know when it's all going to end,' Bella said to June, 'but I do know this. When they open that second front, I hope Les is the first one through it.'

But whoever planned the move that was to affect Bella most of all kept it a secret from the people it would involve most, treated it as confidentially as they would have done the opening of the second front. Not even a rumour leaked out about it. Not even a warning was issued to enable the people who lived on that periphery of the running of the war to tie up the loose ends of their lives.

Chuck and Bill broke the news. They came into Bella's kitchen that night, where she and June were waiting for them, painted and powdered and smelling sweet, ready for a night out. The whole camp was moving out, they said. They would all be gone by the end of the week. They did not know where they were going, only that a new influx of GIs would take over the camp.

There was nothing they could do about it. All they could do was talk about it. They did not go out that night, but instead they spent the evening in Bella's kitchen, sitting around the fire talking about a future that was vague, unseen, a future into which they could only guess where they would fit.

Ronnie and Mavis had gone over to Mrs Bragg's to play with her two boys and Rita was attending a drama class at

112

the technical college, so having none of the children to send, Chuck and Bill went out to get some beer, leaving Bella and June sitting there thinking about all the essentials they were going to lose. No more cheese, no more butter, no more corned beef, no more sugar, no more biscuits, no more cigarettes, no more chewing gum. The list they recited over to one another seemed endless. They kept adding things to it. 'Just imagine having to go back to bare rations like everyone else,' June said. 'We'll starve. We're not used to it. Our Mavis looks real well, too, and her little jaw's never still with that chewing gum.'

When they were drinking their beer, Bella remarked: 'Well, there's one thing. They won't send you abroad. You're only in the stores.'

'If everyone else goes, we go too,' Chuck said, sounding offended. 'Gee, if they do invade France or some place, what do you expect them to do, come back here every time they run out of stores?'

'What I meant, love, was that there's less likelihood of you going,' Bella said, trying to placate him. 'I mean, you can't all go, can you? Who would there be to look after the likes of me and June if you all went?' They all laughed at that, and she went on: 'Anyway, as soon as we know where you're stationed, if it's still in England, we'll come too. We'll move,' she said, with total disregard for what such a happening might mean to anyone else, to Rita. 'We've moved loads of times, June and me. Nothing new. We can carry on just as we are now.'

Somehow, none of them gave the impression that such a thing seemed likely to come about, although they did not turn down the idea. But for Bella it seemed to be the logical next step in her effort to escape. She was so near to getting away that her only thoughts were in going where Chuck went. At that moment she was confident that she was about to spend her last few weeks in that town.

Rita came in at nine o'clock. 'Blimey, what's the matter with you lot? The pubs all shut?' And when Bella told her why they had not gone out that night, she said: 'Oh well, bang goes my long frock.' Only she and Chuck knew what that meant. Since she had been going to the technical college he had been slipping her the odd packet of cigarettes to sell.

There was a bigger market there than there had been at school and stealing a few of her mother's had hardly seemed worthwhile any more. Rita had even begun to look beyond the time when she would have enough money and had been trying to calculate how many clothing coupons it would take to get a long frock. But now, to cover her remark, she said: 'Can I warm my feet? It's freezing out. I wish I had some fur-lined boots like Greta Garbo had in that film about Russia.'

The four of them walked into the town. They got on the bus at the cattle market and went up to the camp. The bus was full. Everyone seemed to have the same idea. They all stood around in the dark by the camp gates, saying goodnight, perhaps goodbye. Chuck and Bill, like all the others, promised to try and slip out once more before they left, not knowing that the short notice of their leaving was arranged on purpose. They were there to fight a war, to defeat an enemy, and to those above them that came first.

'This war won't go on forever,' Chuck told Bella. 'I guess things are on the move now. We're heading for a showdown, and whatever happens, however long the war lasts, I'm coming back for you. I'm taking you back to the States. That's all I want. I want to go back home and I want to take you with me. I don't want to be anywhere without you. When we say goodbye this time, let's make sure we never have to say it again.'

Bella and June did not catch the bus home. They walked through the cold January night without speaking. It was Bella who said eventually: 'I've got one of those feelings, June. It's as if something has just happened and I can't tell what it is.' She was quiet for a while, then she said: 'I wonder if we will see them again?'

And June said: 'Oh, of course we will.' Her face was streaming with tears.

They went into Bella's kitchen. June made a pot of tea and they sat huddled over the fire. Bella turned over the coals with the poker, tried to bring a bit of life into the dead fire and felt depressed that there they were, in her kitchen once more, with tea and cigarettes and their feet on the fender, holding another inquest over a life that refused to go right for them.

'I wonder,' June said, 'how long it would take if they did

114

invade Germany or somewhere?'

'Invade Germany?' Bella queried. 'What with France full of Nazis, I can see our lot leaving it to those Russians.'

'I was wondering about Sid,' June went on. 'I suppose – well, he'll come home won't he, when it's all over?'

'Of course he'll come home. What a daft thing to say. The Germans won't want to keep him. Nobody in their right mind would want him. It was only a dope like you who ever wanted him.'

'But I don't want him now, Bella,' June said, in her simple, childlike way. 'That's what I'm worried about. I don't want him back.'

'Look, love,' Bella said, suddenly sympathetic, 'you left him before the war. Your marriage to him was as good as over when you sent your pay book back. Anyway, he'd never find you now, would he?'

'I don't know. That's what worries me,' she said frowning, anxiety showing on her face. 'It's the thought of him coming back and setting about me again, like he used to. I mean, once I haven't got Bill . . .'

'Well, we can't ask Mr Churchill to keep the war going so that your Sid will remain safely locked up in a prisoner of war camp a thousand miles away, where he can't get at you, can we?' Bella said. June did not reply, just looked perplexed, and Bella went on: 'I never understood why you married him. There were lots of nice lads in Manchester would have married you, and made a good father for Mavis. But no, you had to go sloping off without a word and come back six months later married to that. A great big sergeant in the Coldstream Guards with a head like a pimple and brains you could have put on the sharp end of a needle.'

'He never hit me until we got married,' June said simply. 'I never knew what it was. I never looked at anyone else. But he wouldn't give over hitting me.'

'Les only had one go at me, and that was enough. But you, you kept coming up for more, just like a boxer. But at least Les did have a cause to. I mean . . .' She dried up then.

'Can you divorce someone for being a prisoner of war?' June asked her.

'I don't know. Ask that solicitor who you got your hundred pounds from. The best thing you can do, my girl, is

115

to come to America with me. You'll never get another like Bill.'

'Oh, I don't know,' June said uncertainly. 'I don't think I'd like all those wide roads. They frighten me.'

They sat there for a long time in a cocoon of silence, wondering in their minds how long the war would go on, would rationing end on the day the war finished, would June's Sid turn up again and start hitting her? The technicolour pictures of life when peace came were just a blur in their minds, driven out of focus by the plain reality in black and white of life as it was at that very time.

At the town hall they noticed something different about Bella. It was more obvious to Miss Hackett. Bella worked with her more often than with anyone else. Bella was quiet. The endless, witty, caustic chatter was gone. She still had a polite word for everyone, but not the cheery one for which she would be remembered.

Every Monday she used to bring a little something for Miss Hackett, for her and nobody else. If it was butter, she would say: 'There you are, love, spread that on your national loaf.' And the first time she brought her some dried egg, she said: 'The way our Rita fries that, you can sole your shoes with it.' But now it was: 'A bit of sugar, love. Make it last. I might not be able to get any more.' She never told her where she got it from, just said it was a secret, like Miss Hackett's first name.

'What is it, Bella?' Miss Hackett asked her one morning. 'You don't seem to be with us these days.'

No question could jolt Bella. Nothing would catch her out. She might have had the mind of the devil, but it worked like lightning. Without a second thought, she said: 'I suppose I might as well tell you. I'm expecting. I'm going to bring another ration book into the world.'

'That's a surprise, I'm sure,' Miss Hackett said. 'What does your husband think of it?'

'Pleased as punch,' she lied softly.

'I didn't know he'd been home.'

'Oh, didn't I tell you, love? There look, it must have been all the excitement. I kept it all to myself and didn't even think. Ah well.' Then she said: 'Would you like to tell his nibs for me? He might not want me here when it starts to show. It is a bit upper crust here, isn't it?'

Miss Hackett chuckled at that. It was her only reply. She told Mr Shanklin and later on he came out of his office and put his fat white hand on Bella's bare arm. 'You stay as long as you are able, Mrs Rigby. And if you want to – well, you can come back afterwards. In fact, we shall expect you back.'

'Christ,' Bella remarked, 'what's come over him? He'll be borrowing money next.'

And she went back into her lost world to be with Chuck, living again some of the good times they had had together, and into her new world to be with him, just the two of them with California all to themselves. That was what had made her a ghost of her usual self, most of all that longing for yesterday when she had had the verve to career through life simply because she could meet Chuck, her escape from life, that night.

Bella doubted whether Miss Hackett or anyone else at the town hall knew that the Americans were moving out. A new lot would move in and they would not know that there had been any change. She doubted, too, whether they knew that the town was full of half marriages, children but no wedding ring, or that she was only one of many who were set on going to America. She still hoped that Chuck would get out of the camp just once more. 'They've only got to get under the fence and walk through the cemetery,' she told June. And when the days went by and Chuck and Bill did not appear, she said to June: 'Get on our Rita's bike and go up to the camp. Ask the sentry on the gate if they're still there.'

'Hold on a bit,' June complained. 'I've just got home from work. Haven't got my coat off yet. It's freezing out. Anyway, why don't you go?'

'What me, in my condition? Well, thank you very much,' Bella snapped. 'I've been to work as well, you know. And I do head work, too.'

'All right, all right, I'll go,' June said, giving in. She got Rita's bike and rode off sightless through the blackout, with no lights on the bike.

June might as well have not bothered. Bad news was worse than no news. They had gone. She did not need to ask the sentry. She could tell the place was empty. Even in the dark it looked empty. There was no sound but that of the sentry stamping his feet against the cold. Then she met a woman she knew who told her that lorries had been going out of the camp in long convoys all day.

June did not want any dinner. Neither did Bella. The three children shared it, while the two of them settled down to tea and cigarettes and a new bout of misery.

'It's just like being told that the world is going to end,' Bella said, 'and coming home and finding that it really has.'

The world did not end, life did not end. It just seemed that, while life went on for other people, for Bella and June it halted for a while. Waiting was something they were not good at, something they were not used to having to do. At other times in their lives, as one door had shut another one had opened. But now their lives revolved around waiting to see if the postman was going to bring that letter, the letter that would open the door to their future. When it came, they would go on living.

Had they still been living in Manchester, or London, or Birmingham, there would have been enough distractions to enjoy, even in wartime, that the waiting would have been more tolerable. But in that little town there was nothing. A game of darts at the Plough, a last visit to the Manhattan Lounge before Bella became too pregnant, an evening at a dance in the town to find all the new Americans there. They looked so very young, nothing more than boys. They looked like another generation.

But Bella and June still knew enough about Mr Jerome to be able to claim their free seats in his cinema. He sidled up to them as they sat in the deserted restaurant waiting for the first house to finish. 'You haven't heard from the boys yet? Too bad they had to go away. I know how you must feel. I miss them too. All the time I have people asking me why I can no longer get them this or that, why no more corned beef, why no more cigarettes?'

'Well, the good days have gone,' Bella told him sharply. 'They'll have to learn to go without. Anyway, they made enough money selling it under the counter in their shops. And you did. So that's the end of it.'

Mr Jerome smiled his German Jewish smile. 'Still, there are more Americans at the camp now. I dare say . . .'

'You dare say what?' Bella turned and gave him a stare. Then she said to June: 'You know what he's hinting at, don't you? He's hinting at us getting off with another couple of Yanks so that he can get some more stuff out of the camp.' She sneered at him. 'You've got a bloody cheek. It would serve you right if they gave you a gun and made you go out and fight the Germans. If you were as good at that as you are at running the black market – well, we'd win the war in a fortnight. Rita, come on. The queue's moving.'

They went out to their usual seats in the front row of the balcony and left him there wondering how he could have been so wrong.

Thirteen

A month after the Americans went away, Bella came down the stairs one morning and found a letter on the hall floor. It was from him. She was childlike with joy, not wanting anyone at that moment to share her delight. She put it in her handbag. Rita was on her way down the stairs, still too full of sleep to notice any shade of early morning happiness that might be showing on her mother's face.

There was time after Rita and Ronnie had gone for her to open the letter. But she could hardly read it, the writing was so bad. She put it back into her handbag and went off to work.

June had a letter as well. Hers was readable. They sat in her kitchen that night, read her letter and tried to pick their way through Bella's. 'Stationed in Kent, not far from London,' June said. 'That sounds all right.'

'You'd think, coming from a family as well off as his, that they'd have taught him to write better than this,' Bella grumbled. 'It's like a foreign language. If you reckon that says, "I love you with all my heart dearest," well – it might say that in Chinese.'

They wrote their private letters back, said they would move to London as soon as they could. Had Bella not been pregnant she would have got on the first train and gone to find somewhere to live. She could not trust June to go. She had gone to London once before, Bella remembered. So for a while, life was going to be a matter of waiting for another letter, however bad the handwriting. Bella felt frustrated that she could do nothing until she had had the baby. She got the atlas out to find just where Kent was in relation to London, looked at it and dreamed.

Although they had written straight back to Chuck and

Bill, they did not get the immediate replies they expected. Life became tedious for Bella. She was obviously pregnant now and reticent about going out on an evening. At first, June stayed at home most nights, only going out when Bella did, for a drink occasionally or to the cinema. But a life like that was too monotonous for her, as it was for Bella. But Bella had no option. Eventually, June began to go out without her. At first it was just a bunch of the girls from work meeting for a drink. Then a birthday celebration. Then she came in one night and said she had met such a nice fellow. He asked her out again and June's social life started to pick up once more. She ceased waiting for a letter.

Sitting alone on an evening was unbearable for Bella. If she went over to Megan she was always reading a book or listening to the wireless. And Megan seemed quietly to resent Bella popping into her kitchen almost every evening, said no when she invited her over to share a bottle of beer, dropped the latch sometimes and pretended she was out. Bella could not understand it. She had never been one to force herself on people, had never needed to do that. If that was all Megan thought of her, after all she had done for her, then she would not bother with her.

Rita was no company either. She seemed to be out almost every night. Bella had not realized she went out so often. Drama classes twice a week, students' dance to a gramophone every Friday. One night she would go to Anne's house and every Saturday she and Anne would go to the cinema, to the bughouse where they only showed old films, full of the film stars Rita was sure she would replace one day. Greta Garbo, Claudette Colbert and Jean Harlow.

Ronnie used to sit there reading. 'Just like your father, always behind a book,' Bella said. She had started to knit again and sat there clicking away with her needles. She had not done any knitting since she was first married, when they were living with Les's mother and had no money to go anywhere. 'You'll ruin your eyes with all that reading.'

'I've got it fourteen inches from my eyes,' he replied. 'That's the proper distance. I've got to study or I'll never get to the grammar school.'

'Where do you get all those books from?'

'Library. Now shut up, mam. I keep losing my place.'

'Library?' She could vaguely remember having signed a form to allow him to join. And the grammar school? That was beyond her.

Still she waited for a letter. Weeks went by. Women in the street began asking her when the baby was due. They all had their own theories about the baby. Many of them had heard her screams on that November night, and had peered through the darkness the following night when she had been shouting out of the bedroom window at him. They had always been entertained by Bella and June and their comings and goings, but to the women in the street this was the most interesting incident so far.

Bella was determined to go on working until the very last moment. Life was so boring at home, she could not bear to be there all day as well as nearly every evening. She still kept them entertained with her jaunty sense of humour at the town hall. 'I'll bet you've never had a pregnant receptionist before,' she said to Mr Shanklin when he returned from lunch one day. He winced and looked round to see if anyone else had heard her. 'If you get jammed in a doorway with me,' she said to one of the men, 'then I'd win. It'd be two against one, wouldn't it?'

Coming home on the bus one day, she decided, quite suddenly, to write to Les. She told Rita when she came in from college. 'I think I'd better tell him, Rita. Get it over with. I don't know how to put it. Will you read it through for me, or are you off gallivanting again tonight?'

'I've got a stack of homework,' Rita replied sullenly.

And so Bella wrote her letter. She told him that she was about to have a baby to the American he had seen her with and that it would give him good grounds for a divorce. It was all over between them, she said, and only needed settling properly. 'You should know how to do that,' she wrote bluntly, 'you being an officer. So I'll leave it to you.'

She wrote it sitting by the fireside, leaning the writing pad on her knee. Rita sat at the kitchen table doing her homework. Bella said: 'Rita, love, what do you put if you don't want an answer to a letter, but if you want to know they got it?'

'Something like: "I don't want an answer to this letter, but please acknowledge receipt",' Rita told her, having done so

122

much practice at typing business letters that she felt she could put anything she needed to in writing.

'That sounds good. Write it down on a bit of paper for me and I'll copy it out,' Bella said.

When she had finished the letter, sealed the envelope down and put it behind the clock on the mantelpiece, she got her knitting, studied the pattern for a minute, then got on with the matinée jacket she was making for the baby. Every now and again she would pause, be lost gazing at the fire, then carry on knitting.

Her thoughts were a mile away when Rita said: 'You miss him, don't you?'

'You what, love? Miss who?'

'Chuck. Why don't you write to him again?'

'Oh, I don't think I will. Not yet. I'll leave it a bit longer.'

'I wouldn't,' Rita said. 'I'd have written to Chuck first and dad after.'

'Would you, love?' She was looking at Rita and she noticed that she could talk and write at the same time, just like Miss Hackett at her typewriter. 'You sound all grown up, giving me advice.'

'I am grown up nearly,' Rita said. 'I'm fifteen in a few weeks time.'

Bella went on knitting and when she got lost in thought again, Rita said: 'Where are you now?'

'Where am I? I was having a night out then. One minute I was in the Plough having a game of darts – and winning. Then I was in the Manhattan Lounge having the drinks brought to the table by one of those old waiters in a white coat. Then I was up at the camp at a dance, going round and round the floor. I could even hear the music.'

'You missed out the important thing,' Rita said, still writing. 'You were with Chuck. That's where you were.'

'Ah well,' Bella said, without commenting on that fact, 'I'll get our Ronnie and Mavis in.' She fetched her coat and put it around her shoulders, saying as she did so: 'Your Auntie June ought to be here to see to Mavis. Leaving a child of her age on a winter night,' forgetting that, until just then, she had been quite willing to leave Rita to look after the two children night after night, winter or summer. 'Well, I shan't be so available when I've got the little Anglo-American to look after.'

'The what?' Rita remarked.

But Bella had gone out of the back door, out into the cold and the pitch blackness, down the garden to the bombsite where the children played unseen.

It was not that she did not want to write to Chuck. It was just that she could not. The words that were in her mind one minute were not there when she held the pen above the paper. And the miserable weeks went by, spring showed itself, the nights drew out, but no letter came. She had one from Les. He had written straight back, despite Rita's carefully-worded request for him not to. All was forgiven. There would be no divorce, he wrote, and he would be a father to the baby. He wrote on large sheets of paper and filled one whole page with an explanation of how such things frequently happened in wartime and how they had to be tolerated just the same as other untoward things had to be. After reading that page three times, Bella still could not make head nor tail of it and had to ask Rita to read it and explain it to her.

Afterwards, Rita said: 'He writes a good letter our dad, doesn't he?'

'So he should. He's an officer,' Bella replied grudgingly.

'He could still write a good letter even if he wasn't an officer,' Rita maintained.

Bella gave her a hard look and said sharply: 'Being an officer didn't improve our lot any, did it? How many officers' wives do you imagine live in a rotten little terraced house like this, with nothing but a bombsite and the foundry to interrupt the view?'

'You've hardly given him a chance, mam, have you? After all, there is a war on.'

'I gave him a chance. He had his chance when there wasn't a war on.' She looked into the fire and said: 'I'm taking my chance now. Nobody has ever given me a chance, so I'm taking one.'

One afternoon Bella came home from work and followed her usual routine of making up her kitchen fire and then going into June's house to do the same there. Both of them would bank up their fires with damp slack mixed with tea leaves, potato peelings, anything that would burn slow and keep the fire in all day, anything that would help to stretch the coal ration a bit further. All she had to do was to put the poker under it to get the ash out and let the air in, and the fire would blaze up ready to take the coal she would put on it.

That afternoon she unlocked June's front door and went down the hallway into the kitchen. She knelt in front of the fire and began raking out the ashes. It was a cold, windy day and there was a draught blowing in from somewhere. She had left the kitchen door ajar. She got up to close it and saw a letter on the hall floor. She had walked over it on her way in. Although it was not a letter for her, not a letter lying in her own hallway, she quivered with anticipation. She went and picked it up. It was from Bill, she knew his handwriting. Bella put it on the kitchen table, then dashed back home to see if there was a letter on the dull red tiles of her hallway. But there was nothing there. It was half-past three and she had to contain herself until June came home from work two hours later.

Since Mr Fisher had died, Bella had always cooked dinner for June. She used to come straight into Bella's kitchen to a cup of tea and a chair by the fire. Then she would go into her own house and change out of her working clothes, coming back to find her dinner ready on the table. On that particular evening, Bella never gave her a chance to sit down. She ushered her next door to get the letter. June brought it back, sat by the fire and sipped her tea as she read it. When she had finished she handed it to Bella. 'You'd better read it, Bella,' she said and Bella knew that it could not contain good news.

Part of the letter ran: 'When we got to this place, Chuck sold a whole load of stuff to some guys. They seemed to be waiting. He was getting stuff out of the camp as quick as it came in. These guys had a truck ready to take it away in. I guess I was lucky I was working in another part of the camp. They knew we were buddies, that's why they pulled me in too when they caught him. I guess I didn't write to you while they were holding me in case they read the letter and traced things back to the little bit of business we had going back there. I will post this letter outside the camp anyway, to be on the safe side. The only good thing to come out of this is that Chuck has gone back to the States. He might be in jail, but at least it will be an American jail.'

There was more and Bella read it all. But nowhere did it say why Chuck had not written to her. She gave June back the letter. She was close to tears and she started to dish up June's dinner in silence. Finally she said: 'Well, that's that then. That's him landed up in prison.' She strained to keep the emotion out of her voice. 'Why couldn't they put him in prison here? That's what I'd like to know.'

'It's not as if they've given him six months, Bella,' June said softly. 'They've put him away for years. I don't suppose the Americans have got a prison here anyway.'

'Come and get your dinner, love,' Bella said.

June moved to the table. 'He'll probably write to you when he gets there.'

'I doubt it,' Bella insisted. 'He's a bloody criminal. That's all he wanted me for, so that he could get rid of the stuff. It was me who put him in touch with old Jerome, wasn't it? He must have been frightened I'd split on him. Coming from a family like that too.'

'I should try and forget him,' June said.

'Forget him? I won't forget him,' Bella said with determination. 'You wait till I get to America. I'll find him. I'll cut the bugger's throat for him.'

June breathed a sigh. 'Oh Bella, you do get involved,' she said with an air of exasperation. 'Just forget him. It's over now. It's over between me and Bill too. I'm going to write and tell him. It's no use getting too attached. We'll never see them again, Bella, how can we? It was nice while it lasted. We had some good times, a lot of fun. But it's over now.'

'No it's not,' Bella snapped. 'You've forgotten something. I'm carrying his baby. My marriage is in ruins. He might have finished with me, but I haven't finished with him. Not by a long chalk.'

But Bella could not hate him. She could put on an outward show, but inside her she loved him desperately. She adored everything about him, and to such an extent that her adoration blotted out the fact that he was in prison. An hour after her outburst her mind was full of thoughts of their meeting again. He would write to her, they would wait for the war to finish and then she would go to him. It was all going to turn out fine. One day she would go to America, to Chuck, to the happy life she had always lived for. There was still the chance to escape.

But in the meantime, there was the waiting. There was nothing to occupy her evenings and her weekends but the waiting for the baby to arrive. There was nothing to distract her, nothing to take her mind off it. She could not go out and dreams were not enough. One minute she was morose and down in the dumps, the next minute she was full of sharp remarks, ready to contradict anybody. Only at work was she different. There she was quiet, appreciated their kind remarks to her and was as hardworking as ever.

Bella dreaded having to leave the town hall, knowing full well that she might never be able to go back. The baby would stop that. The baby would stop her going out at night as well. Bella liked a social life. Since the war had started and she had been away from Les, she had had almost the sort of life she knew before she was married. Out every night, always a man, always laughter, nice places to go, a bit of romance. But now the baby would change everything. She could not expect Rita to look after it every night, as she had done with Ronnie and with Mavis. Quietly Rita had established a life of her own. She was growing up. Bella would not even entertain the thought of taking away from her all the excitement and the new things that growing up would bring to her. She recognized the predicament she was in and saw where the fault lay. The predicament was that she was pregnant and the fault lay in the fact that she did not want the baby.

And then, amid all the gloom of it, one afternoon at five o'clock Mr Jerome came to the door. Rita let him in. Bella was preparing the dinner. 'My goodness,' she said, 'look what the cat's dragged in. You haven't come to borrow money, have you?'

'Bella, my dear, I haven't seen you for weeks. I wondered what was the matter.'

'You know very well what's the matter,' she replied. 'It sticks out a mile.'

'Yes, yes,' he said and took a bag from his pocket. 'Here Rita, for you and Ronnie. You share them,' and he gave her his sweet ration. 'You haven't been into the cinema, Bella. You know you can always come, all of you.'

Bella was in no mood to be friendly with anyone just then.

She was finishing at the town hall that week. She had not even asked him to sit down. 'What? You'd be lucky to see me walking past that queue and into your picture house. With me in this condition? They'd all think you'd got me like it. No thank you.'

He grinned and his gold teeth shone. 'But Bella, my dear, you can always come in through the staff entrance.'

'What?' she said loudly. 'If I'm not good enough to come in through the front door, I'm damned if I'll come in through the back.'

Mr Jerome changed the subject. 'I came to ask you, Bella, if you had got a pram. If not, then I think I can help you there.'

'A pram?' She grinned. It was the first time Rita had seen her mother grin for weeks. 'What's on then? Are they selling prams on the black market now?'

'No. I have a friend. He will let you have one a little cheap – as a favour. I just thought that – if you have not got one . . .'

'Oh yes. I bet I wouldn't be able to bring it home in broad daylight, would I?' and she gave him an inquisitive look.

'Bella, my dear, it is not like that. Mr Chambers, my friend, he has a pram shop.'

'Mr Chambers? He's got that double-fronted shop. Well, I never thought he was a Jew.'

Mr Jerome laughed and showed his gold teeth again. 'But he is not a Jew. Why should he be a Jew? He is a business ac-quaintance. And – you are my friend as well and you are not a Jew – well, he will let you have a pram a little cheap.'

'What are you standing up for?' Bella said, suddenly amic-able. 'There's no charge for sitting down you know,' and she pushed a chair near to the fire for him.

Behind his back, Rita stifled a giggle. Her mother had gone back to being her old self with Mr Jerome's visit, but only now could she see how entertaining her manner and her behaviour could be. Never had she realized that her mother was such a comic, never until she had become so solemn, so uncompromising, so overcome by the change in her circum-stances.

Mr Jerome sat by the fire. 'You'll have a cup of tea?' Bella assumed he would and got him a cup and saucer. 'I'm just brewing up for the rest of us. Sugar? We're not down to sac-

128

charin yet. We would have been a long time ago if it hadn't been for the Yanks. Our saucers came from their officers' mess. I don't suppose they missed them. All mine got broken one unforgettable Friday night.'

'Where would we have been without the Americans?' Mr Jerome wondered, stirring his tea. 'Such nice boys.'

'Yes, all we've got now are memories,' Bella said. Then she patted her stomach, grinned and said: 'Well, some of us have got more than memories.'

The following afternoon, Bella said to Miss Hackett: 'I'll work on a bit if nobody minds. Our Rita's calling for me at about four to go and get the pram. Anyway, it'll help me get cleared up before Friday.'

'Don't talk to me about Friday,' Miss Hackett replied. 'I daren't think about next week. It's going to be strange sitting here all alone. I don't know how I put up with it for all those years.'

'Never mind, duck,' Bella consoled her. 'I'll come in now and again and bring the little Anglo-American to see you,' she said without thinking.

'The what?' asked Miss Hackett.

At four Rita came for her mother and they set off for Mr Chambers' double-fronted shop, full of prams and cots, right in the middle of town. Mr Chambers was expecting her. No sooner had she spoken her name than he was all smiles and a handshake. 'This is Rita, my daughter,' Bella said. Mr Chambers beamed at her, gave her a handshake too and a long look, and Bella immediately classed him as another dirty bugger.

Nevertheless, she picked a navy blue pram with big wheels and he let her have it at cost price. She could not understand why. She would never realize that having been one link in that chain that had brought food out of the camp into the bellies of those who could afford to buy it at black market prices would stand her at some advantage now and again.

They wheeled the pram home. When they got to the top of the street, Bella said: 'Slowly now, Rita. Let the nosey devils have a good look. They've had nothing to look round their blackout at since Chuck went away. Stick your nose in the air, Rita. Put on a bit of class. They expect it. You'll never be a film star unless you learn to put on a bit of class.'

People either liked Bella or they disliked her. Whatever remarks she made to Mr Jerome, he liked her and let them all pass. They all liked her at the town hall. Tarty, heavily made up, suggestive, an answer for everything, she was more out of place there than she would ever be anywhere. But on that Friday afternoon they presented her with a cradle for the baby. It was complete, ready to put the child into. Everything was there, right down to the rattle. And Miss Hackett had spent her evenings crocheting a pram cover. She handed it over with her chins quivering and tears all down her face.

Mr Shanklin did not breath a sigh of relief when she left that afternoon. He would have been entitled to. She had blackmailed him into giving her a job and he had given in to her. But for him, like everyone else there, from Eileen on the reception desk to Miss Hackett behind her typewriter, the town hall now seemed a duller, quieter, emptier place. They all hoped she would come back, looked forward to the day.

One of the men from the town hall brought the gifts home for Bella that evening in his tiny Austin Seven. Mrs Bragg was outside sweeping the pavement when the car drew up. Bella waved to her as she came to the front door. After the car had gone, Mrs Bragg went over to Bella's house.

She had not seen much of Bella lately. It was her own choice. Some of the magic had gone out of Bella since the Americans had left, since she had become pregnant. There was no romance in the role she was playing now. She had dropped from being the star in Mrs Bragg's life to being one of those ordinary casualties of war on the home front. Pregnant to another man. Of course, she missed the odd items of food that Bella used to give her, she missed the cigarettes, the boys missed the chewing gum. But most of all she missed the sight of Bella and June all dolled up, Chuck and Bill smart in their uniforms, setting off down the street at seven o'clock for the sort of evening she only knew of by courtesy of the public library and from what Bella told her. And there was something else that kept coming back into her mind. It was the memory of Leslie Rigby standing at her front door, smiling, touching his cap. What more could Bella have wanted than him, she kept asking herself? How wrong could she be to cast him off? Megan could not forgive her for that. She had secret

130

thoughts about Leslie Rigby, thoughts that made it impossible for her to forgive.

'Well, hello stranger,' Bella said as Megan came in. 'I thought you'd joined the navy to be near your husband.' She was in the front room showing Rita and June the cradle. 'What do you think of it then?' She pointed to the pram.

'There's nice,' Megan said, touching it carefully, as if unsure of whether she ought to. 'I bet that cost a pretty penny.'

'Well, not as much as it would have cost some people, love. I got it trade price, through a friend.' Then she said, looking Megan right in the eyes, 'Not everybody cast me off in my hour of need, Megan. See?'

June felt embarrassed. 'It's a lovely cradle, isn't it? They really thought a lot of you at the town hall.'

'Of course they did,' Bella agreed. 'That's the sort of thing people do for you if you're friendly and work hard.' Megan had taken a packet of Craven 'A' out of her apron pocket and Bella said: 'Don't smoke in here, love. I don't want my little one's things smelling of dog ends.'

June could not stand the atmosphere. Bella so hostile, Megan so meek and looking rather hard done by. So she said: 'I'm just taking the mother-to-be down to the Unicorn for a drink. One last fling before she goes pop and lets little Johnnie out. You will come, Megan, won't you?'

'Course she will,' Bella said harshly. 'It's the last chance of a drink she'll have until I get my figure back.'

Fourteen

The baby came, a boy, eight pounds, fair hair. She called him Alan. Rita and Ronnie loved him. So did June, so did Megan, so did everyone who saw him. They all liked him so much that they seemed to forget that he was in fact only a half member of the family. He bore no resemblance to Rita and Ronnie when they were babies. Bella saw straight away that he was the image of Chuck. But why, she asked herself, did he have to have his father's fair hair as well as his looks? In a family of dark-haired people, for as long as he was among them he would always look different enough to make people think.

It was warm that spring. They had a heatwave in May. Bella took a chair out into the back garden, put the pram in the shade and sat there bored stiff, listening to the trains clanking about in the sidings, watching the smoke drifting endlessly up from the foundry chimney. Then she decided that, with all that smoke about, it might be healthier for the baby in the park and she began to wheel the pram there most afternoons. But she was still bored. There was no one to talk to, nothing to do but sit there beneath the trees looking at the still brown water of the pond. There were no ducks, no fish, not even a water lily. It seemed that even those small items had been sacrificed because of the war.

Some days, when she got home from college early, Rita would take the baby out. She and Anne would wheel the pram down to the park. Rita had a part in the play they were putting on at the college that summer and she used to rehearse her lines with Anne's help. Rita was growing up. No longer did she need tissue paper in her brassière. And she was getting shapely in places she would be the last to notice. Often, as she pushed the pram through the park, there were

132

boys lounging about on the bandstand. They would whistle and shout out to her: 'Come on over the shelters, darling, and I'll give you a little brother to keep him company,' indicating the row of brick air-raid shelters that had been built on one side of the park and which had been used for everything except their proper purpose.

Rita would go stiff with embarrassment, look straight ahead and walk firmly on. 'You won't find a future Robert Donat amongst that lot,' she said to Anne and they began going all the way round to the other entrance to avoid them.

June got excited over the invasion of Normandy. She thought the war would be over in no time. Bella brought her down to earth again. 'Sooner peace comes, sooner your Sid will be back in circulation. Hadn't thought of that, had you?'

Bella did not enter into the excitement over the invasion. She read all about it in the papers, followed the Allied progress every day, tried not to miss the nine o'clock news on the wireless. On the couple of nights in the week when she went out, she always silenced everyone in the kitchen at six o'clock and listened through the atmospherics of the old wireless to the news. The bulletins, even those from the battlefront with the sound of gunfire in the background, never stirred her, never brought any exclamation from her. Her interest was a very personal one. Just as the war had brought a change in her life, and the chance of an escape forever from her ordinary existence, so, she imagined, the coming of peace would give her another chance. In the excitement, the hurly burly, the comings and goings that peace would suddenly bring, there might be another chance to escape. Each headline in the newspaper, each news report from the crackling loudspeaker cancelled out a bit of the time she would have to exist before she went away and started to live.

Even though months had gone by, Bella still listened for the drop of her letterbox when the postman was in the street. Still she hoped for a letter from Chuck. But nothing ever came through the letterbox for her. Even Les had not bothered to write again after his last unwanted, unanswered letter. For the first time in her life, she realized, she was without a man.

When Rita was fifteen she had a card, a short letter and a postal order from her grandmother. 'I shall have to write back, mam,' she insisted. 'She's put in a twopence ha'penny stamp and an economy label.' And she made her mother read the letter before she sealed it down. To Anne, she said: 'That's another five bob towards my Paris gown.'

'Paris gown?' Anne exclaimed. 'It was a long frock the last time you mentioned it.'

'Well it's going to be a Paris gown, as soon as the war is over and we've liberated everybody,' she stated.

One of the things Bella missed was the money she had earned at the laundry and the town hall. She envied Rita her five shillings. And yet, since the early days of the war when Les had got his commission, she had got better money than most. Even so, she only just managed to stretch it from one week to the next. She had to buy her cigarettes now. And on her nights out, she would spend all she had. What she missed was having enough money in her purse to be able to give Rita and Ronnie a shilling whenever they wanted it, having enough American food in the pantry to feed any of their friends who happened to be there at tea time. What she hated was the endless queueing for the rations, standing there looking as earnest as all the other women in their head-scarves, with shopping bags made from barrage balloon fabric. For the first time in ages she really depended on that cube of cheese, that sliver of corned beef, hardly thicker than the paper the butcher wrapped it in. Even the fact that she was friendly with the butcher, that in return for the pleasure of her letting him buy her a drink in the Lord Nelson every now and again, in return for the honour of being seen with a woman who looked like her, she would unwrap her joint on a Saturday to find a few sausages in with it, or a piece of liver, never made up for the days of plenty. The manager at the Co-op still repaid her for all the packets of cigarettes she had given him – a couple of eggs, a little extra margarine, things that seemed to go nowhere at all in Bella's disorderly kitchen. And so, like everyone else, she studied her ration books, scoured the shops to see what there was on points and made Rita and Ronnie share the sweet ration out equally. She thought of Chuck coming in and tossing packets of chewing gum at them, or dipping his hand into his greatcoat pocket and saying: 'You kids want some candy?'

She thought of Chuck a lot. Housework was not Bella's

favourite occupation and she shirked it whenever she could. She kept the baby and the children like new pins, but let everything else slide. Right in the middle of a job she would drift off into a daydream. She dreamed her way to America on a liner. Chuck was there to meet her. Then she had a variation on getting from New York to California. At first, he drove her all the way in a long white car. Then they went by train and had dinner in the dining car, served by waiters in white coats who might have stepped straight from the Manhattan Lounge. And finally they flew, and when they landed in California there was the long white car at the foot of the steps with a chauffeur who took off his hat to her and called her Miss Bella.

When she finally woke up from it all, it was to the realization that the money she had been saving to take her to America had almost gone. Most of it had gone on the baby. What she had left was hardly enough for a rainy day. She used to look at the baby and wonder what life would be like without it. All her daydreams left out the baby. In her mind, she felt that Les could provide a future for Rita and Ronnie if she went to America. They were his responsibility as well as hers. But the baby did not enter into the picture of things anywhere. It lay there, clean, healthy, blue eyes and fair curly hair, the image of the man the women in the street had seen her time after time go out with on an evening, so attractive a child that they dismissed their opinions of his coming about as they leaned over the pram to touch his little hand and coo over him. To Bella he was just as beautiful. She cared for him as much as she had for Rita and Ronnie. But she could not see a future for him. Somehow her mind would not conjure it up. His future lay just a day ahead and no further

'You want to get out a bit more, Bella,' June told her. 'You don't look half your old self. Let Rita care for little Alan a bit more. Good practice for her.'

'What do you know about it, June?' Bella contradicted her. 'You've only ever had one child. I've had three. And you've never had a husband to call a husband.'

'That's why I go out, Bella,' she maintained. 'It's the only thing that keeps me going.'

'I'm not getting mixed up with any more men,' Bella

declared. 'Look where the last one got me. He's gone forever and I'm left with his baby. By the time it's off my hands I'll be too old for anything and anyone.'

'Go on,' June said. 'There'll always be someone to keep you warm on a cold night.'

But she did not reply to June's remark. It was stalemate. They sat there in Bella's kitchen in silence. Bella was a little jealous of June at times. She was back in their old routine, out nearly every night. Twice a week they went out together, once to the pictures and once to the pubs that they were used to frequenting. They had long since got into the habit of being regulars at more than one pub. It had stood them in good stead when there was a beer shortage. But now they never went out together on the best nights. On a Friday and a Saturday June always had a date. Not with an American, however. She kept away from them now. She did not want to end up like Bella.

'You not going out tonight?' Bella asked, all of a sudden.

'No. I was, but I don't think I'll bother,' June replied.

'Standing somebody up, are you?'

'Yes. It doesn't hurt them once in a while. Men get too much of their own way. Look where it's got us all.' Then June said: 'Pity your Rita's not about. We could have popped out for a drink.'

'They're rehearsing their play tonight. She's got to have her bit of pleasure,' she told her.

'I'll tell you what,' June said. 'I'll send our Mavis down to the off licence for a flagon of beer. I'll go out and call her.'

Mavis fetched the beer and they sat there smoking and drinking. June said: 'You're going to have to get things sorted out, Bella. Do you think you and Les could get back together again?'

'No I don't,' Bella snapped. 'I've finished with him. As soon as the war is over I'll get a divorce. I'll be off anyway. I'll get to America somehow.'

'Oh Bella, you've got Rita and Ronnie to think of. And little Alan.' June was worried. Bella would do things other people would never think of.

'Look, Rita is sixteen next year, so she'll be at work. She can look after herself.' She did not mean to be unreasonable. Bella had matured young and imagined everyone else was

136

the same. She had had men before she was Rita's age and yet she had not gathered the fact that Rita never mentioned boys, that she had not yet found out about them. 'And our Ronnie, well – he's got a father, hasn't he? Let him have a bit of responsibility. Make up for what he missed through the war being on.'

'There's still little Alan,' June mentioned meekly, touching on the thorny part of the problem.

'You know what I was thinking, love? I was thinking of having him adopted.'

June was shocked. She dropped her cigarette, nearly burned herself. 'You can't, Bella. Never,' she said in a hushed voice.

Bella leaned towards her. 'Look, love, what sort of a future can I offer him? I shan't have a husband, he won't have a father. I shall have to work like hell to keep us both alive. I brought him into the world, I know, but if I can find a better future for him with someone else, then I don't think there's any harm in that.'

June was not convinced. 'How do you think I felt when I had our Mavis, then? I never had a husband. I never had anyone. But I kept her.'

'You had me,' Bella snapped. 'And don't you forget it. It was me who got you two rooms to live in when you were six months gone and never had a home. It was me who was at the midwife's elbow when your Mavis arrived.' She jabbed at June with her finger. 'And here's another thing. Since war broke out and we left Manchester, our Rita has put your Mavis to bed on a night more times than you have. If it hadn't been for our Rita, what would have happened to your Mavis? Tell me that. And we'll have no more about our Rita looking after the baby. If I can't look after him, then I'll make sure there's someone who can. I shan't leave him with a kid. So there.'

June took the verbal assault with her usual look of hurt, of coming tears. She drank her beer, sniffed and said: 'Oh Bella, you don't half go on. You drag everything up.'

'I know I do,' Bella admitted. 'Still, you do let yourself in for it. Come on, let's finish off this beer.' And she filled June's glass.

Although Bella had only thought of adoption the second

before she spoke of it, it seemed to be the answer. That night, she looked down at little Alan asleep in his cradle. There was no doubt that she loved him, and her eyes and throat were full at the thought of losing him. But suddenly she could see a future for him. At last his life stretched beyond the morrow. Before she went to sleep that night, she imagined him in a house with big rooms and in a garden in the sunlight. She saw him growing up with space around him, with air that was fresh and not laden with dust, in a place that he could live in and not have to escape from. She had never imagined a real future for anyone but herself until then, had hardly bothered her mind with what lay ahead for Rita and Ronnie. But for him she saw and wanted a real life.

The heartbreak and the anguish would be hers, not the baby's. He was young enough to know nothing about it. She was old enough to get over it. She would have him adopted.

Fifteen

In the middle of the week, on one of the nights when Bella and June were going out together, June came into Bella's kitchen all dressed up ready. Bella was putting the finishing touches to herself. She had all her old appearance back, a figure that gave no sign of recently having gone through the exertions of bringing a child into the world. Her black hair shone and her face could have passed for that of a twenty-year-old.

Rita was bathing the baby. 'You're making a good job of him, Rita,' June remarked.

'I've just about got the knack of it now,' she replied.

'Good practice for when you've got one of your own,' June went on.

'Oh, I'm not having any children,' Rita stated. 'I might get married, but I'm not even sure about that.'

June was amused. 'What are you going to do then, love, live on your own?'

'No. I shall have a house, and a nice garden,' Rita said seriously. 'I'll have a housekeeper and a maid and a gardener. And I shall have lots of friends round to parties and things. Film stars have a lot of parties.'

'You'll have to have a lot of money to live like that, love,' June said.

That was obvious to Rita. She said: 'I'm going to be a film star, Auntie June. Not just an actress. A film star. And I shall have all the things that film stars have. I shall be able to afford it.'

'That's right, Rita,' Bella agreed. Rita's view of the future never failed to amuse her. 'You go out and get just what you want in life, and let the rest of the world go by. You might not get exactly what you want, love, but you'll have a lot of fun trying.'

They went out then, down the street, greeted by the women who stood by their front doors gossiping in the evening sunlight, greeted and then discussed when the two of them were out of earshot.

'Have you told Rita yet, about having little Alan adopted?' June asked.

'No. That's going to be the hardest thing to do,' Bella admitted. 'She's really attached to him. She's even made plans to take him to the seaside when the war's over. Her and Anne have even decided what they're going to take for the picnic. Funny kid, our Rita. Always years ahead of herself.'

'You were like that,' June told her. 'What you weren't going to do when you grew up.'

'Ah well,' Bella said, 'I hope she has more luck than I've had.'

They went to a dance that night. June had got the tickets for it. It was held in the canteen at the parachute factory, for the airmen from the RAF camp on the other side of the town. They were pouring out of two buses just as Bella and June got there.

When they were inside, Bella said to June: 'Right, here we go then. Now try and get yourself an officer, a squadron leader or something. There must be some here. They'd never let this lot out on their own. Don't have anything to do with anyone with stripes on their arm.' But June took no notice. She did the boogie woogie with a corporal who lifted her over his shoulder and showed all her underwear.

The night out helped to take Bella's mind off her problems. How to tell Rita and how to get the baby adopted were the things she dwelled on most. She did not want to get rid of the baby, did not want only to find it another home. She wanted him to go to someone who could give him the sort of home she had dreamed of him having. It had to be exactly right. Nothing else would satisfy her or give her peace of mind. But how to go about it?

On Friday night June had a date. She did not come home until four the next morning and was too ill to go to town with Bella to get the rations. Bella took her a cup of tea and two aspirins and left her in bed with her headache. She took June's ration books and went to town alone.

140

It was the queueing that took the time. A queue at the butcher's, a queue at the grocer's, a queue at the baker's, a queue at the tobacconist's. When she got to the counter there was the pencilling through of coupons, the clipping out of coupons, the careful cutting of cheese, the exact weighing of butter. It was irksome and tiring. And when she had finished she went into the Unicorn, bought a brown ale and sat in the saloon bar.

Bella was lost in her own thoughts when a voice she knew said: 'Well, hello Mrs Rigby.'

She looked round. It was Mr Shanklin. 'Oh, hello, duck,' she said.

'You are a stranger. We've been expecting you to pay us a visit at the town hall, with the baby.' He put his glass on the table and sat down.

'Oh, you know what it is. What with one thing and another.' Why had none of them ever visited her, she wondered? Had the news got round? Or was it what Miss Hackett had told her, one thing being friendly at work . . .? 'Surprised to see you in here,' she said. 'You don't usually come in here, do you?'

He shook his head. 'I've left my wife in a long queue at the Home and Colonial. Do let me get you another drink.' When he came back from the bar, he said: 'We really have been wondering why we never had a visit from you. Miss Hackett got quite upset.'

Of course, she thought, Miss Hackett would have been upset. And the rest of them must have been mystified. But she could not go, she could not show them her fair-haired child. It was lucky that she had not met any of them before, in the street, in a queue. She was always coming across people she knew while standing in a queue. But Mr Shanklin, whose secret she knew, who paid prostitutes for love, she might as well tell him. It would be better than lying.

She said: 'Well, it's a long story. You see, the baby is mine, but it isn't my husband's. Its father was my American boyfriend. You know how I went round the town hall showing everybody photos of my husband and my two kids? We're all dark, aren't we? And my little one is fair. Lovely blond curls. So I couldn't show him off really, could I?'

Mr Shanklin's face took on an expression of concern. 'Oh,

141

I am sorry. I really am sorry. Causing difficulty for you, is it?'

'It's bound to change life a bit, isn't it? My American has gone – left me. My husband hasn't taken it too bad. He's willing to take the baby as one of his own. But, if you want to know, our marriage is on the rocks. We'll see the war through and then we'll be finished.'

'That is a shame. I'm very sorry for you, Mrs Rigby, I really am.'

'Ah well.' Bella took a drink of her beer. 'These things happen. Blame it on the war. We blame everything else on the war. I'm thinking of having the baby adopted. If I can find a good home for him, that is. Here he is look.' She took a photograph of the baby from her handbag.

Mr Shanklin looked at the photograph. It was a lovely child. He looked at Bella and saw all the good things about her, all the assets that had never been put to any good use. 'You want to have him adopted, do you, Mrs Rigby?'

'Yes. You see, the thing is, I can't offer him much of a life. How can I without a husband? I shall have to go to work. I think somebody else could give him a better chance in life than I could. The trouble is, I don't really know how to go about getting him adopted.'

'Well, it's a big decision to take,' he told her.

'I'm thinking of going to America when the war's finished – start afresh,' she said. 'It wouldn't be fair on the child. I'd rather lose him now, before I get too attached to him.'

Mr Shanklin pondered over what she had said. He looked away, as if it made it easier to think. Then he said: 'If you really want to have the baby adopted, I may be able to help you. Would you like me to see what I can do?'

'I can tell you, love, I haven't got the faintest idea where to start. If you can put me on the right lines, I'd be ever so grateful.'

'Let me see then,' he said. 'What if I make an inquiry or two and come and see you one afternoon?'

She felt a surge of relief go through her. 'All right. And I'll be very grateful for any help you can give me, I really will.'

'We'll leave it at that then,' Mr Shanklin said.

Bella finished her drink and picked up her shopping bag. 'Well I'll leave it with you then, love. And you come round any afternoon. I'll be there. And give my love to everyone at the town hall.' Then she smiled at him and left.

Mr Shanklin sat there, finished his drink and thought. He was not really sorry for Bella. She had, he reckoned, brought it all on herself. But he did like her. She might have been the brassy tart who had brought a sort of colour, a hint of the improper, into the town hall, but still he liked her. In his eyes she was all beauty. Whatever she had done, her looks won her forgiveness from him as they could win her forgiveness from anyone. Since she had left the town hall, every day had been hung on the hope that she would call in and pay them a visit. It had brought him a private misery and the delight of dreams. And now, as a salve to all the heartache and the longing he felt for her, in helping her he was going to try to bring a little satisfaction to himself by forging a link between him and Bella. The idea he had in mind would, at the least, give him access to her for as long as she lived there, he thought, and might, if her plan for going to America did not come about, lead to closer things.

On the following Friday afternoon, at about half-past two, Mr Shanklin came to Bella's front door. She took him into the front room. The baby was in there, in his pram. Mr Shanklin leaned over the pram and looked at him. The baby gurgled and worked its legs up and down. He was enchanted by the child, captivated by its blue eyes and fair curly hair.

Bella picked the baby up. 'There now, isn't he sweet? Alan I've called him. It's going to break my heart to part with him. But what sort of life can I offer him?'

'Charming,' Mr Shanklin beamed. 'Mrs Rigby, what I'm going to say may surprise you. I do believe I have found someone who may want to adopt your baby. I have a daughter – our only child – who, unfortunately, cannot have a child of her own. She and her husband could give the baby a very good home.'

Bella was taken aback. 'My, that's one out of the blue, isn't it? I didn't think you meant . . .'

'Look,' he said eagerly, 'this is where they live. Do you see?' He took a snapshot from his pocket. It was of a large house in the country. 'That's their house. They have a farm. In Cornwall. All they want to make life complete is a child.'

'Well, I wouldn't mind living in a place like that,' she said.

'If I telephone my daughter, she and her husband could come up next weekend.'

'Hang on,' Bella said. 'Rushing things a bit, aren't you? After all, a photo isn't much to go by.'

'Only to see the baby. After all,' he said, 'they would no more go by a photo of the baby than you would go by a photo of their house.'

'That's right,' Bella agreed. 'Only it's all happening so quickly, that's all. I thought you were just going to come here and tell me how to get in touch with the adoption people, not offer to take him into your own family like that.' She looked at Mr Shanklin. His little round eyes were sparkling, there was a smile of expectancy on his lips. 'Oh go on then,' she said. 'You telephone your daughter. And I'll tell you what. I'll give you a snap of little Alan to send to her.' She put the baby back in the pram, opened the sideboard drawer and sorted around for a photograph.

'This really is a good picture of him,' he said, when she handed him the photograph. 'I'll post it off today. And I'll let you know about the weekend.'

Bella could hardly believe it. She closed the door behind him and went back into the front room. She felt no sorrow that she might really be losing the baby, more a strange excitement that the impossible might actually happen. That huge house, and a farm. It was more than she had dreamed of. She looked down at him in the pram. 'Well, sunshine, it seems like you're going to have some of the good luck that has always steered clear of me.'

A letter came on Thursday morning. Could she go to Mr Shanklin's house on Sunday afternoon, with the baby? She was to telephone him at the town hall with her reply. At half-past nine she was in the telephone kiosk, saying she would be there.

Now, Bella realized, she would have to tell Rita. There could be no putting it off, no going out with the baby on Sunday afternoon without her knowing. That afternoon, as soon as she came in from college, the moment she took her coat off, Bella told her. And as soon as she started to speak she knew that telling Rita would be one thing, reconciling her to the fact would be another.

144

There were tears, tears of disbelief, tears of pleading, tears of ordinary sorrow. For an hour Bella talked and Rita cried and argued. She went from offering to take the baby off her mother's hands completely to threatening to run away with him. And Bella put her reasons over and over again, but it was no good. Nothing she said to Rita made a case for her having the baby adopted. It went on so long that eventually Bella began to fear that she would lose her temper. She clenched her fists in an effort to keep control of herself. When she was hoarse from talking, when the atmosphere in the kitchen was electric and it looked as if no one would get any dinner that day, June came in from work.

'Oh, I'll come back later,' she said, sensing what was happening.

'No, don't go.' Bella saw some relief for herself in June's arrival.

'Have you told her – about little Alan?' June mouthed the words.

'Yes. Have a word with her, love. There's no getting it through to her.'

Bella went out, down the garden, and stood by the gate watching the kids playing on the bombsite. She lit a cigarette and a feeling of relief went swimming through her.

Back in the kitchen, June pulled up a chair and sat by Rita. She took her hand. 'Come on now, love,' she said. 'It's going to happen and there's nothing we can do about it.'

'What do you expect me to do, Auntie June? She's giving away my little brother. What do you want me to do, give three hearty cheers?' And she went on sobbing.

'It's for the best, sweetheart. Your mam and dad are finished with each other. She'll have enough on her hands looking after you and Ronnie. I know, love. I had to bring up our Mavis without a dad.'

'Well, you managed all right,' Rita said, not making it sound like a compliment.

'I only had the one, Rita. Your mam's got you two for a start. And she's not as young as I was when I had Mavis. Life looks a bit different when you've turned thirty, never mind there being a war on. She'll have to work full time you know. Who's going to look after the baby all day?'

'You did it with your Mavis. Tell her how you did it.'

'Well, you're forgetting one thing, love. You see, I had your mother. If I hadn't had her, I don't think I would have been able to keep our Mavis. I really don't.'

'You can't tell me that there isn't a way,' Rita snapped.

June looked round at the door. She hoped Bella would come back in. She was lost for something more to say. In desperation, she said: 'Anyway, love, you're a fine one to carry on. You never stop telling us of how you're going to go away and be a film star. You're always telling us you're going to live in Hollywood in a big house. I never hear you offering to take your mother or Ronnie with you. They never enter into it. How do you think your mam will feel when you do go away? It makes no difference how old your child is when it leaves home, be it two or twenty-two. You still feel the same sorrow, Rita. Your mam will feel it for you. Now what do you think goes through her mind when you keep on about it all the time? I don't think she'll give three hearty cheers either.'

Rita had stopped crying. She sat there contemplating her screwed up, soaking handkerchief. 'Oh Auntie June, you've got it all wrong. I don't mean it like that at all.'

'Don't you, love?' June went on. 'If I've got it all wrong about you, there's just a chance that you've got it all wrong about your mother and little Alan. Isn't there? Just you think of this. What would you rather have? An old terraced house to live in, no garden to speak of, a bombsite out the back, dirt from the foundry over everything? Or a big house, a farm, green fields, fresh air? I know which I'd rather have. You're mother isn't thinking of herself in having him adopted, you know. Far from it. It's a sacrifice, Rita. It's breaking her heart, but she's trying not to show it.'

Rita sat there, silent for a while. She did not believe that her mother's heart was breaking. She thought of her mother staying in night after night because of the baby. And she thought of her going out night after night when little Alan had gone. Rita knew exactly where her mother's heart lay. It lay in getting dressed up and going out with men. It lay in going to America and starting life anew. It probably lay anywhere, she thought, except in that little house that was supposed to be home. Wherever it lay, she did not believe it was breaking. At last she said: 'Well, if that's what you think, Auntie June, that's what you think. I just don't believe that it

146

is little Alan's future that is the only thing involved. That's my opinion and I'm saying no more. You can tell my mother to come back in now, if you like.'

'Well I never,' June said. 'I don't know what they teach you at the tech, Rita, but I must say they put some funny ideas into your head.'

June went outside then to fetch Bella, went outside burdened by the lies she had told to Rita. Bella wanted everything for herself, June knew. She wanted an escape for herself, a new life for herself, freedom for herself. And now June feared that Rita knew it too. But there would be no changing Bella, June was certain of that. No one had ever changed Bella. There she was, standing by the gate, smoking, dreaming, seeing herself back at work, going to nice places on a night, getting off the liner in New York while a porter pushed a barrow with her luggage on, all her cases smothered with destination labels.

After dinner on Sunday, Rita went straight out. Bella was relieved. She had not told her who she was taking the baby to. That, she reckoned, would have been too dangerous.

With the baby in the pram, Bella walked the two miles to Belvedere Drive. She was done up to perfection, however unsuitable it all might be for walking. Her feet were dying in her high heels by the time she got there.

It was a big square house with a gravel drive and wide steps up to the front door. She left the pram at the foot of the steps and carried the baby up to the door. Mr Shanklin let her in. They were gathered there waiting. She could see excitement on their faces.

'This is my daughter Alice.' She was a plain little woman and looked about Bella's age.

'Here he is then. My little Alan.' Bella gave her the baby to hold.

Mrs Shanklin sat beaming at what, to her, was a happy event. An only child who could not have children. A mother who could not be a grandmother. The baby meant more to the four of them than Bella or June or Rita put together could ever know.

They had tea then from thin cups that would not have seen the day out in Bella's kitchen, and with the luxury, to her, of a teaspoon each and one for the sugar. She talked to Alice's husband. He was tall and plump, with red cheeks and hair parted on the side and combed straight across like a schoolboy's. Bella liked him. He seemed strong but gentle, with a big hand that had gripped hers firmly and a voice that was soft and cultured. Bella had expected a country accent from a farmer.

He showed her more photographs of the farm. 'That's what our son will grow up to, Mrs Rigby,' he said. 'His own farm. A farm is a business, you know. How many people grow up knowing that they will have their own business to go into when the time comes to earn a living?'

They passed the baby round from one to another. He did not cry, did not even whimper. They were all bright eyes and compliments, and Bella knew that there was a good home for him with them. There was a future for him there, she thought, better than the one she had always wanted for herself. There was a future full of happy people. She had never seen that for herself. She had seen herself and a man and a little bit of luxury. Happy faces, happy people, she had not imagined. But she could see them now, she could see them for little Alan.

They must have decided to say it beforehand, Bella imagined, when tea was over and they were running out of comments to make about the baby. 'We love him,' Alice said. 'I'd like to take him home with me now. But I think we had better look into the ins and outs of adopting him before anything else.'

'That's right,' Mr Shanklin agreed. 'Much as you would like to take him home with you, Alice, there is more to adopting a child than just that.' He looked at Bella. 'I'll get all the necessary information, Mrs Rigby, and I'll be in touch with you. But rest assured that if you do want to have your baby adopted, then I don't think you need look any further for anyone to give him a really good home.'

He said it just as if he were addressing the town council, but Bella smiled and nodded and knew that what he had said was true.

They saw her to the end of the drive. Alice pushed the pram that far. Then they waved her off and when she had one final look at the four of them as they turned to go back to the

148

house, she wondered how on earth a man with a family like that, with such a home and a place in local society, could ever need to pay June two pounds to go down on the grass with him. Bella could not understand it. But for all her experience, Bella did not really understand men. For all her living, she did not really understand life.

'I'll tell you what we'll do,' June said to Bella when she got home, 'we'll go round to the Duke of York's. They've opened the gardens again and we can take the kids. Then you can tell me all about it.'

'Have they now? The war must be going well if they've opened the gardens. There's no danger of any of those flying bombs flying as far as us then, I suppose? You know, it's a blessing we never made off when the Yanks went, isn't it? We'd have been dodging those bloody things now.'

Rita would not go. The play was going on that week and she was still learning her lines. Ronnie did not want to go either. The following day he was sitting the scholarship examination to go to the grammar school and he wanted to stay at home and read. But his mother had taken one refusal, and she would not put up with another. She clipped his ear and told him he was going, whether he liked it or not.

Bella was alone in the kitchen, soaking her feet after her four mile walk. While she was sitting there enjoying the bliss of it, Anne came in. 'I'd just like to say that I'm sorry you're having little Alan adopted,' she blinked. 'My mother won't have him because she said she's got enough on with the rest of us, but I'll look after him on Friday when you go to see Rita in the play,' and her voice tailed off. She broke into tears, and ran out crying noisily.

'Thanks, love,' Bella shouted after her. 'Me and my poor feet say thank you.'

It was a fine evening. They sat in the garden at the Duke of York's, the baby in the pram, Ronnie and Mavis playing on the swings. It was not a very grand place. Trains going by on the embankment nearby drowned all conversation now and again, and people who had been there before the war covered their drinks with their hands.

'You are sure though, Bella? You are sure?' June asked her.

'Sure as I'll ever be,' she replied. 'I want the best for him and the best for me. If I keep him, neither of us will get much out of life. That was the biggest stroke of luck I've ever had, meeting old Shanklin that Saturday lunchtime. I'll bet that in twenty years time, the last thing that baby will long for will be a backstreet home with no father and no prospects. I'm giving him a future, June, something you and I never had. I wish my mother had given me away to a couple who had a farm when I was his age. Mind you, I think my mother would have given us all away, farm or no farm, if there had been any takers.'

Sixteen

Everyone was now looking towards peace. They had been looking forward to victory for a long time and now that it was assured, they saw peace just along the way. The Allies were driving the Germans back through France. 'They'll be liberating Paris soon, Rita,' Bella said. 'You'll be able to get your Paris gown at last.'

But there was no reply from Rita. Little Alan had gone and her mother was back to her old ways, out every night, sacrificing everything for her social life.

Bella had gone back to being her old self on the very Sunday that she had pushed the pram those two miles to Belvedere Drive and had come back without it. June had gone with her, but had not gone to the house. She had stayed at the end of the street waiting, ready to see Bella home should she be overcome at the very last by what she had done. There were a few tears. That night June had taken Bella out to help her get over it. They had come home in a taxi at one o'clock the next morning, singing, drunk. June had been too ill to go to work the next day.

Bella did not show her sadness. It was all kept inside her. That hard defiant exterior hid everything. She knew where her limits lay and she stayed within them. When she took the baby away for the last time, she left him in the pram at the foot of the steps and went up to the front door. She dared not take the baby out of the pram. One more touch, one long look and she would be reduced to ordinary grief just like anyone else. And that would not do for Bella. Bella was not ordinary and did not want ordinary things. She wanted her ambitions. And so she took one brief look at the child and walked off down the drive with her head held high, sniffing and blinking. That was his future settled and now she had to

151

settle her own, once and for all. That was why she had gone through it all. No ordinary person would have done it.

But suddenly the days were empty. She longed to be back at the town hall, but she knew that, for her own peace of mind, she could never go back there, where the daily presence of Mr Shanklin would keep the memory of having the baby adopted forever fresh in her mind. She missed the baby. Even though every one of its belongings had gone with it, there was still the smell of it, of baby powder, there were still spaces that it had occupied, in her bedroom where the cradle had been, in the front room where she had kept the pram. The place that the tiny creature had taken in her life had been huge, and the emptiness that its absence caused haunted her. But it was her own private ghost and no one else ever knew of the weeks of agony she endured before it left her, before time exorcised it.

Bella went to the labour exchange to try to get a job, but all they offered her was factory work. It was an office job or nothing, she had stated, so for a while it had to be nothing. Then a letter came one morning. Ronnie had won a scholarship to the grammar school. Bella made him write to tell his father. 'What did you do that for, Bella?' June asked. 'You don't want to give him an excuse to turn up again, do you?' They were having a cup of tea and a smoke after dinner.

'No, I'm hoping he might send some money,' she replied. 'He'll need a blazer and things. And me without a job.'

'You don't do bad, Bella,' June said. 'You should be able to manage on an officer's money.'

'I might be able to if I stopped in all my life like Megan,' she said sharply. 'What do you want me to do, join the bloody library?'

June looked away, then said: 'He must be brainy, your Ronnie, getting to the grammar school.'

'Of course he's brainy. He takes after Les. You know, I could tell our Ronnie would get on,' she said, 'by the way he was always reading. Never out from behind a book. And you know what?' She leaned towards June as if about to impart something very confidential. 'He reads books without any pictures in them. That's a real sign of brains. How many children do that?'

And June said dismally: 'Oh dear, and I went and bought

152

him the *Beano Annual* for Christmas.'

'He still likes his comics though. What boy doesn't like his comics? But when it comes to a book, it has to be one without pictures in it. I shall never regret signing that form for him to join the library.' She gave a sigh of satisfaction. 'I've got our Rita to the tech, our Ronnie to the grammar school and a home with a good future for our Alan. I don't think I've done bad. I don't think I've done bad at all.'

'All you want now is a job,' June said. 'I should ask that Mr Shanklin if he can fix you up. He must know a lot of people in business.'

'I might do that,' Bella replied.

But she did not. Instead, she answered an advertisement in the evening paper. Rita told her what to put and she got an appointment for an interview.

June was concerned. Bella started going on as if she had the job already. 'But Bella, you've never served in a shop. There must be heaps of people after jobs who have served in a shop.'

'Les's father was manager of a shoe shop, wasn't he?' Bella insisted. 'This is a shoe shop. I'll bet they won't get many people applying whose father-in-law was manager of a shoe shop.'

'He was dead before you even knew Les,' June went on. 'What on earth are you going to say?'

'Oh, you know me,' Bella said, confident to the last. 'I'll make it up as I go along. Hargreaves. That's a posh shop. I shall like it there, I know.'

She did not make it up as she went along. She had it all worked out ready in her mind. Dressed in her best costume and her very best hat, she went to the interview.

Mr Hargreaves interviewed her personally in his little office. He had a shiny pink face and a shiny head with no hair. 'This is a family firm,' he told her, looking into her steady dark eyes. 'We like to think of our employees as part of our family. So perhaps, to begin with, you'd like to tell me what experience you've had.'

Not too much make-up and try to sound refined, Rita had told her. And she tried. 'My father-in-law had a shoe shop in Manchester. I never worked there on a regular basis, just now and again, when one of the girls was on holiday or off

153

sick. They always used to send for me. I seemed cut out for it. Took to it naturally.'

'Have you done shop work at all, other than that?' Mr Hargreaves studied her. She was an extremely good-looking woman, he thought, and he came across a lot of women in his shop. But this woman had such fine features, such glossy black hair, such eyes. He could picture her serving in the shop.

'Well no, I usually do office work. But there's not much about. And of course, I have to be a little bit particular about what sort of work I do, because of my husband. He's an officer in the RAF, so I've got to be a bit choosey.'

'Is he now? Fly does he?'

'Fighter pilot. Hurricanes.' That always impressed. She could get free drinks in pubs on that, when the landlord's wife was not about. 'With the children out all day now, I really do want to get back to work. My daughter is at the technical college, and my boy is starting at the grammar school next term. Scholarship. Now if you want a reference, you can get one from Mr Shanklin, the town clerk. I used to work for him. Do you know him?'

'Not personally,' he replied, when in fact he would not even have known him by sight. 'Well now, we should require you four and a half days. Thursday is early closing and Saturdays my two daughters come into the shop to help. It may take you a little while to get into the run of things, but what with shoes being on coupons like most things, trade is not too brisk. We do our own repairs and that is by far the busiest side of the business at present. Anyway, as you have done this sort of work before, however briefly, I'm sure you'll soon pick it up. Can you start on Monday?'

'Do you mean I've got it?' she burst out excitedly, almost dropping the refined front she had been putting on. And she had so much more to say. She had not even got as far as bringing Mr Bevin into it.

Bella was overjoyed. Before she had got fifty yards down the street she was planning what she was going to do with an extra twenty-two and six a week coming in. Top of her list of priorities was the fare to America. That was definite. And if the Atlantic dried up, she would walk there. For the rest of the day she was all dreams.

154

Her happiness turned into generosity and her generosity overflowed. 'We'll all go to the pictures on Saturday,' she said to Rita and Anne. 'If there's nothing good on at the Palace, we'll go somewhere else. My treat. We'll take Mrs Bragg and her boys. I don't think they've been to the pictures since we took them last.'

To June it was: 'We'll go out Friday night and have a really good time. Celebrate my new job.'

'Wouldn't it be better to wait until you get your first week's wages, Bella?' June asked.

'No. We'll pick up two nice fellows and we won't let them go home until they've spent all their money.'

Bella felt like an eighteen-year-old again. She had got over parting with the baby. That never entered her head now. And Les was out of the way. A new job, a bit more money, her independence back. We were winning the war and life was going to be good again.

On Friday afternoon she got behind the curtain in the kitchen and washed all over. Then she changed and put on a pinafore to guard her clothes while she got the dinner. She was only hotting up the remains of yesterday's stew. They would not like it, but they would either have to eat it or go without. She was cooking nothing else. She was going out and that was that.

When June came in from work she had a sheepish look on her face. She waited until Bella had poured her a cup of tea before saying: 'Bella, I'm ever so sorry but I can't go out with you tonight.'

'You what?' Bella's eyes flashed like lightning.

'I can't go out with you tonight. I've got a date. Do you mind putting it off until tomorrow night?'

'Got a date? What do you mean, you've got a date?' she bawled. 'We arranged to go out tonight. It's been on all week. I'm playing darts at the Plough tomorrow, you know very well. It's a friendly. I said I'd play.'

'He came to the factory gates at lunchtime. I didn't like to say no.'

'You don't mind saying no to me though, do you?' Bella fumed. 'Who is it? That RAF boy with the greasy hair? The one you met at that dance?'

155

June nodded and bit her bottom lip. 'His posting has come through. He's going to Scotland.'

'Well let him go then. There are plenty of women in Scotland.'

'Oh Bella, I couldn't say no. It would have been too mean.'

'You don't mind being mean to me though, do you?' she snapped. 'Fine friend you turn out to be at times. All right, go out with him then. I'll go out on my own. I shan't be short of company, don't you worry.'

'We'll go out Sunday night,' June said passively. 'How about that?'

'Don't talk to me about Sunday,' Bella said bitterly, and set about stirring the stew vigorously.

Nothing would have kept Bella at home that evening. She was bursting with venom at being let down and the only way she knew of getting over it was to go out and drink and enjoy herself. And so she went.

Bella had friends all over the place. There was hardly a pub in the town where she was not greeted by someone the moment she walked in. There was always a drink being bought for her. She could have stayed in the first pub she went into, the Unicorn, and had a good time. The piano was going in the back room and people were dancing. That should have been enough. But somehow she felt restless. She missed having June there. She missed having a man. It was not enough to pick someone up or to be picked up. For it to be right for her meant having a date all arranged. It was the walking out with a man, the swaggering off down the street with him, the never being on her own that made the occasion right. To go out on her own, whatever happened during the evening, was only half the fun. Deep inside her she still wanted Chuck. However badly he had cast her off, she still longed for him. With Chuck she had felt a class above herself, and she had put on airs to match it. With no one else could she ever imagine having that feeling. Of all the men who bought her drinks or asked her to dance that evening, she could not imagine herself going into the Manhattan Lounge with any one of them. None of them brought out that grand feeling inside her. They were all so ordinary.

Bella went from the Unicorn to the Wheatsheaf, then to

the Black Horse, then to the Trafalgar. And she got drunk, and steadily drunker. It was not closing time when she came out of the Trafalgar. Suddenly, in her mind, she felt the need to go home. For some reason she thought of the children. And although she could walk straight, her head was spinning.

Her body got her to a bus stop. Her mind found her sitting on the top deck of a bus and she had a period of clarity sufficient for her to realize that she must be on the wrong one. It was taking her in the wrong direction. All her usual command of a situation was missing. She panicked, set off down the stairs, tripped and knew nothing of what happened then. She knew nothing of hitting her head on the platform of the bus, nor of falling out into the road, nor of the following taxi running over her body.

What Bella did know was that something strange was happening to her. She was in a nightmare world. She tried to move, but people held her down. When she wanted to get up there was an awful pain all over her body that made her scream. But it seemed to be someone else screaming. She listened to the screams rise and fall until the pain was gone and the voice was quiet. Sometimes it was light, sometimes it was dark, sometimes there were figures in white, sometimes no one at all. At one time she saw Rita, then June, then Ronnie. Then they were there together. Megan was there looking down at her, but no sooner did she realize who it was than it was Les. Les was there, in airforce blue, with his pilot's wings on his uniform and his brass buttons shining. But then he was gone and everything was turmoil again. She struggled against the figures in white, succumbed and all was calm once more. Then the faces appeared again. They were all there together, more of them than she had seen before, all looking down at her. Rita and Ronnie, June, Megan, Mr Shanklin, Miss Hackett, Eileen, Mr Jerome, Mrs Sadler, Les and his mother. Their faces were ranged before her in an arc, looking down at her with sad eyes and faltering mouths. And then they were gone.

Seventeen

It was light when Bella woke up. She was not at home. The window was in the wrong place. The small room was all white and she was done up tightly in a strange bed. She was calm now. There was no panic. She had her mind back and she tried quite rationally to remember what had happened. But it was all gone. Whatever it was that had happened, it had got her into hospital. She was aware enough of that.

Presently one of the figures in white came into the room, a nurse. She appeared intent on just glancing in, but when she saw Bella's eyes meet hers she came over to the bed. 'How are you now, Mrs Rigby?'

'All right, love.' Her voice sounded coarse, her throat was dry. 'What day is it?'

'It's Wednesday.' She put her hand on Bella's forehead.

'How long have I been in here?'

'Since last Friday night. You fell off a bus. Don't you remember?'

'No,' Bella said hoarsely. 'I'm dry. Get me a drink, will you, love?'

'Don't you move.' The nurse poured some water and held it to her lips. 'Try to keep as still as you can. Doctor will be in shortly.'

The nurse left her then and the doctor came in straight away. Another of the figures in white. They had sat with her at first, then looked in at her at intervals when her condition had improved during the week. 'How do you feel?' the doctor asked her softly.

'Are you sure it was only a bus I fell off?' she replied.

He smiled. 'Try not to move. You've injured your back. It's important that you do not move.'

'Fat chance I'd have. I'm done up like a mummy.' She did

158

not mean it to be funny. That was exactly how she felt.

He smiled again. 'You've been quite ill. But you are over the worst now.' He was quiet for a while, just leaned over her and looked into her eyes. 'Nurse will come in every now and again. You're going to be all right now. Don't worry.' And he went out.

During that day Bella came to know that, lying there in that bed, she was helpless, unable to do anything for herself. She was to find out soon that everything, however small, however private, had to be done for her. It took all her courage to endure it. She thought of all the wrong things, all the hard things, all the desperate things in life she had done. She thought of the risks she and June had run, the chances they had taken, the fun it had all been. Was it going to be memories from now on, she wondered? Or was she going to go out and carry on living life as she always had done?

Throughout that day she dozed and woke again, slipping in and out of sleep like a baby. When it was dark and her mind seemed to be at its clearest, she wondered about being able to move. Already she felt irked at just lying there. Bella had never been ill. Childbirth had been the only thing to confine her. The nurse's instructions about not moving were, to her, just a caution. And she tried to move her legs, and felt the most searing pain in her back. A scream rang out from her, the room spun, she saw the nurse there above her and knew nothing else until it was light. But she remembered that awful pain. It seemed that the mere thought of moving her legs, the slightest suggestion of a movement, had brought her that sudden agony. From then on she lay still, afraid of the pain, afraid of what she had done, afraid of what she might do to herself if she as much as imagined herself getting out of the bed.

The day passed, the following day came and the nurse said: 'You can have visitors today, as long as you don't move.'

'Visitors? I must look awful. I can't see anyone looking like this. My hair.' She felt it with her hand. 'Can you put a comb through it for me?'

The nurse combed her hair and held the mirror for her to see. She saw her dead white face. There was no colour in it at all. Even her lips were white. It scared her. She said nothing, just turned her head away.

They let Rita and Ronnie come in to see her first. Ronnie looked frightened. Rita smiled, although she found it difficult to do so, leaned over and kissed her mother. 'How are you now, mam? The nurse says you're much better.'

'Does she, love? Oh, I'll pull round. You know me. Aren't you going to say anything, Ronnie?' But he looked embarrassed, grinned awkwardly and stared at the floor. She did not know what to say to him. 'I'll bet the last time you saw me lying in bed on a morning was when I had a hangover.'

'It's afternoon, mam,' Rita said.

'Oh is it, love? I haven't got a clock in here. I suppose I've lost track of time – must have slept through breakfast.' Again there was silence. Then she said: 'Who's looking after you? Auntie June?'

'She was at first,' Rita replied, 'but gran's here now. She's seeing to us.'

Bella's lips tightened. 'Oh, she is, is she? And how did she manage to get in on things?' she asked acidly.

Rita looked at her mother. Her face was dead white but her eyes were suddenly full of life. 'They sent for her, mam. They had to. She's waiting outside now. And dad. They sent for him too. But they let me and Ronnie see you first.'

'Where's your Auntie June then?'

'She's at work, mam. She stayed home until gran came, but she went back to work yesterday.'

Bella's voice became fraught with anxiety. 'Who's looking after Mavis then?'

'I'll see to her, mam,' Rita assured her. 'I'll look after Mavis.'

Bella turned her head to one side. 'Oh God, why did this have to happen to me?' She blinked as she felt the tears coming, bit her lip, felt such anguish at being so helpless. 'She hates your Auntie June. She hates Mavis too. Poor kid. No one to look after her. I've always treated her like one of my own.'

'Oh come on now, mam. Mavis will be all right. I'll see to her. Now stop worrying. If the nurse sees you all upset, she'll blame me.'

Bella brightened up again, although she was full of worry inside. The nurse came in and Rita and Ronnie kissed their mother goodbye.

They sent Les in then. He looked as awkward as Ronnie had done. He did not kiss her, but pulled a chair up to the bed and sat down.

'Well, are you sure the Air Chief Marshal can spare you?' she said hurtfully.

'How are you feeling now?' he asked quietly. 'You've been very ill. They thought at one time that you might not pull through.'

'Oh did they?' she snapped. 'Well, it takes more than falling off a bus and being punched all over by you to put paid to me.'

He was unmoved. 'Bella, a taxi cab ran over you,' he explained.

'So what? Shows what I'm made of then, doesn't it? Still, if I can put up with you and your mother – well, I think I can get over anything.'

'Look, Bella, let's try and be sensible about things,' he began.

But she would not let him go on. 'Oh, why don't you go and get on with your bloody war and leave me alone? Just go away and take your mother with you. Now go on.' And she shouted for the nurse at the top of her voice.

Les was out of the room before the nurse appeared. She leaned over Bella, who said: 'Don't let people just come wandering in here, love. I'd like to have some say in the matter.'

The nurse was taken aback. 'We imagined you would want to see your husband, Mrs Rigby.'

'Well you shouldn't go imagining things, should you?' Bella told her. 'Just you tell me who is out there and I'll say whether they can come in or not.'

The nurse was speechless. She had never heard anything like it. Despite her training and her years of nursing, she felt for the first time that, unless she was very careful, she would succumb to her patient's powerful personality. She had watched Bella come through a terrible crisis and now saw in that exchange what had brought her through. For this patient, life had always been a fight. She had won the toughest round. Anything else would be easily overcome.

The nurse was on her way out of the room when Bella said: 'There's just one thing. If my friend June comes, I want to

161

see her. I expect she'll come to see me. Blonde she is, a nice-looking girl.'

'She's been in every day,' the nurse said. 'I'll send her straight in.'

June would have gone to the hospital straight from work, but Rita had telephoned her at the factory as soon as she had seen her mother. June was like Bella about appearances and wanted to look her best when she saw her. And so she went home first and dolled herself up as if for a night out.

Nevertheless, no sooner had June put one foot inside Bella's hospital room than she was in tears. She had some flowers for her. 'Oh Bella, you haven't half given us all some worry.'

'Never mind, love. The worry's over now. You've brought me some flowers. Let me see. Oh, moon daisies and marigolds and snapdragons. You shouldn't go spending your money.'

'I didn't,' June admitted. 'Our Mavis brought them home for you. I don't know where she got them from. School, she said. I hope she didn't pinch them. I bet she did.'

'Never mind, it's the thought that counts,' Bella reassured her.

June wiped her eyes. 'Oh Bella, you do look awful. You look like death warmed up. You really do.'

'Well, that's nice, I must say,' Bella retorted. 'After all I've gone through. I've been unconscious for nigh on a week.'

'You weren't unconscious, Bella,' June said. 'They had to give you something to put you to sleep until you were over the worst. You must be on the mend now. But you do look awful.' She started to cry again. 'They would only let me and Rita come in to see you, but you were sound off all the time.'

'Only you and Rita?' She remembered all the faces she had seen looking down at her. 'But I could have sworn . . .' she began. But she went on: 'I've had Les here, June. Did you know? And his mother. I wouldn't have her in here though. As if things aren't bad enough. Who had the cheek to go and summon her up from hell just when I was in this state?'

'The doctors sent for her, Bella. And they sent for Les, you were so bad. She turfed me out of your house as soon as she arrived,' June said sorrowfully. 'Never a thank you for looking after Rita and Ronnie. Three days work I lost and not a thank you from your Les either.'

Bella took her hand. 'Well I thank you, June, I thank you. I'll make it up to you. You know what's worrying me, don't you? Who's going to look after your Mavis?'

'Megan said she'd see to her until I get home from work,' June said. 'She said she'd try and get in to see you this evening. I left her giving our Mavis a bit of dinner.'

Bella sighed. 'Oh God, haven't I messed it up for everybody? Haven't I? And the trouble is, I can't remember a thing about it. I don't know how I got here or what I've done to myself. I'm in a right quandary.'

'Perhaps it's just as well you can't remember,' June said. 'After all, with your new job to start. It would have upset you to lie there thinking of that. I went and saw that Mr Hargreaves.'

'That Mr who?'

'Hargreaves. The shoe shop. Your new job there. Can't you remember, love?'

'Oh, the shoe shop.' Bella closed her eyes. 'The shoe shop,' she said again, almost to herself. 'I remember, I remember. I went out, didn't I? I had a right skinfull, June. I remember now. I got on the wrong bus, didn't I? I came down the stairs to get off and . . . That's all I can remember.'

'You fell on the stairs, Bella. That's when you fell.'

The door opened and Megan came in, unobtrusive, unannounced. Megan, so insignificant in her brown coat and her headscarf knotted tightly under her chin, had moved unnoticed through the hospital and had gained entry to the room for herself. 'There's better you look now,' she said. 'Bit like your old self again.'

'Now that's what I wanted to hear,' Bella said. 'It's one thing feeling like death warmed up and another being told you look like it.'

Megan took a packet of cigarettes out of her pocket, but June warned her, 'They won't let you smoke in here, love.'

'Go on,' Bella said. 'You have a smoke if you want one. Open that window. Stand over there. No one will know.' Megan did as she said, gave a cigarette to June and Bella said: 'What have you got there, Megan? A packet of five

Woodbines? Different to the time you always had forty Camel behind your old man's photo on the mantelpiece, isn't it? I remember the first time I went into your house. You were smoking Pashas. Didn't half make your kitchen stink. Good job me and my American came along and saved you from that, wasn't it?' She said it harshly, without a smile.

When they were walking to the bus stop, June said: 'I thought she'd had her share of bad luck, what with Chuck going away and the baby coming along. I blame it all on that wreath. The day her wreath fell off the hearse everything started going wrong.'

Megan said: 'Things always go in threes, don't they? Perhaps it will be different for her now. She can't have any more bad luck.'

When visiting time came round at the hospital the following afternoon, the nurse said to Bella: 'There must be about a dozen of them out there. How do I know who to send in? Or are you out to all callers?' She smiled as she said it.

'Is my mother-in-law out there?' Bella asked. 'She's a fat little party with a face like an old stone wall.'

'She's there,' the nurse nodded.

'Well, what I want you to do is send her in with my old man and the two kids, altogether. I don't want her or him in here alone, never mind together. All this rubbish about no more than two visitors at a time, you can forget that for once, can't you?'

'Of course we can.' She would bend almost any rule for this patient. The doctors had examined her that morning. They had been as gentle as possible, but she had screamed and cried, and refused to be put to sleep afterwards to get over it. And now, although she looked like death, there was something inside her that was very much alive. She was scheming, deciding that what she wanted was what mattered. 'Now look, if you feel you've had enough, just ring the bell. Don't need to shout. Just ring. All right?'

Miss Hackett came in first. 'Nurse said I could have ten minutes,' she said and started crying. She had brought roses from her garden, and two ounces of liquorice allsorts from Eileen, who had not come because the smell of hospitals made her sick. Bella spent the whole ten minutes explaining about the baby, why she had not brought him to the town hall, telling her all except who had adopted him, keeping the second of Mr Shanklin's secrets.

When Miss Hackett had gone, they all traipsed in after each other. Mr Shanklin and his wife, Mr Jerome who was near to tears and kissed her, Mrs Sadler and her husband who smelled of a recently closed pub, people from the town hall whom she had never expected to see again, all those faces that she thought she had seen looking down at her, but which had not really been there.

June and Megan came in together. 'Honest, the things I've had done to me,' Bella said. 'No wonder there aren't any men nurses. I don't know what would happen. They'd have to have double beds for us all.' They took up their station at the window, smoking, and Bella went on: 'June, can you pay my Christmas club at the Unicorn for me, love? And my guesser. And I'm in the victory club at the Plough. See to it for me, will you? As soon as I find out who's got my handbag, I'll straighten with you.' She was rigid in the bed, her face the colour of the pillow, and June looked at her and wondered for a moment whether it was all worthwhile.

Last of all came the four of them. They looked serious, hardly a smile from Rita as she kissed her mother. Mrs Rigby took a chair at the foot of the bed. Bella hardly gave her a glance. It was almost five years since she had last seen her. They avoided each other's eyes.

Bella felt that there was something wrong. She hoped that Rita had upset her grandmother, but when they had finished inquiring of how she felt, Les said: 'I think we are going to have to come to some arrangement about the children, Bella. Mother has a job now, you know, and she'll have to get back. So what we've . . .'

Bella had heard enough. 'Let her go home then. June can see to Rita and Ronnie just as well as anyone. Anyway, I'll be out of here in a week or so. I'll have to pull myself together, won't I? Our Ronnie's starting at the grammar school in a few weeks time. There's his blazer to get and other things he'll need.'

Les remained calm. 'But Bella, you're going to be in here for longer than a week or two. Haven't they told you? Haven't the doctors spoken to you?'

'All I know,' she snapped, 'is that I'm in here with a bad back. And I'm not enjoying it. I want to get out as quick as I can.'

'A bad back? Look Bella, it's going to be a long job,' he said gently. 'It's going to take time. What we had in mind was to send Rita and Ronnie back to Manchester with mother. Ronnie can go to grammar school there and he'll be in time to start the new term. And Rita can . . .'

'You sod,' Bella screamed. 'You've got me helpless in a hospital bed and now you're going to take my kids away from me. You won't, you won't. I'll get the police. You won't go, Rita, will you? Tell me you won't go, love.'

But Rita was in tears. And the nurse came in then, alarmed at the shouting. She ushered the four of them outside. Bella wanted to turn over and cry into her pillow, but she could not move. Instead, she covered her face with her hands and sobbed quietly for a long time.

Outside, Rita saw from her father's face that he was angry. He sent for the sister and demanded calmly, but with authority, to know why his wife had not been told of her condition. He was told that it was for the doctor to do that. And the doctor had gone off duty at four o'clock.

'Contact him immediately and tell him I wish to speak to him,' the sister was told sternly.

'I can't do that,' she said starchily. 'He has gone home. I'm sure the doctor knows . . .'

She was not allowed to finish. 'Telephone him straight away. Or had I better see the matron?'

'It's not really my place to . . .'

'Look, young lady. There is a war on. I should be in France fighting this war. That's where I was a few days ago and that's where I'll be again very shortly. Do you think you could possibly persuade this doctor to come to the telephone to speak to me? Is it asking too much? I've risked my life almost every day for the last five years for you and your doctor. Don't you think that allows me a little priority?'

The sister gave way. Rita felt proud of her father. He had sounded just like her mother, but calmer and more persuasive. Her opinion of him changed in seconds. It had come as a shock to have someone so softly spoken, so aloof, in the house and she had not liked it. In the past, when he had come home

166

on leave, she had never noticed how different he was, with her mother always shouting, arguing, ordering people about. But now she saw him anew. She liked him almost as much as she had liked Chuck.

The doctor came to the telephone, and then he came to the hospital. He came into Bella's room, placed a chair by the bed and sat down. He said: 'Mrs Rigby, I've had a talk with your husband and I feel that it would be best if I told you a little more about your condition. I'm afraid it will be some weeks before you will be able to leave the hospital.'

'As soon as I can crawl, I'm going,' she said firmly.

The nurses had told him what sort of a person she was, so he had no qualms about what her reaction might be when he said: 'Mrs Rigby, you have had a bad accident. It's a miracle that you didn't break your back. As it is, when you have healed up a bit, you will have to learn to walk all over again. You may be able to walk quite normally. You might not be able to walk at all. There again, it might be somewhere in between the two. I don't know. But I will promise you this. As soon as your injuries are sufficiently healed up, you can leave hospital. You'll need looking after, you'll have to learn to walk. But you won't have to stay in hospital for that.'

She looked at him, her eyes unblinking, fixed him with a stare. In a voice that was little more than a whisper, she said: 'I might not be able to walk, did you say?'

'There is that danger,' he said. 'There's a fifty-fifty chance.'

'That's why they want to take my children away then, is it?' she asked, still numb from the shock of it.

'It really is the best thing. It will be a long time before you can fend for yourself, never mind look after two children. And if you like, we can transfer you to a hospital in Manchester.'

That brought her back to life. 'What? Not bloody likely. I don't want to be anywhere near Les's mother, thank you very much. Not until I can defend myself. I'll miss the kids, but I have this feeling that as soon as I can move about a bit, I'll be all right. I just have this feeling.'

'Good,' he said. 'That means you're half-way towards getting better. I'll leave you now. I'll see you in the morning.'

And although he left her sounding so confident, hardly

had the door closed than she was in tears. She might not walk again. She was losing her children. She could hardly believe that she had planned to go to America, that she had only vaguely considered what might become of Rita and Ronnie. It all seemed another world, a world in which she had been someone else. The only consolation she had was in realizing that she had done the right thing in having Alan adopted.

Eighteen

The following afternoon, Sunday, just before two o'clock, the nurse said: 'Visitors. Who do you want to see?'

'Wheel them all in,' Bella said.

June came in first, with Mavis. 'She's not allowed in really,' June said, 'but the nurse said she could just bring her flowers in.'

Mavis reached up and kissed Bella. She had a bunch of pansies wilting in her hot little hand.

'For me? You've been robbing graves again, have you?' Bella joked, as if she had not a care in the world. 'Thanks, love. You're an angel.'

Afterwards, when Mavis had gone, Bella said. 'Have you heard? That old witch is off back to Manchester with our Rita and Ronnie.'

'Rita came in this morning and told me,' June said. 'Oh Bella, I could easily have seen to them for you.'

'I know you could, love. Some cock and bull story from Les about his mother having a job. I can't imagine who'd employ her. Works at the zoo, I expect. Stands in for the ape on its day off.'

But June had a serious expression. 'Oh Bella, I can't help thinking this is all my fault. If I'd have gone out with you that night instead of with that chap, it would never have happened.'

'Don't reproach yourself, love,' Bella told her. 'We might both have fallen off the bloody bus.'

'They had a right time with you,' June revealed. 'You were drunk.'

'Well, that's the best way to go, isn't it?' Bella said. 'Absolutely pickled, a daft smile on your face. That's how I want to go. Just like Mr Fisher. He had the right idea.'

June blinked, thought of the falling wreath, swallowed hard and wished she could speak to Bella of it. But she knew she could not. To anyone else, but not to her.

Bella said: 'I'm glad I got little Alan fixed up like I did. That was a bit of luck, wasn't it? I proved everyone else wrong there, didn't I? Where would he be now, poor little devil? In a home, I expect. No, I shall never regret doing it, never.'

They would have stayed there talking all the afternoon. Bella wanted to see no one else but her. But after a while the nurse came in. June's time was up.

For the rest of visiting time there was a procession of people trouping in. Anne came, fat and silent, lost for words, people from the pubs Bella had frequented, and the flowers piled up. Women from the street, who had watched her from behind their curtains, had discussed her behind her back, now came in as old friends and neighbours.

Bella took it all in good part, saving herself for the end, when Rita, Ronnie, Les and his mother came in. But in her life she had seen her way through all sorts of storms and situations, and her character held, she never let herself down. The anxiety was all on their side. Rita was crying, Ronnie blinking to hold back the tears, Les and his mother solemn and on edge in case she should turn on them.

It was all arranged. They were going, Les told her, early the next morning to Manchester. He had to rejoin his squadron on Wednesday. The furniture would go into store. Mr Jerome would have the house to let again. And as soon as she was well enough to be moved, they would have her transferred to a hospital in Manchester to complete her recovery.

Bella had her own ideas about that. But she let him say it all, she let him finish, and as visiting time drew to its close, she said in a dramatic voice: 'Do you mind leaving me now? I'd like to say goodbye to my children.'

Rita loved the way she said it. It might have come straight out of a film. She lay in bed looking and speaking like a stricken heroine. It would have made them dab their eyes in the one and nines.

But it was Rita who was crying, and Ronnie too, as soon as his father and his grandmother had left the room. Bella went on playing her part, stoical, stiff upper lip, showing those

170

qualities that were always associated with people of a class to which she wanted to belong, but probably never would.

It was a relief when it was all over and they had gone. Bella felt devoid of all emotion. She did not cry, just lay there feeling desolate, empty, as if everything in life had been taken away from her, her emotions as well.

The following morning, the doctor again mentioned sending her to a Manchester hospital. But Bella was having none of it. She would stay where she was, she maintained, until she was better. The only thing she wanted was to move into a ward with other people. She had always been one for company. There was some sort of a life to be lived, even in a hospital.

Later in the week they judged her sufficiently improved to go into a ward. But it was not much different for her. All the other patients had broken legs or injured backs and few of them could move about. Bella was not able to sit up. She felt just as isolated.

But she had visitors. Her visiting times were solidly occupied. When June came next, she said: 'You'll never guess. Your Les came to my door on Sunday evening. Said they were on their way the next morning and would I go in after they'd gone and collect your things? Gave me the key.'

'Oh, I have got some possessions left then, have I?' Bella remarked.

'I'll look after everything, Bella,' June said. 'Don't you worry about a thing. Can I borrow your fur cape next Saturday? I've got a special date on.'

'Of course you can, love. Borrow anything you like. But not my French underwear. I think I'll keep that for our Rita.'

'Go on,' June said, 'you'll be wearing that yourself soon, I'll bet.'

'Yes, to get buried in,' Bella said solemnly.

But she was not down for long. Anne came to see her and brought her some old, dog-eared magazines. Bella had never read a magazine. She had looked at the pictures in *Picture Post*, but that was all. Then, in one magazine, as she flipped through the pages of love stories, reading only the advertisements for Bile Beans and corsets, her eyes were caught by the illustration to one of the stories. There was a handsome air force officer looking sideways at a beautiful girl. The girl could have been Bella. The resemblance struck her. She studied the picture for a long time, went on looking through the magazine, then turned back to it. The caption underneath read: 'The war had brought them together, and only the war could break them apart. But they would not let it.' Bella began to read the story.

Quick as her mind was about other things, fast though she was at explaining her way out of anything or working her way into something, she could not understand the story. She read it twice, and again the next day. All the time she saw herself as that lovely girl, imagined that she herself was saying the words the character spoke. It gave her a strange satisfaction to see herself living the life of the girl in the story. It made her able to understand it eventually.

Bella began to look through the magazines for another story. First she looked at the pictures, but there was no one else who looked like her. So she picked a story at random, read it slowly, then again, got the drift of it and pictured herself as another heroine. Without realizing it, she found herself living life through the stories in the magazines. She was each beautiful woman, she experienced all the emotions, felt all the longing and all the rewarding passion of love requited. But she did not realize that the life she found in her magazine stories was the life that Megan found in her library books.

Later that week she had a letter from Les. She did not write back, but he went on sending brief letters to her that never gave a hint that he wanted an answer. Rita wrote to her once a week. For Bella, sitting at a table writing a letter was hard enough. To do it while she lay flat on her back was impossible. Miss Hackett solved the problem. She took down Bella's reply in shorthand and typed it out for her. Rita's letters were always happy. She liked the technical college she was at, Ronnie liked his school. And she was going to drama classes, proper ones, although Bella did not know what a drama class was, never mind a proper one.

From where she lay she had no idea of what it was like outside. Only the date on the newspaper told her that winter was coming on. The pain in her back gradually went away. She could wriggle about a bit without feeling it and when they moved her about in the bed she had no fear that the agony she had felt before would suddenly return. Bella reckoned that she would be out and about for Christmas.

Then one day they decided to get her out of bed. She had no use in her legs, no strength in them at all, but the doctor did not seem concerned by it. She could not even stand, and it appalled her. At no time during the weeks that she had lain in the bed had she imagined that she would not be able to stand up when the time came. To have to learn to walk again she had accepted. But not to be able to stand frightened her.

Bella was the only one who was upset by it. The nurses put her in a wheelchair and took her off to physiotherapy. At the end of a week her legs would just hold her, if she had someone to cling on to. It took a fortnight for her to get the slightest shuffling movement in them. Finally they got her on to crutches, and she moved along on feet that she could slide a bare three inches with every attempt at taking a step.

It gave Bella an enormous ache in her back that did not go away until she lay down. But she was like a child who was learning to ride a bicycle. It was her first go on the swings, the moment she got her feet off the bottom of the bath and swam. Her mind was so uncomplicated, her thoughts so direct, that she could see no obstacle in the way of her walking again. Come New Year, she reckoned, she would be linking arms with everyone else and dancing in nineteen forty-five.

Even when she fell she never complained. And she fell frequently. Even when, after weeks of physiotherapy and of going up and down the ward on her crutches, she could still only shuffle those few inches, she was not dismayed. She would sit in the chair at her bedside, put a bit of make-up on, comb her hair and set off along the ward. She had a little conversation at each bed. 'There's only one thing we need in here,' she said loudly one afternoon, 'and that's a few men. Well, when I say a few, one each at least.' They all liked her, remarked at all the visitors she had and wondered if she would ever walk properly again. Some of them doubted it. Bella never did.

Her plan for when she got out of the hospital was to go and live with June for a while. June had agreed to it. The children seemed settled and happy and there was that thought emerging from the back of her mind again that, if they were content, perhaps she might get to America after all.

Not for one moment did Bella think that, in her state, she might have to do what other people arranged for her, whether it fell in with her plans or not. So it was that one morning the doctor came to her bedside and said, in a matter of fact sort of way: 'Well, Mrs Rigby, I think you can go home now.'

Bella was aghast. She hardly knew what to say. 'Home?' she said, as if remarking on something silly one of the children had said. 'Home? I can't walk.'

'It will take time, Mrs Rigby, it will take time,' he said amiably. 'You'll still have to go to physiotherapy, but as an out patient. A nice trip out for you a couple of times a week.'

'But I've got no home,' she said, in a voice strained with disbelief. 'I've got a friend to go to, we'd arranged it all. But not until I can walk.'

'A friend?' He smiled. 'Why, you've got a family waiting for you in Manchester. Now don't you worry about a thing. We'll arrange everything.' And he walked away to the next bed.

The thought that things were being arranged for her while she lay there, while she shuffled along on her crutches, unable to do anything about it, worried her. It had never happened before. Bella had always lived her own life. Anything she had got herself into, she had got herself out of. There had always been an escape. One minute she had been imagining again the biggest escape of all, to America and a new life. The next, she found her destiny changed for her. Back to Manchester, back to Les's mother, back to the place she had escaped from all those years ago. To Bella, it seemed so horrible that she could not read, could not eat, could not sleep.

June would have had her. But they were against it. The doctors said no. It was all being arranged. And when finally the date was fixed and the clothes she needed were brought in, June said to her: 'I shan't stay here, Bella, not without you.'

'What will you do, love? Come back to Manchester?'

'No. Sid might find me there. The war will be over soon, we all know that, and he'll be back. No, I think I'll go to

174

London.'

Bella was surprised. 'London? What on earth do you want to go there for? It's been bombed flat.'

'Oh, I don't know. I liked it when we were there before. I've always wanted to go back.'

'What about these flying bombs?' Bella said. 'It's as bad now as when we left.'

'No worse than the ordinary bombs, really,' June replied. 'We avoided them all right, didn't we?'

'You had me with you then. I remember you always wanted to put your make-up on before we went down to the shelter. Pretty close to death you took us a few times.'

'Oh, I'll get by,' June said, and she sighed. 'I've got my hundred pounds from Mr Fisher. I'll get a job. No need to rush. Get our Mavis settled in first.'

Bella was not at all pleased with June's plan. Despite her hundred pounds, she feared that she might go back on the game. She said earnestly: 'Oh June, don't do it. I don't like the thought of you going to London. You always get into some sort of bother. Come to Manchester. You'll be all right. Or stay here. I'd feel better if you just stayed here.'

'I'd stay if you were still here,' June said. 'I don't mind this town, I've got used to it. But now you're going, it just won't be the same. No, my mind's made up.'

'You will write, won't you?' Bella said.

'Every week,' June replied. 'And I'll come up and visit you. You wait until you're walking again. You know, we might even go to America together. How about that?'

'June, would you? What about those wide roads you're so frightened of?'

June laughed. 'Well, look what happened to you on one of our narrow ones.'

On the last visiting day they all came to say goodbye. Mrs Sadler had had to go for a stiffener first and smelt pleasantly of drink, but it did not prevent her crying. Megan was too choked to speak. Mr Jerome wiped his eyes and Miss Hackett had to be led away in tears by a nurse. Even Eileen came, holding to her nose a handkerchief soaked with lavender water.

The next morning Bella was ready in the wheelchair. She

had on her slacks, her fur cape and her hat with the brim that came down over one eye. Rita came into the ward looking taller, more grown up. And Ronnie unbuttoned his raincoat to show her his school blazer. Mrs Rigby stayed in the background, watched Rita wheel her mother round the ward to say goodbye to everyone. There were more tears. 'Not a dry eye in the house,' Rita remarked, as she wheeled her mother out of the ward, down to the ambulance and on to the train that took her back to Manchester.

Nineteen

Mrs Rigby had a pleasant little house. She and her husband had bought it by years of careful living. Bella had not been there since she and Les had left for their own home twelve years before. It was not that Bella did not like the house. She did. Few people had lived in it and that made a difference, one which Bella, from a family of ten, had soon noticed. And she liked the street, liked the area. People lived in those houses, they did not just exist, as they had in the street where she and June had been brought up. The only thing that spoiled it all was Mrs Rigby. Both she and Bella had relied on first impressions of each other, and each never saw the other in anything but the most unfavourable light.

Rita and her grandmother had made the front room into a bedroom for Bella. They had worked hard to get it ready and make it look pleasant. Bella took one look at it and said: 'I'm not sleeping in that double bed. It's too big. I'll freeze to death. I can't curl up in bed like you, you know, not with my back. I'll have to have a single.'

'We'll change it over on Saturday then,' Mrs Rigby said, not caring to think of the trouble she and Rita would have getting the bed back up the stairs. They had had more luck than judgement in getting it down.

But Rita was not so willing to let her mother have her own way. She said: 'But mam, what about dad when he comes home? Where's he going to sleep?'

'He can share with Ronnie,' Bella snapped and the matter rested there.

That night Bella went to bed early. She had become used to it in the hospital and the long train journey had tired her. Rita said: 'Do you want any help, mam?'

'No, love, I can manage,' she said. In fact, she was looking

177

forward to being left alone, to see how much she could do for herself. 'Come in after and say goodnight.'

Rita went in later and sat on the foot of the bed. 'Do you want a cigarette, mam? Did you bring any with you?'

'No, love. I've given it up. I haven't smoked since I had the accident. When you think that every breath might be your last, one thing you don't want to do is die full of smoke. Now come on, tell me about yourself. What's it like at the college?'

'Lovely,' Rita said. 'I go to drama classes twice a week at Mrs Runciman's. Monday and Friday evenings. She's very good. Much better than those we had at the tech.'

'Who's Mrs Runciman when she's at home?' Bella asked.

'She has her own drama school,' Rita told her. Her enthusiasm showed in her face. Her eyes shone and she smiled. 'She's well known is Mrs Runciman. She won't have anybody. You have to pay.' She clapped her hand over her mouth. 'Oh damn, I wasn't supposed to tell you that.'

'Why not, love?'

'Because gran's paying for me and it's supposed to be a secret. You won't let on, will you?'

Bella smiled. 'Of course not. I never say no if someone else is paying, anyway.'

'And what's more,' Rita said excitedly, 'they're holding the drama festival this year. First time since before the war. Of course, it won't be as big as it used to be, being as we haven't shot all the Germans yet, but Mrs Runciman has entered me for the Crombie Cup for drama.'

'The Crombie Cup? Sounds more like something you'd get for rugby league,' Bella said.

But Rita went on: 'Just imagine, being able to tell people I won the Crombie Cup,' talking just as her mother would have done, as if she had won it already.

'You're still going to be a film star, are you?' Bella asked her, amused at her starry-eyed, faraway look.

'Oh yes. Of course,' she said, coming back to reality for a minute, 'I'll have my shorthand and typing as a standby. I mean, I shall only get small parts at first, but I'll be able to earn my living until the bigger parts come my way.' She got lost then, looking at a picture in her mind of a film première, of two people getting out of a limousine before the crowds

178

and the spotlights outside a West End cinema. She saw her mother, with her hair black against her white dress, and her father in his uniform, the spotlight catching the colours of his medal ribbons and his pilot's wings. Then she said: 'Mam, what are you going to do when you can walk again?'

'What am I going to do, love? Well, I know what I want to do. I want to get dressed up and go out every night, just like I used to. Sounds awful, doesn't it? But that's what I want.'

'It's not awful,' Rita insisted. 'It's only natural. I'd love to see you get all dolled up and go off down the street in your high-heeled shoes with your nose in the air. I always think of you like that. That's how I shall always remember you, when you're a grey-haired old lady and I'm a famous film star.'

Bella looked at her for a moment, then said: 'It's not right, though, Rita, is it? I'll bet your gran doesn't go out every night and leave you.'

Rita was surprised. She had never before heard her mother say anything vaguely pleasant about her grandmother. 'Well, if I had to make a choice, you know what it would be.'

'The trouble is,' Bella admitted, 'I always think of myself. I don't seem able to change. I'm still set on going to America.'

'What are you going to do when you get there?'

'Oh, find Chuck, murder the bugger, then settle down,' she said laughing.

And Rita said surprisingly: 'I'm just like you, mam. I want to be a film star and nothing is going to stop me. You want to go to America and find a better life and nothing will stop you either. We've got ambitions and we're both strong-willed. We'll succeed, you see if we don't. Who knows, we might end up going to America together.'

Bella was up early that first morning. They all had breakfast in the living-room, with a cloth on the table and everything layed out properly. That was Mrs Rigby's way. Her husband had been manager of a shoe shop. They had bought their own house. They had never regarded themselves as working class, but had lived to standards that were a little bit higher.

Bella said to Rita, before she set off for college: 'Have you got anything for me to read, love? Any magazines? I left all mine at the hospital. Didn't want to bring any germs out on them.'

Rita was astounded. 'You don't read, do you, mam?'

'I'm a proper bookworm now,' Bella said. 'Nothing else to do in that hospital.'

'I'll see what they've got at the paper shop,' Rita replied.

'I'll drop a line to Miss Hackett this morning. I promised to keep in touch with the old dear. Is that the *Daily Mirror*? I'll have a look at that. Just see what Jane's up to. Heavens, she's got no clothes on again. Better not let our Ronnie see that.'

Mrs Rigby worked as a receptionist at a doctor's surgery. She was gone every morning from half-past eight until eleven, and each evening from five until seven. Over the years, Mrs Rigby had changed. She was more tolerant now, more willing to accept Bella as her daughter-in-law, ready to go more than half way to meet her. It was time, not Bella's injuries, that had made her change. Before she went out that morning, she said to Bella: 'You can have the wireless on. There's the *Radio Times*. You can have "Music While You Work". And there's Sandy MacPherson.'

'No, I don't want it,' Bella said bluntly. 'I don't like the wireless. All sound and no pictures. I only listen to the news.'

'What are you going to do then?'

'Oh, I'll get on my crutches and practice walking.'

'What if you fall?'

'So what? I've fallen loads of times. I hope I fall on something valuable. Teach you to make me come back here.'

There was nothing for it then but to exist. The times Bella liked most were those when Mrs Rigby was at work, especially when she went out at five after they had had dinner, and Rita did the washing up while Bella dried, sitting in her wheelchair. They were very much aware that they were living in someone else's house, even though Mrs Rigby was wise enough not to take Rita and Ronnie out of Bella's control. But the evenings were the worst for Bella. She longed to go out, to have a drink, to meet a few people. But she knew no one and Mrs Rigby did not drink. Bella had to content herself with a bottle of beer from the off licence, and put up with the sound of the wireless which Mrs Rigby switched on the moment she came home from work, listening

do you want me to do?' She was settled in her armchair by the living-room fire.

'We'll do the soliloquy,' Rita said, handing her mother the script. 'You just stop me if I say any of it wrong.'

'Do the what?' Bella asked her.

'The soliloquy,' Rita told her again. 'It's this piece I have to say all by myself. It's from "Sir Damien and the Maiden". I'm the maiden, see, and I'm imagining I'm having to thwart the attentions of one of the rivals for my affections. All right?'

'Yes, love,' Bella said, although she did not have the faintest idea what Rita was talking about. 'Where do we start then, at the top?'

'That's right,' Rita said. 'Now I'm going to do the actions as well, so don't get alarmed if I wave my arms about.' She positioned herself in the middle of the room. 'Ready? Right, I'll begin.' And she started: ' "Fie, Sir Toby, would you treat a maiden thus?" '

'Hang on a minute, love,' Bella said, before Rita could go any further. 'Fie? That's not right, is it? Looks like they've missed a letter out there. Shouldn't it be five or fire? Or perhaps it should be fine?'

'No, mam, it's fie. It's what they used to say in the olden days. It's like we would say: "Get away with you." Now, I'm going to start again. "Fie, Sir Toby, would you treat a maiden thus? I beseech thee, sire – " '

'Wait a minute, Rita, you've missed a bit out,' her mother interrupted her. 'There's a bit here about "clutches bosom". I don't think I'd like to hear you say that on a stage in front of a lot of people.'

'No, mam, those words in the brackets are the directions for the bits of action I have to do. There, do you see?' She ran her finger down the page, pointing them out to her. 'That's why I was standing like this,' she told her, returning to the middle of the room and holding both hands to her chest.

'Oh, is that what it is?' Bella said. 'Well, you haven't got much bosom to clutch yet, have you? Never mind, you've only got small hands. Right, off we go again then.'

Just after Christmas Bella had a letter from June. She had gone to London as she had said she would. Bella was not

183

happy about it. The news was full of reports of flying bombs. One Saturday evening Rita took her to the cinema, and it was on the news, a buoyant, spirited, thumbs up report of Hitler's last crack at London, spoken to pictures of buildings reduced to rubble and firemen rooting about in the debris looking for bodies.

Bella worried, and she had plenty of time to worry when Rita and Ronnie's holidays were over. When she got tired of reading she would think, and when she got tired of thinking she went back to reading. Most of her thinking was worrying. Apart from worrying about June and Mavis, she worried about herself, about the fact that she could still only shuffle those few inches at a time. Try as she might, she could not manage any more, however great the effort she made. Her legs just would not move. She could hardly lift her feet at all. In fact, there was no improvement in her movements that she could detect. None at all. She had reached her present standard months before in the hospital and had got no further. She had gone thin in the hospital too and she had put no weight back on. To herself, she looked thinner than ever. Her legs were like matchsticks, her legs that had been as beautiful as the rest of her.

Occasionally she would look at Rita. Rita was going on for sixteen. Despite the joke she had made at her clutching her bosom, she had filled out, was tall and looked older than her age. And Bella would look at her and see her own legs, her own figure, her own complexion. She was not jealous. She was unhappy. For the first time ever she could see what she herself had really looked like and she wanted to look like that again. That pallid face, those sunken cheeks, those dark marks beneath the eyes, did not belong to her. Inside, Bella was full of energy, waiting to burst into life. But the part of her that needed energy most, that lacked life almost entirely, was her legs, and no effort she made was sufficient to bring any life into them.

Another letter came from June, a week after the first, Monday morning, as regular as ever. The following week there was none, nor the week after that. It was on Bella's mind all the time. 'What shall I do, Rita? Shall I write?'

She wrote and there was still no reply. So she wrote again. And, as if she did not have enough to worry about in her empty life, when she went to the hospital that week, after her session with the physiotherapist, she was told to wait to see the doctor.

In a bland sort of way, the doctor said to her: 'Well, Mrs Rigby, I don't think you need come here twice a week any longer. I'll make an appointment for you to see me in a month's time and we'll see how you are then.'

'What?' Bella burst out. 'Not come again? How am I supposed to learn to walk again? You can't just tell me not to come.'

Gently, he said: 'Mrs Rigby, you have made all the progress we imagine you are likely to make with the treatment . . .'

'Progress? I haven't made any bloody progress,' she blazed at him. 'I'm no better now than I was when I left the hospital.'

He clasped his hands together, looked down at his desk, thought for a second. 'It was made clear to you, Mrs Rigby,' he said calmly, 'that any progress you made towards being able to walk again depended on chance. They told you so when you were in hospital. There was a chance that your legs would respond to treatment. They did, to a certain extent. In some patients we get no response at all. We have had some response in your case. Limited, I will agree, but you can walk, albeit with difficulty.'

Words, it was all words. 'But you can't just cast me off,' she pleaded. 'I'm hardly ever off my crutches. I've fallen over a hundred times, but I've never complained. I always come here as cheerful as you like, as eager as can be. And what do I get? Cast off, just like any other old cripple.' She burst into tears.

'We are not casting you off, Mrs Rigby,' he carried on patiently. 'We will give you some instructions of things you can do at home to try to bring a little more movement back into your legs and . . .'

'Little more movement?' she shouted. 'I want to walk, you silly bugger, not just have a little more movement. Oh, let me get out of here.' She swung her wheelchair round. 'Nurse, nurse, get me out of here. I won't wait for the ambulance. Get me a taxi.'

The despair that she had felt at being sent back to Manchester returned to Bella. She could not eat, she could not sleep, she could not read. No letter came from June. The two things in life that connected her with the real world, hearing from June and looking forward to walking again, were now gone. Miss Hackett's letters were no consolation. They were full of the hope that she herself had now lost.

It was Rita who, for a while, shook her out of the depression she had sunk into. 'It'll be an afternoon out for you, mam, even if I don't win. I've been round to Black and White Cabs and ordered a taxi, because it's too far for gran to push you, up and down all those kerbs. There'll be a man on the door and he said he'll get you up the steps in your wheelchair and he'll put it somewhere safe until afterwards. I've got you a seat on the centre aisle, so you won't have any difficulty hopping out of your wheelchair into your seat.'

Bella listened to her in silence. It was like listening to an echo of herself from the past. Everything was arranged, she could not say no, she was going. It was as if, in one way at least, she and Rita had changed places. If she had protested at all, she imagined Rita turning to her and snapping: 'You're coming and that's that,' just as she herself had said to Rita a short time before.

All the arrangements were faultless, from the taxi driver helping her in and out of the cab, to the man taking her backwards up the steps in her wheelchair, to Rita's performance. While Rita spoke the words, Bella mouthed the soliloquy all the way through, mouthing the actions as well. '"Fie, Sir Toby, would you treat a maiden thus? (Clutches bosom.) I beseech thee, sire . . ."'

If the arrangements were faultless, the result was absolutely perfect. 'The winner of the Crombie Cup for drama,' the man at the microphone said, 'is Miss Rita Rigby. The cup will be presented by Lady Natwick.'

Rita crossed the stage, curtsied and received the cup. And Bella wept the first tear that she had shed for anyone but herself for a long time.

'I've got to take it to have it engraved,' Rita said that evening. 'Where can I put it, gran? Somewhere where everyone will see it.'

The trip out, Rita winning the cup, did Bella no good at

all. It just emphasized for her how other people's lives could go forward, while hers stood still. There was nothing for her but the past. She began to lose herself in a daze of memories. Sitting by the fire behind a book or a magazine, she began to live again happy times from the past. She could see herself, June, Chuck and Bill, right before her eyes, moving and talking and living in the places where they had enjoyed themselves. She went right back to the time when she had first met Chuck, and went through all the experiences that she could remember, in all the detail she could recall, and enjoyed it all again. But it was a sad remembrance. When she came back to reality she was hurt, bitter, miserable, that it had all ended and would never begin again.

She got lost within herself to such an extent that she began to wake up in bed thinking that she was back at home, that June was next door, that Megan was over the road. Sometimes it was the fact that her legs would hardly move that brought her back to reality, sometimes the mystifying fact that everything in the bedroom seemed to be in the wrong place. Occasionally she woke up full of the idea that she was still working at the town hall and she tried to remember what she had been doing the day before, whether she had been helping Miss Hackett, what duties she had been given for the following day. And then it all came back to her, and she died a death that was not complete and gave her no relief from her worries.

Mrs Rigby noticed the graphic change in Bella's behaviour, the faraway look in her eyes, the appearance of living in a world of her own. Gone were the acid remarks, the sharp-tongued rebukes. Despite the differences that still existed between them, Mrs Rigby was worried about her. But she dared not say a thing. Instead, she spoke to Rita. Rita had also noticed the change in her mother, but was too young to comprehend the seriousness of her odd behaviour. But she understood when Mrs Rigby spoke to her about it.

She went into the bedroom that night, and said: 'Is your bottle hot enough, mam? It's really cold tonight.'

Bella was lying awake in the dark. 'Yes, I'm warm enough, love, thank you.'

'You're all right then, are you?' Rita put the bedside light on and sat at the foot of the bed.

'Yes, I'm all right.'

'You're not, you know. You're not all right. You've got us all worried.'

'Oh, don't waste your time worrying about me,' Bella said. 'I'll get by.'

'What is it, mam?' Rita asked earnestly. 'You seem to be in a dream all the time. You hardly eat anything. You never speak unless you're spoken to. It's weeks since you told any of us off, raised your voice even. Just because I won a cup for drama doesn't mean to say you can't shout at me any more.'

'What do you want me to do then, love?' Bella said, with a cynical tone to her voice. 'I can't walk, they've slung me out of the hospital, my best friend has stopped writing to me. My marriage is over, I'm living with a mother-in-law who I hate. Now you tell me what you want me to do.'

'Oh, come on now,' Rita said, with her mother's way of talking to someone as if they were a child. 'Auntie June is probably head over heels in love with some chap, that's why she hasn't written. One day soon you'll get six pages of unreadable scribble from her telling you all about it. And besides, the war will be over soon, dad will be home, we can have a house of our own again. You'll see things differently then.'

'I won't. It's over,' Bella said sullenly. 'I don't want to see your father ever again. So we'll have no more of that.'

Rita was patient. She said: 'You wait until spring comes and the weather gets better. I tell you what we'll do. We'll have a little holiday, you, Ronnie and me. During the Easter holidays. Blackpool. How about that? A week at Blackpool. I'll write to dad and tell him to send us some money. The sea air, the sunshine, that'll put some life back into those legs of yours. What you need are a few sunny days.'

But the only response she got from her mother was: 'All my sunny days are over, Rita. It's not a holiday I want, love, it's my old life back. I want to get all dressed up and go out on the town. Pick up a nice chap. That's what I want. That's what life has always been to me. Who's going to look at me now, on crutches, in a wheelchair?'

'You've got to persevere, mam,' Rita insisted. 'These things take time.'

'I haven't got time, Rita. The older you get the faster time goes by. Don't bother yourself over me, love. Think of yourself. Go out and do the things in life that you want to do. Bugger everybody else. That's what I tried to do. I didn't succeed, but you will. You've had a better start than me. You've got your shorthand and typing, you've won your cup. If you want to be a film star, well go out and be a film star. That's my advice. Don't just sit around dreaming about it, Rita. You'll never get anywhere doing that. I was never one for dreaming. I wouldn't have got out of that scruffy street I was born in, out of that mill I worked in, if I had just sat around dreaming. The world is real, Rita, it isn't all in your imagination. Whatever you want in life is there. It's just a matter of going out and getting it. The only thing I hope is that you have better luck than I had. For all my efforts, look where I ended up. Pole-axed falling off a bloody bus.'

Rita looked at her mother for a while. Their eyes did not meet. Bella was looking away, still with her faraway expression. Rita said: 'Now look, mam, I don't like to hear you talking like that. Life isn't over yet, you know. People have got over worse things. I'm telling you, if you don't buck up, well I'm going to get the doctor in to you.'

And with the last remnants of her sense of humour, Bella said: 'Make sure he's good looking then.'

'This is no time for joking, mam,' Rita said sternly. 'And as for me being a film star, well, that was all childish stuff really.' She swallowed and forced herself to say it. 'When I leave the tech this summer, I'm going to get myself a good secretarial job. You know I like acting, so I'll join the amateurs. Then I shall be here to look after you.'

'No, Rita, no,' Bella said intensely. 'That's not what you want to do. Don't miss all your opportunities for me. I'll manage . . .'

'How will you manage?' Rita asked her. 'You've finished with dad and gran can't look after you. She can't push you far in the wheelchair now and she's not getting any younger. Look, when you can walk a bit and can see to yourself, that's the time I'll think of being anything but a secretary. I'm going to take you out more often when the weather's fine. You're shut in the house too much with nothing but your thoughts. I'll take you into a few pubs, all the places you used to go to with Auntie June, if they haven't been bombed flat.

189

Now you go to sleep and think about that, think of all the places you'd like to go to. Then when the fine weather comes . . .'

'Yes, all right love,' Bella said meekly, and when Rita had turned off the light and gone, she admitted to herself that what she had suggested would never be enough. It would not be enough for either of them. There could never be a substitute for real life, and real life was either trying to achieve all the things you ever wanted or actually having achieved them.

Rita closed her bedroom door that night, put on the light, lay down on the bed and cried. 'Dreams,' she said out loud, 'dreams. That's all I'll ever have. Just like mam. Nothing but dreams.'

The following afternoon Bella was sitting by the living-room fire, leafing her way through a magazine with no interest at all. Someone knocked at the front door. Mrs Rigby went to the door, stood talking, let the person in. They remained talking in the hallway for a while. Bella could hear a man's voice speaking low. Eventually Mrs Rigby came into the living-room, stood just inside the door, clenched her hands tightly together, looked at Bella with eyes that spoke.

'What is it?' Bella asked her. 'What's up?'

'It's June,' Mrs Rigby said softly. 'A policeman has just come. She's dead, Bella. A flying bomb hit the house. She was killed.'

Bella did not move, just sat there for several seconds with her eyes wide open and unblinking, her mouth agape. Then she said in a heightening voice: 'Mavis. What about Mavis?'

'They were both killed, Bella,' Mrs Rigby said, in a voice that was little more than a whisper. Her eyes were softened with tears, as if it had been friends of her own who had been killed. She turned and beckoned to the policeman.

He came into the room. Bella could not see him. All she could see were two faces she would never see again. He cleared his throat and said: 'It was a direct hit. There were no survivors. They had difficulty in the identification. Then your letters turned up and they were able to . . .' He stopped then, could say no more, was silenced by the look of the woman. That raven hair, those wide eyes that now shone

190

with tears, that pale lovely face that was the ghost of beauty The policeman turned away and went out.

The tears ran but Bella did not really cry. She made no sound, just sat there with her memories, while the tears ran down her face like rain down a window pane. She said nothing, sat there for two hours, her face glistening wet. At four o'clock she dried her eyes, blew her nose, got on her crutches to look at herself in the mirror. She did not want the children to see she had been crying.

When they came in, when Bella heard them come in through the back door, she called to them. They came into the living-room and she said in a voice that was steady, firmly in control of her emotions: 'I've got some bad news. Your Auntie June is dead. And Mavis. A flying bomb fell on their house. That's why we hadn't had a letter. Now that's all there is to it. These things happen in wartime. If you want to cry, I want you to go upstairs and cry. Then come down and have your dinner.'

Rita flew out of the room in tears and would not come down from her bedroom until her grandmother fetched her.

At dinner, Bella ate her first proper meal for weeks and chided Rita for only picking at her food. When Mrs Rigby had gone to work and they had done the washing up, Ronnie sat at the kitchen table and did his homework while his mother and Rita sat in the living-room talking.

Bella told Rita all about June, from the early days when both she and June had thought that the sole way to escape from a life where poverty was the only outlook would be to get themselves pregnant by someone well off, right up to the time that June had met Mr Shanklin in the Plough and had gone into the park with him for two pounds. And in telling Rita about June, Bella had to tell her about herself. She told it all, right down to how she had blackmailed Mr Shanklin into giving her a job at the town hall and how she and June had stolen the curtains from the camp.

Their friendship had been a life of little adventures, Rita realized as she listened, and she understood why her mother had worried over June, why she had worried at her going to London, why she had worried when her weekly letter never arrived, when she had been writing to someone who was already dead. They had gone through thick and thin together, their lives had hardly ever been lived separately from each other. Both of them had looked for a bright new beginning in a shining future, and they had both failed. They had had fun playing the game, but they had both lost, and there was no joy in losing. Rita thought, as she listened to her mother talking, that now she knew that she had lost, and that she would come to terms at last with what was left of her life.

That night Bella went to bed early, at nine o'clock. When Rita looked in half an hour later, on her way to bed, her mother was sound asleep. The following morning Bella got up and had breakfast with Rita, Ronnie, and Mrs Rigby in the living-room, looked at the *Daily Mirror*, chatted just like she used to do and said goodbye to the children as they left. Bella seemed to be more her normal self again. Rita went off to college feeling that her Auntie June's death had brought her mother back to life.

When Mrs Rigby had gone to work, Bella got her make-up out and did her face. She did it perfectly, took a long time over it. Then she combed her hair just the way she would have had she been going out one evening, and painted her nails. When she had finished she looked something like she used to at the time that had been the height of her life, with Chuck, June and Bill at a dance at the camp, or in the Manhattan Lounge.

Bella got on to her crutches then and went into the kitchen. She threw a cushion on the floor, lowered herself down slowly on to the tiles, opened the gas oven door, turned on all the jets and lay with her head on the cushion. And she made her escape at last.

Twenty

They buried Bella on a bitterly cold day, when a freezing wind chilled everyone to the bone and their feet went numb standing on the hard ground around the grave.

Rita lost all the feeling in her body, but it was grief, not the cold, that made her feel that all she consisted of was two crying eyes and a sobbing throat. Some strange power made her legs carry her from the graveside to the car and from the car into the house. But the bright crackling fire in the living room did not revive her. It was as if she had left part of herself back in the cemetery, the living part of herself, and had come home with only her emotions.

A silence fell over the house. Weeks passed by, Rita recovered her feelings, but still the silence was there. It was a silence that no amount of noise seemed able to overcome. Even when she was in the kitchen, practising her tap dancing on the red tiled floor, and her grandmother was in the living-room with the wireless on listening to Henry Hall's Guest Night, and Ronnie was outside with some other boys, kicking his football against the house wall, the silence was still there. Bella, with her chatter, with her sharp voice that could be heard above any din, with her comical remarks, with her acid and bitter arguments, with her flashing eyes and her black hair and her arrogant toss of the head, had been the colour in their lives. And now she was gone. There was just an empty silence where she had been. It was like waking up on a spring morning and hearing no birds singing, and knowing that they would never sing again.

By the time summer came, Rita had begun to think of her mother not with sadness but with admiration. She admired the way her mother used to look. She stood in front of the mirror, turned her head from side to side and was pleased at the resemblance. When she walked along she held her head erect, put on a bit of class, looked aloof and was only one point away from seeming high and mighty. Just like her mother, she wanted people to say. But no one said it. None of them around there had ever seen her mother without her wheelchair. And to Rita it was all, as yet, a put on. When she saw Ronnie's football on the path by the house, she could not resist the temptation to give it a kick.

That summer, after peace had been declared in Europe, after the bonfires and the fun and the foolishness of people who thought that life was suddenly going to be very good and very easy, Rita's father decided to stay in the air force. He was posted to Germany. Mrs Rigby was proud of him and was pleased at his decision. To be an officer in wartime, she knew, might have had glamour, but it did not have the distinction of being an officer in peacetime, where she saw it as having the difference between being an amateur and being a professional.

His decision did not effect Rita. The empty space left in her life by her mother's death had gradually been filled by stronger and more vivid pictures in her imagination of the career on which she wanted to embark. She still wanted to be a film star and the time was drawing near when she thought she would be able to take the first real steps towards achieving her ambition. At the end of the summer term she would be leaving the technical college, destined, everyone thought, for a typing pool or a dusty commercial office. But Rita allowed them to go on thinking that, while she spoke to Mrs Runciman about her real desire.

'Don't you think you're rushing things a bit, Rita?' Mrs Runciman asked her. 'Just suppose I *did* get you a screen test and you *did* go to the film studios. What if they said no? What if they didn't offer you a part?'

'I've got to take my chance,' she replied firmly. 'It's what I want to do and I've got to take my chance.'

'But you are only sixteen, Rita,' Mrs Runciman went on. Sixteen she was, but there was a mature look about her. She was one step from being glamorous, Mrs Runciman had to admit to herself. 'There's plenty of time. You leave the technical college in a few weeks. Why not get a nice job, earn a little money and then we'll see about getting you an audition with one of the repertory companies?'

Rita's eyes blazed at her. 'I'm not going into rep,' she said indignantly. 'I'm not going to spend years as an assistant stage manager, learning nothing more than I know already. Anyway, I've got some money. I've been serving in a greengrocer's every Saturday since my mother died. I worked there full time during the holidays. I've saved it all specially. And besides, I did win the Crombie Cup.'

'Oh, I shouldn't try to make too much of that, Rita,' Mrs Runciman said quickly. 'The acting profession is full of people who have won much grander things than that as students.' She sighed. She was in a quandary. Any of her other pupils would have been glad of the chance to get into a repertory company. She was out of her depth. Never before had anyone asked her to get them a screen test. She did not know how to do it. And she did not know how to handle Rita. Rita was so talented. She could act, she could dance, she could sing, she had confidence. She had Mrs Runciman in a corner. 'What does your father say about it?' she asked, looking for a way out.

'My father?' Rita said, speaking with a dramatic mixture of anger and hurt. 'My father's in the air force, as you well know. He's staying in. He's not being demobbed That's his life now. And me without a mother. So what is it to do with him?'

Mrs Runciman was reluctant to pass a remark on such a private topic, reluctant because Rita was fixing her with a steady piercing glare from hooded eyes, the sort of glare that had once transfixed Mrs Runciman when she had looked at a bird of prey at the zoo.

But then Rita lifted her eyes, looked somewhere up above Mrs Runciman's head, her eyes opened wide and the light softened them. She smiled and said: 'My mother was the one you should have asked. She was all for me taking a chance. My mother would not have asked anyone to help her. She would just have got on the train and gone to the film studios.'

That startled Mrs Runciman. Rita was bright-eyed, lovely and talented, and if she got on a train to go to London she feared to think where she might end up. But she had an alternative to offer. 'What would you say, Rita, if I got in touch with a friend of mine in London who is a theatrical agent? What would you say if I asked her to get you an audition for a stage part?'

'Well, that's not exactly a screen test, is it?' she replied bluntly.

But Mrs Runciman had nothing else to offer. The stage, that was where she could learn her craft, she told Rita, the things she could not learn from drama classes. 'Experience is the thing,' she said. 'To be able to go to the film studios with the experience of the theatre behind you, that's the thing. Looks just aren't enough.'

That last remark enraged Rita. She breathed down her nostrils. 'I can't help the way I look, Mrs Runciman.'

'No, my dear, I didn't mean it like that,' she blustered. 'What I mean is – well, you haven't even been to drama classes full time, have you? And I think that to be in the hands of a really good agent will be the best thing for you. I'll arrange it, shall I?'

Somehow, in her faltering way, Mrs Runciman had convinced Rita that it was the right thing to do, for Rita calmly agreed. 'I'll call in one evening and talk it over with your grandmother,' Mrs Runciman said. 'I think that will be best.'

Rita left then. She walked down the street to the bus stop. The bus came, she got on and a man gave her his seat.

To be on the safe side, Mrs Runciman called to see Mrs Rigby on the night that she knew Rita would be at the youth club. She was surprised to find out that Rita had imparted nothing of her plans to her grandmother and she was even more surprised at Mrs Rigby's quiet acquiescence on learning what was planned.

When Rita came home, she and her grandmother talked about it. 'It's what you really want to do, is it?' Mrs Rigby asked her. It was an academic question. What Mrs Rigby wanted to avoid, above all, was the sort of argument that would leave bad feeling, that would ruin forever her relationship with Rita, that would see her packing her bag and leaving.

'Oh yes. Films eventually, of course,' Rita said. 'My mother told me not to dream but to take my chance. And this is my chance.'

Mrs Rigby had never had dreams. Reality had been

196

enough. She said: 'Well, there'll always be a home for you here, Rita. Your bedroom will always be there ready for you. And I'll not see you go empty handed. Neither must you ever be short of anything on my account. You only have to write. Money, anything.'

'Thanks, gran,' Rita said softly. She looked at her grandmother. She had an awkward, self-conscious look on her face, as if the charitable gesture she had made had been offered to a stranger and was not quite proper.

'Are you going to write and tell your father?' Mrs Rigby asked her.

'No, not yet,' Rita replied. 'I'll wait until it's all fixed up. Its's no good going on about anything and then having it all fall through.'

Mrs Rigby left it at that. She would have liked her to sit down and write there and then, thought that would have been the proper thing to do, but she was not going to argue. To Mrs Rigby, Rita looked just like a replica of her mother and she did not want to have the same jagged relationship with her son's daughter that she had had with his wife.

The good news came. 'We were on the stage together, Mrs Brite and I,' Mrs Runciman told Rita. 'You're not the first of my young ladies I've sent to her. As theatrical agents go, you could not be in better hands. The trouble with the theatre, Rita, is that it is full of men. But you'll have to put up with that. Remember, always say no and concentrate on your career. Actresses are, in general, good-looking. And men not only like good-looking women, they want them.'

Rita felt her face going hot. She looked at the floor. Her mother would have put it more bluntly, but would have made a joke out of it.

There was no one now, Rita thought, who could hinder her plans. Ronnie was doing well at the grammar school and was as happy as his quiet manner would allow him to show. Her grandmother, who had paid for her to go to Mrs Runciman's drama classes, seemed unmoved by the news but mentioned to her again about writing to tell her father. Her mother was dead, her father had gone. She was tied up in no one else's plans for the future, no one's but her own.

On the morning that she went away, Rita spent two shillings on the taxi fare to the station, rather than go on the bus and suffer the unladylike procedure of putting her suitcase under the stairs behind the conductor's legs and then having to get it out again. Mrs Rigby saw her off. Rita wore her navy blue pinstripe costume, a white blouse, her black hair shone and on her lips was the same bright red lipstick that her mother had always used. Just like her mother, Mrs Rigby said to herself. The taxi driver took her suitcase, smiled at her and held the door open for her. Life would always be like that for Rita, Mrs Rigby thought. Men smiling and opening doors for her.

When she got to London, Rita followed Mrs Runciman's advice and took a room at the YWCA. She telephoned Mrs Brite to tell her that she had arrived and the following morning she went to see her.

Her office was hard to find. Rita walked up and down the street twice before noticing a door secretly placed between two shop windows. She went inside, up a bare wooden staircase, on to the first floor landing. There was a door with a pane of pebble glass in it and on the glass was stuck a piece of paper with the words 'Come in' written on it in blue crayon. She went inside.

There was a woman in the room sitting at a desk typing. There was no one else there. Rita said: 'I'm Miss Rigby.'

The woman looked up at her. She looked about thirty, was plain and plump with a dead white face. There were no rings on her fingers, Rita noticed. 'She's on the blower at the moment. She won't be long. Sit down,' the woman said.

Rita sat down on one of the little round-seated wooden chairs that were placed around the walls of the room. On the floor there was brown patterned lino and in front of each of the chairs it had been worn in a round patch by the feet of the people who had sat there, had been dented by countless pairs of high heels. There was a track trodden into the lino leading to the door of Mrs Brite's office. The walls of the room were cream, darkened by grime, and Rita reckoned, as she sat there, that if she wet her finger she would be able to write her name quite clearly in the dirt on the walls. The ceiling was browned by the smoke of countless Woodbines and Player's Weights. On a low table there were four thick glass ashtrays advertising Bass, just like the ones her Auntie June had had,

198

Rita remembered, the ones she had stolen from a pub, but which she used to wash regularly and rub up with a duster, just as if she had bought them at a posh shop.

The woman stopped typing, looked up at Rita and said: 'Take no notice of this place. We got bombed out of our other offices. This used to be a vet's.' Then she went on hammering away on her old Underwood.

The telephone tinkled as the receiver in Mrs Brite's office was replaced. The woman stopped typing again, opened the door, put her head around it, said something, then turned to Rita and said: 'You can go in now.'

Rita stood up, and walked along the track worn into the lino, into Mrs Brite's office.

That night she wrote three letters. She wrote home to her · grandmother to tell her that she had arrived safely, she wrote to Anne and she wrote to her father. Her father was shocked to learn that Rita was trying to make all those childhood dreams of hers come true, that she had opted for a world of fantasy rather than for the steady security of the secretarial work for which she had been trained. And in her letter to him, she told him that: 'Mrs Brite is very pleasant. She looks like a prize fighter who has been tamed, but I like her very much,' giving him the awful feeling that Rita had inherited her mother's sense of humour.

She had to go to Mrs Brite's office again the following morning. 'Photographs,' Mrs Brite said. 'I've made an appointment. This afternoon at half-past two. Take a short dress for your legs. Have you got one? Good. And a swimsuit?'

'Oh no, I haven't got a swimsuit.'

She did have one but it was a navy blue woolly one that was too tight, and whenever she got into the freezing cold water in it her nipples used to stick out like chapel hat pegs. She had left it at home.

'Go out and buy one this morning,' Mrs Brite instructed her.

'Will I have to give clothing coupons for one?' Rita asked.

'I don't know,' Mrs Brite replied. 'It's a long time since I bought a swimsuit.'

Rita looked at her in her bristly tweed jacket, with her square jaw and her square body, and thought to herself that the last time Mrs Brite wore a swimsuit she had probably gone down to the sea in a bathing machine, pulled by a cart horse.

'Here's the address,' Mrs Brite said. 'Think you can find it?'

'Oh yes,' Rita said. Of course she could find it. All you had to do in London was to go out into the street and hail a taxi.

And, as if she had read her thoughts, Mrs Brite said: 'Don't go getting a taxi. They'll know you're from up north, take you the long way round and charge you the earth. Get the underground, then ask a policeman.'

The front windows of Laurence's Photographic Studio had been blown in by bomb blast, and were boarded up with wood. Rita pushed open the door, and went into the empty, gloomy interior. A light shone at the foot of a staircase and a notice on the wall said: 'Please ring and come up.' She pressed the bell and went up the stairs. In her hand she had a shiny new attaché case that she had bought that morning in Woolworth's and which contained her short frock and a new swimsuit.

In a small room at the top of the stairs was a girl sitting at a desk. She looked about twenty and had a Veronica Lake hairstyle. Behind her was a window and through it Rita saw all the rubble from the bomb-damaged lower floor piled in the yard.

'He won't be a minute, Miss Rigby,' the girl said. 'Please take a seat.'

As she moved her head, her hair swung in front of one eye and she moved it back with her fingers, something, Rita noticed, that she had to do frequently.

Rita sat down. There was grey carpet on the floor and all over the walls around the desk were glossy photographs of people. She spotted Robert Donat and next to him there was someone wearing a crown.

'That's not the King, is it?' Rita asked.

'Heavens no,' the girl said, laughing. 'That's John Gielgud in one of his Shakespearian roles.' And noticing an expression of awe coming on to Rita's face, she went on: 'Oh, Laurence didn't take these. Most of them belonged to my sister. She was an usherette at our local flicks, but it got bombed and they let her have them. She picked them up in the debris. They used to have them in the foyer and up the stairs to the circle. I thought they would make the place look more like a photographer's. Look, there's Judy Garland, Tyrone Power, Ralph Richardson.' The girl pointed them out.

Rita gazed up at the photographs and remarked: 'A pity your downstairs got damaged.'

'Well, what can you expect?' the girl said. 'It doesn't look very grand, I'll admit, but Laurence has a lot of very nice clients, people in advertising and that and they don't seem to take any notice. He's trying to get more theatricals, people like you. That's why you got an appointment so quickly.'

Theatricals, Rita thought. People like her. And yet she had never set foot on the professional stage. The girl went chattering on, as if she were glad to have someone to talk to, and she made Rita feel glad that she did not have to sit there all day, alone but for Laurence's very nice clients.

Presently Laurence appeared in the doorway. He gave Rita a shock. He had a fat stomach, wore a pair of baggy corduroy trousers that were held up with a necktie around his waist, and had a bushy ginger beard. A puff of blue smoke came from within the beard and Rita imagined that somewhere in there he had a cigarette. 'You're the one old mother Brite sent, are you?' he said. 'Come on then.'

She followed him into the studio. He sat her down and arranged the lights ready to take some facial studies. Then he looked at her, said: 'Oh God,' and walked out. He came back in carrying a tray of make-up and began putting something on her face. 'Sunken cheeks,' he muttered, as if it was something he should have been warned about. Then he began painting her eyelids and said, as he did so: 'Before you have any more photographs done, buy some false eyelashes.'

'Are they expensive?' she asked.

'Well if they're more than you can afford,' he replied, 'catch some spiders and make your own.'

He took the facial studies of her then and when he had finished she went into the changing room and put on her short frock. He perched her on a stool and snapped away, puffed at the dog end that was somewhere amongst his whiskers and said nothing.

But Rita, once she had become accustomed to her surroundings, was as chatty as her mother had been. 'What did you do in the war?' she asked him.

'RAF,' he replied.

'Oh, my dad's in the RAF. He flies Hurricanes. Did you fly?'

'Yes. Photo reconnaissance.' He felt in his beard for the dog end, held it between finger and thumb and drew on it, as if to do so without holding on to it might have meant risking swallowing it. 'Right, all done. Tell old mother Brite they'll be ready tomorrow pm.'

'But what about my swimsuit?' Rita said. 'You haven't taken me in my swimsuit.'

'You're a bit boney,' he said, fiddling with his camera.

'I've only got bones in the usual places,' she replied indignantly. 'And I bought a new swimsuit specially.'

'Oh, go on then,' he said half-heartedly.

Rita changed into the swimsuit. It was a one piece with blue flowers all over it. When she came back into the studio Laurence was half-way down another cigarette and the glowing red end was dangerously near his beard. There was an unconvincing backdrop of the seaside for her to pose in front of.

'You're a bit white, aren't you?' he remarked.

Rita, annoyed at being criticized first for being boney, then for being white, snapped at him: 'I was nut brown until I washed all the muck off.'

He looked at her, drew on the cigarette, and she thought he was smiling, but she could not tell for all the hair on his face. His eyes did crease up, half-closed, and sparkle, but for all she knew it might have been because of the cigarette smoke. He kicked a beachball towards her to pose with and went on taking the photographs.

On her way out, the girl said: 'Don't forget us when you're famous.'

A few days later an audition was arranged. Rita took the things she would require in her attaché case. They went in Mrs Brite's car. It was not a glamorous beginning. To start the car, she had to crank the engine with the starting handle while Rita sat behind the steering wheel holding the choke out and with one foot on the accelerator. The wind blew Mrs

Brite's hair first to one side, then to the other, then into her face, and she went red from exertion before the car finally vibrated into life. It began to rain and as they drove along the windscreen wiper flipped reluctantly to and fro, seeming to go gradually slower, like the heartbeat of someone who is dying.

Rita felt happy. The photographs had turned out well and she was on the way to an audition. Although the day was dull and wet and windy, to her the world was full of sunshine. 'Did you tell the people I am to audition for that I had won the Crombie Cup, Mrs Brite?' she asked.

Mrs Brite, bringing a bit of cold reality into Rita's sunny world, said: 'No. You'd best forget that. The theatrical world is full of people who have won tin vases. Heinz's would have made better use of them.'

They went to a church hall in West London that had been bombed and had only half the proper roof. The other half was a tarpaulin. The rain beat noisily upon the tarpaulin and whenever anyone opened the door the heavy material billowed out then flopped down again on the roof timbers. Beneath all this, five girls were rehearsing a dance routine at one side of the hall, to the accompaniment of an old upright piano. On the small stage a scene was being acted out by some people who were still wearing their raincoats and who were reading their lines from their scripts.

After a brief introduction to a man whose name she did not catch, Rita changed in a little side room and joined the dancers. She picked up the steps and kept at it for ten minutes. They stopped then. She waited for someone to pass some remark on her dancing but no one did. Mrs Brite was nowhere to be seen. The man whose name she had not caught was talking to the woman who played the piano. Rita went across to him and said: 'How did I do?'

'Very good, my dear, very good,' he said, as if he had no real interest in her dancing at all.

'Have I got the part then?'

'Yes, of course.' He seemed surprised that she should ask.

Rita was delighted. 'Oh good, I'll tell Mrs Brite. Where is she?'

'She's gone,' he said. And as if he were tired of her pestering him, he called out to one of the girls: 'Pearl, take care of

Rita here, will you?' and went on talking to the pianist.

Pearl was a peroxide blonde. She looked older than the other girls. She introduced Rita to them. They were friendly and seemed glad to have her with them. 'You're a replacement,' Pearl said. 'Who was that came with you?'

'Mrs Brite, my agent,' Rita said.

'Your agent brought you? First job is it? Well, I hope you last longer than the girl you're replacing. It was her first job too.'

'What happened to her?' Rita asked apprehensively.

'Her father came and took her home,' Pearl said. 'She was supposed to go into a convent. Still, if what she told me about herself is true, she won't get into any convent. She won't pass the medical.'

'I thought there would be other girls to audition,' Rita remarked.

'No, you were the only one,' Pearl told her. 'A good agent you've got in that Mrs Brite. I wouldn't mind getting on her books.' Then she went on: 'Although, let's admit, anyone with a foot on the end of each leg could dance in this show. Still, us six, we're the lucky ones. And if our luck holds out, who knows, this show might last all the winter. Then, once they've cleared the mines and the barbed wire off the beaches, summer shows. Filey, Skegness, who knows? Who cares as long as there's fine weather and full houses?'

'Right,' called the woman at the piano. 'Come on then, girls. Let's run through it once more, shall we?'

When Rita got back to the YWCA that evening, there was a letter for her. It had come by the second post. It was from Anne, who had written straight back. She had started work with a firm of accountants and in her letter she seemed just as excited about that as Rita did about going on the stage. They were both sixteen, and whatever they did at that age was almost sure to be exciting.

Twenty One

There was a strong enough streak of her mother in Rita to enable her to adjust easily to her new life. She had the maturity of someone two or three years older than herself. The ragged life-style that her mother had forced them to lead, living first in one place, then in another, made it easy for her to become accustomed to her new environment. That way of life had hardened her in the same way that her mother had become hardened by her pathetic childhood.

The endless rehearsals tired Rita, but they did not bore her. The show was a revue and they finally settled on calling it: 'It's All Over Now.' The humour in it evaded her. Not only did she have her mother's looks, her mother's startling eyes, eyes that could hurt as much by looking right past someone as they could by looking right through them, but, as her father had feared, she had inherited her mother's accidental sense of humour, a sense of humour so natural that it made the contrived comedy in the revue seem rather flat. All the songs sounded vaguely like songs she had heard before, nobody seemed satisfied with their part and the producer seemed dissatisfied with everyone. It was a small company simply because there was not enough money to engage more people, and because of the financial limitations, Rita was given a small part in one of the sketches. She played a nervous waitress and had to tip plates of soup over people. She enjoyed that for the simple fact that, at rehearsals, for some reason, people laughed at it. 'Make them laugh on the first night and we're home and dry,' the producer kidded her, and she felt important, a part of it for the first time.

The stars of the show were two people called Francine Gurr and Hector Wilsby. Rita had never heard of either of them. They were both in their fifties and Pearl had been in a show with them before the war. 'They were old hat then and they're old hat now,' she told the other girls. 'The only way they'll get back into the West End is on a bus. You know who they wanted for this show originally? Bebe Daniels and Ben Lyon. Well, I ask you. They even wanted Vic Oliver. The thought was enough to make him take up the violin again.'

'Don't you think much of the show then?' Rita asked her.

'Don't I think. . . ? I hope to heavens we don't play Barnsley. I was in a show there much better than this one, and I'll tell you this, it was the only time I'd played to an audience who'd had all had their tongues cut out and their hands tied behind their backs.'

But Pearl was a born pessimist and was having to live with the fact that, at twenty-five, she was still in the same position that she had been in when she had first gone on the stage, a dancer having to audition with a hundred others for the lowest job in the company.

They opened in Birmingham among the ruins of the bombing in the first wet weeks of winter. There were full houses every night. Rita loved it. The first time she tipped the soup over Francine Gurr the house erupted with laughter. The sound thrilled her, she could not resist glancing out towards the audience, and there occurred a pause that should not have been there. And then she tipped the soup over Hector Wilsby, more laughter, and she thought that, even if the show ran for only that night, she had known success.

But the reviews were awful. 'After the bombing, must we be inflicted with this? It was more fun in the air-raid shelters,' one critic wrote.

'You should use that. It's funnier than your jokes,' Rita said to the comedian in the show, who had been allowed to put some of his own material in, and who was making a pest of himself, just as Mrs Runciman had warned her. 'It was all right you being a prisoner of war for five years,' she told him. 'You had a captive audience. We can't afford to have men with guns outside to keep everyone in. And get your hands off my backside. I've told you about doing that.'

Rita and Pearl shared a room in Rita's first theatrical digs. Walking home from the theatre through the wet streets, going from one pool of yellow lamplight to another, past the half-fallen wreckage of the blitz, past the gaunt, empty, hollow black shells of burnt-out buildings, past rows of boarded-up shops, it seemed that on every wall, on every hoarding, there was a bill advertising the show, with the names of Francine Gurr and Hector Wilsby above the title. And although it rained incessantly, although the wet penetrated the walls and soaked into the hoardings, it could not dislodge the posters. For a week it rained and for a week the carping words of the critics hung about the revue. But they stuck to their task and the bills stuck to the shop fronts so that, at the end of the week, only here and there had anything been altered in the revue, only here and there had the rain made the corner of one of the bills become unstuck and begin to curl downwards and flap in the wind.

And so the routine began. On stage six evenings a week, matinées, rehearsals with no kind words from the producer, who spoke to the girls without ever looking at them, and on the train on Sunday to another town, another place looking dull and dirty in the winter rain, another bedroom shared with Pearl in a dismal house looking out over the debris of bombed streets. There were always full houses, always bad notices, always digs that made Rita realize why people strove for success and luxury.

They had been on the road for a few weeks, and Rita and Pearl were sharing a room just like all the other rooms, faded flowers on the wallpaper, someone else's face powder dusting the dressing-table, an empty Capstan packet in one of the drawers. Pearl and the other girls went out to do some shopping that morning. Rita did not go. She was tired. She slept late, she had some stockings to mend, and anyway, they had a matinée that afternoon and she needed all the life there was in her to crawl to that.

She had just put on her dress, had lain her make-up out on the dressing-table, when there was a knock at the door. 'Come in,' she called.

The door opened and the landlady stood there. 'There's a man to see you, dear,' she said. 'Says he's your father.'

'Dad?' Rita's eyes lit up. She dashed out on to the landing and looked down the stairs. He was standing in the hallway in his air force uniform, with his greatcoat on.

The landlady smiled. 'He can come up,' she said. He was

an officer so he would be a gentleman and it would be all right. Anyone else would have had to go into the front parlour and it was cold in there because she had not yet lit the fire. She did not light it on the days when the girls were playing a matinée. The coal ration did not extend to it.

'Oh, dad.' Rita kissed him on the cheek. 'Why didn't you answer my letter? Can you stay and see the show?'

'I saw it last night.' He moved past her and looked through the window into the street. A delivery man had stopped at a shop on the corner and had given the horse its nose bag of oats to eat while he unloaded the cart.

'Last night?' She knew then that something was wrong. 'Why didn't you come backstage? You could have met . . .'

He was still looking out of the window. 'I've come to take you home,' he said calmly.

'Take me home? I'm not going home.' She grinned in disbelief.

'I'm taking you home. Get your things together. There's a train at midday.' He turned to face her and met her diamond-bright eyes.

'I've got a job to do, dad. We've got a matinée this afternoon. You're not taking me home.'

'A job? You call that a job? You ought to be ashamed of yourself. You've had a good education. You should be working in an office, not prancing about on stage with next to nothing on.' He reached up and took a suitcase off the top of the wardrobe. 'Here, get packed.' He threw it on the bed.

'You put that back. It's Pearl's.' She felt a surge of hostility inside her. Her face became set. She clenched her teeth, picked up the suitcase and went to put it back on top of the wardrobe.

Her father pushed her away and she fell back on the bed. The case dropped on to the floor. 'Just you get your things together, young lady. You're coming home with me. Now come on.' His officer's voice was firm. She might have that black hair and those red lips, she might have those sparkling eyes and that sharp voice, but she was not Bella. Bella was dead and all that was behind him.

She got off the bed and stood in front of him. Her staccato voice made the words cut right into him. 'I'm going nowhere with you. You're not treating me like you did my mother. So put your cap on straight and get out.'

He grabbed her by the shoulders and started to shake her. 'You are sixteen. You had no business leaving home. I'm not having you turn out like your mother.'

'Don't shake me,' she yelled in his face. She put her hands against him to push him away but he was too strong for her to move and it was she who moved backwards away from him. 'And what are you bothered about? Gran gave me five pounds to go away with.'

'I know she did,' he said. 'She gave it to you because she is frightened of you. She's as frightened of you as she was of your mother.'

Her whole face blazed with anger. 'Don't you speak about my mother like that. Don't you dare.'

'You're coming with me. You're coming.' He made a lunge at her and caught her by the hair. 'Get your things packed. You're coming.'

Rita struggled. She did not scream, although he was hurting her. She knew he would have to let go. And he did. She shook her head. 'Right, you've bloody well asked for it now,' she said through gritted teeth, and with all the force she could summon up she slapped him across the face.

The blow turned his face sideways. His cap fell off. He could not believe it. It was happening all over again. He was losing to her as he had lost to Bella. She was standing there poised to strike him again, like a wild animal that had just been let off its chain. He picked up his cap and went to the door. He did not look back, for if he did, he knew that he would see them both there, Bella and Rita.

Rita flopped down on the bed. She felt weak, utterly drained, just as her mother had always felt after a row. She looked at her hand. First of all it had gone numb, then it had tingled, then it had hurt. And now it ached and had gone blood red. She closed her eyes. 'Oh God,' she said out loud, 'don't say it's going to happen to me too. Please don't let it happen to me.'

Later, when she had calmed down, she made up her face and got ready to go out. When she got down into the hallway, the landlady appeared. 'Has your father gone then, dear?'

'Yes,' Rita replied.

'Oh, I didn't hear him go out,' she said.

Rita was glad about that. She did not want the girls to find out about the row. She did not want them to compare her with the other girl, the one who was meant to go into a convent. The very thought of it made her feel pathetic.

She went out into the street. The air was still and cold, and she felt the cold more because she had been so hot with anger. No wonder her mother had run away in nineteen forty, Rita thought. No wonder she had risked her and Ronnie against the German bombs. No wonder she had loved Chuck. He had made her sad in the end, but he had made her happy for a while. And one happy moment could cancel out a thousand unhappy ones.

Rita wandered aimlessly round the town, waiting for the anger and the frustration to drain from within her, wondering if he would catch the midday train alone or still try to make her go back with him. She looked at the queues. Everywhere there were long queues of people outside shops, still clutching the ration books they thought they were going to throw away on VE day. Nowhere did she see any sign that this was the country that had won the war. People looked hungry because food was rationed, they looked cold because coal was rationed, they looked shabby because clothes were rationed. No wonder they came to see the show, she thought. It was funny and it was warm and it made them forget the hardships of which victory had failed to rid them. And when her father did not appear again at her lodgings or at the theatre, Rita felt that she too had won a victory that she could not feel happy about, one that left her feeling cold and wanting, like the people queueing in the streets.

Sunday was the only day when Rita could find time to write her letters. She wrote them on the train to their next booking. She heard nothing further from or about her father. She did not mention the affair in her letters and her grandmother did not mention it in hers. Neither did her grandmother give away any sign of being scared of her. Her letters were full of instructions for Rita to wrap up warm and not to go short of anything. Once a month Rita wrote to Ronnie and sent him a five shilling postal order. And she wrote to Anne, but all she ever received in reply were the complete details of life in an accountant's office; the glamour and excitement of life in the theatre, which Rita wrote to her about, evidently counted for nothing.

But really, Rita had to admit to herself, there was no glamour. There was excitement. It was magic to her to be up on the stage before all those people sitting out there in the darkness, dancing and singing and playing her small part in the sketch. But her letters did not give away the fact that the show had never played in a major town other than Birmingham, that it was destined to have its run at second-rate theatres in second-rate towns. No one she wrote to was to know that most of the theatres were shabby, that they were not always in the main street, that in the dressing-room she shared with the other girls they did not have mirrors with lights round them as they did in all the films, that it had brick walls which had been covered a long time ago with a coat of distemper that had been written over with scribbled messages. The one that Rita saw every time she sat down to put her make-up on one week dated from nineteen thirty-seven and said simply: 'We died here too.'

But they did not die, despite the fact that the drama critic on one local newspaper wrote: 'An awfully good show, but more awful than good.'

And Rita leaned to put up with the laborious, repetitive routine, she learned to sense that the comedian was coming up behind her to put his arm around her waist, and so could avoid him. She learned, too, to put up with Miss Gurr and Mr Wilsby treating the girls as if they were invisible until they stepped on to the stage. She managed to resist the temptation to throw the soup in Miss Gurr's face instead of spilling it into her lap, even when she kicked Rita's ankle during the sketch one night and did not bother to apologize afterwards.

There were no flowers in the dressing-room from admirers after the show, no one waiting at the stage door with a taxi. Rita's only relaxation was to go to sleep and her only pleasure was to go to the cinema. Standing in the freezing cold one afternoon, waiting to get into the first house, she thought longingly of those days when they had all used to stalk along behind her mother, right past the queue, straight through the doors of the Palace Cinema, just like royalty. The good old days, she thought. If it was not for the nightly excitement of being on stage, life would be nothing. She was just like her mother, she realized. The night had held an excitement for her as well.

Pearl, being the senior of the six girls, was the one who organized the small amount of social life that they were able to fit into their lives. They were in the north east, in a town with tall factory chimneys and a sky permanently grey with industrial smoke, when she came dashing into the dressing-room before the performance and said: 'I've got six chaps lined up for tonight, girls. They're taking us out to supper. Yours is the tall one, Rita. I've told him you're eighteen. You look eighteen and you're taller than the rest of us.'

That was the trouble, Rita thought. Because she was taller than them and looked older than she was, they forgot that she was not yet seventeen, unused to men, unused to drink and barely used to the late nights that were part of their job. A glass of sherry drunk too quickly would turn her giddy. It made her cautious when it would have been fun to be reckless.

But there they were at the stage door, six young men in dinner jackets. Seeing them, Rita wished she had an evening gown to wear, but for all her saving she did not yet have one and neither did any of the others. The young men had a large car. They all jammed themselves inside and were whisked away to the Carlton Rooms.

The Carlton Rooms were exclusive. They would not let anyone in there. Rita judged that her mother could have got in. She would have got in on her looks alone. But not her Auntie June. Her Auntie June, Rita thought, had had the look of a tart about her. There had been something about the way she had looked at men that gave her away. She had always smiled at them. But Rita remembered that her mother had never done that. She had always looked at a man first, then, if she thought she would, she had smiled. Her Auntie June would have smiled at the doorman and not been allowed in. Her mother would have given him a look that would have gone through him like tracer fire and he would have opened the door for her.

It was a grand place, with high chandeliers, red plush and waiters in tail coats. Rita looked about her at the surroundings, at the other people eating supper, at the waiters leaning over the guests, at the wine being tasted. There was fine china on the tables, slender glasses, but there was not much choice of food. It was all that austerity would allow. There seemed to be more china on the table than there was food to put on it. But the overall effect was one of elegance, of wealth, of being in a different world.

And Rita thought of her mother. This was what she had wanted, she knew; the high life, a little bit of luxury. All those years, all that striving, all that scheming, and she had never got it. It seemed wrong to Rita that she, a few months out of school, playing small parts in a second-rate touring revue, should have stepped in so easily to the place her mother had never found.

Rita looked at her tall young man and said: 'And what do you do for a living?'

'I'm a draughtsman,' he replied. 'I've been trying to pick up the threads of the job again since I got demobbed.'

'Yes, it must be difficult,' Rita said. 'What were you in during the war?'

'The army,' he said. 'Medical corps. Spent a lot of time driving an ambulance.'

And one of the other men said, grinning: 'Go on, tell the truth. In actual fact, he had a very important job. He was a chiropodist in the Foot Guards.'

They all laughed, including the tall young man, and Rita joined in although she did not know what they were laughing at.

They ate their austerity supper, then went into the ballroom and danced.

'That was just my style,' Rita said the following morning, as she and Pearl lay in bed in their room. 'Men in dinner jackets. Pity I haven't got an evening dress.'

Pearl lit a cigarette and blew the smoke up towards the ceiling. 'You wait until you're a film star. We shan't see you for mink and diamonds.'

'He was quite pleasant, that man I was with,' Rita went on. 'It was nice to be with someone who didn't want to get their hands all over me. That used to be the trouble at the tech dances. I used to spend most of the time protecting my left breast from right-handed boys.'

Pearl laughed to herself, laughed quietly because Rita said

213

it so seriously. Then she asked her: 'Have you ever been with a man? You know, had sex?'

'Certainly not,' Rita replied, sounding offended by the question.

'The best time to have sex for the first time,' Pearl said, speaking from experience, 'is when you're about fourteen. Then you can have it with a boy. Otherwise, leaving it until you're too old means having it for the first time with a man, and that's a bit like trying to open a winkle with a crowbar. And when that happens, you'll be playing the part of the winkle.'

Rita went hot and red and defensive. 'Well I'm not getting caught up in things like that,' she said, turning her head in Pearl's direction and seeing the grey smoke from her cigarette rising up in a cloud above her bed. 'That was my mother's trouble. She loved the night life. Lost all her opportunities because of it. Night life, men. A film star or bust, that's my ambition.'

'That's right. Start as you intend to go on,' Pearl said, and as she turned to get out of bed she dropped her cigarette in amongst the bedclothes. 'Oh my God, dropped my fag. Where the hell is it?'

Rita got out of bed. Pearl saw the cigarette and grabbed it. 'Oh look, you've scorched the sheet,' Rita said, pointing to a round brown mark on the white sheet. 'The landlady will have you shot for that.'

'No she won't. It hasn't gone through,' Pearl said calmly. 'I'll just put some blanco on it, then turn thesheet over. She won't see it. It'll come out in the wash anyway.' She stuck the cigarette back in her mouth. 'Take my blanco into the bathroom and wet it, Rita, will you?'

Rita did as she asked. She admired Pearl at that moment. She had been calm and calculating where someone else might have panicked. But what advantage was that ability to Pearl, Rita wondered? Where had it got her? Twenty-five and still kicking up her legs in a second-rate revue. Perhaps, she thought, it all depended on luck. She held the blanco under the tap and let the water drop onto it.

A couple of nights later, after the show, when they were in the dressing-room taking of their make-up, jostling each other trying to get dressed in the cramped space, the stage doorkeeper knocked on the door and said: 'Someone to see Miss Rigby.'

Rita stood stock still. It was her father, her frightened mind told her. He had come again to take her home.

Pearl glanced at her, saw the look of apprehension on her face and called out: 'Who is it, Charlie?'

'Gentleman from the press,' he replied.

Above the babble of conjecture that started in the dressing-room, Rita called with relief: 'I'll be right down.' Then she said: 'I wonder who it is? I'll bet it's that comedian playing a trick on me.'

'He wouldn't do that,' one of the girls said. 'He's too fond of you.'

'It's fame at last, Rita, after all these weeks,' Pearl said laughing.

'If any of you are pulling my leg,' she replied threateningly, 'there are going to be some eyes scratched out, so there.'

If the light had been better and she had been able to see him sooner, she would have gone back to the dressing-room and sent someone out with an apology. For standing there was a thin young man in a fawn raincoat and a brown trilby. He was definitely not from *The Times*, as she had hoped.

Rita gave him one of her hard looks and said one word: 'Well?'

'Good evening, Miss Rigby,' he said politely. 'I'm Ian Chase.'

'If you want an interview, you should contact my agent first,' she said sternly, to put him off.

'Your agent?' he asked, as if unsure of what she meant.

'That's right. To arrange the fee. What do you normally pay?'

'To tell the truth,' he began. 'You see . . .'

'Now come on. You did come here for an interview, didn't you?'

'Well, I didn't actually,' he said. 'I thought you might like to come out to supper.'

'Oh.' That took her back a bit. 'I thought you were from the press.'

'I am. I'm from *The Courier*. I did that bit about the show in

215

Tuesday's issue.'

'*The Courier*? The local rag?' She felt silly at imagining that he could have been from anywhere else, in that far flung bit of industrial England.

'I've seen the show three times,' he said.

'Why? Didn't anyone else want the complimentaries?' She was still giving him that piercing look.

'Oh, I paid,' he replied. 'I only got the one complimentary – to do my report. I thought you were very good. That's why I saw the show twice more. And I thought you might like to come out for a bit of supper.'

Rita still did not realize that it was her that he liked, not the show. And before she could answer, the other five girls made their way to the stage door.

'Don't eat him alive, Rita,' Pearl said as she went past.

'Stun him first,' said one of the others and they went out into the street, giggling.

'All right then,' Rita said when they had gone, feeling indignant at their remaks. 'You can take me to the Carlton Rooms.'

'The Carlton Rooms?' Her suggestion took his breath away. 'I don't go there. It's too dear. I'm not the editor. I'm only a reporter.'

She looked him up and down. 'Hm. I don't suppose they'd let you in looking like that, anyway. All the men had dinner jackets on when I was there.'

'There's a nice little place not far away,' he said quickly. 'Just round the corner.'

'Oh all right,' she agreed reluctantly. He did not look much older than she was – about twenty. And she looked nineteen.

When they got to the little place just round the corner, and he opened the door for her, she noticed as she went in that there was a queue standing at a counter. He guided her to a stairway and as she reached it she turned and said angrily: 'This is a fish and chip shop. You're not getting me in here.' The heat, the smell, the hissing fat had told her.

'It's nice upstairs,' he replied, putting his hand on her arm, and gently he persuaded her to go up the stairs to the neat, cosy dining-room.

The tables were covered with chequered cloths, a waitress

stood in attendance. A year before, Rita would have been in her element going into such a place. He took her coat and hung it on the stand by the door, took off his trilby and his fawn mac and hung them by it. And he held her chair while she sat down.

They studied the menu. 'Can I call you Rita?' he asked.

'You may,' she replied haughtily. 'What did you say your name was?'

'Ian Chase,' he told her again. 'Shall we order?'

'All right then, Ian Chase, I'll have haddock and chips, with brown bread and butter.'

'What would you like to drink?'

She forgot herself for a moment, felt more at home there than she had at the Carlton Rooms, and said: 'Have they got any Tizer?'

He smiled. 'I didn't think ladies of the theatre drank Tizer.'

She realized her mask was about to fall away. But her mother's gift for quick thinking was hers, and it saved her. 'Well, they don't serve wine here, do they?' she stated, as if it was logical, 'and if I drink tea at this time of night I shan't sleep a wink. What would you prefer me to have – a glass of water?'

Rita enjoyed the meal. She liked it more than the food she had had at the Carlton Rooms. And as he was paying for it, she found it twice as tasty.

'Did you read my column?' he asked her.

'No,' she replied. 'The producer did. You gave it the thumbs down like everyone else, so he said.'

She was not so hard and icy towards him now, and he liked her all the more because of it. 'Not entirely. I wrote: "Six lovely young ladies working their hearts out do not save the show. But if 'It's All Over Now' was a sinking ship, that half dozen would be the only ones worth saving."'

She looked up from her haddock and chips. 'Did you write that about us? Well, we should be taking you to supper then, shouldn't we?'

'I didn't see the show three times to watch the other five girls,' he said, looking right into her eyes, which were soft and dark now and had a shine in them like the shine on her jet black, smooth hair.

At last Rita realized that he was soft on her and she wished she had become aware of it before. If he had been different she would not have minded. But him, this sallow, badly-dressed cub reporter, who could afford nothing better than a fish and chip shop to take her to, he would not do at all. Their next booking was only forty miles away and she did not want him turning up there as well. If he did, and the girls found out, she would never live it down. She was going to have to put him off, and she had her mother's way of doing it.

'Tell me,' she began, 'is that your reporter's outfit? That old mac, that grey suit that's never been pressed and that awful brown trilby?'

'Well, yes, it is actually,' he replied, feeling disturbed at her description of his clothes.

'Don't you believe in dressing up a bit when you take a girl out?' she asked him acidly. 'I mean, look at you. Wherever do you live? Underneath the arches?'

'I came straight from work,' was his excuse. 'I was out on a job. Never got back into town until half-past six.'

'Do you always want to be a reporter on the local rag?' she went on. 'How far do you think you are going to get going around dressed like that? You look just like a reporter on a small town evening paper and that's what you'll always be. If you think you look like Humphrey Bogart, you've got another thing coming. And for goodness sake, get rid of that trilby. It looks awful. Go to a hat shop and get something else. When we go out of here tonight, leave it on the peg.' She stopped then and drank her Tizer.

He looked hurt, did not know what to say. Then he came up with: 'Well, I'm glad it's only Tizer you're drinking. Heaven knows what you might have said to me if you'd had anything stronger.'

When they got up to go, Rita said to him: 'Are you going to leave it there?'

'Yes,' he said, 'just to please you,' and he left his brown trilby on the hook.

Rita's lodgings were not far away. While they walked along, he told her of some of the reporting jobs he did, of how that day he had gone out of town to where the fire brigade were trying to rescue a cow that had fallen into a muddy stream.

Finally, at the door, Rita said to him: 'Now remember, when you're a famous reporter and I'm a famous actress, we'll meet up and have dinner together. Properly. At the Carlton Rooms. And we won't drink Tizer.' Then she was gone.

She told Pearl when she got up to their room: 'He took me to a fish and chip shop. Can you imagine it? I'd rather have come back here and soaked my feet and had a cup of cocoa.'

A strange thing happened to Rita then. She woke up at six o'clock the next morning thinking of how badly she had treated him. She could not go back to sleep. Every time she closed her eyes she saw his brown trilby hanging on the hat-stand in the dining-room of the fish and chip shop. Whereas her mother had been almost entirely without a conscience about the way she treated people or the wrong things she did, Rita was now experiencing a part of her character that came from her father. He had gone back to her mother at her time of need in spite of everything, had written letter after letter to her which he knew she would never answer. Those were things he had felt he had to do in order to come to terms with his conscience. Rita lay in bed having similar thoughts.

But the time she spent lying there was not wasted. When it was time to get up she had it worked out. She found a large paper bag and went back to the fish and chip shop. It was closed. Through the glass door she could see a woman scrubbing the floor and she tapped on the glass to draw her attention. The woman opened the door.

'My friend left his brown trilby on your hat-stand upstairs last night,' she said. 'Can I have it, please?'

'I'll get it, love, save you treading on my wet floor,' the woman replied and she went up the stairs and fetched the hat.

Rita put it in the paper bag, then set off for the newspaper offices. They were in an old building in a back street and it seemed a fitting place for Ian Chase in his fawn mac and crumpled suit. There was a counter with a glass top and underneath the glass were samples of classified advertisements cut from the newspaper. A girl appeared, looked at Rita, and wondered why on earth she could not look like her.

'I'd like to see Mr Chase, please.'

'He's out, madam, on a job,' the girl said. 'He's up the

cemetery, covering a funeral.'

Rita, going on seventeen, looked old enough to be called madam. She said: 'Would you give him this then? It's his hat. He left it at the Carlton Rooms last night.'

'At the Carlton Rooms?' the girl said in disbelief.

'Yes. We had dinner together there last night and he left his hat behind. They telephoned me this morning. They know me – I'm appearing at the Grand this week. They remembered he was with me. So I collected it for him.'

'I'll see he gets it, madam, directly he returns.'

Rita had known that he would not be there. He had told her the night before, as they walked back to her lodgings, that he was covering a funeral at eleven that morning. And knowing that, she had put a note in with his hat. It read: 'Never believe all an actress tells you. The trouble with actresses is, they never stop acting.'

It was Saturday, they had a matinée and an evening performance. Then it was straight to bed and up in time to get an early train to their next booking. Rita said to the stage doorkeeper: 'Charlie, if that chap comes round here for me again, I'm not available. Tell him something, will you? Miss Rigby regrets. You know.'

He knew. He had been saying that to men at the stage door for years. Whether he had to say it to Ian Chase, Rita never found out. Charlie did not mention it to her. And her mind was in the next theatre, in the next town, in a place she had never seen.

Twenty Two

They did not have a booking for Christmas week. It was the pantomime season and Pearl reckoned that the worst pantomime in the world would beat their show to a booking. They were still in the north, so Rita did not have too long a journey to get home. She wanted to ask the girls to come back early, to come to Manchester and stay the night so that they could all have a day out together, but there would not be room for them all and she could not imagine her grandmother making room for five dancing girls. Her mother would have let them stay, would have told them to grab two chairs each and left them to it. Then she thought of asking just Pearl, but one look at her peroxide blonde hair and her darkening roots would have been too much for Mrs Rigby.

And so Rita let the idea die, wrote home to her grandmother and asked her to leave the key under the mat, and caught the midnight train back to Manchester. The train was full, but she had bought a first class ticket and was able to get the last seat in a compartment. A naval officer lifted her case up on to the rack for her and they all sat there, jammed together, in silence. She had bought a copy of *Everybody's* magazine and she sat behind it reading in the dim light.

The train seemed to empty at Manchester. Rita knew there would be a queue to get a taxi. That was why some men got off the train almost before it had stopped and raced off along the platform. But she could not have run, whatever the necessity, not in her high heels which, although they looked smart, made her feet freeze to death. Instead, she thanked the naval officer, who was not getting off there and who not only took her case down from the rack but took it to the door for her, and she proceeded down the platform with her handbag and magazine in one hand, her suitcase in the other, the collar of her white raincoat pulled across to keep out the cold against which her silk scarf gave little protection.

As she walked along among the crowd, one figure was coming the other way. She saw him walking slowly against the tide of people making for the barrier, saw that he was looking for someone, recognized her father in his air force blue and realized too late that he was looking for her. There was no time for her to dash into the ladies' to avoid him. It had not entered her head that he would be there, at home. As far as she knew, she had slapped his face and he had gone back to Germany.

He smiled. 'Hello, Rita. Thought I'd come and meet you.'

'Hello,' she said and went walking on.

'Let me take your case,' he offered.

'I can manage,' she replied starchily, looking straight in front of her, her head up, her face set.

'Let me.' He took hold of the case and pulled it away from her, and the people walking behind looked and wondered.

She flashed a fierce glance at him. It annoyed her, the way he took her case, the way it would have annoyed her mother. But unlike her mother, Rita did not cause a scene.

'How's the show going?' he asked.

'All right,' she replied.

'Home for the week then?'

'Yes,' she said.

They got out of the station and there was a queue of people waiting for taxis. They stood there and he said: 'Rita, I'm sorry about what happened.'

She said nothing and he said again: 'I said I'm sorry, Rita.'

'I heard you,' she said irritably.

'Do you forgive me?' he asked her.

'Yes,' she said, 'I'll forgive you. But I won't forget.'

He heard the hard reply as he would have heard it from Bella, and it hurt him as much, for she might have been Bella standing there with her head held upright, with her black shiny hair, her red lips, her pencil thin eyebrows, her raincoat belted tightly round her waist to show off her figure. She might have been Bella.

222

It was cold. People stamped their feet. Rita longed to wriggle her toes to get some life back into them, but there was not room to do that in those shoes. She longed to be able to slip one shoe off, to clench her toes then, to hold her foot against her leg to win a bit of its warmth, but she could not, not while she was standing there with him. She knew she should have worn her slacks to travel in, and some other shoes. Then she would have been able to wear her woolly socks as well. But she had got herself all dolled up, just as her mother would have done, just as if she was going to be seen by somebody. And why not, she thought? She was good-looking, she was smartly-dressed. She would be seen by everybody and she would freeze to death to let them see her. There was a young man at the front of the queue who looked round at her every ten seconds. He had an army haircut, with his hair shaved right up the back, but he was in civvies, in a demob raincoat that was too wide at the shoulders. Let him look, she thought, and the other man who moved his eyes but not his head. Let them look. Because that was all they could do. When Rita decided it was time for a man to do more, then she would say so. Until then, they could just look.

Finally they got a taxi, and her father broke the silence. 'Where are you playing next?' he asked her.

'Rotherham,' she said and the name of the place sounded just like the name of the end of the world. No glamour, no imagined pictures of anything grander than any of the other places they had played at. They had all sounded like the end of the world, and had all looked like it too, all grime and grit and industry, and theatres where, when the girls danced, the disturbed dust rose up from the boards of the stage and hung in front of the footlights like factory smoke.

'I've been home a week,' he said. 'I go back on Boxing Night.'

'Germany?' she asked, looking sideways through the window.

'No, I'm in East Anglia now. Flying jets. You know, those aeroplanes without a propeller.' He nudged her to get her attention, pulled up the sleeve of his greatcoat and said: 'See? Squadron leader now.'

But it made no difference to her what he was, or what he flew, or whether he was in Germany or East Anglia. They

223

had fought, she had won and she had no respect for anyone she had beaten. With him, although she did not realize it, she was picking up just where her mother had left off.

There was a bright fire in the living-room. The kettle steamed on the hob and there were sandwiches on the table, covered over with a serviette. Ronnie had hung up the trimmings and there was a Christmas tree with Jack Frost sprinkled on it, and Rita imagined the fuss her grandmother must have made when some of that went on the hearth rug. Although she wanted something to eat and would have loved a hot drink, she declined them both. To stay down there with him would only mean talking and she did not want to talk to him. Instead, she slipped off her shoes, stood in front of the fire with one hand resting on the mantelpiece and thawed out her frozen feet, holding each one up in turn close to the flames. Then she went up to her room, to her photographs of Robert Donat, Eric Portman and the late Leslie Howard smoking his pipe. There was a hot water bottle in her bed. She took her nighdress out of her suitcase and wrapped it around the bottle. There was a smell in the room, a pleasant smell, one she thought she knew but which she could not remember smelling before. It was the smell of her books on the shelf, of their cardboard covers, the school smell that comes from paper and ink and pencils. It was the smell of her past, more pungent than any pictured memory.

Rita was glad when her father went back off leave. To have him and her grandmother there was too much for her. They were so alike. He was as much like his mother as Rita was like hers. She watched them moving about in silence, their minds working with thoughts they imparted to no one, their mouths full of words they never spoke. Rita and Ronnie made all the noise. Rita had bought her brother a table tennis set for Christmas, and they fixed it up on the kitchen table and played with a complete lack of skill, laughing and shouting, while Mrs Rigby watched them through the open doorway from where she sat in the living-room, wincing as she saw the ball bouncing off her crockery that stood white and shining in regular rows on the kitchen dresser, the crockery that Hitler's bombs had not even disturbed.

It was not until their father had gone that Mrs Rigby suggested to Rita and Ronnie that the three of them should take flowers up to Bella's grave. Only then did she make some of the remarks that Rita had expected her to make upon her arrival home, such as how pasty Rita looked and how she hoped she had not started smoking. With Leslie Rigby not there, it seemed as if the blue touchpaper had gone and there was nothing to set off the explosion. Her father, Rita realized, must have told her grandmother what had happened and the old lady had gamely kept the peace.

But now her attitude was relaxed. As Rita's week at home drew to a close, her grandmother said to her: 'You've been sitting in front of that fire reading for days now, with your knees up the flue. I'd like to see the sort of places you've been living in.'

'They've got all the comforts of home,' Rita said, 'only they're not home.' Then she looked at the chair opposite, the chair that her mother had used to sit in, pictured her sitting there with her library book and her crutches near at hand in the corner. 'I remember last Christmas night,' she said. 'Mam sat in that chair drinking a glass of this and a glass of that and said it was the only time she'd ever got drunk sitting down.'

Rita looked round, expecting to hear some remark from her grandmother. But she saw her go through the doorway into the kitchen in silence, leaving Rita to wonder what she thought of when she looked at that chair, whether she still heard the silence that Rita had heard for so long after her mother had died. For Rita, the silence had gone now. It had been replaced by pictures in her mind, pictures that she could smile at now and which did not make her sad.

The company reassembled. Rita danced and sang and tipped soup through another week before they all got on the train again and went to a seaside resort in North Wales.

There was talk there of someone called Randall Axter being in town to see the show. 'Who's Randall Axter when he's at home?' Rita asked.

'He's the impresario who put the show on the road,' Pearl told her. 'He's probably come to tell us how wonderful we've all been, before we start our next stretch of unemployment. What have we got? Two more bookings in Wales, two more in the Midlands and that's it. Back to the labour exchange.'

225

After the curtain came down that night, they all had to hang around backstage while the important man came up from his seat in the front stalls to speak to them. The girls stood there awkwardly, like children who were being kept in after school. To show their seniority, Francine Gurr and Hector Wilsby left the stage, then came back again, making an entrance from one side of the stage as Randall Axter came on at the other. They crossed to meet him and there was much hugging and kissing and clasping of each other.

He had a shiny bald head, a pointed nose and the trace of a foreign accent. As a bonus for all their hard work, he told them, he was giving them a final week in London. It was not the West End, but it was London. And on top of that, there would be a part in his new production, going into rehearsal shortly, for all of them. It was a musical, with a big cast, and it would have a brief tour before going into the West End.

They gave him a round of applause and voiced their grateful thanks, before drifting off to their dressing-rooms. On the way, the comedian said: 'He can keep his musical. I've got something else up my sleeve.'

'The only thing you've got up your sleeve,' Rita said, 'is a sweaty armpit.'

'I'll have you know I've got a summer season at Margate,' he said indignantly. 'So there. First summer of peace. Should be great.'

'Yes, all your old jokes should go down a treat at the seaside,' Rita said acidly. 'The kiddies will love them.'

'At least my contract is signed, darling,' he snapped back. 'I wouldn't bank on Randall Axter too much. All he had in nineteen thirty-eight was a pierrot show on the beach at Ilfracombe. And that was a darn sight better than this show.'

'That's never right, is it?' Rita asked Pearl as she closed the dressing-room door.

'I don't know,' she said. 'And I don't suppose I shall get close enough to him to ask.'

But if things had always been that way for Pearl, they were going to be different for Rita. She had almost finished changing when she was wanted outside. Randall Axter was waiting a little way along the passage. He beckoned to her. 'I liked your performance, Miss Rigby. You have a good voice. You sing very well, very well indeed.'

226

'How could you tell?' she asked with her usual frankness. 'We all sang together, me and the other girls.'

'My dear Miss Rigby, I can listen to a whole symphony orchestra playing and hear only the third oboe.'

She did not believe that. From then on she believed the comedian.

'Anyway,' he went on, 'I think there is definitely a part for you and your voice in my new show. In fact, I've got some of the songs with me. How would you like to go through a few of them?'

'Well, if you like,' she said uncertainly.

'Good. Come up to my hotel suite. When shall we say – two-thirty tomorrow? We'll run through a few numbers from the show and see what becomes of it.'

He went then. Miss Gurr and Mr Wilsby had appeared, all dressed up, it seemed, for a night on the town.

Back in the dressing-room, Rita recited what he had said as if it were a tale of woe. 'I don't think I'll go,' she said. 'I think I'll be ill instead.'

'Give me a black wig and stretch me a couple of inches and I'll go,' Pearl said. 'Talk about looking a gift horse in the mouth.'

'But how does he know what I'm like? He couldn't have told me from you from where he was sitting.'

'Look, sweetheart, you've got a great voice. You can really belt out a good number.' Pearl, who had never been given even a half a chance, was not going to let Rita or any of the others pass up an opportunity like that. 'He's been in the business a long time. He knows what to look for.'

'But he only had a pierrot show at Ilfracombe,' Rita reminded her.

'Oh, don't take any notice of what he said. He's only jealous because Max Miller's got a funny ending to all the jokes he hasn't even got the beginning to.'

Rita looked at her and frowned. 'But that doesn't make sense, Pearl.'

'Nothing makes sense in this business, love. It doesn't make sense that I'm still hoofing it in the chorus line after ten years. It doesn't make sense that you're not over the moon at being given the chance the rest of us are always dreaming of. I envy you, but you'll go to that hotel tomorrow even if I have

227

to drag you there by your hair. That doesn't make sense either, does it? But I'll do it.'

At two-thirty the following afternoon, Rita went up in the lift to Randall Axter's hotel suite. She knocked on the door. He let her in, guided her to the settee. On a small table were some musical scores.

'A drink perhaps?' he asked her.

'Gin and orange, with plenty of orange if I'm going to sing,' she replied.

'And I'll have a gin and orange with plenty of gin,' he joked, and poured the drinks at the cocktail cabinet.

It was a large room, well furnished, the sort of room that she had only seen before in a film. She looked around. It had never occurred to her that she would be the only one there. She had imagined that perhaps Francine Gurr would be there, or Hector Wilsby. 'Is there anyone else coming?' she asked.

He sat down beside her, handed her the gin and orange. 'No, my dear, there are only us two.'

'Oh, I thought there would be someone else.' She sipped her drink. There was too much gin in it. 'Where's the piano?'

'Piano? Oh, I haven't got a piano. I think we can manage without.'

'How am I supposed to pick up the tunes? I can read music a bit, but I'm not all that great at it.' She leaned forward and took one of the scores off the table. 'Hey, this is "Rose Marie",' she said. 'I thought you said. . . ?'

He snatched the score off her. 'Yes . . . well, that's nothing to do with it. I'm thinking of putting on a revival of "Rose Marie", but that's a different project.' He seemed flustered and put the score back on the table.

'Well, what am I supposed to sing then?' she asked.

'Let's sit and talk a bit first,' he said. 'Now, it's Rita isn't it? I may call you Rita?'

'I suppose so.' Her voice sounded high and nervous. He was sitting rather close to her. She looked towards the door and wished there was someone else there with her.

'Tell me about yourself,' he said. 'What have you done in the theatre so far?'

'Nothing much,' she said. 'I'm only seventeen.'

'Seventeen?' He chuckled.

'Well, I shall be in a few weeks,' she admitted.

'In a few weeks,' he repeated. 'Your first show?' He rested his arm on the back of the settee so that it just touched her shoulders.

'Yes,' she said. 'I want to get into films.'

'Films? Then, Rita, you've come to the right person. That is where I may be able to help you,' he said, beaming at her.

'Oh, you make films do you?' She felt his arm settle gently around her shoulders and her whole body cringed.

'I don't actually make films, but I do know a lot of people in the film world, the sort of people it's useful to know should anyone want to get into pictures.'

'Oh, who do you know then?' She did not believe him. And if her nervous voice got any higher, it would be nothing more than a squeak.

'Well, Alexander Korda, Herbert Wilcox. All the right people.'

As he spoke, he turned towards her and slipped his other arm around her waist. She could feel his hot palm beneath her heart. Rita was frightened. Had he been anyone else, she would have just shoved him away and told him to get his bloody hands off. But him, the impresario, the man who might be able to get her into films, she could not do that to him. Instead, she said: 'Do you mind not doing that?' But she did not say it firmly enough, and, as if he had not heard her, he moved even closer to her.

'Yes, it's people who count when you want to get into films. People first, looks next, then talent,' he said and he grinned a grin that Rita imagined showed that he was very satisfied at having got that far.

She swallowed and said: 'Knowing such famous people, Alexander Korda and so on, must be very nice.'

'Oh it is,' he said, enjoying the pleasure of having his hands on her body. 'Such people as Phyllis Calvert, Valerie Hobson . . .'

But Rita did not hear what he said about them because his hand was moving up her body and she knew that very soon she was going to have to protect her left breast. She wondered what her mother would have done in her situation. Her mother had always been in command of things, had always had an answer for anything. Nothing that Rita could remember had ever rattled her. In moments of crisis she had always stayed calm until it was time to act otherwise. And that was what Rita did, while his hand began to quarter inch its way up her rib cage towards her vulnerable left breast.

It was then that he made his mistake. Not satisfied with feeling her body, he pushed his face towards her as if to kiss her.

'No,' Rita squealed and she pushed him away and went to get up.

But she was held by his arm round her shoulders. In the excitement of the moment, while he struggled to hold her on the settee, his accent cracked. 'You wanna get into films, you gotta be nice to people . . .' He had lost the chance to feel her breast because she was struggling and had half turned away from him. And so he shot his hand up her leg and clutched at her.

Rita screamed. She clamped her legs together, but his hand grasped at the bare flesh above the top of her stocking. She tried to stand up, but his hand remained up her leg and seemed to be holding her back somehow. He was chuckling with delight, as if the struggle was what he enjoyed, and he was talking in little staccato bursts, but she could not understand what he was saying because his accent had broken completely.

He tried to pull her onto her back. She screamed again. She found strength from somewhere and pulled herself upright, put her hand in his face and pushed him away. Again she tried to stand up, but his hand was still up her leg, was still holding her back. 'I'm caught, I'm caught,' he seemed to be saying.

Breathless with fright, too breathless to scream again, she put her hand in his face once more and pushed him away, and although his body bent backwards, still his hand remained up her leg until, with one great push with her hand that squashed his features, he shot backwards across the settee away from her. Something went snap against her thigh and only then did she realize that his watch strap had caught in her suspender and had held his hand there.

Rita took two steps towards the door and no more, for he bounded off the settee and locked his arms around her. He turned her towards him and tried to pull her towards the settee. His eyes glittered, his mouth was open and he made little grunting sounds of exertion in his throat.

She braced herself, tried to pull herself away but could not, and as a grin of impending triumph crept across his face, she brought her right knee up hard between his legs. His eyes closed, his face crumpled, he let go of her and doubled up. And in desperation, unaware of the extent to which she had disabled him as he bent double in agony, she clenched her fist and punched him with all her might on his pointed nose. He yelled and collapsed backwards on to the settee, putting one hand up to his face as the blood spurted from his nose.

Rita grabbed her coat and made for the door. She turned as she went out, saw blood running through his fingers. She had no fear now. She was on top. And in the strident voice she had heard all through her childhood, she shouted at him: 'I hope you bleed to death, you dirty pig.'

She slammed the door. She went past the lift, did not want to risk him coming out while she stood there waiting, and went all the way down the stairs, out into the street, into a tea shop on the front, drank two cups of tea and stared blankly through the window at the grey, glittering sea.

Rita could not make herself out. One moment she had been frightened to death, the next she had found the strength to fight, the courage to kick him in his parts, punch him on the nose and shout at him. It seemed as if it had been someone else doing it, not her. But it had been her. There was a red mark on her knuckles to prove it.

'And that was it. I grabbed my coat and left,' Rita told Pearl and the others. They were in the bedroom at their digs, sprawled about listening in awe. 'So that's me finished. Thank goodness I'm not far from home.'

'Oh, I shouldn't bother, love,' Pearl said. 'We've only got a few more bookings. It's hardly worth them getting anyone else to take your place, is it? You're a great little soup dropper. They'll put up with you for another few weeks.'

'It's put the tin hat on my career though, hasn't it?' Rita said dismally. 'And I was only defending my honour.'

But Pearl said reassuringly: 'I'll bet you're not the first one he's tried it on with, so look, if anyone takes you up about it, just you write to that agent of yours and tell her what's going on. She should be able to settle his hash. She looked warlike enough the time I saw her.'

'I don't think I'll go to any extremes,' Rita replied.

They went down to the theatre and everything seemed normal but for the fact that Miss Gurr gave Rita a look that was as frosty as the North Pole. Rita could not imagine how Randall Axter dare speak to anyone about what had happened, let alone Miss Gurr. And anyway, she thought, she always did look a bit arctic.

But after the final curtain, as they were drifting away to their dressing-rooms, the producer suddenly appeared. 'A word with you, Rita,' he said.

Rita was as tall as him with her outdoor shoes on. With the high heels she wore for the last scene, she could look down at him. The tall pink feathers she wore on her head gave her a feeling of even greater height.

He did not look very composed. He said: 'Needless to say, I've been to see Mr Axter. Now, Rita, there are people in this business who have it in their power to help you, to help you a great deal, and you do not go punching them on the nose. Now I want you to go straight to Mr Axter's hotel and apologize.'

It was then that he noticed her eyes. They were dark and they glittered and they looked right into his. They fixed him like a snake fixing a rabbit. Even before she spoke, he wished he had not said the little that he had.

Rita forgot all about not going to extremes. She prodded him on the chest with her forefinger. She went on prodding him as she spoke. 'Look here, you,' she said, looking down at him. 'Apologize yourself. That dirty devil got me in his room and tried to do things to me that he could go to prison for. And not only did I punch him on the nose, but I kicked him where it hurts too. Now if you want to make a fuss about what I did, or if anyone else wants to make a fuss, then I'll make a fuss too. Only I'll make a fuss down the police station. I'm only sixteen, but I can look after myself. If you don't believe me, just put yourself in the place of that Handell Rackstraw or whatever he calls himself.' Then she turned on her high heels and strode away to the dressing-room.

232

For the second time that day she had a tale of woe to tell the girls. 'I think I've cooked my goose now. That's two of them I've had a go at in one day. One physically and one verbally. I think I'll pack tonight.'

'Rubbish,' Pearl snapped. 'They daren't do a thing now you've mentioned the police.'

'My first show too,' Rita went on miserably. 'I shouldn't think anyone would want me now.'

'Heavens, Rita, they don't give references in this job,' one of the others said. 'No end of tour reports, either.'

'Look, kid,' Pearl told her, 'you'll get along all right. You've got starlight shining all over you. I'll bet when you're my age you won't be kicking your legs up in the chorus or touring in a slow-death show like this one. By the time the tour ends, we'll all be having a drink and laughing like hell over this little episode. And you'll be laughing loudest of all.'

The following morning there was an unscheduled rehearsal call. The six girls traipsed down to the theatre to find the producer already there in the wings, a clipboard in his hand, with Francine Gurr perched on a chair and Hector Wilsby at her side.

'Right,' he bellowed in the direction of the girls. 'We're going to change the routine a bit. Mr Axter's idea. He thinks the show needs a little more sparkle and so do I.'

The comedian appeared at Rita's elbow. 'What's happening? What have I missed?'

'You've died. We've just held your funeral,' Rita said out of the corner of her mouth.

'First change, the restaurant sketch. Beryl, you'll be taking the part of the waitress,' the producer said.

'Hang on a minute,' Rita said loudly. 'That's my part.'

'Do you mind letting me finish?' he said tartly. 'Now, the trio, the Andrews Sisters routine. I want you in there, Pam.' He looked at his clipboard. 'So that's Pearl, Alice and Pam for the trio. All right? And in the finale I want you, Alice, to take the centre spot, with Rita moving to your old place at back row left. Okay, that's it. Let's get started.'

'Hang on a minute,' Rita yelled. 'That's my three spots gone. That's hardly fair.'

'Oh, isn't it?' the producer said sarcastically in the silence that followed Rita's complaint. 'Well then, you'd better speak to Mr Axter about it, hadn't you? Only he's gone back to London this morning, so you'll have to telephone him later on. Come to me after and I'll give you his number. Right, come along Beryl. The restaurant sketch. Miss Gurr and Mr Wilsby don't want to be here all day and neither do I.'

Rita stood there looking grim and fierce, and feeling unhappy and wretched. The girls murmured little words to her, as if in apology for what had happened, and Beryl rehearsed the restaurant sketch and made a mess of it. But the producer did not mind. He seemed to have become blessed suddenly with endless patience and went about the job smiling the self-satisfied smile of a rat that had just swallowed a fat cat.

Words of solace did nothing for Rita, although the girls were all over her with commiseration when the rehearsals had finished. She was hurt, she was bitter and she wanted to cry. And cry she would have, had there been the privacy. But there was worse to come. The show was already in progress that night when the producer decided on another change. He cut Rita out of the hornpipe. The five girls would do it, with Sylvia dancing in the middle of a square formed by the other four. And Rita had already changed into her sailor suit ready to go on. They left her in the wings with her throat tight and her eyes full, watching them dance the hornpipe, watching the comedian totter on to the stage as a drunken sailor, with too much red on his nose.

The morning after, Pearl got out of bed and went over to the dressing-table to get her cigarettes. She put one between her lips, lit it with the fourth flick of her lighter and looked at Rita lying there with her eyes half open, seeing nothing but her own thoughts. She sat down on the edge of Rita's bed and said: 'You're not still thinking about it, are you?'

'Of course I am,' Rita replied sullenly. 'I shall think of it every minute of every day until the show's finished.'

'Oh come on, love,' Pearl said softly. 'You're going to make the rest of us miserable as well, you know.'

'It's not fair,' Rita said. 'Why should I have my parts in the show taken off me just because I refused to be raped?'

'Well I'm afraid, love, we're at the butt end of the business

234

and there's very little we can do about such things, is there? I mean, if you won't get in touch with your agent . . .' She flicked her ash on to the bedside rug, drew on her cigarette and went on: 'The trouble is, Rita, that you did it all wrong. I know you're only sixteen and you don't know much, but the thing to have done with Randall Axter was to play him along a bit. Let him have a grope around but not let him go too far. You see, a man like that with a girl like you is a bit like a little boy let loose in a sweet shop. He wants more than is good for him, more than he can really appreciate at one go. Play him along, that's the thing.'

'That's what you'd have done, is it?' Rita asked her in a doubting way.

'I did it,' Pearl said.

Rita turned and looked at her. 'You did what?'

'I played somebody along, just like I've been saying. Then, when I thought it would be worth my while, I let him have me. It was before the war. Mind you, he was a bit more presentable than Randall Axter. He was on the way up in the theatrical world. I wanted work and he wanted me in bed. So I played him along. He got me some good jobs. A whole year in a show in London. Only in the chorus, naturally, but it was grand. Then straight into pantomime and after that a summer season in Blackpool. George Formby. And this man of mine used to come up to Blackpool once a week just to get into bed with little old me.'

'Disgusting,' Rita said. 'And where did it all get you?'

'Well, that was the war, wasn't it?' Pearl told her. 'I mean, he joined up and got killed. So that was that. And all the clothes and things he bought me I lost in the blitz. Everything. Nothing but memories now.' She got off the edge of Rita's bed, took one last draw on her cigarette, then stubbed it out in the ashtray on the dressing-table. Then she got back into bed.

'I'm sorry about that,' Rita said. 'I suppose you thought you were doing the right thing, though. But I know one thing. They wouldn't have treated my mother the way they treated me. She wouldn't have let them get away with it.'

'I don't suppose she was much different to you when she was sixteen,' Pearl said.

But Rita thought about it for a long time, while Pearl got

up, dressed and made up her face. Rita lay in her bed and wondered what her mother would have done, what little scheme or trick she would have thought up to get her own back. And she got an idea from somewhere, an idea that would settle the whole thing.

Rita went with the others to the theatre that night. The producer was still looking smugly happy at the way Randall Axter had made it possible for him to get his revenge on Rita for the way she had spoken to him, the way she had jabbed him in the chest with her finger, the way she had looked down at him. The girls went into the opening number, the show got under way and later, while the other five were dancing the hornpipe, with the comedian standing ready to make his entrance, Rita shut herself in the dressing-room, quickly changed into her outdoor clothes and slipped out through the stage door into the street. She went back to her digs, went in silently and unseen, packed her suitcase and went out again, any noise she might have made being drowned by the sound of dance music coming from the land-lady's wireless.

Twenty Three

Rita went to the station and took a train to Crewe. From there she caught a connection to London, where she arrived in the early hours of the morning. She took refuge from the winter cold in the airless warmth of the waiting-room and spent the rest of the night there with the other sleeping, murmuring people. Some of them left at various times to catch trains, to be replaced by others who had just got off trains, and who joined the residue there who had no luggage, who neither came nor went, but slept and smoked and complained every time the door was opened, as if the place was home to them.

When she had booked in at the YWCA, Rita telephoned Mrs Brite and told her the whole story in one long sentence, with as few pauses for breath as was possible. Mrs Brite passed no comment but told her to come and see her at her office at four-thirty.

Even when Rita went to the office, sat in front of her and told her the whole story again, Mrs Brite expressed neither rage nor disgust, not even amazement. She did not do what Rita hoped she might, grab the telephone and get Randall Axter on the line. Instead, she said: 'Well, you've had a rotten start, haven't you? Still, that's show business. To tell you the truth, I didn't think you'd stick with the show as long as you did. Sixteen, no mother, father away from home, living with your grandmother. Most girls in that situation would think about leaving home.'

'But it's always been my ambition . . .' Rita began.

But Mrs Brite cut her short. 'I honestly thought that putting you in a show that was touring the Midlands and North would make it easy for you if you wanted to give it up and go back home. Have you been back home?'

'No,' Rita said, 'I came straight here. What was there to go back there for? I'd never become a film star by doing that.'

'All right,' Mrs Brite said, smiling. 'Let's put the past behind us. No good bothering ourselves with that any more. I must admit, Rita, that I took you on because of your looks as much as for anything else. But I reckon you've got more than looks. So, we'll see what else we can get you a part in.'

'Of course, I'd prefer a screen test,' Rita burst out, 'but if there's no chance of that, then I'd love to get back on the stage. I really liked it, I did. And now the war's well and truly over, there should be plenty of jobs going, shouldn't there?'

'I don't know about there being plenty of jobs,' Mrs Brite told her, 'but there are plenty of people after jobs. I've had every girl who ever appeared in a WAAF or ATS camp concert coming up the stairs, confident that what pleased a tent full of bored servicemen during the war will send West End audiences wild. You'd hardly believe it. No, you just bide your time, Rita, and we'll see what turns up. Just come in every day and see if there's anything. Call at the outer office and leave the rest to me.'

Call at the outer office, Rita said to herself as she went back down the stairs. That was exactly as she had seen it in films. Girls calling at agents' offices day after day, never getting any further than the woman in the outer office. Misery was written all over her face as she went out into the street. It had rained and the air was cold. The streets were full of the bright headlights of buses and cars, the pavements thronged with people who had just left work, people who were hurrying home, disappearing into the underground, joining bus queues. Everyone was moving briskly along with a purpose, except for Rita. A bus stopped, the queue began to shuffle forward, the conductor shouted: 'Move down inside.' A girl looked down from a steamed-up window on the top deck, looked out into the wet street at Rita in her white mac and her headscarf, slowly walking along among the teeming rush-hour tide. The conductor gave the full bus three bells and the girl went on homewards. Rita walked slowly back to the YWCA.

The following morning she added up all her money, did a bit of arithmetic, counted the clothing coupons she had bought and saved over the months and gave Mrs Brite a fortnight. Then she went out and bought herself a long black evening gown, leaving herself two weeks from starvation, an office job or a dismal trip back to Manchester. The gown was what she had longed for. It was low cut, showed off her cleavage, accentuated her salt cellars, but clung to her like a coat of shiny black paint. It was a dream come true.

There was nothing at the outer office. Every morning she went there, to the dowdy room and the woman who did nothing more than shake her head and say: 'Nothing today, dear.' There were always girls there, sitting with their hand-bags on their knees and smoking. One morning the woman said to her: 'Don't forget to sign on at the labour exchange, dear. Mrs Brite said to tell you.'

Rita thought of her dwindling exchequer and went to the labour exchange, but she did not go inside. The sight of the queue put her off, the way they all looked at her as she went by in her white mac, her high heels, with a sheen on her jet black hair and that red lipstick on her lips. She could not bring herself to join the queue. There was nothing but problems. There was everything but an answer. Life became a wet day beneath a leaden sky.

The fortnight stretched into three weeks, but too many visits to the cinema and the theatre made her money dwindle quickly. 'Why don't you get yourself a job to tide you over?' the woman at the outer office said one morning. 'Get the *Daily Telegraph* and find yourself a little job.'

'I suppose Mrs Brite told you to say that too,' Rita said grumpily, stalked off down the stairs and went window-shopping at jewellers and expensive gown shops, slipping into a store now and again for a warm when she got too cold.

Whether she was being cruel to be kind, Rita was not mature enought to detect, but the next remark did it. 'You can phone in instead of traipsing here every day,' the woman said as Rita stood once more on the worn lino in front of her desk.

Rita turned on her heel and vowed to herself that she would never again step inside that office unless she was asked to by Mrs Brite. Her money had almost gone. Only pride and her ambition were keeping her going. But the way the woman was casting her as a failure was too much; the schoolmistressy way in which she spoke to her seemed intended as discouragement. Rita decided there and then to choose independence. She went into the first newsagent's she came across, bought the *Daily Telegraph*, went into a café and bought a cup of very weak, very hot tea, and then looked through the female vacancies. There were dozens of jobs for shorthand typists. She sipped her tea. Shorthand, she thought, shorthand. I must be rusty. It was last July . . . She took a pencil out of her handbag and tried writing an imaginary business letter along the edge of the newspaper. But it had gone. Her shorthand had gone. She had forgotten almost all of it.

She spent the rest of the day trying to recall something from those hours she had spent taking dictation at the technical college, but only the elementary stuff came back. Desperately, she tore a sheet of paper out of her writing pad, drew the keyboard of a typewriter on it and practised typing. With relief she found she could remember how to type, knew where every letter lay.

The following morning she bought the *Daily Telegraph* again, prayed as she walked down the street to the café, and looked for a job as a copy typist. And not only did she see one, but it was temporary. There was a telephone number. She rang, was told to go for an interview straight away, got on the tube, and found herself in a street of tall terraced houses, each with a title in gold letters on the front window. She was looking for Patterson's Graphics, an advertising agency. When she found it she went up the steps, through the front door and tapped on a glass panel marked: 'Inquiries.' A woman came out of the office and took her to a room on the first floor.

Mr Patterson, a grey-haired man sitting at a desk that was inches deep in paper, gave her the job straight away. His heart gave her the job. That face, those eyes, that black hair, that figure. 'Our other girl has had to go into hospital for an operation, but she's coming back when she's well again. It's thirty-five shillings a week.'

'Is that all?' Rita retorted. 'I was getting more than twice that . . .'

'Well, you're not on the stage here, Miss Rigby,' he said, not unpleasantly.

'Oh, all right then,' she said. 'Do you want me to take a typing test?'

'No.' With her looks, he decided to take a chance. 'When can you start?'

'Now,' she said. It was freezing outside, but it was warm in there, and it would be another day's wages, she thought.

Mr Patterson took her back downstairs to the office with the inquiry window, to Mrs Phipps, who was about forty, and who sat at her typewriter with a cardigan around her shoulders. The office almost glowed with warmth. There was the odd smell of scorching furniture from Mrs Phipps's desk, which was too close to the electric fire. Only the two of them worked in there. Rita's typewriting technique soon came back to her, her speed increased and by lunchtime she was rattling away on her typewriter confidently.

In the middle of the afternoon, Mrs Phipps said to her: 'Nip round the corner to the tobacconist's and get me an ounce of AI cigarette tobacco, will you? If he says he's got none, say it's for me.'

Rita got the tobacco and telephoned the agency from a call box. 'Nothing today, dear,' the woman said, almost before Rita had told her who she was.

When she got back to the office, she gave Mrs Phipps the tobacco and was surprised to see her take out a leather tobacco pouch and put the ounce of AI inside. She then took out a cigarette roller, rolled three cigarettes, put two into a small silver cigarette case and put the other in her mouth. As she lit it, she said: 'I started rolling my own during the war, when there weren't any fags about. Got to prefer it.'

'My mother always did well out of the Yanks for cigarettes,' Rita remarked. 'Never without her Camel or her Lucky Strike.'

'That was all right if you knew any Yanks,' Mrs Phipps commented.

The casting off of the anxiety she felt over her money dwindling away helped Rita to settle into the job. She wrote home for the first time since she had left the revue and told her grandmother that she was in London rehearsing a new show. But she could not forget the revue. We would just be starting the matineé now, she would think to herself on an afternoon.

About now I would be doing the restaurant sketch. Just at this time we would be in the dressing-room helping to put each other's feathers on for the finale.

It was the same in the evenings, even at the cinema. She relived it all. One glance at the cinema clock would bring to mind exactly what she would have been doing at that time, even if it was just standing in the wings watching Francine Gurr and Hector Wilsby trying to do as well with a number as Jeanette MacDonald and Nelson Eddy would.

The pay packet she received every Friday gave Rita the satisfaction and the patience to remain at the job, rather than put into action the odd schemes to get into films that she conjured up in her imagination. Mrs Phipps let her ring the agency on the office telephone and used to giggle as Rita mouthed the answer the woman in the outer office always gave: 'Nothing today, dear.' Then, when a month had gone by and Rita had copied down the addresses of all the film companies she could find in the telephone directory and had begun to type out a letter that got no further than 'Dear Mr Rank,' because she did not think that the YWCA was a good enough address to write from, someone barged into the office without knocking one morning, and said: 'Hello, how's old mother Phipps?'

Rita looked up and saw the baggy corduroys, the fat stomach bulging through a well worn jacket, the dense ginger beard with the end of a cigarette just visible in the middle of it, glowing red like a traffic light as he drew on it. 'Oh, hello Laurence,' Rita said.

He looked at her, squinted as the cigarette smoke drifted up into his eyes, but said nothing.

'Rita Rigby,' she said. 'You did my photographs. Mrs Brite sent me to you.'

'Ah yes,' he said, 'I remember you.' He looked at Mrs Phipps and said: 'Is he in?'

'Yes, you can go up,' she said.

He turned to Rita. 'What are you doing here?'

'Earning an honest living,' she said brightly.

'I thought old mother Brite had launched you,' he said, taking the cigarette out of his mouth and spitting a bit of tobacco indiscriminately in her direction.

'Well, the show ended, so I'm doing this until something

242

else turns up.'

He put the cigarette back between his lips. 'You shouldn't be here,' he said. 'You don't want to end up smoking AI like old mother Phipps, do you? A bit of modelling would be better. What are they paying you, thirty bob?'

'Thirty-five.'

'Five bob for your big blue eyes,' he said and came towards her. He caught hold of her hands. 'You've buggered your nails,' he said, showering her with cigarette ash.

She had. They had broken and split from typing and she had had to cut them down from long rounded points to short half circles. She looked up at him as he studied her hands and she could see where all the hair around the middle of his lips was burnt from his cigarettes.

He let go of her hands. 'Could have used you for the Van-creme ad, but you've got no nails. Still, something might come up.' And he turned away and went out.

'Fancy you knowing Laurence,' Mrs Phipps said. 'He's done a few jobs for us lately. I'm surprised really that you don't go in for being a mannequin. I mean, being tall and slim and knowing Laurence.'

'I don't think my accent's posh enough,' Rita replied and went back to thinking of the revue, of being in a different town every week, another theatre with a shabby dressing-room, another audience alive out there in the darkness, another band just like all the other bands never quite able to start a number altogether. Then somehow her memory brought to her the fact that the anniversary of her mother's death had passed and she had forgotten to keep a promise she had made to herself, to visit the grave on that very day every year. When she wrote to her grandmother that weekend, she sent her a ten shilling note to buy flowers.

A couple of weeks later Rita was seventeen. She had cards from her grandmother and Ronnie and Anne. That Saturday morning, she said to Mrs Phipps: 'I went to the pictures last night. Fred Astaire. Quite frankly, I don't think he's worth all the fuss they make of him. I'll admit, he can dance, but he just doesn't look right for the parts he plays. No good-looking woman would give him a second glance. I mean, he's too old and too thin and he's got a face like a dented kettle. He came on wearing a white suit, with his little bit of hair

243

flattened down, and he looked just like a safety match. And as for his singing, well, Jack Buchanan could give him a lesson or two there.'

Mrs Phipps listened as she typed. She had become used, over the weeks, to having to listen to Rita's morning discourse on the film she had seen the night before. Usually she had to listen to the whole story and her own personal criticisms as well. She waited until she had finished with Fred Astaire, then said: 'Nip round to the tobacconist's for me, will you? An ounce of AI and a packet of flints for my lighter.'

Rita walked round to the shop, took her sweet coupons with her and bought an ounce of pear drops, and although she did not feel unhappy, she felt now that everything had gone so wrong that it would never come right again. It would have been better, she thought, if she had let her father take her home. It would have been better if she had taken Mrs Runciman's advice and gone into weekly rep. That, she admitted to herself, would have been real acting. She walked slowly back to the office and got on with her work, watched Mrs Phipps roll herself a cigarette, noticed how she always pinched the end of it together with her fingers before placing it between her lips, and smiled at her inability to keep a cigarette alight, always having to relight it at least three times before she got to the end of it. There was nothing she could do now, Rita thought, but work there with Mrs Phipps and wait for something to turn up.

At midday, the door was flung open. It banged back against the wall. It was Mrs Brite. Her hair was awry and her eyes wide and staring. 'Come on,' she yelled at Rita, 'come on. Train to catch.' She grabbed Rita by the arm and dragged her off her chair.

'Hang on,' Rita protested. 'What's happening?'

Mrs Brite let go of her. 'I've got you a part. There's a train to catch. Come on.'

Rita reached for her coat and at the same time she said: 'I can't go just like that. I'll have to work a week's notice.'

'No time, no time. They're waiting for you,' Mrs Brite shouted, pulling her towards the door. 'You'll explain it, dear, won't you? You'll explain it,' she said to Mrs Phipps, who was sitting there looking startled by what was going on, unable either to speak or move.

Rita grabbed her handbag and the last Mrs Phipps saw of her she was being pulled by her arm through the doorway by the excited, panicky Mrs Brite. On her desk, Rita had left a paper bag with her pear drops in it.

Twenty Four

It was a sunny day, the sea was blue, there were white waves coming up the beach and the theatre was on the promenade. Mrs Brite had given Rita a copy of the play to read on the train. Hers was a small part, the maid in a country house. In one place she noticed the instruction: 'Pinches maid's bottom again,' pondered over that for a moment, then remembered that it was a comedy. And there was the title on the front of the theatre: 'A Blue Moon Rising.'

The Saturday afternoon matinée had finished when she got to the theatre. She went to the stage door and asked for Mr Fox, the director. Everyone else had gone but he was still there. He saw her before she saw him. He saw her tall, with the first curves of a beautiful body, black hair, dark eyes full of life, skin like silk, and red, red lips.

'So you've come to save the show, have you?' he said, in a voice that was quiet with surprise. 'We've been touring the south of England. One more booking along the coast, two weeks in Brighton and then we're going into the West End. I suppose Mrs Brite told you?'

'Yes, she told me,' Rita said.

'We're taking a chance with you,' he went on, 'but if you're as good as you are beautiful, you should do. Have you learned your lines?'

'I read the play through quickly on the train,' she replied.

'Well, we're depending on you. The girl who originally played the part broke her leg. And the understudy dies a death in a different part of the play every night.'

'Heavens,' Rita said 'I hope they haven't gone to all that trouble just for me.'

He laughed. 'Come and see the performance tonight,' he said pleasantly. 'Take no notice of the girl playing your part.

246

All that training and she ends up with stage fright. She threatened suicide rather than go on after tonight. Locked herself in the lavatory and made us promise.'

'Hard to commit suicide in a lavatory,' Rita said casually. 'Limits one's choice somewhat.'

He laughed again. He liked the girl. She had confidence and did not seem afraid of someone else's failure. 'Be here at ten tomorrow morning and we'll run through your part, just you and I. I shall play all the other parts. Then you'll have to get word perfect ready for a run through with the cast on Monday morning. All being well, you'll tread the boards on Monday night. All right?'

'Fine,' she replied. 'Any idea where I can get digs?'

'Come, we'll see George, the stage doorkeeper. He'll tell you of a place where the young virgins may rest unmolested.'

She saw the play. The girl who took the part of the maid was awful. She had to be prompted time and again and had a look on her face more of horror than of fright. But the rest of the cast were good and were not shaken out of doing their best by the girl's performance. It was a good play too. Rita enjoyed it. And she had no qualms about playing the part at all. In the revue it had been all quick changes and something different in every scene in which she had been involved. To play just one part, and the part she had just watched, was going to be easy in comparison.

After the performance she met the cast. They all gathered for a drink in the theatre bar before going their separate ways for one day. The woman who played the lead had long silver hair, the like of which Rita had only ever seen in a Technicolor movie. She looked about thirty-five. She was not good-looking, but she was very attractive. 'Welcome, darling,' she said in a baby voice that seemed to be put on. 'I'm Lottie. This is Thorpe, my husband.'

Thorpe had the part of Lottie's husband in the play, as well. He was a slim man with a moustache, who looked and sounded as upper crust as the character he played. 'Greetings, dear child,' he said.

'Humphrey, come and meet Rita,' Lottie said to the red-faced fat man who had romped gruff and belligerent about the stage. 'Come along, Shirley,' to the other member of the small cast, and Rita felt that she was going to like being with them, was going to be happier in the play than she had been in the revue.

'Arnold, you really are clever,' Lottie said to Mr Fox. 'Where did you find this lovely sweet thing? Isn't she lovely, Thorpe?' It was all said in her comical baby voice and all Rita wanted to do was go away and laugh at it. In the play, Rita recalled, Lottie had used the same silly voice and it made her wonder how on earth she got parts to play.

'Lovely,' Thorpe agreed. 'More suitable for having a maid than being one.'

All this fuss, Rita thought, and they had not seen her act yet. She could hardly keep a straight face and when Humphrey wanted to get her another sherry, she said: 'I shouldn't really. I shouldn't drink at all. I'm only seventeen, you know.'

'Only seventeen,' Lottie whooped. 'Thorpe, did you hear? Only seventeen. And so sweet.'

And Rita realized that Lottie had not yet stopped acting.

That night, Rita could not sleep. Her mind was kept awake by the unbelievable, magical good luck of it. On her seventeenth birthday she had been given the chance of a part in a play that was going into the West End, where all the best cinemas were. She would be able to go to the cinema on every afternoon that they did not have a matinée, she dreamed. She might be spotted on stage by a big film producer sitting in the third row of the stalls.

It was just the way things had happened for her mother, she thought, only much grander. In a way, it was the equivalent of Mr Jerome renting her mother a house, of her getting a job at the town hall, of there always being something or someone turning up in a crisis. It was her mother's sort of luck which had enabled her so often to turn up her nose at the hard world in which she had been placed. Her mother had been right, she realized. It was no use just dreaming. But then Rita felt that she had no need to dream.

She and Mr Fox did a hotchpotch rehearsal of her part in the play. They finished at one o'clock. He was pleased with the way she had performed and as they went to the stage door he said: 'I think you'll save our bacon. I shall have to say a big thank you to Laurence if you do, shan't I?'

'Laurence? What's it to do with Laurence?' she asked,

248

raising her eyebrows.

'He was down here the other day,' he said as they went out into the street, into the warm sunshine. 'Said he knew just the girl. Wanted her for modelling work but the suggestion got her agent's back up. You've got Laurence to thank.'

'Well, fancy that,' she said, her face as sunny as the day. 'If he wasn't so hairy and scruffy, I'd go straight up to London and kiss him.'

'Don't take any notice of his appearance. That's his trade mark,' Mr Fox said. 'There'll come a day when people will give their eye teeth to have his name in small letters under their photographs in all the best magazines.'

'And I've already got it,' she said triumphantly.

'Don't get too starry-eyed,' he said laughing. 'Just be ready at three o'clock when I call for you. Our next booking isn't far away, but you'll need time to get acclimatized.'

It may have been only a minor part, but the importance of it had been made obvious to the rest of the company during the previous week. But Rita was a born actress. She lived her little part, and the fact that she was tall, slim and beautiful, did not look like a maid in a country house, and still had more of her Lancashire accent left than she realized, made no difference. She was a maid in a country house, she acted so much like one that the audience saw her as nothing else.

Rita could not make out what all the fuss was about. After her first performance Lottie and Thorpe took everyone out for a drink, and although Rita did not mind being kissed by them all for doing it so well, Lottie piped on and on in her childish voice with as much praise as Rita imagined Flora Robson had received in a lifetime. It was a relief when she stopped for breath or a drink. But no one seemed at all surprised by her manner.

'My father is in the RAF,' Rita said to Humphrey, when Lottie had run out of words extravagant enough to describe Rita's performance. 'He flew Hurricanes during the war and now he's flying one of those aeroplanes without a propeller, you know, one of those gas jet things.'

'A jet aeroplane, you mean,' Humphrey corrected her. 'He must be pretty well up to fly one of those.'

'Well, he's a squadron leader,' Rita said, using her father's position just as her mother had done, forgetting the animosity for a while and making capital out of him being an officer.

'I decided straight away not to lower my standards one inch because of old Hitler and his war,' Lottie suddenly declared in the fluting tones of a determined six-year-old. 'And there was I, sleeping under a bed at the Savoy, while Thorpe was away in the army enduring that awful khaki suit they made him wear and minus all the hair above his ears.' She leaned against Thorpe, gazed up at him and went on: 'Thorpee, darling, I can't ever believe that you fired off that gun they gave you. I just can't, so there.'

At the end of that first week, Rita had a birthday card from her father. It had reached her via the YWCA, Patterson's Graphics, Laurence and Mrs Brite. There was a cheque and the message: 'I understand young actresses never get enough to eat, so have a blow-out on me.'

She did not look upon the card and the gift as creating an excuse to heal the breach between them, but she had the courtesy to write and thank him and she managed to expand on her solitary week with the play to make the letter read as if she had been with it during the whole of its tour. The weeks as a copy typist were not mentioned. She wrote a similar letter to Anne, full of the small, sweet lies that her mother used to trot out at the drop of a hat to get what she wanted or to impress. And Rita wanted to impress.

She saved the money. It did not seem the time to spend rashly. Even there in the south of England there were bomb-sites as a reminder of the time that had just passed and although they looked different in the sunshine, with the stately look of ancient ruins, an impression that the grime and the rain of the north had denied the bomb damage there, they seemed to stand as a warning to be cautious. There were still endless queues at the shops, rations seemed to get smaller and clothing coupons could be bought at half a crown each from people who, for reasons that no one ever went into, had them and did not want them for themselves. That was the difference in character between Rita and her mother. With her mother it had been spend, regret, hope. With Rita it was all hope

On the Sunday, Humphrey drove Rita and Shirley to Brighton in his MG. They sat in the back, cramped up with not enough room for their legs, surrounded by luggage, with the hood up, the wind making their hair stream out behind them, and only able to communicate by shouting.

'Lottie and Thorpe were in the West End before the war,' Shirley said at the top of her voice, 'so it's nothing new to them. I couldn't believe my luck when I got my part. I mean, the West End. Heaven knows what will follow.' She took a deep breath. 'Lottie's going to throw another of her parties while we're at Brighton,' she yelled. 'We've had a couple of wizard ones on tour. You'll be able to meet Desmond then, my boyfriend. He always comes to Lottie's parties.'

'I hope they're not wild drunken affairs,' Rita said, managing to sound prim while bellowing at full force.

'No, we only go for the food,' Shirley replied, her voice forcing its way through the wind. 'I mean, there's always lots of food.'

'Food?' Rita screamed back. 'Wherever does she get food from?'

'The black market, I suppose,' Shirley replied, lowering her voice as they started to go slowly up a long steep hill, the engine of the MG whining with the strain, sounding just like a kettle singing on the hob.

'Well that's not right,' Rita declared, 'not with half the country crying out for a crust of bread to mop up their gravy with.' She fell silent then, because suddenly she remembered the smuggling that had gone on from the American camp, the sugar, the dried egg powder and the corned beef that had been stacked up behind the sofa in the front room.

'You won't say that when you walk into Lottie's party with your stomach rumbling,' Shirley told her. And as the car crept to the top of the hill, she said: 'You do understand about me saying I didn't want to share a room in Brighton, don't you? With Desmond coming down now and again, it just wouldn't work. I mean, you'd just have to wait outside sort of, wouldn't you?' she observed awkwardly.

'Oh, I understand,' Rita said pleasantly as the car swept down the other side of the hill making the air whoosh suddenly past her ears. 'Anyway, I expect he has enough trouble clambering down drainpipes.'

They had a wonderful opening in Brighton. Lottie and Thorpe were besieged in their dressing-rooms on some

251

nights and Lottie told Rita that the people were all friends from London who had travelled down to see the play, the sense of which Rita could not see since the play was going to London anyway. But she did not raise that point with Lottie because, even when she said sensible things, with her canary trill of a voice she sounded absolutely ridiculous, and Rita knew that her mother would have made mincemeat of her in seconds.

One afternoon, when they had finished a matinée, Lottie called Rita into her dressing-room. She was sitting before the mirror in her petticoat, brushing her long, silver hair. 'Rita, darling,' she said in her little girl's voice, 'you will come to our party, won't you? I shall play up no end if you say no.'

'Of course I shall come,' Rita said. 'I'm looking forward to it.'

'You must go to lots of parties if you want to be a great actress or a film star. It's the only way,' Lottie declared. 'You meet such important people at parties.'

Rita watched her brushing her hair and wondered what she dyed it with to turn it that colour. Then she asked her: 'Is Carlotta Trevane your real name, Lottie?'

'Of course it is my sweet, truly,' she replied.

'I thought I'd keep my own name because it doesn't take up much space on billings and programmes and things,' Rita stated. 'When I was at school, I used to think of using my mother's name. Her maiden name was Isabella Ackerman, but whenever I wrote it out to see how effective it looked, it seemed so long. I thought that if they ever had to put that up in lights they'd have to send out for more bulbs, and borrow a bit of the building next door.'

'Names are very important in the theatre,' Lottie agreed. 'Do you know, I bought a little book full of names when I was expecting our little one, to be sure that Thorpe and I made the right choice.'

'Heavens,' Rita exclaimed, 'have you got children?' Lottie looked the sort of person who had never exerted herself. She gave Rita the impression that she would be unable to eat a grape unless it had been peeled for her and had had all the pips removed.

'Child, Rita,' Lottie corrected her. 'Our little Sebastian is twelve now. He's at boarding school. Come the hols and he'll be all over the place, asking questions, doing things he shouldn't.'

Lottie put on her dress and Rita zipped it up for her. 'I'm not getting married,' Rita said firmly. 'My mother was let down by a man. I'm not having that happen to me.'

'Really? And that photo you have of your daddy, he looks so nice in his air force uniform,' Lottie commented.

'It wasn't my father who let her down,' Rita said. 'It was her American boyfriend. Let her down very badly.'

'Was that before she was married?' Lottie asked her gently.

'No. My mother had lots of boyfriends. Everybody liked my mother. Of course, she shouldn't have done it, being married, I know. Still, it serves as a warning to me.' She thought for a minute, then said: 'I wouldn't mind getting married if I met someone really suitable, like you met your Thorpe, but I don't really fancy all that carrying on in bed. From what I've heard, it doesn't seem very hygienic.'

'That is the trouble with a man in bed,' Lottie admitted. 'He does tend to come between a girl and her top sheet.'

Lottie held her party on the Sunday evening that began their final week in Brighton. The food that Shirley had spoken of was layed out on a long table and was of such an array that, in Rita's mind, it made her mother's wartime Sunday teas seem both miserable and innocent in comparison.

Rita grabbed a plate and began eating, oblivious of the other people there, deaf to the music that the quartet was playing, careless of the fact that there might have been someone there from the film world who would have listened with interest to her inquiries on how to get a screen test.

'This is real meat,' she said excitedly to Shirley, lifting the top slice from one of the tiny triangular sandwiches on her plate. 'And look. Those are peaches in that trifle.' She jabbed a finger at the dish of trifle that Desmond had just cut into with his spoon. 'Peaches,' she said again in amazement and she looked at the table, wondered how many trifles she would be able to eat without it becoming noticed and began stuffing the meat sandwiches into her mouth in order to get started on them as quickly as possible.

She wolfed as much food as she could as inconspicuously

as possible, with no thought for the consequences, and no sooner had she sat down, feeling very full and a little uncomfortable, than Lottie came across to her with a face that was all pouting lips and pleading expression and asked her to sing. 'Sing us something from that lovely musical show you were in, please, darling, do.'

'None of those songs were singable anywhere else,' Rita proclaimed. 'And anyway, I've got an awful voice. I've got the sort of voice that would stop ships going aground on the Goodwin Sands.'

'Well, we're by the sea, so that won't matter,' Thorpe said and they dragged her away to the piano.

Rita sang 'Blue Moon', full of the feeling that at any moment she was going to be sick over everyone. The moment they had finished applauding she went through the french windows on to the veranda where it was dark and a little too chilly for anyone else to venture and made loud relieving noises.

She stood behind some potted plants, leaned against the wall and remained there until she felt better, until she felt that the food had gone down so far that it would not come up again. While she was standing there she thought of one of her mother's instructions to her. 'If you're anywhere posh and you want to let go of your wind, always go outside and do it. Don't go sneaking it out in company and sharing it with everyone else.'

Rita laughed at the memory of it. She realized that she must have a little of her mother's fault of doing things to excess, when she remembered the nights she had lain in bed and had heard her mother come home, had heard her come in through the front door, dash down the hallway, through the kitchen, out of the back door, into the outside lavatory and be heartily sick. And yet, the following morning, she had always been full of talk about the wonderful time she had had the night before, how she had not enjoyed herself so much for years. Rita was glad she had never contradicted her.

Twenty Five

❦

They completed their run in Brighton and then off they went to London, to the West End, to a first night audience, black and white with shirt fronts and dinner jackets, shining with silk evening gowns and sparkling jewellery.

Rita had no nerves. To her it was no different from any other opening night. It was just a posher house. She went into Lottie's dressing-room and found it to be a mass of flowers. There were telegrams all over the place. 'Lottie, you really are famous,' she said with amazement. 'Can I come in after the show and read all your telegrams?'

'Of course you may, my darling,' Lottie told her.

The first night audience laughed uproariously at all the funny parts in the play, hooted with enjoyment even when Rita had her bottom pinched again. And after the cheers and shouts and curtain calls, and all the yelling for Carlotta and Thorpe, and a speech from the old man who had written the play and whom Rita saw for the first time that evening, she went into Lottie's dressing-room to read the telegrams, while people came and went, kissing and gushing, and Lottie's baby voice squeaked away higher and higher.

The opening-night party was held at a nightclub. Rita went in her solitary black evening gown, feeling that success had arrived and that fame was just around the corner, although Lottie was the centre of attraction to the exclusion of the others, squealing with delight and babbling away like a tiny tot at every word of praise she received. Rita saw Laurence at the party, looking smarter than she could ever have imagined him in his dinner jacket. She went straight over to him. He had a drink in one hand and was smoking a cigar which, unlike when he was smoking a cigarette, he did not keep permanently in his mouth, but had a puff at it and then held it between his fingers. A safety precaution, she thought as she approached him.

'Laurence, it really was sweet of you to put a word in for me with Mr Fox,' she began. If he had not been so hairy she would have kissed him, but there did not seem to be a suitable place left on his face for anyone to do so.

'That's all right,' he said, hardly looking at her. 'Next time you want any photographs done, make sure you come to me.'

'Oh, I will,' she assured him.

'That's good. Now you're in the West End, I'll charge you double,' he said, his eyes twinkling with a smile that could not penetrate through his beard.

'Come on,' Rita said, 'let's dance.'

He finished his drink and they took to the floor, but dancing with him, she found out, was not an easy thing to do. It was impossible to get close to him because his bulging stomach got in the way; it had the effect of making his arms seem short so that he could only just reach her with his hands.

'What made you think of me?' she asked him. 'I mean, you must know dozens of actresses.'

'Wasting your time at Patterson's,' he said, looking round at the other people rather than at her. 'Could have got you some modelling work. Suggested it to old mother Brite. Looked at me as if she'd wet herself and had just found out that when it runs down your leg it's warm, not cold.'

'Laurence, don't be disgusting,' she chastized him. 'Anyway, now I'm in the West End I don't suppose I shall ever have too much difficulty getting work, shall I?'

'You're not playing Lady Macbeth,' he said. He had three or four hard puffs at his cigar to keep it alight, then said to her: 'Your trouble is you're too glamorous too young. That's why you ended up working at Patterson's. Photographic modelling would suit you. Pays well. You want to remember that when you're unemployed again. Might be able to make a mannequin out of you. I could help you in that direction, if ever you're interested.'

'Oh Laurence, that is kind of you,' she said, trying to sound grateful even though she had no intention at all of becoming a mannequin.

'You're tall and slim,' he said, unintentionally blowing his cigar smoke in her hair, 'but we'd have to get rid of your Lancashire accent. You still sound as if you work in a tripe and onion factory.'

'Well, thank you very much,' she retorted. 'If ever your beard catches fire, don't expect me to run for a bucket of water.'

The party went on all night. They were still drinking and dancing when Rita left at four o'clock, when she went outside to be hit by the cold morning air, sent as giddy by it as she had been by the too many drinks she had drunk. A taxi took her home. It was raining gently then, but when she woke up at midday with her mouth tasting as if she had drunk metal polish, there was a beam of sunlight streaming in through the gap where she had failed to draw the curtains together that was too bright for her eyes.

After a while, when she came to the opinion that the only way to go on living was to struggle a bit, she got out of bed and went into Shirley's room next door. Shirley was in bed asleep, with all her clothes on.

'It's funny,' Rita said, 'we've been here a month now. It's the longest I've ever been in one theatre. I'm beginning to feel quite at home.'

Shirley laughed. 'In six months time you'll be sick of the sight of the place.'

It was the middle of the week. They had finished the evening performance and were back in their dressing-room, changing. Rita had taken off the little white apron and the short, tight, dark blue dress she wore in her part and was sitting in front of the mirror, removing her make-up. She said: 'I think I'll start looking round for a flat soon. I mean, the thing is going to run, isn't it?'

'It'll run,' Shirley assured her. 'The reviews were marvellous and Thorpe said the advance bookings cover us for weeks ahead. Anyway, what do you want a flat for?'

'Well, I can afford one,' Rita said. She had wanted to get a flat the moment they had arrived in the West End, but Shirley had advised her to wait just in case the play did not run and they had taken rooms in a theatrical boarding-house instead. 'I want somewhere I can lounge about in,' she went on, 'somewhere I can be untidy in.'

257

'Don't forget you'll have to clear up after yourself too,' Shirley warned her. 'I think I'll stay put for a while.'

There was a knock at the door. It was the stage door-keeper. 'Gentleman to see you,' he told Rita as she poked her head round the door. 'Says he's an old friend.'

'How old?' she asked him.

'Early twenties. Wouldn't give his name. Surprise, he said.'

'Oh, tell him to wait,' Rita said irritably. She closed the door. 'Can't think who it can be. Perhaps he'll get fed up and go away. Now, what did you say? You're going to stay put? Well, you're hardly ever there anyway, are you?' She pulled her dress on over her head and said from inside it: 'You're always getting on the underground and going off to Desmond's.'

'Well his parents do make me very welcome,' Shirley said.

'It's not his parents making you welcome that keeps you out all night,' Rita said, emerging from her dress. 'You want to be careful. He might get you into trouble. Then how welcome would his parents make you?'

Shirley smiled at Rita's attitude, her stern warning, given as if she were the elder of the two of them. 'I did think I was pregnant once,' she said. 'Of course, that wasn't Desmond. It was when I was in North Africa.'

'In North Africa? Whatever were you doing there?'

'Doing my bit in the war,' Shirley said. 'I was in Ensa. Did troop concerts, dancing and singing. I didn't fancy joining the ATS and marching around in khaki bloomers. And when we went to North Africa, I fell in love with the pianist. Grantly Harcourt, his name was. I used to dream of marrying him and appearing on the stage as Mrs Grantly Harcourt, you know, just like Mrs Patrick Campbell. We used to make love under the desert palms, until I thought I was pregnant.'

'Why did you think you were pregnant?' Rita asked her. 'I mean, I thought men always used one of those rubber things.'

'Well of course he used to use one, but . . . Don't you know anything about love, Rita? Don't you know what passion is? Making love with a man isn't always a calculated thing.'

'It was with my Auntie June,' Rita said. 'She got paid for

258

it.'

'Well anyway,' Shirley went on, 'he was taken ill with a dicky stomach and they put him in the military hospital in Alexandria. And while he was in there he fell in love with a nursing sister. So that was that.'

'How rotten of him,' Rita sympathized. 'What did you do then? It must have been awkward, him playing the piano for you as well.'

'Oh, he didn't, not any more,' Shirley told her. 'They sent him home because of his stomach. The ship he was on got sunk in the Bay of Biscay. Poor Grantly was drowned.'

'How dreadful,' Rita said in a hushed voice. 'I'll bet that knocked your performances for six.'

'I didn't find out about it until sometime afterwards,' Shirley said. 'We were a bit out of touch, traipsing around Egypt and Libya in the back of an army lorry. Saw the pyramids and the sphinx. You do miss civilization when you're in the desert, though, Rita. I can't tell you what a luxury it was to sit on a proper lavatory again, to pull the chain and see it all disappear.'

'Lucky you weren't pregnant after all,' Rita commented gently.

'I was glad Grantly and I had each other when we did, though,' Shirley admitted. 'After all, you never know when it's all going to come to a sudden end, even in peacetime. That's why Desmond and I are together so much. You never know.'

Rita agreed but said nothing. She thought of her mother getting all dolled up to go out that night, and never being able to get dolled up to go out again. She thought of herself, the things she wanted in life, and realized that, young though she was, this might be the only chance in life she would have to get those things; the screen test, success as a film actress, the sort of home her mother had always wanted, revenge on a man called Chuck.

'Right, are you ready?' Shirley asked her. 'Hey, I wonder if that man's still waiting?'

'Couldn't care less,' Rita stated. 'The only man I'll ever hurry for is the big film producer who offers me a starring part.' And she put on her coat, buttoned it up, checked her face in the mirror, taking her time as if no one mattered at that moment but herself, just as her mother would have done.

But he was still there when they left the dressing-room, standing in the dim light just inside the stage door.

'What are you going to say to him if he only wants your autograph?' Shirley asked her, as they looked at him from a safe distance.

'Wouldn't have stood there all this time waiting for an autograph, not mine anyway,' Rita replied.

'Well come on then,' Shirley said, 'if we're going to get a taxi.'

'Let's just walk along and see what he says,' Rita decided. She could cut anybody dead, she knew that.

But he heard them coming, turned towards them, smiled and said: 'Hello, Rita. Do you remember me?'

She knew him from somewhere, though she could not immediately recall the place. He was a pleasant-looking man, fresh faced, neat hair, smart in a double breasted overcoat and a silk scarf.

'I'm afraid not,' Rita said, still walking towards the stage door, her nose in the air.

'Perhaps I should have worn my brown trilby,' he said.

She walked a few more paces, then stopped. She turned and looked at him in silence, saw him smiling at her. 'You,' she said. 'You've come to get your revenge.'

'Nothing of the kind,' he said laughing. 'I work in London now. I've just seen the play – thought we might go out to supper.'

Rita smiled at him. 'Oh, what a pity. I can't.' She glanced at Shirley who was standing just behind her, then said to him: 'I've promised to see Shirley home. She's not feeling very good. She was unwell all through the performance. I'm so sorry.' He said nothing, just stood there looking at her, and so she said: 'Why don't you telephone me one day and we'll have lunch together?'

'Yes, all right,' he said, unable to disguise his disappointment.

Then she said: 'I'm sorry, but I can't remember your name.'

'Ian Chase,' he told her.

'Ah yes,' she said, and they turned and went out through

the stage door, leaving him standing there.

In the taxi, Shirley said: 'Who was that? Who was that man who you thought had come to get revenge?'

'Oh, he's nobody,' Rita told her. 'Just someone I met when I was touring with the revue. I can't say I ever expected to see him again. I couldn't even remember his name. Thank goodness I thought of an excuse.'

The following evening, just before the curtain went up, Rita was called to the telephone. It was Ian Chase. He wanted her to go to lunch with him the following day.

'I'm sorry but I'm lunching with my agent tomorrow,' she said truthfully. 'No, Saturday isn't a good day. We have a matinée, you see . . . Monday? No, Monday I'm having my hair done. What about Tuesday?' She hoped that he would find Tuesday unsuitable, but he did not.

On Friday, for the first time since the occasion months before when she had stormed down those bare wooden stairs in a rage, Rita went to Mrs Brite's office. She opened the door of the outer office. There were three girls sitting on the little wooden chairs. Another girl came out of Mrs Brite's office and the plump, white-faced woman at the desk said: 'Hello, Miss Rigby. Will you go straight in, please?'

Rita did not answer, did not even smile at the woman who had said no more than three unpleasant words to her over the telephone every day for weeks. She just stalked into Mrs Brite's office with her nose in the air and an expression of superiority on her face.

'How many out there, Marjorie?' Mrs Brite said into the telephone. 'Three? Tell them to come back at two-thirty, will you?'

Hearing that gave Rita a grand feeling. Make way for the star, she thought to herself, as she set off to have lunch with Mrs Brite.

'Of course I still want to get into films,' Rita said. 'I know I've been lucky, getting into the West End as quickly as I have. But I want to play my luck before it runs out. I want a screen test.'

Mrs Brite could not avoid those dark eyes that were looking at her, that dominated and were half the case that was being put to her. She said: 'Let's give it a while longer,

261

Rita. I'll get someone to come and see the play just to watch you, someone from films.'

'They're not going to learn much from that, are they?' Rita maintained. 'I only play a maid. The biggest part I had in the revue was as a waitress. I mean, all that qualifies me for is a job in Lyons Corner House.' She turned her head and looked across the restaurant. Her black hair swung, her chin tilted upwards, her red lips parted a little.

Arrogant, Mrs Brite thought, arrogant. But with a little bit of magic. Rita, she reckoned, could have got into a taxi, gone to the film studios and got a screen test for herself. They would not have turned her away, not with her looks and her confidence. The only thing she did not have was knowledge of the business, and Mrs Brite thanked God for that. There would have been a film part easily enough, she knew. And there would have been someone to look after Rita until the next part came along, someone with the same ideas as Randall Axter, but with a bit more finesse. 'The thing is,' Mrs Brite said, 'that you don't have to play Hedda Gabler for a film director to know if he could use you. Get accustomed to the play so that you can give the same good performance week after week, then you won't find it too much of a strain to nip down to the film studios during the daytime to play a small part in a film. That's the way I plan it. What do you think?' She sipped her coffee, looked at Rita and could tell that half her mind was trying to fathom out who or what was Hedda Gabler.

'Yes,' Rita said, 'yes. Small parts, of course.' Then she gathered her thoughts together and said: 'Do you know, Arnold, the director, says we'll run for at least nine months or he's a monkey's uncle. Well, I told him not to bring his relations into it. Anyway, if we get into the autumn, I think I'll have been long enough in the West End by then for it to mean something to J. Arthur Rank or whoever.'

'That's the idea, Rita,' Mrs Brite said. 'And we'll have some more photographs done of you beforehand.'

'Oh yes, I'll nip along to Laurence's when you want me to.'

'Well, you needn't go to Laurence,' Mrs Brite said carefully. 'There are other photographers, you know.'

'No, I'd rather have Laurence take them,' Rita said, and

those dark eyes challenged Mrs Brite and won.

'Very well, dear,' she said.

'Did that revue I was in do any good in London?' Rita asked her.

'It didn't come to London,' Mrs Brite replied. 'It only got as far as the home counties. Guildford or Richmond was as near as it got.'

'It was supposed to come into London. Then there was going to be a musical,' Rita told her.

'Hogwash.' Mrs Brite dismissed Rita's statement with a wave of her hand. 'By the way, I had a girl from that show come to see me one day. Mentioned you.'

'Pearl, was it?' Rita asked, her white teeth flashing as a smile of expectancy crossed her face.

'Girl with bleached hair, mid-twenties.'

'That was Pearl,' Rita proclaimed. 'Did you get her a part?'

Mrs Brite shook her head. 'Don't want any showgirls on my books,' she said and looked at her watch. 'Showgirls are ten a penny. Even you should have learned that in your short time.'

Rita felt disappointed for Pearl, but she had a very quick dream of one day being the famous star who takes her long lost friend out of the back row of the chorus and into the limelight.

'Half-past two. Better be going,' Mrs Brite said.

By the time they reached the street, Rita reckoned, it would be twenty-five to three. Five minutes trying to find a taxi, ten minutes for Mrs Brite to get back to her office. It would be getting on for three o'clock before she saw anyone, and those three girls would have been there at half-past two on the dot, knowing that however much they would like to stub out their last Woodbine in Mrs Brite's face, when they walked along the track in the lino into her office, they would have to be all sweetness and light, and treat her like God.

Rita spent half a minute realizing how lucky she was, then she went to the pictures.

Twenty Six

The taxi came round the corner and drove down the street. Rita could see Ian Chase standing on the pavement outside the restaurant, but he did not notice her until she was closing the taxi door because he was unfamiliar with the life style of an actress and had expected her to come walking down the street or to get off a bus.

To him, she looked more grown up, more beautiful, more of an actress than she had been when he had first seen her all those months before. The sight of her made him feel excited, took his appetite away so that the food stuck in his throat and he had to swallow hard to make it go down.

And he looked different to her, looked very much different to the shabby young man she had frantically rid herself of that Friday night. He was better dressed and seemed more grown up. 'What are you doing in London?' she asked him.

'I'm on the *Daily Herald*,' he said.

'Are you?' she asked with genuine surprise. 'You mean to say you've actually left that comic paper you used to work for?'

'Yes,' he said, lost for words, overcome by the occasion, conscious of the way men at other tables in the restaurant glanced at her. It made him feel inadequate and her remarks did not help.

'I didn't know whether to come out with you or not,' she said. 'I suppose it would be my own fault if you slipped something in my drink and poisoned me. The way I treated you.'

'It was the way you treated me that got me on to the *Daily Herald*,' he told her. 'I mean, after what you said to me I just had to prove you wrong, didn't I? If only for my own satisfaction.'

She wished she had not gone to lunch with him. All the

time he talked he kept looking right into her eyes. He still had that fascination for her, she realized, could not disguise his fondness for her for a second. And yet, although he looked different and had a job on the *Daily Herald*, she had no more feeling for him than she had had the night he had bought her a fish and chip supper. 'There's a lot of water gone under the bridge since then,' she said.

'Yes. We've both come a long way, haven't we?' he replied. 'Me from *The Courier* and the funerals, you from that terrible revue.'

She agreed. 'What are you on the *Herald*? Something important?'

'I'm a reporter. Only a very junior one as yet. But it is a national daily. And they get applications every day from people wanting to get on to a big newspaper.'

'And here's me on the West End stage,' she said. 'Who would have imagined it?'

Who would have imagined, he thought to himself, that he would ever have seen her again, that face and that figure and that voice that had never ever left him, that girl who had hurt him and then apologized, who had helped him and whom he wanted to thank, that girl whom he had been in love with from the moment he had first seen her. But just being with her was overwhelming, she fogged his mind so that all the things he wanted to say were lost in his head. There was nothing but small talk, and when she decided it was time to go he had been unable to make another date with her. For all he knew it might be goodbye for ever.

She was getting into the taxi. She was closing the door, smiling at him, and he had not asked her. His tongue seemed to be paralyzed. His brain told him there were bound to be other men. Could he telephone her again? Where did she live? Had he been able to speak he would have been too frightened to ask. She held the door open a little and said to him: 'Nice to see you again. Do keep in touch.' And she closed the door and the taxi drove away, and all the life and hope came back into his body too late.

'Is that reporter chap still ringing you up?' Shirley asked Rita one Sunday evening. They were at Lottie's flat for a party and Lottie was hugging everyone and squealing at

265

them as they came in. But no one took any notice. They all knew Lottie.

'Is he? Ten out of ten for persistence,' Rita told her. 'I'm running out of excuses. I had to have lunch with him again the other day and quite frankly I talked non-stop the whole time just to prevent him saying what was in his eyes.'

'Lovelight?' Shirley asked.

'Blinding,' Rita admitted.

'You'll have to do something,' Shirley told her. 'Surely you can put him off.'

'I put him off once,' Rita replied. 'That was when I was touring the north. But it didn't work.' She was not going to admit that it was her own fault, that she had been as soft the next morning as she had been hard the night before.

'You really should have a steady,' Shirley advised her. 'It's such an asset when you're in the theatre. You're bound to be pestered, but if you've got a steady you can always use him to put someone else off. You don't have to be in love with him or anything. I'm surprised you don't cotton on to somebody.'

'Oh no,' Rita said firmly. 'I'm not being caught like that. When I'm on the road to fame, then I might think differently. But until then . . .'

'Then I'm afraid you're going to have to break the world record for saying no,' Shirley said.

'Oh, I wish I could think of something,' Rita went on. 'My mother was the one. She would have found a way to get rid of him.'

'What do you reckon she would have done?' Shirley asked her.

Rita thought for a moment. 'She would have told him straight,' she said. 'Mind you, she had plenty of practice doing that. When you looked like my mother, you were always putting men off.'

Shirley could see Rita having to go through life doing the same thing, when she had grown out of the precociousness that, despite her looks, gave her away when she talked. 'Try it,' Shirley said. 'Be blunt, be cruel to be kind. It might work. And now, let's have some food.'

There were always parties and there was always food from the black market. Lottie and Thorpe had a large flat in St

John's Wood and life for them, despite the austerity, the shortages, the rationing, was full of fun and parties. There were parties at their flat, parties at someone else's flat, house parties, parties at hotels and nightclubs, days in the country.

But after one of Lottie's parties, Rita used to wonder sometimes whose food they had been eating, who was going without so that they could enjoy themselves, who had unlocked a door one morning and found their cupboard bare? Her conscience never troubled her a great deal. It just came alive inside her now and again to remind her that she did have one.

Lottie always asked Rita to sing. Her voice was loud and high and she could reach easily all the high notes that everyone else had to strain for. That night Rita sang 'Tangerine' and afterwards Shirley saw her talking non-stop to a refined, silver-haired old actor who was discovering how great an error he had made when he had congratulated her on her singing.

'I bought the music in Woolworth's,' Rita was saying. 'It's a lovely song and I liked the way they used it in the film 'Double Indemnity'. Did you see that film? I thought Fred MacMurray was magnificent, by far his best role. And Edward G. Robinson, I think that was his best part to date too. All those gangster parts he played had to be in preparation for something, didn't they? And I think this was it. As for Barbara Stanwyck, I remember the time I found out she was married to Robert Taylor. Well, I went green with envy, I can tell you, green all over, but I mustn't hold that against her, must I? I will say that she turned in a very creditable performance, equally as good as some of her other starring roles, such as . . .'

The man was too well mannered to interrupt Rita. He just stood there while she chattered away without ever seeming to stop for breath. Her refined tone disappeared and was replaced by flat Lancashire vowels that battered against the man's ears like slates being blown from a roof on a windy night and smashing on the pavement.

Rita admitted to Shirley that it was really her own fault that she had allowed Ian Chase to become such a nuisance to her. She admitted it the following morning while she sat in Shirley's room, watching her paint her toenails scarlet.

267

Rita's eyes hardly blinked, remained unconsciously focused on Shirley's toes, while her voice miserably admitted that it was her own fault.

He had telephoned her so often that she had practically run out of excuses not to go out to lunch with him, or to tea in one of the depressing little cafés that, she imagined, only newspaper reporters could feel comfortable in. 'We could go to the cinema,' he had said, 'but what with you being at work every night and wanting Sunday to rest, when on earth do you get a chance to go?'

'I go on an afternoon,' she had blurted out, 'when everyone else is at work.'

'Well, I'll get an afternoon off then,' he had said and had left Rita cursing herself at the other end of the line.

'And he keeps getting afternoons off,' Rita said, as Shirley finished one set of toes and started on the other. 'He just spoils my enjoyment of the film. I'm conscious of him all the time, just sitting there next to me in the darkness.'

'You don't cart lame ducks around with you in this business,' Shirley told her. 'Cotton on to successful people like Lottie and Thorpe, that's the thing to do. Success is one of those things that rubs off on to people. In the theatre it does, anyway.'

There was no way in which Rita could get out of going to the cinema with Ian Chase that week. She spent the whole afternoon sitting there in the dark trying to think of a gentle way in which she might be able to tell him that she did not want to go out with him at every touch and turn.

When they came out of the cinema and went to have tea in a little café she knew where they did not have thick, bulletproof cups and where the tea was not brought to their table by a man with hair growing all over the backs of his hands, Rita said to Ian: 'Do they mind you having all these half days off?'

'Oh no. In my sort of job, no one ever knows where you are,' he said.

Rita did not believe him and with his lie she saw a way of dislodging him. She said gently, in the well spoken way she used when she was calm: 'I don't believe that, Ian. You should not put your job in jeopardy.'

'I would never see you otherwise,' he said. 'Whenever I'm

free, you are at work.'

'London is full of girls,' she told him.

'Yes,' he agreed, 'but there's only one of them I want to be with.'

'Ian,' she said softly, trying to sound as grown up as she could at seventeen, 'don't sacrifice your career for me. After all, I wouldn't sacrifice mine for anybody. You've got to be realistic. The next job I get might take me anywhere. We might not see each other for ages.'

'That doesn't comfort me any,' he said disconsolately.

She looked at him. He looked so sad, so much like the boy who had taken her to supper at a fish and chip shop. 'Now I'm going to be firm with you, Ian, for your own good,' she stated in a kindly way. 'You must not miss work for me. You must put your career first. That's what I do. I put my career before everything. I do not want to be dated by you or anyone else. And I do not want you telephoning me every five minutes. Once a month we could have lunch together and you could tell me all about the reporting jobs you've been doing for the *Daily Herald*, but that is all. That is sufficient.' She stopped then and waited to see his reaction. She was pleased at the way she had said it. Her mother would have shouted, would have sworn, would have been cruel without thinking.

He was silent for a moment, then he said very quietly: 'It's not enough, Rita. Since I met you I haven't gone out with another girl. I can't. I'm in love with you, don't you understand?' He could not look at her now. He looked down, unseeing, at the table.

'Well,' she said, just as quietly, 'the only cure for that is to go out with someone else. Go out with lots of girls. I don't love you and I don't believe you love me.'

He said nothing, just covered his eyes with his hand.

It was not working. He remained silent for a long while. She began to feel desperate. If only he would say something. A waitress looked across at him, wondered if he was ill. 'Ian, everybody's looking at you. Now I'll tell you what we'll do. The next time we have a party at Lottie and Thorpe's flat, I'll take you. There will be lots of pretty girls there. You'll never have seen such a lot of pretty girls in your life. I'll telephone you. I'll leave a message at the *Daily Herald*. How about that then?'

He uncovered his eyes. 'All right,' he said. He would go anywhere as long as she was there.

'Good. Now brighten up. You go and pay the bill and I'll leave a shilling under my plate for the waitress.'

And he did as she asked, looking sad, looking doleful, wishing that he had not gone to London after all. He was in love with her and she did not care.

The telephone did not ring for Rita for a whole week and when it came to the Wednesday of the following week and Ian had still not rung, she was tempted to think that her little talk with him in the tea-shop had been sufficient. But she decided not to take that chance and she said to Lottie: 'Can I bring a young man with me on Sunday, Lottie? That one who spent his life savings telephoning me.'

'Of course you may, my dear. Have you decided to love the poor boy after all?'

'Certainly not,' she replied. 'I want to get him fixed up with a girl. I don't want him. And you do have lots of pretty girls at your parties. In fact, other than you and I, I think they must be the prettiest girls in London,' she said ingratiatingly.

Ian came to the party, smart in his dinner jacket, was kissed by Lottie and startled by her voice. He danced with Rita and then with Shirley, and Thorpe did as Rita asked and introduced him to all the girls. Thankfully, Rita noticed that he was circulating, that he was talking to people, that he was not hanging around her all the time, although it seemed that whenever she looked round, whatever he was doing, talking to someone or dancing, his eyes immediately met hers and would not look away. Nevertheless, she felt relieved that he was not acting like the pathetic, scorned creature who had been on the verge of tears in the tea-shop.

She knew for certain that he had not found himself another girl at the party, could tell that he had no intention of doing so. Fearing what he might say to her, what she might let herself in for if he took her home in a taxi, she said to Shirley: 'How am I going to get home? I feel for certain that his love is going to boil up all over me. I didn't think of it when I asked him to come.'

'We'll share a taxi,' Shirley said. 'The four of us. Desmond pranged his car the other day, so we'll have to get a taxi.'

A surge of gratitude welled up inside Rita and she said excitedly: 'Oh, what a relief. Of course, I wouldn't have asked you to give me a lift home if Desmond did have his car, because I know how you always drive away into the night and do things in the dark that you wouldn't dare to do in the daylight . . .' Her voice tailed off. Shirley was grinning at her and Rita knew that she must have sounded just like her mother.

Desmond got out of the taxi with Rita and Shirley. There was a lot of night left for him to say goodnight to Shirley in, down the dark alley that ran along the back of the houses. Ian was driven away alone, feeling upset, cast off and bitter.

'I'll be back at lunchtime,' Rita said, poking her head round the bathroom door at Shirley who was soaking in the bath reading a copy of the *Daily Graphic* that had gone limp through the steam.

Lightheartedly, she set off. Three weeks and she had not heard a thing from Ian Chase. Today she was going to collect her new evening gown. She was buying it from a man Lottie had sent her to, a man who never took a cheque, never issued a receipt and did not want clothing coupons. It was a lovely dress, cream in colour and made of something that was not quite silk. It was purchased as a much needed supplement to her solitary black evening dress, which she had worn to every function she had attended, every nightclub Lottie had led them all off to, every restaurant she had been to dinner at, every party at the flat where she had always hoped to meet a big film producer but had not done so.

Rita ran up the stairs and burst into Shirley's room. She put the box on the bed, tore it open and took out the dress. 'There, what do you think of that then?' She held it up against her body, turned to look at herself in the dressing-table mirror and said to Shirley, who was sitting at the dressing-table making up her face: 'Shift over a bit.'

Shirley moved out of the way so that Rita could have an uninterrupted view of herself. 'Looks lovely,' Shirley said. 'Going to try it on?'

'Later,' Rita said. She sat on the edge of the bed admiring the dress. 'Do you think I should wear it on Sunday at

Lottie's place? Will it be that sort of a do, do you think?'

'I don't know,' Shirley replied. 'All I know is that it's damned extravagant of her and Thorpe to go renting a house at the seaside just to keep little Sebastian from under their feet while he's on holiday from school. That and having to pay someone to look after him.'

'Well, it is Thorpe's auntie who is going to look after him, but I do agree it does seem odd,' Rita said. 'You'd think Lottie would want to mother him a little, cook his dinner and turn the collars on his shirts.'

'She's acting like the human equivalent of a cuckoo, in more ways than one,' Shirley burst out hotly.

'Well, I suppose that's nothing to do with us,' Rita said. 'All I know is it's a house by the sea and I've got a bathing suit that has never seen water, let alone got wet.'

'Well I'm not going,' Shirley stated. 'I'm not going on a beach until I'm sure they've dug up all the mines they planted in nineteen forty.'

'Humphrey says they didn't put mines down on every beach,' Rita told her. 'He says they just put signs up saying there were mines and rolled out some barbed wire, because they didn't have enough mines to go round.'

'Is that so?' Shirley asked. 'Well, I didn't see Humphrey paddling in the sea when we were down on the south coast. If I had done, I might have had second thoughts. By the way, your agent rang up for you. Said you've got to go and see her today at two sharp.'

Rita leapt off the bed. 'Did she? Well why didn't you say straight away?' She began folding up her dress.

'You didn't give me a chance, you were so excited over your new dress.'

'I wonder if it's a screen test? Oh, I hope so. Hey, it's lucky I've bought it then, isn't it? I mean, if I have to go out to dinner with a producer, well . . .'

Shirley heard no more. Rita was still talking as she rushed through the doorway back to her own room.

However important her seeing Mrs Brite might be, Rita decided not to go by taxi. She had spent enough money for one day, so she went on the underground. A clock was striking two as she went through the doorway and up the bare wooden stairs. The door to the outer office was open. The woman was not there, was still at lunch, she imagined. Mrs Brite's door was open too and she called Rita into her office. Rita went in, sat down and saw that Mrs Brite did not have a pleasant look on her face, not one that would go with good news.

'Have you been giving people interviews, Rita?' she asked.

'No I haven't,' she replied. 'Who would want to interview me?'

'You are telling the truth? You know that I am the one who arranges everything for you, be it a photograph, an interview, anything.'

'Mrs Brite, I would not lie,' she said sternly.

'Have you read this?' She held up a small magazine, did not hand it to her, just held it up so that she could see it. It had a plain black cover, with just the title *London Chat* printed on it in white letters.

'No. I can't say I've ever seen it before.'

'Well, it's got something about you in it.' She flipped through the pages. 'And about a few other people. Carlotta and Thorpe North. Listen to this. It's headed: "West End Life." It starts: "One of the most sought after events in the theatrical circles of the West End is an invitation to one of the parties given by Carlotta Trevane and Thorpe North. These munificent hosts take their guests far away from the world of the ration book and the meagre allowances it affords us, back to pre-war days of the heavily-laden table and the choice of dishes. At the latest of their Sunday night gatherings, the buffet laid out, recently fallen from the back of a lorry, no doubt, was as follows." There is then a list of everything that there was to eat at the party.'

'What's that to do with me, Mrs Brite?' Rita asked indignantly. 'Just because they manage to buy stuff through the black market is none of my concern.'

'First things first, Rita. If this tatty little book, which only comes out once a month, thank God, fell into the hands of the police – or other interested parties – I don't think it would be very good for Carlotta Trevane and Thorpe North, do you? And anyway, listen to this: "A regular guest at these functions is up and coming young actress Rita Rigby, who appears with her hosts in their very successful play 'A Blue Moon Rising'. To be in a West End hit at the age of seven-

273

teen needs talent and this Miss Rigby has in abundance. She also has determination, as she recently told me: 'I would advise anyone to put their career first. I always put my career before everything. I wouldn't sacrifice it for anybody or anything. One has to be realistic. A year ago I was touring in the north of England in a not very good revue. I did not get into the West End by being anything but single-minded.'" There's more, Rita, but the rest is just innocuous gossip. All written by someone called Paul Lindsey. What have you got to say to that?'

'Paul Lindsey? I've never heard of him. I've never given anyone an interview either.' A fierce expression was developing on her face, her eyes began to blaze, but she sat there calmly. She had the self-control to simmer where her mother would have boiled over. 'May I see the magazine please?'

Mrs Brite handed it to her and watched her read the article to herself. It was not the interview as such that concerned her. It was the reference to all the food at the party. With shortages, austerity and everyone still having to do their bit as they had done all through the war, put that in the popular press and a few careers would take a knock. And it seemed, from what was written, that Rita had spoken to someone. That, Mrs Brite feared, was what implicated her.

Rita recognized her own words. Eventually she looked up and said: 'I'm afraid I did say that, Mrs Brite. Or something very much like it. But I never gave an interview. I said it to a friend.' Her expression had changed. She looked very solemn now and she paused before going on. 'We went to the cinema one afternoon. Then we had tea in a café. And I said those things. You see, he said he was in love with me and I told him I was putting my career before anything else. He's been hanging after me and I don't really like him. But I felt sorry for him. I asked Lottie if I could bring him to one of her parties. I thought he might catch on with someone else.' She paused again. The worst bit had yet to be said. 'He's a reporter on the *Daily Herald*. His name is Ian Chase. I don't know who this Paul Lindsey is.'

Mrs Brite leaned back in her chair and breathed a deep sigh. 'Probably one and the same person, Rita. For Ian Chase read Paul Lindsey. Well, we'll have to act and quickly. Ian Chase, *Daily Herald*. Who do I know on the *Daily*

Herald?' She opened a drawer in her desk, took out a leather-bound notebook and began flipping through the pages. 'He's not a freelance, is he? How did you get to know him?'

'He's nothing important, Mrs Brite. He's not much older than me,' she told her. She looked at the pages of Mrs Brite's notebook. They were covered with her hurried handwriting that looked like birds' footprints in the snow. 'He was on a local evening paper in the north when I first met him, when I was in the revue. He hasn't worked on the *Herald* for long.'

'Well, no joy there.' She closed the notebook and threw it back into the drawer. 'When he went to this party, Rita, was he sociable? Did he mix, speak to people?'

'Oh yes,' Rita said.

'Did you notice if he wrote things down?' she asked her keenly. 'These sort of people often collect so much gossip that they can't remember it all.'

'No, I didn't see him doing that. Although I was at a party at Lottie's once when somebody did that,' Rita admitted. 'He wrote down something I said. Said he could use it, whatever he meant by that.'

'Oh yes,' Mrs Brite said seriously, 'and who was that?'

'I don't know. An old man he was,' Rita said. 'I was saying how my mother was not much of a cook and how she baked these cakes one day and she said: "These are what I call King Alfred cakes, on account of I've burnt them." And he wrote it down. Then I said about the time she tried to make a sponge and it turned out a bit flat and how she said: "I think I'll call this sponge the Titanic. It got three quarters of the way there and then it sank." He wrote that down too. Said he could use it. I can't imagine where.'

'Neither can I,' Mrs Brite said and gave her a long blank look. Then she said: 'Well, I suppose I'd better go and sort this creature out, Rita. If they find out at the *Daily Herald* that he's been freelancing, he'll be on the train home before his feet can touch the ground.'

'But Mrs Brite, what about Lottie and Thorpe? What if they read it?'

'I shouldn't think they would,' she told her. 'One of the girls in my husband's office was reading this magazine. He just happened to glance through it and saw that article. And he had to go to three or four bookstalls before he found it on sale, which is a point in our favour.'

'Will you tell them, Mrs Brite?'

'No, and neither will you. Mum's the word, Rita. By the way, you don't know this chap's address, do you?'

'I'm sorry, I don't,' she said. 'He's in lodgings somewhere.'

'Doesn't matter. Just you leave it to me. I'll sort him out, you see if I don't. Now you toddle along. I'll be in touch.'

And Rita found comfort in that masculine face, that determined nature, and felt frightened for Ian Chase.

The woman was back at her desk in the outer office when Rita went out. She smiled the sort of smile at Rita that seemed to say that she knew why she had been asked to come in. 'Hello, Miss Rigby,' she said. 'And how are you enjoying being in the West End?'

Rita remembered her mother's instructions, stuck her nose in the air, put on a bit of class and said with a cut-glass accent: 'Fine, really fine. Of course, the social life does take up more of one's time than one would wish, but when one is on the West End stage, one has to make sacrifices.'

She went down the stairs into the street, her face betraying none of the turmoil that was going on inside her, her one urgent desire at that moment being to go to the lavatory.

She went into a public convenience, put a penny in the slot and shut herself in the little green-painted cubicle. While she was in there, she had an awful picture of herself and the rest of the cast standing in the dock at the Old Bailey, of the story of the trial being on the front page of every newspaper, of newsboys standing by their placards in the street calling out the verdict: 'West End star jailed.'

It was going to be her mother's story all over again, Rita felt. Just when things had been going well for her mother, something had always happened. And it was happening to her too. The fall-out with her father, the affair with Randall Axter and now, whatever Ian Chase had done, she felt it would be she who would be to blame for whatever happened to Lottie and Thorpe. It was just like a curse, she thought, a curse that had been passed on to her by her mother. She had her looks, her sense of humour, her ability to turn on a bit of arrogance, a bit of class. And she had her bad luck too, she thought. But right up to the end, she realized, her mother

276

had fought her way through all sorts of problems and come out proudly with her nose in the air. Even the awful affair of having little Alan adopted had been a victory for her mother. How did she do it, she wondered? Why did people still like her, in spite of everything? Why had they cried the day she had left the hospital? It was, Rita surmised, her personality, that little bit of magic in her make-up that she had probably taken for granted because she never knew she had it. It was her ability to tell lies that would bring her some good and do no one any harm. Those things had balanced all the bad luck, right up to the end, when the bad luck had finally won.

Rita decided, while she sat there in the toilet, listening to the banging of the closet doors, the pulling of the chains, that if she had the looks, the humour, the put-on class of her mother, if she had the bad luck, then she must have the other things too. She must have the magic in her personality, the ability to act her way through life when being ordinary would not be enough. Realizing all this, she pulled the chain, washed her hands and went out into the street feeling more relieved than she imagined she would do when she went in.

She decided not to take the underground but caught a bus instead, so that she could sit on the top deck, look out of the window and let whatever caught her eye attract her mind away from her problem. It came on to rain. London looked a dismal place in the wet. The wreckage from the blitz lay everywhere and weeds had flourished on the bomb sites that summer so that it seemed as if they were being let go back to nature. At the end of every street, around every corner was another building in ruins, another whole row of houses gone, another shop-front boarded up. When Rita got off the bus and began to walk the rest of the way to the boarding-house, the sun came out and on the acres of destruction that she passed, on the vast brick-strewn spaces, amongst the half walls and the dark entrances to still-standing lower floors, children came out to play, running and shouting across the left-over playground of war, thin children, poorly dressed in clothes that were patched and did not fit, children who had very little of value in life except their freedom.

Rita got through her performance that night, and the matinée the next day, and another evening performance. She was glad they had a matinée that day because it took away

277

from her the time she would have spent dwelling on things, sitting in an easy chair at her lodgings pretending to be reading, when all the time she would have been waiting for the telephone to ring.

The call came while she was still in bed. The landlady brought the message up to her. She had to meet Mrs Brite in a café at ten-thirty. The café was not far from the agency. It was a little place with stools along the counter, a big chromium tea urn that someone must have polished lovingly every morning and a tumbler full of wax straws on the counter for anyone who bought a lemonade. Mrs Brite was already there, sitting at a table in the corner, when Rita went in. Rita bought herself a cup of tea and joined her.

'I come in here now and again,' Mrs Brite said. 'I like a change from Marjorie's tea. I know we have to economize but you can see the bottom of the cup through her tea.'

'How did you get on?' Rita asked her.

'I'm going to tell you straight, Rita,' she said, 'because there's no alternative. If there was a way round telling you, I'd take it. But there isn't one.'

'Go on then,' Rita said and she took a sip of her tea. It was scalding hot and burned her tongue; she knew that she would have a sore patch in her mouth for days because of it.

'You certainly picked yourself a little Tartar, Rita,' Mrs Brite began. 'He said that if I reported him to the *Daily Herald* for freelancing, he would sell the story to the Sunday newspapers. I think he meant it too. In fact, he said he might as well sell the story to them anyway, because now I'd poked my nose into it he reckoned I would give the game away. But he did have an alternative. In fact, he had two alternatives, in return for which he said that if the police made any inquiries, he would say that he made the whole thing up to hurt you. The first alternative was to sell the story to me for a thousand pounds.'

'A thousand pounds?' Rita said loudly, so that the woman serving at the counter looked across at her.

'A thousand pounds,' Mrs Brite said again. 'I don't know where he imagines I can get a thousand pounds from, just like that. Have to sell myself into white slavery.'

Rita did not know exactly what white slavery was but she had a vague idea and she did not reckon that selling Mrs

Brite into that sort of thing would fetch the money. She said: 'What was the other alternative?'

'He said he'd drop the whole idea on condition that you quit the play,' she said quietly.

Rita could not speak. She could not move. She could not believe what Mrs Brite had just said. She just sat there unable to do more than stare at her cup of tea, the tea dark brown against the shiny white china of the cup.

'Well I told him he could forget that idea,' Mrs Brite went on quickly, 'and I told him that an actress could not walk out of a West End play just like that. I said I'd think things over, and went and found the creatures who turn out *London Chat*. That was the only satisfactory part of things. They definitely don't want any trouble. They've already had a writ issued against them over an article they published about the high life of generals during the war. Written by some ex-batman with a grudge. So there's no danger there, but no help either.'

'What are we going to do then?' Rita asked her in a voice that was hardly more than a whisper.

'I don't know,' Mrs Brite said. 'I just don't know.'

Rita wrapped her fingers round her cup of tea. It was cooler now and she drank some of it. 'Well he's not getting me out of the play,' she said bitterly, her emotions starting to come to life. She blinked her eyes quickly and drank some more of the tea. 'I'd sooner kill the little bugger.' She took another drink, the final drink, drained the cup and put it down on the saucer with a clatter.

'Now Rita . . .' Mrs Brite began.

But Rita said fiercely: 'Nobody's doing that to me. I'm only seventeen and I'm not having my opportunities spoiled, not at my age. If neither of us can come up with a better idea . . .' She got up from the table and dashed out into the street, her anger transforming itself into an energy that gave her the ability to walk all the way back to the boarding-house, straight along the pavements, bumping into people, marching over roads amongst the traffic, so full of fury that, had anyone challenged her, she would have clenched her little white fist and punched them with it.

That night, after they had come home from the theatre, Rita put her dressing-gown on over her pyjamas, slid her feet into

279

her slippers, went out on to the landing and tapped on Shirley's door. Shirley was lying in bed with the light on reading *The Star*. Rita said: 'Where's Desmond this week then?'

'He's travelling Kent,' Shirley said. 'Back on Saturday.'

'Miss him?' Rita asked, lounging across the foot of the bed.

'I'll miss him when we're married and he's not home,' Shirley replied.

Rita began picking at a loose thread in the bedspread and, without looking up from this preoccupation, she said: 'You know when you have sexual intercourse with Desmond, do you do it in the dark?'

'Not if we do it in the daytime,' Shirley replied, smiling to herself behind the newspaper.

'If you do it at night then, in bed?' Rita tried.

'Depends,' she said. 'Sometimes we keep the light on, sometimes we turn it out. It just depends. Anyway, why do you want to know?'

'Well, I've never done it.'

Shirley looked over the top of the newspaper. 'Are you planning to do it then?'

'No, but I'd just like to know in case I do.' She got tired of picking at the bedspread, rolled over on to her back, put her hands behind her head, drew up her knees and said: 'When you have sexual intercourse, do you take all your clothes off?'

'Sometimes,' Shirley said, going back behind the newspaper to smile. 'When we were on tour and Desmond came down, if I managed to smuggle him into my room and he decided to stay until dawn, then we used to take all our clothes off. But of course, when we spent an afternoon amongst the bracken on a cliff top we didn't. Nor the night we did it in a shelter on the sea front. On that occasion, naturally, we did it standing up. You can do it standing up, you know, either dressed or undressed.'

Rita got off the bed. She knew that Shirley was laughing at her. 'Thank you for giving me the benefit of your experience,' she said and went back to her room.

The following morning, Rita went downstairs into the hallway to the telephone, dialled the *Daily Herald*'s number and crossed her fingers. Luck was with her. They gave her Ian Chase's number and he was there when she rang. 'I'd like to talk things over with you,' she said. 'Could we meet somewhere?'

He sounded very sure of himself on the other end of the telephone, no longer had the apprehensive manner that he had had when trying to arrange a date with her. Sure he would meet her. In a pub near Fleet Street at twelve o'clock.

Rita got ready. She made up her face perfectly, painted her nails and put on a blouse that had a neckline which plunged down her chest in a deep V. Then she went out and hailed a taxi.

She was going to do the only thing she could think of doing. Her career depended on it. The reputation of Lottie and Thorpe depended on it. It was going to be a sacrifice, she knew, but it was the sort of thing her mother would have done. Thinking of what her mother would have done was what had brought the idea into her head, as if her mother had sent down a message from above telling her that it was the only thing to do. It was part of the magic her mother had possessed, Rita thought, knowing that she had something no man could resist, something to be used in times of trouble.

He was not in the pub when she got there. She bought a gin and orange and sat down far away from the bar, by the frosted glass windows where she could hear the sounds of the traffic outside in the street. Some men standing at the bar watched her buy her drink, saw her take it and sit down, turned round and glanced at her while they talked. But to her it looked a decent place, the sort of place where all they would do would be to look.

Ian Chase came in five minutes later, went to the bar and bought half a pint of beer. He was wearing a trilby again, a grey one with a wide brim, and he had pushed it on to the back of his head. With his fawn raincoat unbuttoned and with the belt dangling, she imagined that he was trying to look like somebody he had come across and admired. The men at the bar watched him as he went across and sat down by her.

'What do you want?' he asked her.

She looked at him. He had pushed his hat too far back on his head and when he sat down the brim of it rested on the collar of his raincoat, but she knew he would not dare to spoil his image by moving it. 'I want you to stop this silly, spiteful thing you are doing, Ian,' she said.

'No,' he said, staring at her with eyes that would never look at anything or anyone else while she was there. 'You were rotten to me, now I'm going to be rotten to you. Revenge.'

Rita sipped her drink. 'No one knows I've come to see you, Ian. I believe Mrs Brite's busily rounding up a few big men to persuade you to change your mind. Actresses often get harassed by men, but luckily there are always those willing to defend them.'

'You don't scare me,' he said, grinning at her.

'I didn't come here to scare you,' she replied. 'I came here to offer you something in return for you dropping this whole silly affair.'

He looked at her for a minute before he spoke again. She looked so calm, so adult, so much more like an actress than he felt he looked like a reporter. He knew that her smart appearance made him look ordinary, for all his attempts to look the part he was playing, the reporter with a hot story and a price. 'What's your offer?' he asked her.

She took a deep breath, looked him straight in the eyes and said: 'In return for you not blackmailing me and not selling the story to the Sunday papers and saying that you made the whole silly thing up to spite me if anyone wants to know, then I'll let you make love to me. In bed, with nothing on. Sex, the whole thing, tonight in my room. I've never done it before, but I don't suppose . . .' She stopped then. His expression had changed. He frowned a little, almost looked worried, while she had expected him to grin and say yes. He was not looking at her now, he was looking away, and she felt that it was not going to work, that that was his way of saying no. Desperately, speaking a thought that flashed into her mind that very second, she said: 'Or are you the only man in London who doesn't want to get into bed with me?'

That made him turn his head. That forced him to answer and there was only one answer he could give to those steady dark eyes that were waiting for him when he turned his head. 'Yes, all right,' he said, when he wanted to say no, when the sickly fear he felt in his stomach at giving his answer was the same feeling she felt at hearing it.

She took another sip of her drink. 'Right then, that's that,' she said. 'And I don't want you going back on your word afterwards. Because if you do, I'll sell *my* story to the Sunday papers. How you got me into bed and so on.'

'You can trust me,' he said, in a voice that betrayed the fact that they had practically changed roles.

'You'd better meet me at the stage door tonight, then. We'll go up to my room. I'll keep my part of the bargain and you had better keep yours. And make sure you buy one of those thingummybobs. I don't want you getting me pregnant.' She finished her drink. He was in too much of a daze to ask her if she wanted another, but she would have said no anyway. 'I'm off. Bye for now.'

The men at the bar watched her walk to the door, with her face and her figure and her head-high arrogant look that would have made them cautious and, they admitted only to themselves, so grateful.

'It's a taxi for one then,' Shirley said. 'I thought you had seen the last of him.' Ian Chase was at the stage door and she imagined he had just turned up out of the blue.

'So did I,' Rita said. 'I'll try and get rid of him for good this time.'

'Try pushing him in the river,' Shirley said and she went out laughing.

Rita took as long as she could to change and when she finally left the theatre he was standing outside in the street. They walked along in silence, got a taxi and when they reached the boarding-house she made him wait outside in the shadows while she went in to see if the coast was clear.

The light was on in the hall and a rim of light shone from round the kitchen door at the gloomy far end of the hallway. She went up the stairs. Shirley's light was still on. Rita quietly opened her bedroom door, put on her bedside lamp, then went back downstairs to fetch him. As she went down the stairs, she prayed for him to have taken fright and gone, but he was still there, seeming nervous, unsure of himself, not looking half so cocky with his trilby hat on straight and his mac buttoned up. She took him upstairs, closed the bedroom door on him and went back down into the hallway. She tapped on the kitchen door, opened it, peeped inside and said: 'We're in now, Mr Gregory. Goodnight.'

He looked up from his paper, took his pipe from his mouth and said: 'Goodnight then, Rita.'

Ian was still standing in her room just as she had left him, as if in a quandary over what he should do. She felt for a moment that if she tackled him then, gave him a good talking to, he would take back all the threats he had made to Mrs Brite. But, just as quickly, she realized that she could not risk losing face if his expression masked his real desire. And anyway, she did not feel forgiving. She had not inherited from her mother any great ability to forgive.

'Get your clothes off then,' she said brusquely. 'Put them on that chair.'

The quick changes of costume that she had had to make in the revue had taught her how to undress and dress again quicker than she would otherwise have imagined possible. She was out of her clothes in a flash and Ian turned to see her climbing naked into the bed. She lay on her back and watched him undressing in silence. He looked thin, white and harmless in the dim light of the bedside lamp. And while she lay there, she suddenly wondered how long it would take. She had forgotten to ask Shirley that. Whether it would hurt or not did not bother her. Whether to do it with clothes on, whether to keep the light on, how long it took: those were the things she had meant to ask her. And how long it would take was the most important thing of all. For all she knew, once he got started he might be going at it all night.

Ian slid into bed beside her. They lay there, while she waited for him to make the first move. He lay quite still, said nothing and did nothing. 'Well come on, get on with it,' she said impatiently.

He turned towards her suddenly and kissed her hard on her lips. There was a pause and he turned towards her again, put his hand on her breasts and started fondling them as if, Rita thought, he imagined that was the thing to do, rather than for the effect it might have on her or any pleasure he might get from doing it. Then he stopped, lay back on the bed again, while she waited for him to do something else.

A minute or two passed and he did not move. Rita's body, tense with anticipation at the beginning, relaxed as suspicion and anger began to brew up inside her. 'Well come on, come on,' she said sharply.

284

He half turned towards her and remained in that position as if he expected her to reciprocate his move. But she lay there stock still, putting all the onus of the anticipated event on him. And he moved back and lay there motionless while another couple of minutes went by.

Rita could stand it no longer. For all she knew, it could have been all over by then. She sat up in the bed. 'Well are you going to do it or aren't you?'

He did not answer, just turned his head away from her.

She tore the bedclothes off him and looked at his body, looked at the part of it he had gone there to use. It hardly looked any different to Ronnie's miserable little thing, except that it had hair on it. 'Hey,' she said, using the small amount of knowledge that she had on the subject, 'why hasn't it gone stiff? It's supposed to go stiff. You can't do it, can you? You can't do it,' she said in a voice that triumph had made happy and sneering at the same time.

He sat up and swung his legs round on to the floor. 'It's you . . .' he began, but he said no more.

She pushed him in the middle of the back with her hand. 'Well if you can't do it, get your clothes on and bugger off.'

Ian retreated to the corner where he had put his clothes and began to get dressed with his back to her.

Rita put on her pyjamas, her dressing-gown and her slippers, and released a torrent of words at him. 'You had the audacity,' she snarled, 'to ask Mrs Brite for a thousand pounds, to demand that I leave the play, to risk Lottie and Thorpe going to jail, and you can't even do it. Well, any more malarky from you, my lad, and I'm the one who'll be selling their story to the Sunday papers. You'd better make up your mind to deny the whole thing, wherever the food at Lottie's party came from, because if you don't, if ever the police decide to make inquiries, then I shall go straight round to the *News of the World*, *The People* and the *Sunday Pictorial* and sell them my story about you. You wait until your family read it. You'll never be able to go home again. And look at the colour of your underwear,' she went on wildly. 'Whoever does your laundry? Don't they know that Rinso has been invented?' She stopped then, because once more she could hear her mother's voice ringing around the room.

He took it all in silence, finished dressing, buttoned up his

285

raincoat and put on his trilby, while she stood there with her arms folded, glowering at him. Then he followed her out of the room. She put on the landing light and they went down the stairs towards the dark hallway.

They had reached the foot of the stairs when they saw Winston, Mrs Gregory's bulldog, lying in his basket by the hatstand just inside the front door. It showed its teeth and growled very deeply, as if daring them to step off the last stair on to the floor. Rita held on to the bannister rail, crouched down and spoke soft baby talk to it in a voice a bit like Lottie's, but the moment she went to put her foot down, Winston moved his shoulders and showed all his teeth, even the ones at the back which Rita knew, from school, were used for biting through bones.

Ian shot halfway up the stairs. She looked round at him. His mouth had dropped open and his eyes were staring. She went up towards him and he retreated back to her bedroom as if afraid she might drag him back down to the bulldog.

He spoke in a quavering voice. 'I'll get out of the window,' he said. 'I don't like dogs. I'll get out of the window.'

'All right,' she said and she went over to the window and pushed it open. 'There's a shed just below. You can drop on to there, go across the yard and out of the back gate.'

Ian looked out of the window. There was a flat-roofed shed built against the house. With the same eagerness that he had shown in retreating from the bulldog, he clambered over the window sill. He began to lower himself but just before he got to the point where he would not have been able to draw himself up again, he stopped, hugged the window sill and said: 'It's a felt roof. I'll go right through. It's not slates, I'll go through,' and he began to heave himself back up through the window.

'No, you'll be all right. It's not far. Go on,' Rita insisted. She did not want him to get back into the room. There was no other way out and she did not want him in there all night.'Jump, Ian, jump,' she said and she pushed against his shoulders. He gave a cry of anguish and disappeared through the window. But he managed to hold on to the bottom of the window frame with his fingers.

Rita looked out of the window. 'It's only a few feet. Let go.'

'No, I'll go through,' he said in a strained voice. 'Please

286

help me back up, please.'

'I'm buggered if I will,' Rita said to herself, drawing her head back into the room. She went across to the dressing-table, picked up her hair brush, went back to the window and began hitting him on the knuckles with it with all her might. 'Jump, you bugger, jump,' she said, while he whimpered and pleaded and she hit all the more remorselessly at his knuckles. 'Jump, jump . . .'

She did not hear the door open, but suddenly someone caught hold of her and pulled her backwards. She struggled, looked round and saw that it was Shirley. 'What on earth are you doing, Rita? You'll wake the whole household.'

'It's Ian,' she said. 'Winston won't let him out of the front door and he won't jump on to the shed roof because he's frightened he might go through.'

Shirley did not bother to inquire on what pretext he was in her room. She looked out of the window. 'He would go through too,' she said. 'Come on, let's try and pull him up.'

Rita could not protest. They got an arm each, but they could not move him. He dangled there making faint noises of fear, while his fingers, reddened at the knuckles where Rita had hit them, clung grimly to the window frame.

'Oh heavens, Rita,' Shirley said angrily and she swept from the room and went down the stairs. She came back very quickly. 'Winston's fierce,' she said, 'but he's got a soft spot. Have you any chocolate? He likes chocolate. I saw Mrs Gregory give him some the other day. She had a box of Caley's and she gave him two, one after the other.'

'To a dog?' Rita said in amazement. 'What an awful waste. Anyway, I haven't got any. I've got some liquorice comfits.'

Shirley said nothing, sighed a fierce sigh and left the room.

Rita looked through the window. 'This would look great in the Sunday papers,' she hissed. 'Can't do it to a woman, frightened of a dog, scared of dropping a few feet on to a flat roof. I could make a fortune.'

He whimpered. Shirley tapped her on the shoulder. 'Here you are.' She handed Rita the last four squares of a bar of milk chocolate. 'Give Winston a piece of this and while he's eating it nip into the kitchen, out through the back door, climb on the dustbin, up on to the shed roof, get hold of his

287

legs and help him down. Then come back in, give Winston a bit more chocolate and nip up the stairs.'

Rita looked horrified. 'Oh no, he might bite me. We might go through the roof.'

'Not unless you jump up and down,' Shirley said. She pushed Rita towards the door. 'It's either this or wake up Mr Gregory. The choice is entirely yours. So go on.'

There the dog was, like a little heap of muscle slumped in his basket. He showed his teeth and gave a growl that sounded in his throat like someone rolling an 'r', as Rita stretched out her arm with a square of chocolate held lightly between finger and thumb. 'Come along, Mr Churchill,' she said softly. 'Eat, eat.'

The smell of the chocolate reached his nose. He stopped growling, opened his mouth and she popped the chocolate inside. He closed his eyes and chewed and Rita took three cautious steps backwards towards the kitchen.

The key to the back door was in the lock. She reached up and slid back the bolt, went out into the yard and opened the back gate. The dustbin was handily placed by the shed. She got on to it, put one slippered foot on the narrow sill of the shed window and hoisted herself on to the roof. The felt gave a little under her weight.

'Take his shoes off,' Shirley said in a loud stage whisper. 'Let him stand on your shoulders, then go slowly down on to your knees.'

Rita did as she was told. But she could hardly bear his weight and before she could lower herself on to her knees her body gave way. She rolled sideways and Ian hit the shed roof with a dull thump and fell over the side into the yard. By the time Rita had recovered, he was getting to his feet. 'Shoes,' she said. She threw them down to him. He did not stop to put them on, but picked them up and went out of the back gate limping, hardly able, it seemed, to put one foot to the ground.

No sound came from the house. No lights came on. She climbed down off the shed roof. His trilby was on the ground. She picked it up and stuffed it into the dustbin.

Winston, uncharitable to the last, heard her emerge from the kitchen, looked at her through one eye and growled until his jowls quivered, until the scent of the proffered chocolate wafted to his nostrils. 'Good boy, Mr Churchill,' she said and he opened his mouth wide. Rita placed the square of chocolate on his tongue, the jaws closed, he rested his chin on his paws and lay there with the contented look of an overfed old man enjoying an after dinner mint.

By the time Rita got back upstairs, Shirley had gone back to bed. 'Oh Shirley,' she said, bubbling over with gratitude, 'you are a genius. The next thing I was going to do was to slam the window on his fingers. I couldn't control myself.'

'Rule number one,' Shirley said. 'Never take a man up to your room unless there's a drainpipe handy.'

'Oh Shirley, I really am grateful,' Rita went on. 'If you were a man I'd kiss you.'

'I'm glad I'm not, the way you treat your men,' Shirley replied.

'And now I'm going to tell you the whole story, in strictest confidence of course, because if . . .'

'Not now, Rita,' Shirley said wearily. 'Tomorrow. Let's get some sleep now and when we wake up it might all turn out to have been a strange dream.'

They looked through the window down at the shed roof. There were dents in it. 'If they ever see that,' Rita said, 'I'll get the blame. They can't blame that on tomcats, unless the cats around here have very big feet. I think now is the time for me to get a flat. I'll buy the *Daily Telegraph* and *The Times* and have a look through the adverts to see what there is going.'

She went off to see Mrs Brite then, to tell her that she could forget all about Ian Chase. But she did not give her any details, just dropped odd vivid hints of what had happened. 'Yes,' she said, 'I'll bet it's not every night of his life Ian Chase falls off a roof.'

'Falls off a roof?' Mrs Brite echoed.

'The last I saw of him, and ever shall see of him,' Rita declared, with all the fearlessness of the heavyweight champion of the world, 'he was limping off into the night with his shoes in his hand.'

From Rita's exuberance and her confidence, Mrs Brite decided that it was safe to assume that the whole affair was

289

over, for there were lights dancing in Rita's eyes, her excited voice had lost all the poise of its proper accent and she had begun to sound just like a Lancashire mill girl.

Twenty Seven

Rita went down to the coast with the rest of them that Sunday, but the shock of the affair with Ian Chase came home to her, and while it did not prevent her from enjoying herself, it made her feel that she wanted to withdraw from adult life and go back to being a child again. Instead of staying with the rest of them, who lay out on the sands under the warm sun and talked of the theatre, she larked about with Sebastian. They played with a beachball, one minute being in the sea with it, the next on the sand, one minute cold and wet, the next warm and damp, not noticing the discomfort of it for the fun they were having.

Later on, they went searching around in rock pools for anything that moved, and after they had had a picnic tea on the sands, the two of them played around in the incoming tide, screaming and shouting as the foam-topped waves roared up the beach and washed over them, submerging them briefly under a rush of green water.

The others left them there and retreated up the cliff path to the house, talking of cocktails and of getting dressed for dinner. Later, when Rita had dried her hair and had changed into her new evening gown, she did not find the pleasure in wearing her new dress that she thought she would. She did not feel that she was yet an adult, but that she still belonged in that world where, although there was fun and pleasure, there was still innocence.

The following Saturday, after a week in which Rita had been able to wear off the shock of her experience, she and Shirley were in their dressing-room at the theatre, changing for the matinée. 'It has been quite a relief,' Rita said, 'to be able to go to the pictures on my own. I can concentrate better alone. Although you wouldn't have thought it would have

291

made much difference if you had seen us all going to the pictures when I was at school. My mother used to take a great crowd of us, on account of she knew the manager and we all got in for nothing.' She glanced at Shirley to see that she was listening, and Shirley knew that Rita was now her normal self by the way she was chattering, by the way her voice seemed to get louder and higher as she warmed to her subject. 'Talk about disturbance, though. Mavis was in and out to the lavatory the whole time. My mother used to say that if ever she came back to life as something else, it would be as a water melon. My mother could not resist passing remarks. We saw "Rebecca" twice and the second time we saw it she said that if that housekeeper had treated her the way she treated Joan Fontaine, she would have biffed her in the chops.'

'It sounds as if your mother would have been more suited to the part of the housekeeper,' Shirley said, while Rita stopped for breath.

'Mrs Danvers,' Rita said, as if she had inadvertently left out an important detail. 'That was the housekeeper's name.'

There was a knock at the door and the stage doorkeeper said: 'Gentleman at the stage door to see Miss Rigby.'

Rita went white. 'Oh God,' she said, 'not again.'

'Gentleman in uniform,' he said.

'The police, the police,' Rita said with fright, drowning the stage doorkeeper's next words. 'Oh Shirley, they've found out.'

'Who is it?' Shirley called out. 'Curtain goes up in a minute.'

'I've just said.' He repeated his unheard words. 'Says he's her father.'

'All right, she'll be out in a tick.' Shirley grinned at Rita, sitting there looking petrified. 'Come on now. Try acting like the daughter of the woman who would have biffed Mrs Danvers in the chops.'

Rita regained her composure. She put her coat on over the short blue dress of her costume and went down to the stage door. 'Hello,' she said. She stopped about eight feet away from him.

'Hello.' He smiled. 'How are you? How's the show?'

'Oh fine,' she replied. 'Have you seen it?'

292

'No, we've got tickets for this evening. I thought I'd come and see you first. I'm getting married again, you see, and I've brought her to see the show and I thought we could go out to dinner afterwards and you could get acquainted.' He said it all in one breath, all in a rush, not as he had meant to say it, calmly and slowly for it to be a shock to her. But she looked so grown up, so aloof in the way she stood away from him, that thoughts of trying to shock her were instantly swept from his mind.

'Getting married? Well, you shouldn't break news like that to someone who is about to go on stage, you know.' She smiled as she said it.

'I'll book a table then,' he said.

'That's right. And come round to the stage door after the curtain.'

'Right.' He did not know what else to say, could not help thinking that if he said one wrong word, she would snap at him. 'I'll see you after the show then.'

'All right. And it's not a show, it's a play.' And having corrected him, she turned and went back to the dressing-room.

'You've been called,' Shirley told her.

'I've only got my apron to put on,' Rita replied. 'He's getting married again,' she said offhandedly. 'What a time to come and tell me that. I've got to meet the bride. We're going out to dinner.'

The call-boy tapped on the door. 'Two minutes, Miss Rigby.'

She glanced at herself in the mirror. 'No consideration,' she said half to herself, then she went out, down to the wings, round to the back of the stage where she was to make her first entrance through a door in the scenery.

Humphrey and Thorpe were on the stage. She heard Humphrey say: 'Well there must be someone here. I'll ring again.' And he tugged on a bell pull. He and Thorpe went on talking. She smoothed down her apron, although it did not need smoothing down, then waited for her cue line from Humphrey: 'And I said to him, if that was all he thought of the girl, I would marry her myself. So I did and that was how she came to be the first Lady Stitchley.'

She paused for laughter, opened the door and stepped on to the stage.

Her father came backstage that night and brought with him Helen, the woman he was to marry. At first, Rita did not think that she looked her father's type. She seemed to be about his age, but she was plump and healthy-looking and filled her evening dress full. But then she realized that her mother had not been her father's type either, and that putting appearances aside, he might have made a correct second choice.

She introduced them to the cast. Lottie put on her usual, overplayed performance for them, piping away with her little voice. 'Oh, you lovely man,' she said to Rita's father, kissing him on both cheeks and then on the lips. 'To think that I was down here in nineteen forty feeling all afraid, while you were up there being brave for little me.'

'And for the rest of us,' Rita butted in.

Lottie took no notice. 'Quite frankly,' she carried on, 'nothing would induce me to go up in an aeroplane. There's such a big space between your feet and the ground, isn't there?'

'They do have a floor in the aeroplane,' Rita said, but when Lottie was performing she was oblivious to everything.

The three of them went out to dinner. Her father seemed happy and relaxed with Helen. She was well spoken, came from a good family and fitted in well with him in his role of an air force officer. Rita could more easily picture Helen at a function in the officers' mess than she could her mother. Helen would attract no one's attention. Rita's mother would have claimed glances and stares from everyone.

Helen found Rita both attractive and charming. Having met her made her feel sad at what Leslie Rigby had told her about the rift that had occurred in their relationship, and it made more obvious to her the care he took in the way he spoke to her. And so, when they had finished dinner and had gone into the bar, Helen knew that somehow she would have to allow them five minutes together, whether they wanted to get things off their chests or just carry on the pretence that everything was normal between them. She excused herself, took her handbag and went to the ladies.

Rita sipped a gin and orange. Her father looked at her and said: 'You look just like your mother sitting there.'

'How do you know?' she asked. 'I don't suppose you ever

took my mother to a place like this. You never even bought her an evening dress to go in.'

He had heard that voice before, that sharp edge to it, that confident tone. He said: 'Your mother will never be dead while you are alive, Rita.'

'I don't suppose she will be,' Rita admitted. 'After all, there's more of her in me than there is of you.' And, in order not to make him feel too let down, she added: 'I think Ronnie takes after you.'

He was quiet for a while, and then he said, without looking at her: 'You've never really forgiven me for trying to take you home, have you?'

'No,' she stated. 'I'm afraid I don't forgive easily.'

'That's where we differ,' he said quietly. 'I can forgive. I forgave your mother . . .'

'You what?' she burst out, her eyes beaming in on him like searchlights. 'You did not forgive her. You gave in to her like everyone else did. She had a little bit of magic about her that no one could resist. It was more than looks. You gave in to her.'

She sounded so grown up for seventeen, and she looked so much like her mother. But he could see that there was a subtle difference between the two of them. He had never won an argument with Bella. She had always screamed and shouted at him, that had been her way. But Rita remained calm and articulate and she seemed more dangerous than her mother because of it. He wished there were something else they could talk about, something else besides Bella. But he could think of nothing. He said:'I wanted things to be so different for you and Ronnie. I had such plans. But the war came along and . . .'

She cut him short and without looking at him she said in a hushed but firm voice, as if she had said it a hundred times before: 'Don't go blaming everything on the war. I'm sick of hearing people blaming all their mistakes on the war. You had your chance and you muffed it.' She looked up at him then and he looked just like someone who had been put in their place. She sipped her drink, toyed with the glass and went on in a more pleasant way: 'How I always saw it, the only way I was ever going to get the things I wanted in life was by going out and seeking them. I think mam always had the same idea. We had no illusions. There was not much of a view from that terraced house we lived in, of the future or of anything else. All we had was a bombsite and a foundry. Nobody told us there was ever going to be anything else. You certainly never did.'

'Well I never got you into a terraced house near a bombsite and a foundry,' he said, defending himself.

'No,' Rita admitted, 'you didn't. Mam with her crazy way of life did. But, whatever you think of her, just you remember this. For me, life with mam was a lot of fun. I wouldn't have swapped her. Most of the things she did were not quite proper, but they raised a smile when there was very little to smile about. Do you remember all those people who turned up at the hospital? They'd never had anyone so popular. Speaks for itself, dad, doesn't it?'

He took a long drink from his glass, then he looked down into it and said: 'Don't let's have an inquest on it. They held one inquest and that didn't prove anything. Nothing at all. Why she did it . . .'

She looked at him. He looked so sad. Every time he thought of her mother, Rita imagined, all through his life, he would look sad. She did not know what to say to console him and so she said what was in her mind at that moment, what she herself believed. 'They didn't need to hold an inquest. I could have told them why she died. She died because the American she loved had left her and because a friend she loved had died. She didn't die for you, dad, nor for me, nor for Ronnie. She died for a GI who got her pregnant and deserted her, and for a friend who was little more than a prostitute. It's funny the things people die for, isn't it? Whatever we do in life, dad, whether you become Air Chief Marshal and I become another Greta Garbo, I don't suppose either of us will do anything as brave as she did. I don't suppose either of us will die because of a friend. And if neither of us ends up as anything at all, I don't think we will die for our lost ambitions.'

Helen came back then and Rita's thoughts and her conversation changed just as they would have done between the dramatic end of one act in a play and the calm beginning of another.

Her father noticed Rita's pleasantly refined accent. And

he noticed too how she used the gift that her mother had had, that Lottie possessed, to go on acting in real life when the occasion demanded it. But he had the fear that behind that facade lay a different person, just as behind the sweet face, the enticing body, the black hair and the bright eyes of Bella he had found someone he never imagined existed. There was a gulf between him and Rita, he felt, and he was glad that there was, because he did not want to encounter the other person she might be. Even if he was wrong about her, he was willing to live with his mistake, and for safety's sake hope that they would always be friends rather than father and daughter. Helen, he thought, would be more of a wife to him than Bella had ever been, more of a wife than Rita had ever been a daughter.

Twenty Eight

Rita got a tiny flat in an elegant house in a pleasant square, and her windows looked out on to the little park in the centre of the square, the grass a lush green from the wet summer.

The flat was furnished, but it lacked one important thing. 'There aren't any blankets or sheets or anything,' she told Shirley. 'There's just the bed with a striped mattress on it.'

'Of course, there wouldn't be,' Shirley said. 'You'll have to buy some. I think they're still on ration too, aren't they? Don't you have to have dockets to buy bedding?'

'*I* don't know,' Rita said, as if it was silly of Shirley to assume that she might.

'I suppose they'd tell you at the Ministry of Food.'

'I'm not going to the food office to ask about bedding,' Rita stated. 'That can't be the place to go to.'

'Well I can loan you a thick coat to help tide you over,' Shirley offered.

'No, I can manage. I'll write to my gran. She's bound to have some spare sheets and things,' Rita said. 'She's got loads of beds that no one sleeps in any more. I only hope I look my best in the morning. I've got to go to Laurence's to have some pictures taken for the film people. Mrs Brite said someone called Hector Point is coming to watch me in the play one night this week. He's a film director, evidently.'

'Hector Point? He's well known,' Shirley remarked.

'He should be with a name like that,' Rita said. 'Hector Point. Sounds like a place at the seaside.'

She wrote to her grandmother the following morning, then took a taxi to Laurence's studio. The front of the studio was still boarded up and there were two posters stuck on to the boards, a coloured one advertising a circus and a black and white one announcing a sale of bomb-damaged goods. The

298

girl with the Veronica Lake hairstyle was still there. 'Hello, Miss Rigby,' she said. 'Laurence is in the studio just setting up. Please go in.' And she clawed her hair from in front of one eye.

'So old mother Brite's getting you a screen test, is she?' he said, as he fiddled with his lights. He looked at her, puffed at the cigarette end that was hidden in his beard and discovered that it had gone out. He lit his lighter, held it to his lips and puffed. Something caught alight, either the cigarette or his beard, probably both, Rita thought, she could not tell; but there was a brief glow of fire and blue smoke. 'Just because you photograph well doesn't mean a thing,' he went on. 'Movement, that's what counts. Cows film well because they move well. You study a cow. Bulky, but moves with grace. If ever you want to move gracefully, think of a cow and try to move like one.'

'Down on all fours with everything swinging about beneath me, do you mean?' she said, glaring at him. 'Laurence, I've come here to have some photographs taken, so do you think you can tell me what you want me to wear first, without bringing cows into the conversation?'

For the first picture she put on her shorts and a sweater. He told her to sit on the floor with one leg straight and the other one bent, leaning on her hands with her arms braced out behind her. 'Stick your chest out, come on, I want a nice profile of your tits. No, pull your sweater down a bit, it's not tight enough. Now, again, tits out, nipples bristling. Don't look at the camera, look up there.' He pointed to the top of the studio wall.

'Where, up there?' She was annoyed at his remarks. 'All right, I'll look at that cobweb up in the corner. How's that?'

Laurence looked quickly up into the corner, saw no cobweb, saw a little smirk of revenge on her face, grinned, blew smoke and cigarette ash all over the camera, said: 'Don't smile,' and took the picture.

A week after Rita had written to her grandmother, the railway delivered to her a large cardboard box containing everything she needed, from pillows to a bedspread. She was unpacking it excitedly when she was called down into the hall to take a telephone call. It was Mrs Brite. 'You've got a screen test tomorrow afternoon at three. Come to the office at two and we'll go in the car. Hello, Rita, are you there? Hello . . .'

Rita was there, but she was stunned into silence by the news, and although it was not unexpected, she was rendered both speechless and motionless by the realization that a dream she had dreamed a hundred times was going to become reality at last.

It was an awful day, just like the day of her first audition, and it made her wonder if all her important days were to be marked by bad weather. It was windy and it kept coming on to rain in short showers, as if unable to make up its mind whether to pour down or not. They got into Mrs Brite's car and, as usual, it would not start. She tugged away at the starter, held the choke out and Rita said: 'Aren't you going to get out and wind it up?'

'Gremlins,' Mrs Brite said and went on pulling on the starter until the engine burst into life with a roar, as if it had been summoning up all its power to start.

'I thought this Hector Point would have come backstage to see me,' Rita said. 'I got all tensed up nicely every night but he didn't come.'

Mrs Brite gave no reason why he had not done so, but said as they drove along, as the wind buffeted the small car and smudged the raindrops into long wet streaks across the windscreen: 'There's a small part in a film going into production soon. Just the sort of beginning you need.'

Rita said: 'Are you sure this dress will be all right?' The dress she had on under her coat had a flower pattern all over it, and she had worn it on Mrs Brite's instructions, although Rita thought it was the least fashionable thing she possessed.

'It will photograph well,' Mrs Brite told her and they drove on to the studios, where there was a man in uniform at the gate and where all the long buildings made the place look just like a factory.

It came on to rain again just as they got out of the car and they ran to the front office. As soon as they were inside Rita went into a daze, as if she were seeing and hearing everything, but was not actually there. Somebody whisked her off down a long corridor. She looked over her shoulder as she

300

went. Mrs Brite had disappeared. A door opened and she was ushered inside and put into a swivel chair in front of a mirror, where she sat looking at her own dead-white, scared face.

A woman wearing a smock said: 'A little make-up dear, for the camera,' and started with her eyes, putting a lot of blue on the lids and thick lines beneath. When she had finished, the voice of someone else said: 'Do you always wear your hair like this?' And the woman held Rita's long tresses on the palms of her hands, as if gauging it in some way.

'The wind messed it up coming from the car,' Rita said, beginning to recover from the shock of what was happening to her.

The woman ran a comb through her hair and just as Rita felt her confidence returning, the door opened, a man came in, looked at her and said, as if she could not answer for herself: 'Is that what she's going to wear?'

No one answered but the woman combing her hair said: 'Go with him now, dear,' and Rita went with the man, further down the long corridor, through a doorway to where a group of people were standing before a stage setting of a room in a house; a settee, a low table with a telephone on it and french windows showing the painted backcloth of a garden.

Mrs Brite was sitting down, hidden from sight by the man standing by her, until he saw Rita coming and walked towards her. She was relieved to see that Mrs Brite was still there. The man looked about thirty and was not bad looking in Rita's opinion. She thought he must be Hector Point.

'Right, come on then,' he said, taking Rita by the arm and leading her on to the set. 'Now that's the camera,' he said, 'and that thing on that fishing rod is the microphone. The lights won't bother you because you're an actress. Now what I want you to do is this.' He led her to the back of the set, through the french windows to the bit of painted garden. 'Just walk downstage, sit on the settee, pick up the telephone as if it was ringing and answer it. Say those few words there.' He gave her a piece of paper with four lines of telephone-answering dialogue on it. 'Should have given you that to learn,' he admitted. 'But you're an actress,' he told her again, 'so you'll have no difficulty there. I'll put it on the table by the telephone.' He took the script off her and left her standing there while he went off the set and stood by Mrs Brite.

Rita looked out at them grouped around the camera. There should have been a man with a green eyeshade on, she thought, and someone with a megaphone, but there was not. It was not at all how she had always imagined it would be. There was not even anyone smoking a cigar. It seemed as if all the small details that she had remembered from films had been made up especially for the pictures.

She walked down the set, round the low table with the telephone on it and sat on the settee. But the settee was very wide and deep, she sat back too far, sank down into the soft seat so that her feet came off the ground, and she gave a little squeal of surprise as she tipped backwards.

'Sit on the edge, Miss Rigby, sit on the edge,' the director called out, as she drew herself upright and pulled her dress back over her knees. 'Try it again, but sit on the edge.'

She did it correctly the second time, perched on the very edge of the settee and spoke her lines into the telephone. And then he asked her to do it again from the other side of the set, coming round the settee instead of the table, which she thought was the best way to do it anyway. No sooner had she done this and said the last word of her lines than the director said: 'Right, that's good. You can see the rushes tomorrow at four-thirty,' and everyone started dashing around as if they were in a hurry to get somewhere more important.

It was pouring with rain when Rita and Mrs Brite got outside. When she was a famous film star, Rita thought as she dashed towards the car, there would be a limousine waiting for her at the door and a man with an umbrella to make sure that not one spot of rain touched her. But her hair was all wet and bedraggled by the time she reached the car and she dreaded to think what she looked like as they drove past the man in uniform on the gate.

'I've suddenly realized,' Rita said. 'We've got a matinée tomorrow. I shan't be able to come to see the rushes. Not that I mind really. I don't particularly want to see myself going backwards on that settee. Lord knows what Hector Point thought.'

'He wasn't there,' Mrs Brite told her. 'Hector doesn't do

tests. But he'll see the rushes. I'll come tomorrow afternoon and see them. And don't worry. You looked all right from where I was sitting. Lots of girls would have gone to pieces.'

But Mrs Brite's words were not enough. That dream of having a screen test, of going out to dinner afterwards with the director to discuss a film part, would be nothing but a dream. There Rita was in Mrs Brite's car with her hair wet, her feet wet, the smell of damp clothes, the danger that at the next set of traffic lights the car would refuse to move and they would have to push it, and with a performance to get through that night. The event seemed to contain everything except the most important ingredient of all, glamour.

It was a jinx, the jinx that had caused the scene with her father, that had got her into trouble with Randall Axter and had cost her her small part in the revue, the jinx that had brought about the affair with Ian Chase. It had made her sit too far back on the settee and had spoiled her big chance, the chance she had been so confident about that she had even filled her fountain pen with blue ink and had put it in her handbag before going to the film studios, ready to sign a contract, preferring, when she signed her name on that important dotted line, to do so with her own pen rather than with anyone else's scratchy thing.

The jinx sat with her in Mrs Brite's office, while she told Rita that she had not got the part, that they had thought she looked too young. But it was just as well, Mrs Brite went on, because it would have meant playing in several scenes and having to go down to the studios at every touch and turn, and it might have been too much for her, having to do the play as well. Anyway, there was a part for her in another film, just one scene to be shot in a fortnight's time. 'It's not much, but it's a start,' Mrs Brite told her, 'and you've got to start at the bottom, Rita.'

'At the bottom? I'm starting at the very bottom,' she exclaimed.

But she took the part and although she did not feel happy and excited about it, by the time she got back to her flat that morning she had come to the decision that she was going to have to put on a false front of joy and happiness, just as her

303

mother would have done. And so she telephoned Shirley and told her the news, then rang Lottie's flat where Thorpe answered the telephone and gushed praise on her in his upper-crust accent. Lottie was in the bath. He took the telephone in to her and she splashed about excitedly when Rita told her she had a small film role, chattering away in a voice which made her sound, in the echoing emptiness of the bathroom, just like a duck learning to quack.

Rita took a taxi to the studios one morning, they dressed her up as a nurse, she stood by a doorway and said: 'You may come in now, Mrs Watson.'

'First part, one take, that's the ticket,' the man who had directed the scene said.

She changed and left and thought that, but for the money, it hardly seemed worth the journey. But when she got to the theatre that evening, everyone crowded into the tiny dressing-room she shared with Shirley to hear how it had gone, and although she had the odd feeling of being touched by their reaction, she remembered her mother's way. She stuck her nose in the air, smiled, felt proud and exaggerated a little.

Lottie thought the occasion was momentous enough to drag everyone off to a nightclub after the performance. Rita woke up at twelve the following day, with memories of being helped into a taxi in the early hours, falling off her high heels as if she were trying to walk on stilts and having a conversation with Humphrey during which he had said that he reckoned the play might transfer to New York, in which case she would only be a bus ride away from Hollywood, if she did not mind spending a week in a bus. And she remembered saying something to Humphrey which seemed ridiculous to recollect, something about her mother having wanted to go to America to find a certain man and kill him dead, telling him of how she was going to do the deed her mother did not live long enough to commit.

It seemed so silly to have said such a thing. Even if, one day, she did go to America, if she did find Chuck, she would not kill him. She would just like to tell him what he had done to her mother, tell him calmly and coolly just what he had done, that was all. It was one of her ambitions to do that. She felt she owed it to her mother to do it, her mother, who had tried so hard and had achieved so little, who had had a lot of fun on the road to nowhere, but had known only bitterness and regret at the end.

Twenty Nine

Autumn came and the leaves began to fall from the trees in the square to lie in wet brown patches on the grass and on the road. When Rita went out that afternoon and caught the bus to go to Lottie's flat, she looked down from the top deck at the people in the streets, bundled up against the autumn cold, stamping their feet as they stood at bus stops and outside shops. The little glimmer of success that shone into her life seemed out of place in such a dull world.

They had tea in the drawing room of Lottie's flat in St John's Wood. Shirley was there. There were just the three of them and Rita was bursting to tell them about her second film part, which she had played the day before. 'There were four of us girls,' she said, 'all dressed up in crinoline gowns. We sat in this carriage and we went through these gates, along a gravel drive, to the front steps of this mansion. And a couple of flunkeys came down the steps bowing and scraping, helped us out of the carriage and we went into the house. Only it wasn't a proper house. It was just the front, propped up at the back with thick pieces of wood. So that was it. Or at least, it should have been. But they made us do it all over again, because the flunkeys hadn't been bowing and scraping enough, I think. Then one of the horses did its business and somebody had to shovel it up, and wipe the horse's behind for it too, I shouldn't doubt, because you know what they're like in films; you daren't have a hair out of place. So off we went again, but then the sun went in and everything came to a halt while we all stood around looking up at the sky trying to tell which way the clouds were going. That happened several times. And just when I thought we'd done it so often it would be fun to try it with our eyes shut, the director said we were not chattering and laughing gaily enough when we got out of the carriage, so back we went and did it all again. But I ask you, Lottie, how can you chatter gaily when you're frozen to the marrow? Why on earth they didn't film it in the summer, I can't imagine. Anyway, where was I? Oh yes, so that's why I was there all day. And when we had walked a million miles all covered in smiles back to the dressing-room, the director chappy told me not to go taking any acting jobs in Katmandu or New Delhi or places, because they might need me again.'

There was a pause then while they sipped their tea and wondered if she had finished, before Shirley said: 'That sounds promising, if they want you again. Doesn't it, Lottie?'

'It does, my sweet,' Lottie agreed. And then she said, in a voice like the tinkling of a tiny bell: 'And now, I have a little secret to tell you. Not to tell anyone else. Fingers on lips.' And she put her index finger to her lips just like a small child in kindergarten. 'A little bird has told me that we might all be going to New York with our lovely play. I'm not sure, but I think so. You see, Thorpe and I were having a little lunch at the Savoy and we saw Arnold and some other influential people to do with the play, lunching with a certain impresario from New York. Confirmed our suspicions, as Thorpe put it. There now. What do you think of that?'

Rita could not be so hard on soft little Lottie to tell her that she already knew. Instead, she said: 'Well, if New York is nowhere near Katmandu or New Delhi, I suppose I'll be able to go.'

What occupied her mind more at that time was not going to New York but going back to the film studios. The weather had turned cold and she hoped that she would not have to sit in the carriage and do umpteen takes of the scene again. But, to her relief, filming took place in the studio, at a ball, with Rita wearing a lovely yellow ball gown. She had a little scene where she sat on a chair and a young man came across to her and said: 'I saw you at the hunt last week, I believe,' and took her off to dance.

When she told Lottie about it, she was ecstatic with delight. 'You had a scene, Rita darling, you had a scene. Thorpe,' she shouted, 'Rita had her own little scene in the picture.'

'Means something that, old girl,' Thorpe told her knowledgeably. 'Means something.'

'But I never set eyes on Stewart Granger,' Rita said. 'That's all I was doing most of the time, casting my eyes round for just a glimpse of him, wondering if I might be able to sidle up to him and just have a touch. The nearest I shall get, I suppose, is having my name on the credits about ten feet below his.'

Later on, when Rita saw the film, there was a shot of her dancing with the young man, then a shot of two old ladies watching and one said to the other: 'Isn't that the Yarborough girl Nigel is dancing with?' And for all Lottie's excitement, that was all it amounted to. The carriage scene, which had taken practically all day to shoot, lasted for one minute on the screen. But whereas with the first film she had made, in her one speaking role, her name had been the very last one on the cast list, on her second it had risen about a quarter of the way up, which, she thought, was something.

The landlady put the envelope on the table on the landing outside Rita's door. It was there when she got up at midday and went along the landing to the bathroom. It was an invitation to her father's wedding. He was to marry Helen one mid-week morning at the old village church near the air base. There would be no matinée that day and Rita sat down and wrote to say that she would be there.

And then, late that afternoon, she suddenly had an odd feeling about the wedding, about her father. She was sitting in front of the mirror combing her hair before setting off for the theatre, when for no apparent reason she thought of the Friday night her father had come home, the night he had fought with her mother. It all came back to her vividly, the blow that had sent her mother reeling back into the kitchen, his hand hitting her again, hitting her so hard in the face that it jerked her head sideways and made the blood spurt from her nose. She remembered the screams, the shouts, the bangs and the bumps she had heard while she had sat sobbing at her Auntie June's fireside. The black eye, the bruises, the blood, she could see it all, could see it in the mirror as if she were looking at her mother. She could see it in the mirror as if she herself bore all the marks of that night.

The memory of it shocked Rita. The reason for her suddenly thinking of it mystified her. She felt bitter inside. She felt bitter towards her father. In spite of all the wrong things Bella had done, he should not have hit her, because she had done no evil, had left no sadness behind her, had only left friends with happy memories of her.

She took the letter she had written and tore it up. Then she tried to think of an excuse not to go the wedding. She knew what her father wanted. He wanted to parade her before his fellow officers, his beautiful, glamorous daughter who was an actress on the West End stage, who had appeared in films. She was going to deny him that. The following morning she wrote a false letter, full of the little untruths her mother used to say to people. She wrote a letter to her father and in it she said, in her actressy way: 'We've got this big charity do on that very day. I can't back out, they expect me to be there. This sort of thing is very important to a young actress. Simply everyone will be there. Anyway, I'll come to your next wedding for sure.'

When she had written the letter and had posted it, she spent the cold afternoon sitting in front of her gas fire. She wished for a while that she had not had to write the letter, wished that there had been someone there to persuade her not to, someone who could have explained the vivid image of her mother that she had seen in the mirror. But there was no one. Rita was alone. She was a seventeen-year-old girl looking after herself, making her own decisions, at an age when most girls were still locked safely within the family. And when she had thought about it long enough, she came to the decision that she had done the right thing after all, for she had no happy memories of life with her father. All her happy memories were of her own success and of life with her mother. She had a feeling of nostalgia that made her look back with an odd longing for those days at home with her mother and Ronnie; with Auntie June and Mavis next door and Mrs Bragg across the road; finishing school at four with every evening to herself; weekends to be squandered with boredom if she so pleased; tea dances and visits to the bughouse with Anne. All gone now, replaced with the actress's life, the relentless, monotonous regularity of work that spelled success, of Sundays off, but with her more dead than alive, parties at Lottie's flat that she just dare not miss when she would rather have been asleep in bed. On a Sunday morning she longed for someone to bring her a cup of tea in bed, as she had done for her mother. But her only pleasure was the one that had always brought her more enjoyment than anything else, to go to the cinema. That was a pleasure above all others.

She received a brief, regretful note from her father in reply to her letter. After the wedding they sent her a photograph. Her grandmother was on it, looking fierce. And Ronnie, tall and good-looking, a credit to somebody – who, Rita could not decide. But Rita had no regrets about not going to the wedding. For her mother, she felt, would always come between her and her father. Her mother, she realized, had been two people. Her father had known Bella as a wife who had let him down. Rita had known her as a mother who had been sufficient. Rita and her father had lived in different worlds and neither of them would ever accept the other one's view of Bella, who had lived in both worlds. There was nothing she could share with her father. Not even the past. She had her past and he had his, and the two would always conflict.

Thirty

Winter ran on towards Christmas and the play ran on before full houses. Rita had one more film part, which consisted of Dermot Walsh dashing through some swing doors after another woman, bumping into Rita and knocking her handbag out of her hand. The scene, she discovered later, ended up on the cutting-room floor, but at the time she was making it all thoughts of what effect actually being on the screen with Dermot Walsh might have on her career were pushed into the background when it was officially announced that the cast of 'A Blue Moon Rising' were to take the play to New York.

It was good news to take back to Manchester that Christmas. She caught the train on Christmas Eve after the performance. This time her father was not at the station to meet her. The key was under the mat, the house was warm, the kettle was singing on the hob. There were sandwiches left out for her, and she ate them, made herself a drink and got warm by the fire. The trimmings were hung, the tree was decorated, just as it had been the year before. She arranged her presents beneath it and went up to bed.

'Do you mean to tell me,' Rita said to her grandmother on Christmas morning, 'that dad has left you and Ronnie to have Christmas all on your own? I've got to go back in the morning, you know. We've got a matinée in the afternoon.'

'Oh, we could have gone to have Christmas with him and Helen,' her grandmother replied, 'but I wasn't all that keen and Ronnie didn't want to go. There was the carol concert at school and he's in the choir, so he didn't want to miss that. And he's in the football team at the church youth club. They've got two matches during the holidays and he's a right one for his football is Ronnie.'

311

For a moment it seemed strange to Rita that Ronnie had not wanted to go to his father, strange that their father had not taken him to live with him permanently, with his new wife as Ronnie's new mother. She wondered if there had been rows about it, but she did not ask. And she would not ask Ronnie, because she realized then that he probably had that trait in him that she had herself, that their mother had had, that streak of independence that had made her mother set off with her two children into an uncertain future at the outbreak of war, that had made Rita pursue her ambitions regardless of anyone else, that would make Ronnie set out on his own road in life and not complain if it was uphill all the way.

'Well, I didn't go much on that chicken,' Mrs Rigby said, while she and Rita were washing up after dinner. 'It was a bit tough. Still, I suppose we were lucky to have one.'

'Oh, it wasn't too bad, gran,' Rita said, when in actual fact she was dying to get a piece of cotton to draw through her teeth to get out the bits of stringy meat.

'I'll cut the bits of skin up for next door's cat,' Mrs Rigby said. 'At least he'll get some enjoyment out of it.' And then she said suddenly: 'When you go to America, I've got a friend I'd like you to visit. The address is on a piece of paper behind the clock.'

'You've got a friend in America?' Rita said with surprise. She took the piece of paper from behind the clock. 'I didn't know you knew anyone . . . Mr and Mrs J. Hoffman . . . California. Well, that's where Hollywood is. Fancy you knowing someone in California, gran. Who are they?'

'It's just someone I used to know who married an American,' she said reticently. 'I write to her now and again.' And without lifting her eyes from the washing-up bowl, she carried on: 'You will go and see them, won't you? I'll write and say you will. I thought it would be nice to have someone there to go and see, if you go to Hollywood, that is.'

'Oh, I shall go there,' Rita stated. 'After Broadway, it's Hollywood next stop. Fancy you knowing someone in California,' she said again.

Later in the afternoon, Rita went up to her bedroom. She kept all her mother's belongings there, locked in two battered suitcases, the ones her mother had packed each time she had decided to make her escape. Rita sorted through them. She was looking for two things. One was Chuck's address. There were photographs galore spread about in the bottom of one suitcase, and American coins and a badge off his uniform. She sorted through the photographs and wondered why her mother had not bought an album to put them in, wondered why there was not a letter of any sort amongst them, not a diary, not a scrap of paper with the address written on, nothing but photographs, of Rita and Ronnie when they were babies right through to those of her mother and Chuck, the ones that had been taken during that last happy wartime year they had been together. There they were, in a country lane with their arms around each other, smiling and looking in love. Rita blinked back the tears and searched on. At the bottom of the suitcase was a photograph of Chuck, young, smiling, with his pile of blond wavy hair. It was mounted on cardboard, as if it had once been in a frame. She turned it over. On the back, written in her mother's handwriting, she read: 'Chuck Bradwell, Hurst, California.'

Rita fetched her diary and copied down the address. She was determined to find him. If he had moved, she would track him down. She put that before going to visit her grandmother's friend. She sorted through the other contents of the suitcases, came across some terrible black lace underwear, threw it aside and found the other thing she had been looking for, her mother's fur cape. It looked fine after she had brushed it out. 'Remember mam wearing this, Ron?' She put it on, turned from side to side in front of the mirror, admiring herself. And she packed it carefully in her own suitcase and took it back to London with her.

After the curtain came down on New Year's Eve, Lottie carted everyone away to a nightclub to bring in nineteen forty-seven. Rita wore her mother's fur cape and when Lottie saw it she said: 'Ooh Rita, you've got a bit of cat,' and she stroked the fur.

'It's not cat,' Rita retorted indignantly. 'It's fox – or something that's hard to catch.'

'But that's what I always call fur. I always call it cat,' Lottie explained. 'It's lovely.' She stroked it again. 'I'll bet it came off something beautiful and precious, something it was a shame to kill.' She had redeemed herself.

'My mother used to look lovely in this,' Rita said proudly. 'All done up with her best frock on and this fur cape round her shoulders – well, it wasn't fair on the men really. She'd have had your Thorpe down on all fours carrying her slippers around between his teeth.'

Lottie pictured it and gave a laugh that would have sounded ridiculous coming from anyone else.

A new cast took over the play in the West End and everyone had a little time off before going to America. Rita did not go straight back to Manchester. She wanted to see Anne again. She had liked Anne, although sometime during the hectic months of the previous year she had stopped writing to her, had imagined that Anne owed her a letter without thinking that it might be the other way round.

Rita wanted to tell Anne of all the good things that had happened to her, the parts she had played in the revue, how she had suddenly been whooshed off to the south coast to save the play, being in the West End, having her own flat, being in a film with Stewart Granger without ever seeing him. She wanted to tell her of how Laurence, right up to the last moment, had tried to talk her into becoming a manne-quin, of how much money he had told her she could earn modelling clothes. She was not going to tell Anne that, in Laurence's opinion, the play would die on Broadway, that the American audience would not stay in the theatre long enough to laugh it off the stage, and that they would all be on the next boat home, unemployed, eager for work. Neither was she going to tell her of her father trying to take her home, of Randall Axter, of Ian Chase. Those were Rita's private disasters; as interesting, she thought, as her triumphs, but not as important as points of conversation.

She telephoned the Shire Hotel to book a room and caught the train from Paddington. But even on the short taxi ride from the station to the hotel, she knew that she was not coming back to the place that she remembered. In her memory, the streets of that town were not so narrow, the buildings were not so small, the shops were not so dull. That evening, by the time she had been to visit the Plough, one of her mother's old haunts, and had found it to be such an ordinary place, and had seen the little park that her mother had told her about, where it had happened, only to find it grown into a jungle, all tall grass and overgrown bushes, with rubbish tipped there, she began to wonder if she might find the people she wanted to see just as uninteresting, just as much of a let down. Even the Manhattan Lounge was a disappointment, although Rita had never been there before. It had been her mother's idea of luxury, a good imitation of the real thing. There was a man in a dinner jacket playing the piano, waiters in white coats, deep chairs, low lighting, tall stools along the bar. But it was nothing to Rita. Lottie had led them all off to the Savoy, the Dorchester and to countless nightclubs, and after that Rita felt that there could be nothing else to come on this side of the Atlantic.

Despite the let down she felt at seeing the town again, she knew that fame would bring her back there. Fame would take her into her old school, but that morning she just stood outside and watched the girls playing rounders in the yard as she had done, saw one of them stumble and fall on the coke heap by the boiler room, as someone always used to. At the technical college she went into the entrance hall and read all the notices on the board. They were auditioning for the summer play.

One day, she thought, fame would take her into the town hall and then to see her little brother, and it would make him proud to know that he was related to her. But what had possessed her, she wondered, to want so much to have her photograph hung in the foyer of the Palace Cinema? There was a fat woman, with her hair in curlers and a cigarette drooping from the corner of her mouth, kneeling down scrubbing the steps, and the sight of her took away all the glamour Rita had associated with the place.

After lunch, Rita went into the Unicorn. It was a very ordinary place. She bought a drink and sat down. What, she wondered, had her mother ever found in the pub, with its brown walls and hard, battered furniture? A drink on the way to the cinema had been one thing, but to go there on a night – as Bella had done on the night of the accident – was something Rita found difficult to understand. Was the company like the place, or entirely different? Who were these people who could sit in a pub at two o'clock on a weekday afternoon, when everyone should be back at work? It was all

315

a mystery to her, but she did not want to solve it. She wanted no part of it. It was not her world.

She could not avoid the eyes of a sailor who was standing at the bar. His eyes and his fixed grin were always there whenever she looked in his direction and she hurried to finish her drink rather than be stared at by the grinning, unblinking man.

But he left the other men he was with and came towards her. He was short and fat, middle-aged and seemed to be all stomach and no chest. He had a florid complexion and a sparkle in his eyes that did not come from good health. 'Would you like another drink, darling?' he asked her.

'No thank you,' Rita said.

'Come on darling, the navy's buying.'

'Then the navy can buy itself one,' she replied.

He looked down at her, the fixed grin unmoved by her reply. He had brass buttons round his cuffs. 'New in town, are you, darling?' And when she did not reply, while she tipped up her glass to finish her drink, he said: 'I know all the best places in town. If you fancy a nice evening out, I could take you to all the best places.'

Rita stood up. She was inches taller than him. She sent a piercing look down into his round little eyes and said with an actress's mixture of amusement and slight horror: 'What, you? I wouldn't be seen dead with a little squirt like you.' And she went out.

Anne was no longer at home. She had joined the WAAF. 'I wondered why she hadn't written,' Rita said. 'She owed me a letter, but it never came.'

'She thought you owed her one,' Mrs Phelpstead said and showed Rita a photograph of Anne in her uniform, fatter than ever, a face like a pudding. 'Oh, she loves it in the WAAF. She's secretary to a group captain. Her father's ever so proud of the way she's got on.'

Rita's career counted for nothing with Anne's mother. Nevertheless, she gave her a photograph of herself, signed it and on the back she wrote the names of the films she had been in. 'Make sure you go and see them when they come here.'

'Oh, we will Rita, father and I will go.'

'I'm sorry Anne isn't here,' Rita said. 'I was so looking

forward to going out with her tonight, to all the old places, just like we used to.'

'Never mind. I'll give you her address and you can write to her.'

'When I get back from America,' Rita said, 'well, we'll just have to get together then, Anne and I. There'll be so much to talk about.'

'Yes,' Anne's mother agreed. 'Our Anne will sit talking about the WAAF for hours. She'll keep you engrossed, she really will.'

Mrs Bragg greeted Rita unceremoniously, as if it were only days since she had last been in her house. They talked about her mother's death and her own success.

Megan's kitchen was the same neat, bright place, the grate black-leaded so that you could see your face in it, the library books on the window sill, the packet of Craven 'A' handy. 'How are your boys then?' Rita asked her.

'Fine,' was her solitary reply.

'Our Ronnie's doing well at grammar school. Talks about going to university. Fancy that.'

'There's nice,' Megan remarked.

'Well, what's life like here now? Do you still go to the Palace? Does Mr Jerome let you in for nothing? What about Archie, is he still the commissionaire?'

'Now and again I go. They gave Archie the sack. Got too daft for the job, you see. Still stands outside shouting: "Two standing at one and nine," even when there's no queue there. Mr Jerome has to get the police to him sometimes. They'll put him away eventually, I think.'

'Seems a shame really,' Rita said. 'But I suppose once you're daft, you're daft.'

'That's it. Cup of tea?' Mrs Bragg asked her.

She boiled the kettle and made the tea, while Rita chatted away, sounding just like her mother, only much better spoken. With her back to her, Mrs Bragg could have sworn it was Bella putting her talk on, and when she turned round it was almost Bella sitting there in the chair by the dresser. The looks were all there, but there was a touch of elegance to go with them now. And listening to Rita talking about life in the theatre set Mrs Bragg to feeling the same enviousness that she had felt at Bella. What Mrs Bragg would not have given to have been able to live like Bella had lived, to have had the life that Rita was now living. And as Rita went on talking about a party here, lunch there, dinner somewhere else, nightclubs until the early hours, seeing herself for the first time on film, Mrs Bragg felt the same admiration for her that she had had for Bella, recognized all the limits her lack of courage put on her own life and suffered a hopeless longing to be different.

'What about your husband?' Rita asked her. 'Has he been demobbed yet?'

'Oh no,' Mrs Bragg replied. 'He's still in the navy. He's a regular, you see. Couple more years and he'll be finished.'

'What will you do then?'

'He always talks about having a little place in the country,' she said, without enthusiasm. 'Keep chickens and grow fruit, he says. Don't know if we will, like.'

'Where is he now? Still abroad?'

'No, on leave at present. Should be in shortly. Likes to have a drink lunchtime when he's home.' She paused. It was four o'clock. 'He's a chief petty officer now.'

It was only a few minutes later that Mr Bragg opened the front door and stumbled into the hallway. Megan went hurriedly out to meet him and Rita heard his gruff, uncompromising voice, then looked through the kitchen doorway and saw the sailor who had tried to pick her up in the Unicorn.

Mrs Bragg made an effort at introducing them, ashamed as she was at the state he was in, still the worse for drink at four in the afternoon. But he recognized Rita as quickly as she had recognized him. The silly grin was still on his face. He said something unintelligible to Rita, who neither spoke nor moved. He looked foolish but, as Rita imagined, fools usually do, and he turned away and went up the stairs, ignoring his wife as she spoke softly to him.

'They like a drink, bit of company. Being at sea so long, you know,' Megan said by way of an explanation.

When she left shortly afterwards, Rita stood at Mrs Bragg's front door and looked across at the house she had lived in. 'Sounds silly really,' she said, 'but I always think of this street as home. You'd hardly think that such a drab place could be so special to somebody,' she added, without making the remark sound hurtful. Then she said: 'Still, it was better then, wasn't it?'

'Yes, it was better then,' Mrs Bragg agreed, and she watched Rita cross over the road and walk up the street, just like her mother, the same figure, the same long black hair, the same way of walking with her head tilted upwards to give an impression of arrogance, the same magic that made people look, then look again.

Megan closed the front door. He was upstairs snoring, the smell of drink was all over the house. She went into the front room and stood at the window, looking across at the house where so much life had been lived, so much interest provoked for her, an unobtrusive onlooker. There was nothing in the street now. It was drab. It was dull. When Bella had gone, all the life in the place had gone with her. All Mrs Bragg had now were memories, memories that were all concerned with Bella and June, and with Leslie Rigby, standing at her front door on that cold winter night, tall, slim, good-looking, the face she saw in the fire. And where was she, but still there, unchanged, with a husband who drank, a husband who now made her happy only by being away from her. Life was a treeless plain. There was nothing to break the monotony. She was haunted by a dream of having her life to live all over again, and of living it differently, tortured by an impossible longing to be able to walk out through the front door into a totally different existence. For Mrs Bragg life was all regret and no hope.

The train took Rita north to Manchester. As it rattled on its way, she realized what tricks the memory can play. Memories have only a certain percentage of truth; they are always too highly coloured to be totally true. The town, she felt, would always look better in her mind than it had ever been in reality. Her friendship with Anne would probably have suffered the same disappointment had they been able to meet. It was better to be like her mother, she thought, who had hurried on through life without a backward glance, confident that all the hardship and sadness would someday be left in a past to which she would not return, and that happiness and success could only be found in the future.

'Have you got a photograph of yourself that I can send to my friend in America?' her grandmother asked her. 'I've

319

written and said that you'll be going over there and that you'll call and visit her.'

'I've got several in my case,' Rita replied. 'I'll fish them out and you can take your pick. But I can't for the life of me imagine why you should want to send them a photo of me.'

'So that they'll know you when you arrive,' Mrs Rigby said, and before Rita could question such a flimsy answer, she went on: 'A head and shoulders one will do, like that one I've got framed on the living-room sideboard.'

Rita gave her the photographs, and when her grandmother gave them back to her, when she found them on her bedside table, she could not help noticing that she had taken three. Rita smiled to herself; she imagined that in her grandmother's eyes she was famous already and that she would give two of the photographs away. She heard her grandmother coming up the stairs and slipped the remaining photographs into a drawer.

Mrs Rigby came into the bedroom. 'Oh, are you up here?' she said. She took a duster out of her pinafore pocket and began dusting the dressing-table. 'Do you know, rooms get just as dusty with no one using them as they do when they're in full use.'

Rita sat on the edge of the bed and said: 'I wonder how long it will be before I come back into this room and unpack my suitcase?'

'However long it is, it will still be here waiting for you,' her grandmother told her.

'You really are behind me in what I'm doing, aren't you, gran?' Rita asked her.

Her grandmother moved to the bedroom door, ran her duster over it and said: 'Of course I am. It was the same with your father. He always wanted to fly. Aeroplane mad, even when he was a boy. But we always told him, get a trade behind you first. Something to fall back on. And he did. Just like you with your shorthand and typing. You've always got that to fall back on. Better than just dashing off blindly, chancing your neck and ending up . . .' She went out on to the landing and ran her duster down the bannister rail as she went down the stairs.

And ending up just like your mother, Rita thought. That was what her grandmother had been frightened of, she realized. She had not been frightened *of* her, as her father had maintained, but had been frightened *for* her, frightened of seeing her wander off the path she had set out on, just as, she imagined, she had seen her mother do, being distracted by men and happy nights, being left with dreams and having no chance at all of ever making them come true.

But Rita was different. Her father, she reckoned, must know that by now and her grandmother certainly knew it. That was why she had a framed photograph of her on the living-room sideboard. That was why she had the Crombie Cup there, right in the middle of the sideboard, set there prominently for everyone to notice and inquire about.

If only there were something there of her mother's, Rita thought. If only there were a photograph hanging on the wall or a framed snapshot on the mantelpiece. But there was nothing. On her last afternoon, she bought some flowers and she and Ronnie went to the cemetery. Under a winter sky that was black and threatening, in a biting wind that froze her fingers, Rita arranged the flowers in the vase on the grave. And she read the little headstone and cried. Other than memories, that little headstone was all there was.

That night, she lay in bed and thought about America. She thought about Broadway, about finding Chuck and giving him his just desserts, of visiting her grandmother's friend, of going to Hollywood. And she thought of her mother, of the night she had sat on the edge of her mother's bed and joked about them going to America together. She thought of herself getting off the ship in New York, standing on the quayside and saying: 'Well, mam, we finally made it,' as if they had really gone there together, after all.

Thirty One

New York was bleak and windswept and covered with snow. There was no glamour in disembarking from the ship at the dockside. It was not at all as Rita had seen it in films. After several days of inactivity at sea, everyone seemed to be in a rush to get ashore and her dream of descending the gangway gracefully, to the popping of flash bulbs as the cast of one of London's most successful plays arrived, did not come true. Instead, she hurried along anonymously in the midst of the crowd, failing even to look upon her arrival in America as an ambition achieved for her mother as well as for herself. It had been her intention to step ashore with that thought, but she did not. It was too cold and there was too much bustle.

The play was not to tour, but was to go straight on to Broadway after rehearsals. Rita and Shirley shared a flat. It was not in a skyscraper, as Rita had hoped it would be, but was on the top floor of what had once been someone's house. When they had been there a few days, she said to Shirley: 'Right, now I've written to all and sundry to tell them I've arrived in little old New York, let's make a list of all the places we want to see. You write them down. We'll have to go to the top of the Empire State building.'

'Not until the weather's fine,' Shirley said, 'otherwise we won't be able to see a thing.'

Rita walked to and fro, looking thoughtful. 'All right. Next one is the Statue of Liberty. Lottie wants to go there. You go there on a boat, evidently, and you can go right up inside it. Central Park. There'll probably be ducks to feed there, which will be fun. I hope the pond isn't frozen over, though. What do they do with the ducks in a park when the pond freezes over?'

'I don't know,' Shirley said. 'That's a problem I've not yet come across.'

'Well if they take them indoors, perhaps they'll shoo them outside just for us, being as we've come so far,' Rita said. And, ignoring Shirley's giggles at what was meant to be a serious statement, she went on: 'Then when the weather's fine we'll go to Coney Island. That's by the sea and there's a funfair. Oh, and you'd better put down Greenwich Village. Thatched cottages, I imagine. Then we'll have to go to a ball game.'

'Is that football?' Shirley asked her, in a voice that lacked enthusiasm.

'No, it's baseball,' Rita told her. 'It's only rounders for men, but it should be good. My Auntie June's American boyfriend was always on about the New York Yankees and the Boston Bedsocks.'

'The Boston Bedsocks? That's not their name, surely,' Shirley said with amazement.

'Well, it was something like that,' Rita replied, dismissing the matter. 'And we've got to eat hamburgers and hot dogs.'

'And doughnuts,' Shirley added.

'Yes, you can dip those in your coffee,' Rita said, 'a bit like we dip biscuits in our tea.'

'Oh, I don't think I'll do that. It sounds a bit common,' Shirley stated.

'Popcorn. We must try that too. They eat that in the pictures, you know. That Yank my mother fell for, the one whose come-uppance is about to come up now that I've arrived, he said they always used to eat popcorn in the pictures. Now, that's a few things to be going on with. If we think of anything else, we'll add it to the list. Although this rotten weather takes away your enthusiasm for anything, doesn't it?'

Rita stood at the window and looked down into the street. They had had more snow and the freezing wind was blowing it along the street and piling it up against walls and in doorways. She had not realized that they had hard winters in New York. She had imagined that it was always summer there, that they only had snow in the Rockie Mountains.

The play opened, they had a grand party afterwards and Lottie's baby voice went squeaking on through the night, right up until the moment when the newspapers came out.

323

But the reviews were unpromising. The fun stopped. Inquests were held. Humphrey maintained that they should have toured with the play first, but one critic described it as being held over from before the war. They were stock characters in the usual country house, he asserted, acting as if there had never been a war. Thorpe agreed with him, but Rita disagreed with Thorpe and she thought that she was right because, for the first week, they played to full houses. But after that, when the curtain went up, there were empty seats, and when the lights went up and they took their bows, there were often more empty seats than they had started with.

The bad reception the play was getting took all the enjoyment out of everything else they did. Even getting answers to the letters she had written did not cheer Rita up. The reply from Anne was a big disappointment. There was page after page of boring detail of life in the WAAFS, so much detail that Rita felt she could have sat at Anne's desk and done her job without a fault. Hardly a mention was made of Rita's success, not a word about her having made two films, nothing at all about their West End run. She did not even comment upon Rita having met Eric Portman when he had dropped in to one of Lottie's parties in London. And Anne had been very passionate about Eric Portman. Anne, who had loved food despite the fact that she could even get fat on rations, had ignored what Rita had written about there being no rationing in America, of how the shops were filled with food, of how for the first time she had eaten peanut butter that had not been solen from an army camp. And to cap it all, in return for the glamorous photograph that Rita had sent her, one with her autograph in the bottom right hand corner, there was a snapshot of Anne, a picture of a fat WAAF in uniform.

Rita did not know what to do with the snapshot. She could not put it in her album. That was for her show business photographs only and it would have looked odd, especially next to the one that Humphrey had given her and on which he had written, for some reason: 'Yours forever, Rita, Humphrey.' She put Anne's photo back in the envelope with the letter and wondered whether it would not be better to forget friendships from the past. Perhaps, she thought, they were just like places from the past, better to remember than to revisit.

They all knew that things could not go on as they were. Secretly, Rita wrote to Mrs Brite and asked her if she knew anyone in Hollywood she could put her in touch with. But it was no secret that the play was turning out to be a flop. Lottie went around telling everyone to keep their peckers up, trying to encourage them to carry on, saying things would buck up when the weather got better. But it had no effect, which was only to be expected when the words were spoken in a voice that would not have been out of place in a nursery.

On Sunday evenings, they all went up in the lift to Lottie and Thorpe's flat high in a skyscraper. 'When we moved in,' Lottie piped, 'I didn't realize we were so high up and when I looked through the window at the road down there, well, it looked like a twig and the cars looked like beetles crawling along it and I was so frightened that dear Thorpe had to take me away to lie down. I haven't dared look out of the window since. Anyway, Thorpe said that if we are still here in the summer, we will take a house on Long Island. But it doesn't look as if we . . .'

Her voice tailed off, she was near to tears, and Rita thought that it would not have looked out of place if someone had gone up to Lottie, held a handkerchief to her nose and told her to blow.

It was not like the Sunday evenings in London. No one asked Rita to sing. There was a piano that remained unplayed. All the talk was of the theatre and it always got round to their dismal contribution to the New York stage. It made Rita irritable and short-tempered. 'No, no,' a man said to her, 'the team is called the Boston Redsox.'

'Well I call them the Boston Bedsocks,' Rita snapped back. 'After all, they sent me to sleep.' And she stalked away from him.

The following morning, she lay in bed and tested the warmth of the air with her nose. Even with central heating she could detect a drop in the temperature outside. The postman had been and Shirley came into the bedroom and said: 'Who have you written to who lives here? There's a letter for you with American stamps on.'

Rita took the letter off her, opened it and read it. Then she said: 'It's from that friend of my grandmother's. I wonder how she knew I was here. Gran must have written and told her.'

'I thought you said you had written to everyone,' Shirley said.

'Well, not these people,' she admitted. 'After all, I don't suppose I shall get to Hollywood now. The play's a flop, no one I have spoken to has seen either of the films I was in and Mrs Brite's instructions to me are to return home, because she doesn't know a soul in Hollywood and won't admit it. I think I'll go back to London and get signed up as a mannequin, just like Laurence suggested.'

'Are you serious?' Shirley asked her.

'Of course I am,' she replied.

'Oh good, because I can see Desmond and I having a summer wedding and you can be a bridesmaid.'

Rita passed no comment on what Shirley had said, because she was dwelling on her own train of thoughts. She said: 'Something always happens. There was that mess-up in the revue, then there was Ian Chase, then there was the screen test and me going backwards on the settee and showing all my legs. The same thing happened to my mother. She always went her own way and never got anywhere. Trouble all along the line. I've been just the same. I think that if I do what someone else wants me to do, for a change, everything might turn out all right. I think I'll take Laurence's advice. Hollywood can go to hell.'

Shirley said: 'I've never heard anyone say anything so silly in the whole of my life.' She sat in front of the dressing-table mirror and began combing her hair.

'Oh well,' Rita retorted, 'you should keep your ears open more, shouldn't you?'

'Be serious,' Shirley went on. 'And for goodness sake forget about what your mother did or what she didn't do. You've got this odd notion that your life is going to be just the same as hers. Whoever heard of anyone's life running along exactly the same lines as one of their parents? Forget it and live your own life.'

Rita wriggled about under the bedclothes. 'But you've got to admit, the pitfalls I've had in my life are just the sort . . .'

'Rubbish,' Shirley said hotly. 'Stop looking at the things

that have gone wrong and look at the things that have gone right. You're not eighteen yet, but look how you've got on. The West End, films, Broadway. And you've done it purely by pursuing your own ambitions. You're not telling me that you've ever really allowed anything that happened to your mother to stand in your way. I can tell you straight, if what happened to you in that hotel room had happened to me when I was sixteen, I'd have run home screaming, mother or no mother. But you didn't. You steamed straight on. You took to the play like a duck to water, you badgered your agent to get you into films. I don't care what you say, you've gone your own way and succeeded, and that's how you should keep on.'

Rita was a little taken aback by Shirley's outburst. She was quiet for a moment, then she said: 'What do you think then of my decision to go back to London and work for Laurence?'

'I do not think it's what you want to do,' Shirley said. 'Look at it this way. Laurence only wants you to do modelling for the good it will do him. He's trying to build up his business, isn't he? Maybe you will make a lot of money, but . . . There again, you take Mrs Brite. She could easily put you in touch with a Hollywood agent, but I imagine she's a bit tentative about letting you loose in Hollywood because of your age. So, you're just where you like to be, really. Making up your own mind, deciding for yourself. Just like your mother, I expect. So go to Hollywood and don't let anyone put you off.' Shirley looked round at Rita and saw that she was wearing the same kind of expression of bored tolerance that she herself used to adopt when Rita was talking endlessly about the latest film she had seen. She said: 'Well, what's in the letter then?'

Rita looked back at the sheet of notepaper. 'It's from the woman's husband, Jerry Hoffman. Says his wife isn't much good at letter writing and he sure hopes I don't mind him writing. He sure hopes the play is going well. He sure hopes I am going to visit them. Very sure of themselves, these Americans,' she commented, 'by the way they use the word. The trouble with being that sure of things is that it causes size problems when buying a hat.'

'Are you going to write back?' Shirley asked her. 'If you

do, don't go saying the play is a rip-roaring hit. Say we are enjoying a moderate success.'

'Oh, that sounds good,' she said, getting out of bed. 'I'll write that down.'

'I wish Desmond could write love letters,' Shirley said distantly. 'All I get is a page of awkward, disjointed sentences and half a page of multiplication signs. On one letter, he tried drawing a heart in each corner of the page and they turned out looking just like kidneys.'

Rita laughed and said: 'Well, if ever he tells you he loves you with all his kidneys, you'll know he means his heart, won't you?'

Despite her conversation with Shirley, Rita was undecided over what to do. She thought it might be best to dwell on the whole thing for a few days, but no sooner had she come to that decision than the cast of the play were told the inevitable news. The play was to run for another two weeks, then close. The future, in which she would have to decide what to do, had suddenly arrived. It surprised her to realize that the most important thing to decide was whether or not to visit the Hoffmans, and she pondered over the problem of going back to Manchester and facing her grandmother without having made the visit as she had promised. Hollywood could wait. What chance, she wondered, would she have there, knowing no one and being English? Almost all the films she saw were American and all the people in them were American. She could picture no sudden success for herself in Hollywood, but wondered instead what opportunities might be occurring in London while she was all those thousands of miles away, lacking the one thing that she imagined would be necessary for her to get a film part in Hollywood – an American accent.

She wrote to Mr Hoffman, a non-committal letter, saying that the play was closing and that whether she would be able to come to California depended on whether she was needed back in London or not. After she had posted the letter, she thought of Chuck. Chuck, she said to herself, could go to hell, which was just where he belonged.

At the beginning of their final week, Shirley called into the bathroom to Rita: 'There's another letter for you from that man in California.'

Rita did not hurry out of the bath. It was, she imagined, just another letter full of sure hopes. She dried and dressed herself, then came out of the bathroom and looked at the envelope lying on the table. It looked thick, as if it were a long letter. She opened it. It was not the sort of letter that she had expected. It not only asked, it almost insisted that she visit them. And with the letter was an airline ticket. She was booked on a flight to Los Angeles during the week following the closure of the play.

'Funny?' Shirley said when Rita showed her the letter. 'It's not funny. It's exciting. An airline ticket to Los Angeles, an hotel room booked for you to stay overnight, a railway ticket at the desk for you the following morning, someone to meet you when you get off the train. Honestly, Rita, I wouldn't mind being in a play with a plot like that.'

Rita did not feel as happy and confident about the letter as Shirley did. With the play closing, with no other work waiting for her, she felt that life was suddenly as empty and as dismal as it had been when she had left the revue and had found herself in London in winter with no job and no prospects. She looked through the window into the street. The snow had been cleared away, all except for the little frozen mounds that had set hard in corners and could not be moved. The sky was dull and grey and evil-looking, and the wind cut straight along the street as a warning not to go out. She might as well go to California, she thought. At least it would be warm there. She turned away from the window and got out her writing-pad.

At the theatre that night, she told them of her mysterious letter and they all showed the same enthusiasm that Shirley had shown. After the performance they all went out to supper together and Rita's strange news gave them a diverting topic of conversation, made them forget for a while that they were not the toast of the town, that they were not a success, that on Sunday morning they would all be unemployed.

It was a dismal ending on Saturday. They had run on Broadway for six weeks, when they had expected a run of six months at the very least. No one except Rita would stay in New York after the play closed. There was nothing to stay there for. It was too cold, too bleak, for them a place of failure. They had booked their passages home the moment they had heard the play was closing.

Rita went down to the ship to see them off. She wished she was going too. She loved them all and she had none of her mother's hardness at being parted from them. She cried, Humphrey hugged her and could not speak, and Lottie squalled as loudly as a cat with its tail caught in a door. Rita stood on the quay and watched the liner steam away. She listened to the deep, sorrowful moan of its siren, a sound that could say nothing but goodbye.

Thirty Two

The frightening experience of going up in an aeroplane, the way it clawed its way into the air like a man climbing up a mountain, dominated Rita's mind right until the time that the aeroplane seemed to be flying level and was going along steadily like a ship on a calm sea. It was then that she wondered what would have been waiting for her had she gone back with the others, what Mrs Brite might have had lined up for her after she had climbed the bare wooden stairs and walked across the worn lino into her office. She could hear her voice saying to her when, eventually, she did go back: 'Well there's nothing at the moment, Rita, but if you had come back when you were supposed to . . .'

Then, she imagined, she would find herself doing what Laurence had suggested and becoming a model, at least until something else turned up. Laurence, she thought, who had predicted that the play would not run on Broadway, that they would all soon be catching the boat home.

It was too late now to turn back. It was too late to do anything but dwell on the fact that she might end up blaming her grandmother's friend for causing her to miss her big break. Just who was her grandmother's friend anyway, she wondered? Obviously she was someone who had married a rich American, to be able to send her an airline ticket. Undoubtedly they had a fine home and would entertain her well, but the thought of it did not fill her with enthusiasm. In some way, she realized, she lacked something that her mother had had. Her mother would have boiled over with excitement, would not have bothered whether she should have been somewhere else doing something more important, but would have got herself all dolled up and not cared whether the Hoffmans were rich or posh. She would have gone, she would have relied on that strange magic she had and acted her way through. That was what she had done so often, Rita realized, acted. Acting was only telling lies convincingly, and Bella had lied her way in and out of all sorts of situations, Rita knew. Perhaps that was where Rita's own enthusiasm and talent for acting had originated, in her mother's ability to do so. What a place to discover that, she thought, thousands of feet up in the air in an aeroplane flying across America. What a time to have to thank her mother for giving her not only her looks, but her talent, and to thank her too for not giving her that reckless attitude that had made her fly blindly into the future, dragging her children behind her, getting drunk, falling off a bus, and ending it all when she could fly no more. What a place to realize that she was only seventeen, that there was no need to rush, that she had time to do things her own way, that it was possible to be determined and cautious at the same time.

After the long flight Rita felt tired and stiff from sitting so long, but she stepped down from the aeroplane into the bright California sun and felt warm again far from the winter cold of New York. She followed the other passengers into the airport building, thought about getting a taxi, imagined there would be a queue and looked for the way out.

She heard her name. They were calling her name over the loudspeaker. She went to the desk. They had sent a car from the hotel to collect her. The driver was standing there smiling at her. He took her suitcase off her and she followed him in a daze, realizing all at once that she was walking along with her mouth open. She closed it, put her shoulders back, held her head up high, her nose in the air and followed the man out to the car. He opened the door for her and she got inside. This is what it must have been like for Jean Harlow, she imagined. Jean Harlow must never have had to queue in the cold for a taxi, or sat in a wet raincoat on a bus. Jean Harlow must have sped down these same wide, sunny avenues in a car sent by the film studio to collect her, past all these people who looked as if they had always lived in the sun. But Jean Harlow would have been driven to Hollywood and Rita was not going there. Hollywood, where she had always wanted to go, was probably just down the road. Being so near made her previous doubts fade momentarily under a flutter of excitement. It would be easy, she thought, to go to a film studio, to call at the front office and tell them that she had been in two films, on the West End stage, on Broadway. Suddenly experience and looks seemed to be the important things, more than having an American accent. Ronald Colman still spoke impeccable English. And then the feeling passed. Her former opinion took over again. She was not going to rush off into the future. She was a week away from her eighteenth birthday and there was plenty of time. Certainty was better than chance. To go to Hollywood one day and be expected there, to be welcomed, that was the way it would have to be. Visit her grandmother's friend, fly back to New York, get the boat back to Britain. That was her plan and she vowed to stick to it, just as her mother had stuck to her harebrained schemes and had lifted two fingers to caution.

The driver was waiting for her again at the reception desk in the hotel the following morning, to take her to the railway station. He carried her case on to the train for her and she gave him a dollar tip.

Her destination was a town called Ferndale. It was a long journey through the green valleys and gentle hills where they grew fruit, the sort of place where Chuck must live, she imagined, the sort of place that he had described to her mother. It was countryside all the way, countryside looking healthy and bright under the clear, sunny sky. The little towns where the train stopped looked new with white buildings, a million miles and a million years away from the cold, grey, grimy north of England towns she had seen every Sunday from the carriage window, while travelling to the next booking with the revue.

It was after she had had lunch on the train that they rolled slowly into Ferndale. It seemed to be a small place. Two other people got off the train there and she followed them along the platform. The man at the barrier looked at her, took her ticket, looked at her again and said: 'You the lady for the Hoffman place.'

'Yes,' she replied.

'Waiting for you right over at the drugstore,' he said.

She went out into the dry, dusty main street. There was no

traffic, few people, a dog asleep in the shade of a parked car. The buildings were small, there was little relief from the hot afternoon sun which shone from a sky that had lost its blue and had gone white with the heat. She carried her suitcase across the road towards the drugstore. She was halfway across when a man came out of the building and walked towards her. He smiled as he approached her, held his hand out to shake hers long before he reached her and said: 'I guess you must be Rita.'

'That's right,' she said.

'I'm Jerry Hoffman. Sure glad you came. I have the car along here. We'll go straight up to the house.'

He took her case and she followed him down the street. He was not quite as tall as she was, his hair was neatly parted and shiny with grease, and he had a brown Californian complexion. The car was a long white convertible.

'It was very good of you to make all these arrangements for me,' Rita said, 'the airline ticket, the car to take me to the hotel and everything. Did you know my grandmother, Mrs Rigby?'

'I guess not,' he replied.

'Your wife must have known her then.'

'Sure did.'

'Does she know me?'

'I guess you'll have to ask her that.'

'But surely . . .' Rita began, but she did not go on. It was a mystery and he was enjoying it, she could tell, because he had a faint smile on his lips.

Instead, she sat there in silence while the car swept along the road away from the little town. The road was bordered by trees and bushes, with a house here and there standing back in its own grounds. Suddenly they swept into a driveway and when they went round a curve the house came into view from behind the shrubbery that concealed it from the road. It was a grand house, a bungalow, with the roof sweeping low from a gable, big windows that went almost to the ground and smooth green lawns all round.

Rita got out of the car, looked at the house and envied whoever it was who had had the good fortune to marry an American and come to live there. They walked towards the house and a woman came out of the french windows onto the veranda. She stood and watched them for a second, then walked towards them.

Rita saw the woman and stopped. She stared and could not believe her eyes. The woman was the image of her Auntie June, and as she came nearer and nearer, Rita saw that it was her, it was her Auntie June. She was frightened by the sight of her, was struck dumb with fear. She could not believe that it was her, because it could not possibly be her. She put her hands up to her face and looked over the tips of her fingers, found her voice and said shakily: 'No, it can't be you. It can't be. You're dead, you're dead.'

The woman was right in front of Rita now. 'I'm not dead, love,' she said, smiling.

'No, you died,' Rita answered in a voice high with fear. 'It can't be you, Auntie June, it can't be.'

'It is, love,' she said and she caught hold of Rita's hands, took them from her face and drew her close to her.

Rita felt her Auntie June's body, felt her face warm against her cheek, then knew nothing more until she was sitting indoors by a little table with a glass on it. She had a strange taste in her mouth and imagined that they must have given her something to drink.

'Are you all right now?' her Auntie June was saying. 'Are you all right, love?'

Rita's head was spinning. She felt she must be dreaming, yet she heard the voice so clearly.

'Is it really you, Auntie June?' she said, staring at her. 'Is it really you? Am I dreaming? I haven't died as well, have I?'

'No, and I haven't died, either. It would take more than Hitler and one of his rockets to kill me,' she said, smiling.

'Oh Auntie June, I don't understand, I don't understand.' Rita flung her arms round her and buried her head against her shoulder. Her eyes felt hot, but she did not cry. She was too confused to cry. And when she took her arms from around June and lifted her head up again, she knew that it really was her. She was the same chubby blonde Rita remembered, but with a healthy-looking sun tan now. 'I feel as if I've just woken up from a funny dream. I expect my mother to walk into the room at any moment.'

'You haven't been dreaming, love.' June took hold of Rita's hand and held it tightly. 'That wasn't me who got killed. It was some poor devil, but it wasn't me. All sorts of people lived in that house, that's why me and our Mavis got out.' She paused and corrected herself. 'Well, what really happened was that Jerry was on a weekend's leave in London and we met, and when he went back to base in Lincolnshire, I went too.'

'But why didn't you write?' Rita asked her. 'Mam thought you were dead, we all did. Why didn't you write?'

June bit her bottom lip and said: 'Oh, you know me. I meant to write again, but by the time I got round to it your mam had died.' She blinked and the tears began to flow. 'Your gran answered my letter and said that she had died just after they said me and Mavis had been killed, and I've had that awful feeling ever since that she did it because . . .' The tears won then and June wept into her hands.

Rita opened her handbag and gave her a handkerchief. What a thought to have to live with, she said to herself. But she could not let her think that. Rita had the same protective feeling for the soft little blonde that her mother had had. She said: 'It wasn't what you think at all, Auntie June. She had been going downhill for some time. You know what my mother was like. She always wanted to be at the front, leading the way. She would never have come to terms with having to spend the rest of her life in a wheelchair.' She looked at June blowing her nose and making foghorn noises into her handkerchief, and said in an offhand way, reminiscent of her mother: 'Fancy my gran writing to you. She couldn't stand the sight of you.'

'Times change, and so do people,' June said, wiping her nose and blinking. 'We've kept in touch ever since.'

'I thought you would have written to me,' Rita said. 'I mean, why keep it such a secret?'

June fiddled about with Rita's handkerchief, as if she were trying to find a dry place on it, and said: 'Well, I asked your gran not to tell you that me and Mavis hadn't been killed, because I thought you might blame me for your mother dying, even though your gran wrote and said not to think any such thing, that Bella hadn't been her old self for a while. Still, she said that you were doing so well, told me of everything you did, right from your first going on the stage. And then she wrote and said that you were coming to America, and I said that if Jerry and me could help you in any way, it would be the least . . .' She stopped then and looked out through the french windows. 'Well, who do you think this is then?'

A girl was coming across the lawn. She looked to be about twelve. She had shoulder-length, straw-coloured hair, wore shorts and had long brown legs. 'That's never Mavis, is it?' Rita proclaimed.

Mavis came in through the french windows. 'I guess you're Rita,' she said and stood with her weight resting on one leg.

'Isn't she tall?' Rita said. 'She's taller than you already, Auntie June.'

'A proper little Yankee too. Hark at her talk,' said June, who still had her pure Lancashire accent.

'I guess you sure do look like Auntie Bella,' Mavis said.

'She's got a little brother now,' June said proudly. 'You can see him later, only he's having his afternoon nap at present so that he can stay awake all night and scream. We call him Clifford Alan.'

'Mam would have liked that,' Rita said softly. She felt for one quick moment that she was going to have to control her emotions, and to avoid having to do so she said: 'When I found out we were coming to New York with the play, I had every intention of finding that Chuck my mother got involved with and killing him stone dead.'

'I don't know why your mother fell for him the way she did,' June told her. 'I mean, for all his talk, he was only a private. And your mother had some really nice chaps in her time too.' She looked away, as if she had said something she should not have said. Then she went on: 'Jerry was a captain in the air force when I met him, and I thought, what if I do go to America with him and I don't like it? So, you remember that hundred pounds old Mr Fisher left me? Well, I kept that by me just in case, so that I could get me and our Mavis back home if needs be. It's the sort of thing your mother would have told me to do. She was so bright at times, too bright to go wasting her time on anyone like Chuck, however well off his people were supposed to be.'

'I suppose you're right,' Rita admitted. 'I don't suppose he would be worth blunting a sharp knife on.'

'Well now,' June said, 'I'll show you to your room. I expect you'd like to change and that.'

As they went through the house, Rita stopped suddenly and went to a window. 'You've got a swimming pool. Isn't it big? Oh, you are lucky.'

'Jerry's firm makes them,' June told her. 'It's his father's firm really, but Jerry practically runs it.' They went on through the house and she carried on: 'I have to have a woman in every day to help look after this big house. And a man comes in a couple of times a week to do the gardening. Who would ever have thought years ago. . . ?' They reached Rita's room and June left her to change.

It was not fair, Rita said to herself, as she looked round the neat room. It was not fair that her mother should have striven so hard for all the things that her Auntie June had got, and should have died frustrated at having nothing. The house, the pool, the garden, the white convertible were all the things she had lived for and had died without. For a moment Rita wished she had not gone there after all. She wished she had never known that June and Mavis had not been killed, that they had lived happier ever after than they had lived before.

She changed her clothes, began unpacking her suitcase and the bitterness was still inside her when June knocked on the door. She came into the room and sat on the edge of the bed.

'That's nice,' June said, watching Rita hanging her cream evening dress in the wardrobe.

'Yes, I bought it in London,' she said. 'I've got a black one, too.'

June watched her in silence for a while, then she said: 'You'll never know what a burden it's been, Rita. I always blame myself for your mother's accident. If only I'd gone out with her that night as I promised to, instead of going with that chap. If only I'd written to her instead of getting so wrapped up with Jerry. If only . . .' She began to blink and sniffed loudly. If only the wreath had not fallen off the hearse, she wanted to say, but she could not.

Rita looked at her sitting there. She looked so pathetic trying to keep back the tears, trying to stop her voice from breaking. The bitterness began to go from inside her and she said: 'You've got to stop having thoughts like that, Auntie June. None of them are true. You could not have altered what happened to my mother. It was meant to happen. None of it was your fault and let's admit it, you had a hard enough job keeping your own life on the rails, never mind thinking you could have managed my mother's life for her as well. It was all you could do to look after Mavis. After all, half the time she didn't quite know who her mother was, you, me or her Auntie Bella.' She stopped then. They could both hear that voice, not a voice from the dead, but a voice that was still alive.

June cleared her throat, wiped her nose with the back of her hand and said: 'When I first met Jerry and he asked me to come back to the States with him, I always used to imagine your mother coming too. I used to imagine me getting settled in first, then sending for her. Even when I knew she was dead, I still had those same thoughts. They wouldn't go away. And when we came to live here and I saw that I had all the things that Chuck used to promise your mother, well – it was almost too much to bear. It seemed so wrong. It nearly drove me to drink. One of the things that helped me to get over it was the thought that one day you might come here and . . . Well, what I've got to tell you, Rita, is . . .'

The door was flung open then and Mavis stood there: 'Dad says to come. The ice is melting.' Then she dashed away again.

'Oh, we'd better go, love,' June said. 'Jerry's mixing some drinks out by the pool.'

They walked back through the house. Rita found it strange that her Auntie June should have had the same feeling that she had had about the injustice of gaining all the things her mother had wanted. June's confession of remorse cancelled out all the bitterness that remained inside Rita and settled the matter for her.

They sat by the pool and Mavis, who appeared to Rita to be brown all over, dived into the water and swam up and down. Jerry mixed the drinks in tall glasses and put too much ice in them for Rita's liking. 'Did you tell her?' he asked June.

'Oh no,' she said. 'I've been trying to get on to it, love. You

339

see, Rita, I said we wanted to help you if we could, on account of your mother dying the way she did, and so some time ago Jerry was in Los Angeles putting a new swimming pool in this film director's garden in Beverly Hills, and he had a word with him about you. He said you'd been in a couple of films, and had been in the West End, and that you were coming to Broadway, and . . .'

'And the outcome is,' Jerry said, butting in to prevent June dragging it out too much, 'that he wants you to call and see him at the film studios the day after tomorrow. I'll drive you down in the car. It'll only take about ninety minutes on the coast road.'

'A film director? Wants to see me? In Hollywood? Oh, I can't believe it, Auntie June. What can I say?'

'Jerry showed him the photos of you and . . .'

'Photos? What photos?'

'The ones your gran sent, love. I wrote and asked her. She sent three. They were ever so good.'

'So that's why she took them,' Rita said, half to herself. Then she went on: 'Have you seen the films I was in yet? Did gran tell you the titles?'

'Sure. We saw the one you made with Stewart Granger. You were just great,' Jerry answered. 'Everyone we've spoken to liked the movie, which is unusual, because few of your British movies do well over here. In fact,' he went on, grinning as if it were a joke, 'I think most of them are pretty awful.'

And to that, Rita retorted: 'Well, I've sat through so many boring cowboy films, I would recognize the horses anywhere.'

Jerry looked at her. At that moment she looked as hard as a diamond, cutting him to pieces with her eyes, but the next moment, when June spoke, Rita's expression became soft and warm, like the sun coming out on a chilly day.

'Oh Rita,' June said, as if with pride, 'you're just like your mother. Dead spit. Taller, naturally, and I must admit, you do talk a bit posh.'

'Of course,' Rita said, 'I'm still a Lancashire lass at heart, but I would never have got on to the West End stage talking like one.'

'And I thought you were smashing in that film,' June went

on. 'As soon as you appeared on the screen I said: "That's Rita," right out loud, and everyone turned round and said shush. Me and our Mavis saw it three times.'

'I guess Mr Lockshott liked the movie too,' Jerry said.

'Mr who?' Rita asked him.

'Mr Lockshott, the film director you have to see in Hollywood,' he told her.

'That's Gregory Lockshott,' June added, with pride in her voice.

'Oh, is it?' Rita said, trying to sound impressed. But she had never heard of Gregory Lockshott. She could rattle off the names of Hollywood film stars by the dozen, but when it came to Hollywood directors, Gregory Lockshott was placed first in a list of one.

That evening they had dinner at a table lit by candles. Jerry and June laughed over the subterfuge they had employed to entice Rita to go there, and she showed concern over the expense they had gone to. But Jerry laughed the expense away as, Rita realized, the rich can.

Afterwards, Rita and June sat by themselves by the pool and watched the lights coming on in the hills as dusk turned the sky into an autumn of colours, red and purple and gold.

'Are you coming to Los Angeles with us?' Rita asked.

'No, love, I don't like to leave the children,' she said, to Rita's surprise, and she turned away as she said it and bit her bottom lip, as if the guilt of former years were showing on her face. 'I can't say I like the place. I prefer San Francisco. Anyway, Jerry is down there all the time. Stays for days sometimes. They put pools in all the film stars' homes, you know. He's met them all. But I don't go there much.'

That did not sound like her Auntie June. Although she did not look so very different, had the new environment that she was living in made her change her ways at last, Rita wondered? She hoped that was what had happened, and that the days when, at two nods and a wink from a man, she would go into the bushes with him and come out again counting the money, were gone forever.

'I sigh for the old days at times,' June admitted. 'What wouldn't I give to have a night out with your mother, to go into a good old British pub and have a glass of beer.'

'But Auntie June, you've got all this,' Rita said in amazement. 'This big house, the pool, even a woman to help out with the housework.'

'Yes,' June agreed halfheartedly, 'but you can't beat the old times. I mean, all this sunshine is all right as far as it goes, but what's wrong with rain? I'd like to live in a house with a neighbour right next door. Here, you have to go to the end of the garden and stare if you want to get a glimpse of the next house. I'd like to walk down a cobbled street again, smell a fish and chip shop, queue for a bus on a cold winter's night with my breath coming out like little clouds of fog, and know that nothing in trousers was safe from your mother and me.'

Darkness had fallen completely now. The light of the moon lit up the ripples on the water in the pool. In one way, Rita thought, her Auntie June had ended up just like her mother. Despite the life of comfort and plenty that marriage to Jerry had brought her, memories and dreams were what she had most of all. She said: 'Memories might be better, Auntie June. I went back to see that place we lived in. I went to see Mrs Bragg. And quite frankly, it was a bit of a let down. It wasn't like it was when we lived there. It made me more determined than ever to get the things I want, the things my mother always wanted; a house on a hill, a place where I can be warm in the winter and cool in the summer, a little bit of luxury.'

'I've been wondering,' June said softly, 'what would have happened to your mother if she hadn't died. She never made it up with your dad, did she? And she never did get on with your gran, which was a pity, because she didn't turn out to be such a bad old stick in the end. I mean, with you gone, I can't imagine what sort of a life your mother would have had.'

'I wouldn't have left her, Auntie June,' Rita stated. 'I had already told her that I was putting all my ambitions aside and that I was going to get a secretarial job. We had words about it shortly before she died. She didn't want to hold me back. But she knew I wouldn't leave her. I couldn't, could I? So don't go taking all the blame because she died. We are all to blame, me as well. Me most of all, I suppose.'

June had started crying again. Rita could see her in the darkness, wiping away the tears with her hand because, yet again, she did not have a handkerchief. Then June said, in a faltering voice: 'I'll just nip in the house and see to our Mavis. She's just like your Ronnie was. She'll sit up in bed all night reading if I don't stop her. I'll be back in a tick.' And she got up and went towards the house.

Until then, it had never entered Rita's mind that her mother might have been thinking of her most of all when she had died. The sacrifice that she had always thought Bella had made because of June and Chuck had really been made for her. Why it had not dawned on her before, she could not imagine. Why she did not have an overwhelming feeling of grief, of responsibility, she did not know. What she did know, what she learned at that very moment, was that if her mother had not died, then she would not have got on to the West End stage, she would not have been on Broadway, she would not be sitting there by the pool on a dark, warm, Californian night, she would not be going to see a film director in Hollywood.

Thirty Three

'I had no intention of going to Hollywood,' Rita said. 'I thought, what chance would I have, not knowing anyone and being English? Get established a bit more, I decided, and then one day they might ask me to go to Hollywood, they might send me a film script to read first, they might even ask me . . .'

Her voice went on and on. They joined the coast road and drove south towards Los Angeles, and all the time she talked, hardly stopping for breath, not giving Jerry the opportunity to comment upon anything she said. She was so excited that half the things she told him she had already talked about back at the house.

They had been on the road for an hour and he was wondering if she would have any voice left by the time they got to Hollywood, when suddenly she shouted: 'That's it,' and she swung round in the seat beside him and looked back through the rear window. He slowed the car. 'That's it,' she said again. 'On that signpost.'

'That's what?' he asked her, stopping the car.

'The place he came from. That Yank my mother got mixed up with. Hurst, that's the place. It's back there on a signpost.'

Jerry knew all about Chuck. He had heard it all from June a long time ago and he had heard it again as she and Rita had talked about it. 'Do you want to go and take a look at the place?' he asked her.

'I don't know,' she said, 'I don't know.'

But she was still looking back through the rear window, as if unable to drag her eyes away from the signpost, so he put the car into reverse and they went back. 'If you want to go and see the place, we've got plenty of time,' he said.

'Oh all right,' she said, almost reluctantly, as if she would go just to please him.

They turned off the road and drove away from the coast into the hills. It was fruit-growing country and they drove along a valley amid orchards of regimented trees that spread away on either side of the road. Eventually they passed a side road with a gate across it and a guard on duty, and Rita looked along it and saw a factory building. On the side of the building it said in big letters: Hurst Canning Co. She wondered if he was there, in a big office, or whether he was at his house somewhere in the surrounding hills.

The town of Hurst came into view along the valley. 'Do you want to find this guy?' Jerry asked her.

'I don't know,' she replied, sounding as uncertain about that as she had about going there.

He glanced at her and knew that as long as she was in California, whatever success she had in Hollywood, she would always be trying to make up her mind whether to go to see him or not. He thought that it would be best to get it over with, and better if she did not go to find him on her own, not with her looks which, he imagined, could bring trouble to her as well as to someone else. 'Let's ask about him,' Jerry suggested as they drove into the town. 'There's a cop over there. This is only a small town, so I guess he might know the guy.'

He might tell them to go back to the canning factory, Rita thought, or he might send them to a big white house in the hills. And they could always go to the castle gates, even if they did not go to the castle.

'Chuck Bradwell?' the policeman asked. 'Sure. Go straight through the town. Carry on for about a mile. House on the right. Stands on its own. You can't miss it. Nothing else out that way.'

They drove on and Rita began to wish that she had not spoken when she had seen the name on the signpost. She was not prepared for a confrontation. Up until the moment that she had seen that name, her mind had been full of the happy things in life, and the next big thing in her life was to take place in Hollywood, not there in that little valley full of fruit trees. But the car took her on, out of the town, past the last houses, towards the end of the valley where the hills crowded in on the road.

They had travelled over a mile when Jerry stopped the car. 'Well, where is it?' he asked. 'There's nothing here.'

'We passed a place back there. They might be able to tell us where it is,' Rita said.

He turned the car round and they drove back. He had seen the house too, but had not imagined that to be the place. They reached it and he stopped the car. 'Do you reckon this is it?' he asked her. 'He said about a mile and there's nothing else.'

Rita did not answer. She looked at the house. It was built of wood and the paint was peeling off it. An old Packard with a flat tyre was parked at the side of the house and the rusting body of another car lay in the overgrown garden. There was a veranda with broken steps leading up to it. Was this the big white house, she wondered, where her mother had wanted to go? It looked less than the little brick terrace that they had called home.

'Shall I go in and ask?' he said.

'No,' she said, 'not just yet.'

There was an old man sitting on the veranda, just sitting there and looking. When they had been there about a minute he stood up, stared out at the car, went towards the house door and stared again. He was frail and sad-looking, with a face like a fallen leaf. He went into the house.

Another face appeared at the window, a face obscured by the grimy pane. Then it was gone. The door opened and a man stood there, came down the broken steps from the veranda and walked towards the car.

Although his appearance had changed, Rita knew it was Chuck. He was lean now, not so muscular, and the boyish look had gone from his face. He pushed his face through the open window of the car and stared at Jerry. The healthy complexion had gone too. His face was lined and it had the grey pallor of someone who had spent a lot of time indoors, out of the sun. His once wavy hair was cropped short. The blue eyes narrowed and he snarled in a hostile voice that Rita had never heard him use before: 'What's the matter, buddy? What're you stopped here for? Better get moving, otherwise I'll have to move you myself.'

Rita felt angry at the way he spoke, but she kept control of herself. She touched Jerry on the shoulder and said:

'Drive on.'

Until then, Chuck had hardly noticed that she was there. But when she spoke he looked past Jerry at the woman sitting beside him, just had time for one brief look at her as the car moved away. He saw the black glossy hair, the dark eyes with the wild look in them, the red lips, the neat-looking young woman whose expression was a challenge to him. Then she was gone and he was left wishing that he had seen her first, that he had said something different.

'Was that him?' Jerry asked her.

'Yes, that was him,' Rita replied, 'that was him.'

In the couple of seconds that they had looked each other in the face, Rita had seen Chuck's hard eyes soften with recognition. She turned and looked through the window, back along the road. He was still standing there, looking down the road, watching the car disappear towards the town.

Jerry knew the shock and the disappointment that she must be feeling and he said, as if it would help: 'There were a lot of guys made up stories about the great life they lived in the States, just to impress the British girls. We had one guy on the base told his girl he lived on a cattle ranch in Texas. That guy came from New York city and the only things he'd ever seen with horns on were taxi cabs.'

But Rita did not smile, did not comment, just sat there with her thoughts as they drove back through the town, past the canning factory, past the orchards and the groves of fruit trees, back on to the coast road, and headed once more for Los Angeles.

Her first thought was that it had been a mistake to go there. Although he was Chuck, he was not the man who had treated her mother the way she had wanted to be treated, like a lady, like someone with class, someone who could go into the Manhattan Lounge and feel at home there. He was the man who had got her mother pregnant and had abandoned her. It all seemed such a mess. She had not got revenge on him after all.

And yet, while she thought about it, while she sat there silent in the car, she gradually realized that she might have had her revenge on him in a way. What better revenge than for Chuck to be left wondering who he had seen in the car? Had he seen Rita? Or had he seen her mother? Better for

347

him, she thought, to have the torment of never knowing. Better for him to spend his days thinking and wondering and looking through that grimy window every time a car drove slowly by, in anticipation of her coming there again and giving him a second chance. It was the sort of revenge that settled the matter and made her feel pleased.

Jerry glanced at Rita, as silent now as she had been talkative before, and saw a faint smile on her lips. He did not want to intrude on her thoughts, was not inquisitive to know what it was that caused her to smile. He just said: 'When we get to the top of this rise, we'll be able to see Los Angeles.'

She made no reply. It was better for her mother to have died, she thought, rather than to have gone all that way and have her dreams turn to nothing, to have seen that neglected wooden house and to have realized that the escape she had spent her whole life seeking had evaded her once more. It pleased Rita to know that her mother had been spared that disappointment.

She looked through the car window. So that was the Pacific Ocean, washing against the shore just like any other ocean. They reached the top of the rise and there below them, in the distance, was Los Angeles. The sun was bright and warm, the sky was blue and it seemed fitting that it should be so for her entry into Hollywood, for a dream come true. Although she would not mind if it rained. It had rained on some of her most important days, and there was nothing wrong with rain.